In 1956 *The Return of the King* was published by Houghton Mifflin in the United States—thus completing the publication of the first edition of Tolkien's epic trilogy THE LORD OF THE RINGS.

As Tolkien's American paperback publisher, we are proud to bring one of the world's most beloved classics to readers everywhere.

## And what is a Hobbit?

Hobbits are little people, smaller than dwarfs. They love peace and quiet and good tilled earth. They dislike machines, but they are handy with tools. They are nimble but don't like to hurry. They have sharp ears and eyes. They are inclined to be fat. They wear bright colors but seldom wear shoes. They like to laugh and eat (six meals a day) and drink. They like parties and they like to give and receive presents. They inhabit a land they call The Shire, a place between the River Brandywine and the Far Downs.

THE HOBBIT is a story of these delightful creatures—a story complete in itself yet full of portent. For this is the book that tells of Bilbo Baggins, the far-wandering hobbit who discovered (some say stole) the One Ring of Power and brought it back to The Shire.

And so this is the absolutely necessary beginning to the great story of the War of the Rings which J. R. R. Tolkien completes in his epic fantasy trilogy *The Lord of the Rings*.

# About the "Lord of the Rings" Trilogy by J. R. R. Tolkien:

PART I    *The Fellowship of the Ring*

"Filled with marvels and strange terrors . . . an extraordinary, a distinguished piece of work."

—Dan Wickenden, New York *Herald Tribune Book Week*

"For anyone who likes the genre to which it belongs, the Heroic Quest, I cannot imagine a more wonderful Christmas present. . . . No fiction I have read in the last five years has given me more joy than *The Fellowship of the Ring*."

—W. H. Auden, *The New York Times Book Review*

PART II    *The Two Towers*

"This, the second part of Tolkien's trilogy, reinforces the conviction that we have now in the making one of the great literary achievements of our time. . . . For the world of the Ring bears striking, terrifying resemblance to the world we know, and for all its fantasticality, the moral principles which govern it are uncomfortably familiar. . . . To sum it all up, here is a wonderful story, set in a world which paralyzes the imagination, and told in magnificent prose. What more can an author give?"

—Edward Wagenknecht, *Chicago Tribune*

"One of the best wonder tales ever written . . . if you know a great book when you see one, you will want all of these."

—Julian Forest, *Boston Herald Traveler*

PART III    *The Return of the King*

"The great tale of wonder, like the great novel, is not a preoccupation of children . . . the adult mind has, if anything, greater need of fantasy than that of the child. . . . In *The Lord of the Rings* a whole Secondary World is created and successfully sustained through three large volumes. These are sure to remain Tolkien's life work, and are certainly destined to outlast our time."

—Loren Eiseley, *New York Herald Tribune Book Week*

"I have read Professor Tolkien's *The Lord of the Rings* not once but twice. In the highest and most complimentary sense, this is escapist fiction at its finest, yet at the same time it has profound relevance to our troubled age."

—Arthur C. Clarke

"There are very few works of genius in recent literature. This is one."

—Michael Straight, *The New Republic*

It's been fifteen years at this writing since I first came across THE LORD OF THE RINGS in the stacks at the Carnegie Library in Pittsburgh. I'd been looking for the book for four years, ever since reading W. H. Auden's review in the *New York Times*. I think of that time now—and the years after, when the trilogy continued to be hard to find and hard to explain to most friends—with an undeniable nostalgia. It was a barren era for fantasy, among other things, but a good time for cherishing slighted treasures and mysterious passwords. Long before *Frodo Lives!* began to appear in the New York subways, J. R. R. Tolkien was the magus of my secret knowledge.

I've never thought it an accident that Tolkien's works waited more than ten years to explode into popularity almost overnight. The Sixties were no fouler a decade than the Fifties—they merely reaped the Fifties' foul harvest—but they were the years when millions of people grew aware that the industrial society had become paradoxically unlivable, incalculably immoral, and ultimately deadly. In terms of passwords, the Sixties were the time when the word *progress* lost its ancient holiness, and *escape* stopped being comically obscene. The impulse is being called reactionary now, but lovers of Middle-earth want to go there. I would myself, like a shot.

For in the end it is Middle-earth and its dwellers that we love, not Tolkien's considerable gifts in showing it to us. I said once that the world he charts was there long before him, and I still believe it. He is a great enough magician to tap our most common nightmares, daydreams and twilight fancies, but he never invented them either: he found them a place to live, a green alternative to each day's madness here in a poisoned world. We are raised to honor all the wrong explorers and discoverers—thieves planting flags, murderers carrying crosses. Let us at last praise the colonizers of dreams.

—Peter S. Beagle
Watsonville, California
14 July 1973

*Works by J.R.R. Tolkien*

The Hobbit*
Leaf by Niggle
On Fairy-Stories
Farmer Giles of Ham*
The Homecoming of Beorhtnoth
The Lord of the Rings*
The Adventures of Tom Bombadil
The Road Goes Ever On (*with Donald Swann*)
Smith of Wootton Major

**Works Published Posthumously**
Sir Gawain and the Green Knight, Pearl, and Sir Orfeo*
The Father Christmas Letters
The Silmarillion*
Pictures by J.R.R. Tolkien
Unfinished Tales*
The Letters of J.R.R. Tolkien
Finn and Hingest
Mr. Bliss
The Monsters and the Critics & Other Essays
Roverandom

**The History of Middle-earth**
I. The Book of Lost Tales, Part One*
II. The Book of Lost Tales, Part Two*
III. The Lays of Beleriand*
IV. The Shaping of Middle-earth*
V. The Lost Road and Other Writings*
VI. The Return of the Shadow
VII. The Treason of Isengard
VIII. The War of the Ring
IX. Sauron Defeated
X. Morgoth's Ring
XI. The War of the Jewels
XII. The Peoples of Middle-earth

*Adapted by Charles Dixon with Sean Deming:*
The Hobbit: An Illustrated Edition*

*By Robert Foster:*
The Complete Guide to Middle-earth*

*\*Published by The Random House Publishing Group*

# The Hobbit

or

## There and Back Again

*(Revised Edition)*

by
J. R. R. Tolkien

A Del Rey® Book
THE RANDOM HOUSE PUBLISHING GROUP • NEW YORK

A Del Rey® Book
Published by The Random House Publishing Group
Copyright © 1937 by George Allen & Unwin Ltd.
Copyright © 1966 by J. R. R. Tolkien
Copyright © renewed 1994 by Christopher R. Tolkien, John F. R. Tolkien, and Priscilla M. A. R. Tolkien
Copyright © Restored 1996 by the Estate of J. R. R. Tolkien, assigned 1997 to the J. R. R. Tolkien Copyright Trust
Introduction Copyright © 1973 by Peter Beagle
Maps of Middle-earth copyright © George Allen & Unwin (Publishers) Ltd. 1980

All rights reserved under International and Pan-American Copyright Conventions. Published in the United States by Del Rey Books, an imprint of The Random House Publishing Group, a division of Random House, Inc., New York.

Del Rey is a registered trademark and the Del Rey colophon is a trademark of Random House, Inc.

www.delreybooks.com

Library of Congress Catalog Card Number: 77-8025

ISBN 0-345-33968-1

This edition published by arrangement with Houghton Mifflin Company

Manufactured in the United States of America

First Ballantine Books Edition: August 1965

*Revised Edition*
First Printing: January 1982

OPM  145  144  143  142  141  140

# CONTENTS

In this reprint several minor inaccuracies, most of them noted by readers, have been corrected. For example, the text on pages 19 and 53 now corresponds exactly with the runes on Thror's Map. More important is the matter of Chapter Five. There the true story of the ending of the Riddle Game, as it was eventually revealed (under pressure) by Bilbo to Gandalf, is now given according to the Red Book, in place of the version Bilbo first gave to his friends, and actually set down in his diary. This departure from truth on the part of a most honest hobbit was a portent of great significance. It does not, however, concern the present story, and those who in this edition make their first acquaintance with hobbit-lore need not trouble about it. Its explanation lies in the history of the Ring, as it was set out in the chronicles of the Red Book of Westmarch, and is now told in *The Lord of the Rings*.

A final note may be added, on a point raised by several students of the lore of the period. On Thror's Map is written *Here of old was Thrain King under the Mountain*; yet Thrain was the son of Thror, the last King under the Mountain before the coming of the dragon. The Map, however, is not in error. Names are often repeated in dynasties, and the genealogies show that a distant ancestor of Thror was referred to, Thrain I, a fugitive from Moria, who first discovered the Lonely Mountain, Erebor, and ruled there for a while, before his people moved on to the remoter mountains of the North.

East lie the
where

the
Lonely
Mountain

Here of old was
King under the

Far
to the North
are
the Grey Mountains
by
the Withered Heath
whence came the
Great Worms.

Thror's Map

West lies

M.

Þ. ←→ ᚺ

P.

Here was Girion
lord in Dale

the Running River

here is
the gateway
of the Long
Lake

the Desolation
of Smaug

ᛉ·ᛒᚱ·ᚦᛖ·ᚷᚱᛗᚪ·ᚻᛏ
·ᚻᚠᛗᛄ·ᚦᛖ·ᚦᚱᚾᚻᚻ·ᚻᛏ
ᛄ·ᚠᛁᛉ·ᚦᛖ·ᚻᛗᛏᛏᛁᚷ·ᛄ
ᛁᛒ·ᚦᛖ·ᚠᚷᛄᛏ·ᚱᛁᚷᚻᛏ·
ᛄᚾᚱᛁᛄᛄ·ᛉᚠᛒ·ᚦᛁᛚᛚ·ᛄᚻ
ᚾᚻᛄᛏ·ᚦᛖ·ᚻᛗᚪᚾᚠᛖᛗ·

In Esgaroth upon
the Long Lake
dwell Men

Here flows the
Forest River

...Elvenking

...od the Great
there are Spiders.

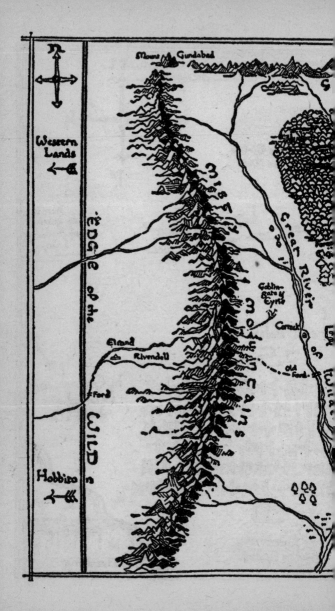

Withered Heath

ntains

Desolation
of
Smaug

Iron Hills

Forest River

Thranduil's Halls

Lonely Mountain

Long Lake
Esgaroth

River Running

Mountains of
Mirkwood

Old Forest Road

River Running

WOOD

WILDERLAND

*Chapter I*

# AN UNEXPECTED PARTY

In a hole in the ground there lived a hobbit. Not a nasty, dirty, wet hole, filled with the ends of worms and an oozy smell, nor yet a dry, bare, sandy hole with nothing in it to sit down on or to eat: it was a hobbit-hole, and that means comfort.

It had a perfectly round door like a porthole, painted green, with a shiny yellow brass knob in the exact middle. The door opened on to a tube-shaped hall like a tunnel: a very comfortable tunnel without smoke, with panelled walls, and floors tiled and carpeted, provided with polished chairs, and lots and lots of pegs for hats and coats—the hobbit was fond of visitors. The tunnel wound on and on, going fairly but not quite straight into the side of the hill—The Hill, as all the people for many miles round called it—and many little round doors opened out of it, first on one side and then on another. No going upstairs for the hobbit: bedrooms, bathrooms, cellars, pantries (lots of these), wardrobes (he had whole rooms devoted to clothes), kitchens, dining-rooms, all were on the same floor, and indeed on the same passage. The best rooms were all on the left-hand side (going in), for these were the only ones to have windows, deep-set round windows looking over his garden, and meadows beyond, sloping down to the river.

This hobbit was a very well-to-do hobbit, and his name

was Baggins. The Bagginses had lived in the neighbourhood of The Hill for time out of mind, and people considered them very respectable, not only because most of them were rich, but also because they never had any adventures or did anything unexpected: you could tell what a Baggins would say on any question without the bother of asking him. This is a story of how a Baggins had an adventure, and found himself doing and saying things altogether unexpected. He may have lost the neighbours' respect, but he gained—well, you will see whether he gained anything in the end.

The mother of our particular hobbit—what is a hobbit? I suppose hobbits need some description nowadays, since they have become rare and shy of the Big People, as they call us. They are (or were) a little people, about half our height, and smaller than the bearded dwarves. Hobbits have no beards. There is little or no magic about them, except the ordinary everyday sort which helps them to disappear quietly and quickly when large stupid folk like you and me come blundering along, making a noise like elephants which they can hear a mile off. They are inclined to be fat in the stomach; they dress in bright colours (chiefly green and yellow); wear no shoes, because their feet grow natural leathery soles and thick warm brown hair like the stuff on their heads (which is curly); have long clever brown fingers, good-natured faces, and laugh deep fruity laughs (especially after dinner, which they have twice a day when they can get it). Now you know enough to go on with. As I was saying, the mother of this hobbit—of Bilbo Baggins, that is—was the famous Belladonna Took, one of the three remarkable daughters of the Old Took, head of the hobbits who lived across The Water, the small river that ran at the foot of The Hill. It was often said (in other families) that long ago one of the Took ancestors must have taken a fairy wife. That was, of course, absurd, but certainly there was still something not entirely hobbitlike about them, and once in a while members of the Took-clan would go and have adventures. They discreetly disappeared, and the family hushed it up; but the fact remained that the Tooks were not as respectable as the Bagginses, though they were undoubtedly richer.

Not that Belladonna Took ever had any adventures after she became Mrs Bungo Baggins. Bungo, that was Bilbo's father, built the most luxurious hobbit-hole for her (and partly with her money) that was to be found either under The Hill or over The Hill or across The Water, and there they remained to the end of their days. Still it is probable that Bilbo, her only son, although he looked and behaved exactly like a second edition of his solid and comfortable father, got something a bit queer in his make-up from the Took side, something that only waited for a chance to come out. The chance never arrived, until Bilbo Baggins was grown up, being about fifty years old or so, and living in the beautiful hobbit-hole built by his father, which I have just described for you, until he had in fact apparently settled down immovably.

By some curious chance one morning long ago in the quiet of the world, when there was less noise and more green, and the hobbits were still numerous and prosperous, and Bilbo Baggins was standing at his door after breakfast smoking an enormous long wooden pipe that reached nearly down to his woolly toes (neatly brushed)—Gandalf came by. Gandalf! If you had heard only a quarter of what I have heard about him, and I have only heard very little of all there is to hear, you would be prepared for any sort of remarkable tale. Tales and adventures sprouted up all over the place wherever he went, in the most extraordinary fashion. He had not been down that way under The Hill for ages and ages, not since his friend the Old Took died, in fact, and the hobbits had almost forgotten what he looked like. He had been away over The Hill and across The Water on businesses of his own since they were all small hobbit-boys and hobbit-girls.

All that the unsuspecting Bilbo saw that morning was an old man with a staff. He had a tall pointed blue hat, a long grey cloak, a silver scarf over which his long white beard hung down below his waist, and immense black boots.

"Good morning!" said Bilbo, and he meant it. The sun was shining, and the grass was very green. But Gandalf looked at him from under long bushy eyebrows that stuck out further than the brim of his shady hat.

"What do you mean?" he said. "Do you wish me a good morning, or mean that it is a good morning whether I want it or not; or that you feel good this morning; or that it is a morning to be good on?"

"All of them at once," said Bilbo. "And a very fine morning for a pipe of tobacco out of doors, into the bargain. If you have a pipe about you, sit down and have a fill of mine! There's no hurry, we have all the day before us!" Then Bilbo sat down on a seat by his door, crossed his legs, and blew out a beautiful grey ring of smoke that sailed up into the air without breaking and floated away over The Hill.

"Very pretty!" said Gandalf. "But I have no time to blow smoke-rings this morning. I am looking for someone to share in an adventure that I am arranging, and it's very difficult to find anyone."

"I should think so—in these parts! We are plain quiet folk and have no use for adventures. Nasty disturbing uncomfortable things! Make you late for dinner! I can't think what anybody sees in them," said our Mr Baggins, and stuck one thumb behind his braces, and blew out another even bigger smoke-ring. Then he took out his morning letters, and began to read, pretending to take no more notice of the old man. He had decided that he was not quite his sort, and wanted him to go away. But the old man did not move. He stood leaning on his stick and gazing at the hobbit without saying anything, till Bilbo got quite uncomfortable and even a little cross.

"Good morning!" he said at last. "We don't want any adventures here, thank you! You might try over The Hill or across The Water." By this he meant that the conversation was at an end.

"What a lot of things you do use *Good morning* for!" said Gandalf. "Now you mean that you want to get rid of me, and that it won't be good till I move off."

"Not at all, not at all, my dear sir! Let me see, I don't think I know your name?"

"Yes, yes, my dear sir—and I do know your name, Mr Bilbo Baggins. And you do know my name, though you don't remember that I belong to it. I am Gandalf, and Gandalf means me! To think that I should have lived to be good-morninged by Belladonna Took's son, as if I was selling buttons at the door!"

"Gandalf, Gandalf! Good gracious me! Not the wandering wizard that gave Old Took a pair of magic diamond studs that fastened themselves and never came undone till ordered? Not the fellow who used to tell such wonderful tales at parties, about dragons and goblins and giants and the rescue of princesses and the unexpected luck of widows' sons? Not the man that used to make such particularly excellent fireworks! I remember those! Old Took used to have them on Midsummer's Eve. Splendid! They used to go up like great lilies and snapdragons and laburnums of fire and hang in the twilight all evening!" You will notice already that Mr Baggins was not quite so prosy as he liked to believe, also that he was very fond of flowers. "Dear me!" he went on. "Not the Gandalf who was responsible for so many quiet lads and lasses going off into the Blue for mad adventures? Anything from climbing trees to visiting elves—or sailing in ships, sailing to other shores! Bless me, life used to be quite inter—I mean, you used to upset things badly in these parts once upon a time. I beg your pardon, but I had no idea you were still in business."

"Where else should I be?" said the wizard. "All the same I am pleased to find you remember something about me. You seem to remember my fireworks kindly, at any rate, and that is not without hope. Indeed for your old grandfather Took's sake, and for the sake of poor Belladonna, I will give you what you asked for."

"I beg your pardon, I haven't asked for anything!"

"Yes, you have! Twice now. My pardon. I give it you. In fact I will go so far as to send you on this adventure. Very amusing for me, very good for you—and profitable too, very likely, if you ever get over it."

"Sorry! I don't want any adventures, thank you. Not today. Good morning! But please come to tea—any time you like! Why not tomorrow? Come tomorrow! Good-bye!" With that the hobbit turned and scuttled inside his round green door, and shut it as quickly as he dared, not to seem rude. Wizards after all are wizards.

"What on earth did I ask him to tea for!" he said to himself, as he went to the pantry. He had only just had breakfast, but he thought a cake or two and a drink of something would do him good after his fright.

Gandalf in the meantime was still standing outside the door, and laughing long but quietly. After a while he stepped up, and with the spike on his staff scratched a queer sign on the hobbit's beautiful green front-door. Then he strode away, just about the time when Bilbo was finishing his second cake and beginning to think that he had escaped adventures very well.

The next day he had almost forgotten about Gandalf. He did not remember things very well, unless he put them down on his Engagement Tablet: like this: *Gandalf Tea Wednesday.* Yesterday he had been too flustered to do anything of the kind.

Just before tea-time there came a tremendous ring on the front-door bell, and then he remembered! He rushed and put on the kettle, and put out another cup and saucer, and an extra cake or two, and ran to the door.

"I am so sorry to keep you waiting!" he was going to say, when he saw that it was not Gandalf at all. It was a dwarf with a blue beard tucked into a golden belt, very bright eyes under his dark-green hood. As soon as the door was opened, he pushed inside, just as if he had been expected.

He hung his hooded cloak on the nearest peg, and "Dwalin at your service!" he said with a low bow.

"Bilbo Baggins at yours!" said the hobbit, too surprised to ask any questions for the moment. When the silence that followed had become uncomfortable, he added: "I am just about to take tea; pray come and have some with me." A little stiff perhaps, but he meant it kindly. And what would you do, if an uninvited dwarf came and hung his things up in your hall without a word of explanation?

They had not been at table long, in fact they had hardly reached the third cake, when there came another even louder ring at the bell.

"Excuse me!" said the hobbit, and off he went to the door.

"So you have got here at last!" That was what he was going to say to Gandalf this time. But it was not Gandalf. Instead there was a very old-looking dwarf on the step with a white beard and a scarlet hood; and he too hopped inside as soon as the door was open, just as if he had been invited.

"I see they have begun to arrive already," he said when he caught sight of Dwalin's green hood hanging up. He hung his red one next to it, and "Balin at your service!" he said with his hand on his breast.

"Thank you!" said Bilbo with a gasp. It was not the correct thing to say, but *they have begun to arrive* had flustered him badly. He liked visitors, but he liked to know them before they arrived, and he preferred to ask them himself. He had a horrible thought that the cakes might run short, and then he—as the host: he knew his duty and stuck to it however painful—he might have to go without.

"Come along in, and have some tea!" he managed to say after taking a deep breath.

"A little beer would suit me better, if it is all the same to you, my good sir," said Balin with the white beard. "But I don't mind some cake—seed-cake, if you have any."

"Lots!" Bilbo found himself answering, to his own surprise; and he found himself scuttling off, too, to the cellar to fill a pint beer-mug, and then to a pantry to fetch two beautiful round seed-cakes which he had baked that afternoon for his after-supper morsel.

When he got back Balin and Dwalin were talking at the table like old friends (as a matter of fact they were brothers). Bilbo plumped down the beer and the cake in front of them, when loud came a ring at the bell again, and then another ring.

"Gandalf for certain this time," he thought as he puffed along the passage. But it was not. It was two more dwarves, both with blue hoods, silver belts, and yellow beards; and each of them carried a bag of tools and a spade. In they hopped, as soon as the door began to open—Bilbo was hardly surprised at all.

"What can I do for you, my dwarves?" he said.

"Kili at your service!" said the one. "And Fili!" added the other; and they both swept off their blue hoods and bowed.

"At yours and your family's!" replied Bilbo, remembering his manners this time.

"Dwalin and Balin here already, I see," said Kili. "Let us join the throng!"

"Throng!" thought Mr Baggins. "I don't like the sound of that. I really must sit down for a minute and collect my wits, and have a drink." He had only just had a sip—in the corner, while the four dwarves sat round the table, and talked about mines and gold and troubles with the goblins, and the depredations of dragons, and lots of other things which he did not understand, and did not want to, for they sounded much too adventurous—when, *ding-dong-a-ling-dang,* his bell rang again, as if some naughty little hobbit-boy was trying to pull the handle off.

"Someone at the door!" he said, blinking.

"Some four, I should say by the sound," said Fili. "Besides, we saw them coming along behind us in the distance."

The poor little hobbit sat down in the hall and put his head in his hands, and wondered what had happened, and what was going to happen, and whether they would all stay to supper. Then the bell rang again louder than ever, and he had to run to the door. It was not four after all, it was FIVE. Another dwarf had come along while he was wondering in the hall. He had hardly turned the knob, before they were all inside, bowing and saying "at your service" one after another. Dori, Nori, Ori, Oin, and Gloin were their names; and very soon two purple hoods, a grey hood, a brown hood, and a white hood were hanging on the pegs, and off they marched with their broad hands stuck in their gold and silver belts to join the others. Already it had almost become a throng. Some called for ale, and some for porter, and one for coffee, and all of them for cakes; so the hobbit was kept very busy for a while.

A big jug of coffee had just been set in the hearth, the seed-cakes were gone, and the dwarves were starting on a round of buttered scones, when there came—a loud knock. Not a ring, but a hard rat-tat on the hobbit's beautiful green door. Some-body was banging with a stick!

Bilbo rushed along the passage, very angry, and altogether bewildered and bewuthered—this was the most awkward Wednesday he ever remembered. He pulled open the door with a jerk, and they all fell in, one on top of the other. More dwarves, four more! And there was Gandalf behind, leaning on his staff and laughing. He had made quite a dent on the beautiful door; he had also, by the way, knocked out the se-cret mark that he had put there the morning before.

"Carefully! Carefully!" he said. "It is not like you, Bilbo, to keep friends waiting on the mat, and then open the door like a pop-gun! Let me introduce Bifur, Bofur, Bombur, and especially Thorin!"

"At your service!" said Bifur, Bofur, and Bombur standing in a row. Then they hung up two yellow hoods and a pale green one; and also a sky-blue one with a long silver tas-sel. This last belonged to Thorin, an enormously important dwarf, in fact no other than the great Thorin Oakenshield himself, who was not at all pleased at falling flat on Bilbo's mat with Bifur, Bofur, and Bombur on top of him. For one thing Bombur was immensely fat and heavy. Thorin indeed was very haughty, and said nothing about *service*; but poor Mr Baggins said he was sorry so many times, that at last he grunted "pray don't mention it," and stopped frowning.

"Now we are all here!" said Gandalf, looking at the row of thirteen hoods—the best detachable party hoods—and his own hat hanging on the pegs. "Quite a merry gathering! I hope there is something left for the late-comers to eat and drink! What's that? Tea! No thank you! A little red wine, I think for me."

"And for me," said Thorin.

"And raspberry jam and apple-tart," said Bifur.

"And mince-pies and cheese," said Bofur.

"And pork-pie and salad," said Bombur.

"And more cakes—and ale—and coffee, if you don't mind," called the other dwarves through the door.

"Put on a few eggs, there's a good fellow!" Gandalf called after him, as the hobbit stumped off to the pantries. "And just bring out the cold chicken and pickles!"

"Seems to know as much about the inside of my larders as I do myself!" thought Mr Baggins, who was feeling positively flummoxed, and was beginning to wonder whether a most wretched adventure had not come right into his house. By the time he had got all the bottles and dishes and knives and forks and glasses and plates and spoons and things piled up on big trays, he was getting very hot, and red in the face, and annoyed.

"Confusticate and bebother these dwarves!" he said aloud. "Why don't they come and lend a hand?" Lo and behold! there stood Balin and Dwalin at the door of the kitchen, and Fili and Kili behind them, and before he could say *knife* they had whisked the trays and a couple of small tables into the parlour and set out everything afresh.

Gandalf sat at the head of the party with the thirteen dwarves all round: and Bilbo sat on a stool at the fireside, nibbling at a biscuit (his appetite was quite taken away), and trying to look as if this was all perfectly ordinary and not in the least an adventure. The dwarves ate and ate, and talked and talked, and time got on. At last they pushed their chairs back, and Bilbo made a move to collect the plates and glasses.

"I suppose you will all stay to supper?" he said in his po-litest unpressing tones.

"Of course!" said Thorin. "And after. We shan't get through the business till late, and we must have some music first. Now to clear up!"

Thereupon the twelve dwarves—not Thorin, he was too important, and stayed talking to Gandalf—jumped to their feet, and made tall piles of all the things. Off they went, not waiting for trays, balancing columns of plates, each with a bottle on the top, with one hand, while the hobbit ran after them almost squeaking with fright: "please be careful!" and "please, don't trouble! I can manage." But the dwarves only started to sing:

> *Chip the glasses and crack the plates!*
> *Blunt the knives and bend the forks!*
> *That's what Bilbo Baggins hates—*
> *Smash the bottles and burn the corks!*
>
> *Cut the cloth and tread on the fat!*
> *Pour the milk on the pantry floor!*
> *Leave the bones on the bedroom mat!*
> *Splash the wine on every door!*
>
> *Dump the crocks in a boiling bowl;*
> *Pound them up with a thumping pole;*
> *And when you've finished, if any are whole,*
> *Send them down the hall to roll!*
>
> *That's what Bilbo Baggins hates!*
> *So, carefully! carefully with the plates!*

And of course they did none of these dreadful things, and everything was cleaned and put away safe as quick as lightning, while the hobbit was turning round and round in the middle of the kitchen trying to see what they were doing. Then they went back, and found Thorin with his feet on the fender smoking a pipe. He was blowing the most enormous smoke-rings, and wherever he told one to go, it went—up the chimney, or behind the clock on the mantelpiece, or under the table, or round and round the ceiling; but wherever it went it was not quick enough to escape Gandalf. Pop! he sent a smaller smoke-ring from his short clay-pipe straight through each one of Thorin's. Then Gandalf's smoke-ring would go green and come back to hover over the wizard's head. He had a cloud of them about him already, and in the dim light it made him look strange and sorcerous. Bilbo stood still and watched—he loved smoke-rings—and then he blushed to think how proud he had been yesterday morning of the smoke-rings he had sent up the wind over The Hill.

"Now for some music!" said Thorin. "Bring out the instruments!"

Kili and Fili rushed for their bags and brought back little fiddles; Dori, Nori, and Ori brought out flutes from somewhere inside their coats; Bombur produced a drum from the hall; Bifur and Bofur went out too, and came back with clarinets that they had left among the walking-sticks. Dwalin and Balin said: "Excuse me, I left mine in the porch!" "Just bring mine in with you!" said Thorin. They came back with viols as big as themselves, and with Thorin's harp wrapped in a green cloth. It was a beautiful golden harp, and when Thorin struck it the music began all at once, so sudden and sweet that Bilbo forgot everything else, and was swept away into dark lands under strange moons, far over The Water and very far from his hobbit-hole under The Hill.

The dark came into the room from the little window that opened in the side of The Hill; the firelight flickered—it was April—and still they played on, while the shadow of Gandalf's beard wagged against the wall.

The dark filled all the room, and the fire died down, and the shadows were lost, and still they played on. And suddenly first one and then another began to sing as they played, deep-throated singing of the dwarves in the deep places of their ancient homes; and this is like a fragment of their song, if it can be like their song without their music.

> *Far over the misty mountains cold*
> *To dungeons deep and caverns old*
> *We must away ere break of day*
> *To seek the pale enchanted gold.*
>
> *The dwarves of yore made mighty spells,*
> *While hammers fell like ringing bells*
> *In places deep, where dark things sleep,*
> *In hollow halls beneath the fells.*
>
> *For ancient king and elvish lord*
> *There many a gleaming golden hoard*
> *They shaped and wrought, and light they caught*
> *To hide in gems on hilt of sword.*
>
> *On silver necklaces they strung*
> *The flowering stars, on crowns they hung*
> *The dragon-fire, in twisted wire*
> *They meshed the light of moon and sun.*
>
> *Far over the misty mountains cold*
> *To dungeons deep and caverns old*

*We must away, ere break of day,*
*To claim our long-forgotten gold.*

*Goblets they carved there for themselves*
*And harps of gold; where no man delves*
*There lay they long, and many a song*
*Was sung unheard by men or elves.*

*The pines were roaring on the height,*
*The winds were moaning in the night.*
*The fire was red, it flaming spread;*
*The trees like torches blazed with light.*

*The bells were ringing in the dale*
*And men looked up with faces pale;*
*Then dragon's ire more fierce than fire*
*Laid low their towers and houses frail.*

*The mountain smoked beneath the moon;*
*The dwarves, they heard the tramp of doom.*
*They fled their hall to dying fall*
*Beneath his feet, beneath the moon.*

*Far over the misty mountains grim*
*To dungeons deep and caverns dim*
*We must away, ere break of day,*
*To win our harps and gold from him!*

As they sang the hobbit felt the love of beautiful things
made by hands and by cunning and by magic moving through
him, a fierce and a jealous love, the desire of the hearts of
dwarves. Then something Tookish woke up inside him, and
he wished to go and see the great mountains, and hear the

pine-trees and the waterfalls, and explore the caves, and wear a sword instead of a walking-stick. He looked out of the window. The stars were out in a dark sky above the trees. He thought of the jewels of the dwarves shining in dark caverns. Suddenly in the wood beyond The Water a flame leapt up—probably somebody lighting a wood-fire—and he thought of plundering dragons settling on his quiet Hill and kindling it all to flames. He shuddered; and very quickly he was plain Mr Baggins of Bag-End, Under-Hill, again.

He got up trembling. He had less than half a mind to fetch the lamp, and more than half a mind to pretend to, and go and hide behind the beer-barrels in the cellar, and not come out again until all the dwarves had gone away. Suddenly he found that the music and the singing had stopped, and they were all looking at him with eyes shining in the dark.

"Where are you going?" said Thorin, in a tone that seemed to show that he guessed both halves of the hobbit's mind.

"What about a little light?" said Bilbo apologetically.

"We like the dark," said all the dwarves. "Dark for dark business! There are many hours before dawn."

"Of course!" said Bilbo, and sat down in a hurry. He missed the stool and sat in the fender, knocking over the poker and shovel with a crash.

"Hush!" said Gandalf. "Let Thorin speak!" And this is how Thorin began.

"Gandalf, dwarves and Mr Baggins! We are met together in the house of our friend and fellow conspirator, this most excellent and audacious hobbit—may the hair on his toes never fall out! all praise to his wine and ale!—" He paused for breath and for a polite remark from the hobbit, but the compliments were quite lost on poor Bilbo Baggins, who was wagging his mouth in protest at being called *audacious* and worst of all *fellow conspirator*, though no noise came out, he was so flummoxed. So Thorin went on:

"We are met to discuss our plans, our ways, means, policy and devices. We shall soon before the break of day start on our long journey, a journey from which some of us, or perhaps all of us (except our friend and counsellor, the ingenious wizard Gandalf) may never return. It is a solemn moment. Our object is, I take it, well known to us all. To the estimable Mr Baggins, and perhaps to one or two of the younger dwarves (I think I should be right in naming Kili and Fili, for instance), the exact situation at the moment may require a little brief explanation—"

This was Thorin's style. He was an important dwarf. If he had been allowed, he would probably have gone on like this until he was out of breath, without telling any one there anything that was not known already. But he was rudely interrupted. Poor Bilbo couldn't bear it any longer. At *may never return* he began to feel a shriek coming up inside, and very soon it burst out like the whistle of an engine coming out of a tunnel. All the dwarves sprang up, knocking over the table. Gandalf struck a blue light on the end of his magic staff, and in its firework glare the poor little hobbit could be seen kneeling on the hearth-rug, shaking like a jelly that was melting. Then he fell flat on the floor, and kept on calling out "struck by lightning, struck by lightning!" over and over again; and that was all they could get out of him for a long time. So they took him and laid him out of the way on the drawing-room sofa with a drink at his elbow, and they went back to their dark business.

"Excitable little fellow," said Gandalf, as they sat down again. "Gets funny queer fits, but he is one of the best, one of the best—as fierce as a dragon in a pinch."

If you have ever seen a dragon in a pinch, you will realize

that this was only poetical exaggeration applied to any hobbit, even to Old Took's great-grand-uncle Bullroarer, who was so huge (for a hobbit) that he could ride a horse. He charged the ranks of the goblins of Mount Gram in the Battle of the Green Fields, and knocked their king Golfimbul's head clean off with a wooden club. It sailed a hundred yards through the air and went down a rabbit-hole, and in this way the battle was won and the game of Golf invented at the same moment.

In the meanwhile, however, Bullroarer's gentler descendant was reviving in the drawing-room. After a while and a drink he crept nervously to the door of the parlour. This is what he heard, Gloin speaking: "Humph!" (or some snort more or less like that). "Will he do, do you think? It is all very well for Gandalf to talk about this hobbit being fierce, but one shriek like that in a moment of excitement would be enough to wake the dragon and all his relatives, and kill the lot of us. I think it sounded more like fright than excitement! In fact, if it had not been for the sign on the door, I should have been sure we had come to the wrong house. As soon as I clapped eyes on the little fellow bobbing and puffing on the mat, I had my doubts. He looks more like a grocer than a burglar!"

Then Mr Baggins turned the handle and went in. The Took side had won. He suddenly felt he would go without bed and breakfast to be thought fierce. As for *little fellow bobbing on the mat* it almost made him really fierce. Many a time afterwards the Baggins part regretted what he did now, and he said to himself: "Bilbo, you were a fool; you walked right in and put your foot in it."

"Pardon me," he said, "if I have overheard words that you were saying. I don't pretend to understand what you are talking about, or your reference to burglars, but I think I am right in believing" (this is what he called being on his dignity) "that you think I am no good. I will show you. I have no signs on my door—it was painted a week ago—, and I am quite sure you have come to the wrong house. As soon as I saw your funny faces on the door-step, I had my doubts. But treat it as the right one. Tell me what you want done, and I will try it, if I have to walk from here to the East of East and fight the wild Were-worms in the Last Desert. I had a great-great-grand-uncle once, Bullroarer Took, and—"

"Yes, yes, but that was long ago," said Gloin. "I was talking about *you*. And I assure you there is a mark on this door—the usual one in the trade, or used to be. *Burglar wants a good job, plenty of Excitement and reasonable Reward*, that's how it is usually read. You can say *Expert Treasure-hunter* instead of *Burglar* if you like. Some of them do. It's all the same to us. Gandalf told us that there was a man of the sort in these parts looking for a Job at once, and that he had arranged for a meeting here this Wednesday tea-time."

"Of course there is a mark," said Gandalf. "I put it there myself. For very good reasons. You asked me to find the four-teenth man for your expedition, and I chose Mr Baggins. Just let any one say I chose the wrong man or the wrong house, and you can stop at thirteen and have all the bad luck you like, or go back to digging coal."

He scowled so angrily at Gloin that the dwarf huddled back in his chair; and when Bilbo tried to open his mouth to ask a question, he turned and frowned at him and stuck out his bushy eyebrows, till Bilbo shut his mouth tight with a snap. "That's right," said Gandalf. "Let's have no more argu-ment. I have chosen Mr Baggins and that ought to be enough for all of you. If I say he is a Burglar, a Burglar he is, or will be when the time comes. There is a lot more in him than you guess, and a deal more than he has any idea of himself. You may (possibly) all live to thank me yet. Now Bilbo, my boy, fetch the lamp, and let's have a little light on this!"

On the table in the light of a big lamp with a red shade he
spread a piece of parchment rather like a map.

"This was made by Thror, your grandfather, Thorin," he
said in answer to the dwarves' excited questions. "It is a plan
of the Mountain."

"I don't see that this will help us much," said Thorin disap-
pointedly after a glance. "I remember the Mountain well
enough and the lands about it. And I know where Mirkwood
is, and the Withered Heath where the great dragons bred."

"There is a dragon marked in red on the Mountain," said
Balin, "but it will be easy enough to find him without that, if
ever we arrive there."

"There is one point that you haven't noticed," said the
wizard, "and that is the secret entrance. You see that rune on
the West side, and the hand pointing to it from the other
runes? That marks a hidden passage to the Lower Halls."
(Look at the map at the beginning of this book, and you will
see there the runes in red.)

"It may have been secret once," said Thorin, "but how do
we know that it is secret any longer? Old Smaug has lived
there long enough now to find out anything there is to know
about those caves."

"He may—but he can't have used it for years and years."

"Why?"

"Because it is too small. 'Five feet high the door and three
may walk abreast' say the runes, but Smaug could not creep
into a hole that size, not even when he was a young dragon,
certainly not after devouring so many of the dwarves and men
of Dale."

"It seems a great big hole to me," squeaked Bilbo (who had
no experience of dragons and only of hobbit-holes). He was
getting excited and interested again, so that he forgot to keep
his mouth shut. He loved maps, and in his hall there hung a

large one of the Country Round with all his favourite walks marked on it in red ink. "How could such a large door be kept secret from everybody outside, apart from the dragon?" he asked. He was only a little hobbit you must remember.

"In lots of ways," said Gandalf. "But in what way this one has been hidden we don't know without going to see. From what it says on the map I should guess there is a closed door which has been made to look exactly like the side of the Mountain. That is the usual dwarves' method—I think that is right, isn't it?"

"Quite right," said Thorin.

"Also," went on Gandalf, "I forgot to mention that with the map went a key, a small and curious key. Here it is!" he said, and handed to Thorin a key with a long barrel and intricate wards, made of silver. "Keep it safe!"

"Indeed I will," said Thorin, and he fastened it upon a fine chain that hung about his neck and under his jacket. "Now things begin to look more hopeful. This news alters them much for the better. So far we have had no clear idea what to do. We thought of going East, as quiet and careful as we could, as far as the Long Lake. After that the trouble would begin—."

"A long time before that, if I know anything about the roads East," interrupted Gandalf.

"We might go from there up along the River Running," went on Thorin taking no notice, "and so to the ruins of Dale—the old town in the valley there, under the shadow of the Mountain. But we none of us liked the idea of the Front Gate. The river runs right out of it through the great cliff at the South of the Mountain, and out of it comes the dragon too— far too often, unless he has changed his habits."

"That would be no good," said the wizard, "not without a mighty Warrior, even a Hero. I tried to find one; but warriors

are busy fighting one another in distant lands, and in this
neighbourhood heroes are scarce, or simply not to be found.
Swords in these parts are mostly blunt, and axes are used for
trees, and shields as cradles or dish-covers; and dragons are
comfortably far-off (and therefore legendary). That is why I
settled on *burglary*—especially when I remembered the existence of a Side-door. And here is our little Bilbo Baggins, *the*
burglar, the chosen and selected burglar. So now let's get on
and make some plans."

"Very well then," said Thorin, "supposing the burglar-
expert gives us some ideas or suggestions." He turned with
mock-politeness to Bilbo.

"First I should like to know a bit more about things," said
he, feeling all confused and a bit shaky inside, but so far still
Tookishly determined to go on with things. "I mean about the
gold and the dragon, and all that, and how it got there, and
who it belongs to, and so on and further."

"Bless me!" said Thorin, "haven't you got a map? and
didn't you hear our song? and haven't we been talking about
all this for hours?"

"All the same, I should like it all plain and clear," said he
obstinately, putting on his business manner (usually reserved
for people who tried to borrow money off him), and doing his
best to appear wise and prudent and professional and live up
to Gandalf's recommendation. "Also I should like to know
about risks, out-of-pocket expenses, time required and remu-
neration, and so forth"—by which he meant: "What am I
going to get out of it? and am I going to come back alive?"

"O very well," said Thorin. "Long ago in my grandfather
Thror's time our family was driven out of the far North, and
came back with all their wealth and their tools to this Mountain on the map. It had been discovered by my far ancestor,
Thrain the Old, but now they mined and they tunnelled and

they made huger halls and greater workshops—and in addition I believe they found a good deal of gold and a great many jewels too. Anyway they grew immensely rich and famous, and my grandfather was King under the Mountain again, and treated with great reverence by the mortal men, who lived to the South, and were gradually spreading up the Running River as far as the valley overshadowed by the Mountain. They built the merry town of Dale there in those days. Kings used to send for our smiths, and reward even the least skillful most richly. Fathers would beg us to take their sons as apprentices, and pay us handsomely, especially in food-supplies, which we never bothered to grow or find for ourselves. Altogether those were good days for us, and the poorest of us had money to spend and to lend, and leisure to make beautiful things just for the fun of it, not to speak of the most marvellous and magical toys, the like of which is not to be found in the world now-a-days. So my grandfather's halls became full of armour and jewels and carvings and cups, and the toy market of Dale was the wonder of the North.

"Undoubtedly that was what brought the dragon. Dragons steal gold and jewels, you know, from men and elves and dwarves, wherever they can find them; and they guard their plunder as long as they live (which is practically for ever, unless they are killed), and never enjoy a brass ring of it. Indeed they hardly know a good bit of work from a bad, though they usually have a good notion of the current market value; and they can't make a thing for themselves, not even mend a little loose scale of their armour. There were lots of dragons in the North in those days, and gold was probably getting scarce up there, with the dwarves flying south or getting killed, and all the general waste and destruction that dragons make going from bad to worse. There was a most specially greedy, strong and wicked worm called Smaug. One day he flew up into the

air and came south. The first we heard of it was a noise like a
hurricane coming from the North, and the pine-trees on the
Mountain creaking and cracking in the wind. Some of the
dwarves who happened to be outside (I was one luckily—a
fine adventurous lad in those days, always wandering about,
and it saved my life that day)—well, from a good way off we
saw the dragon settle on our mountain in a spout of flame.
Then he came down the slopes and when he reached the
woods they all went up in fire. By that time all the bells were
ringing in Dale and the warriors were arming. The dwarves
rushed out of their great gate; but there was the dragon
waiting for them. None escaped that way. The river rushed up
in steam and a fog fell on Dale, and in the fog the dragon
came on them and destroyed most of the warriors—the usual
unhappy story, it was only too common in those days. Then
he went back and crept in through the Front Gate and routed
out all the halls, and lanes, and tunnels, alleys, cellars, man-
sions and passages. After that there were no dwarves left alive
inside, and he took all their wealth for himself. Probably, for
that is the dragons' way, he has piled it all up in a great heap
far inside, and sleeps on it for a bed. Later he used to crawl
out of the great gate and come by night to Dale, and carry
away people, especially maidens, to eat, until Dale was ruined,
and all the people dead or gone. What goes on there now I
don't know for certain, but I don't suppose any one lives
nearer to the Mountain than the far edge of the Long Lake
now-a-days.

"The few of us that were well outside sat and wept in
hiding, and cursed Smaug; and there we were unexpectedly
joined by my father and my grandfather with singed beards.
They looked very grim but they said very little. When I asked
how they had got away, they told me to hold my tongue, and
said that one day in the proper time I should know. After that

we went away, and we have had to earn our livings as best we could up and down the lands, often enough sinking as low as blacksmith-work or even coalmining. But we have never forgotten our stolen treasure. And even now, when I will allow we have a good bit laid by and are not so badly off"—here Thorin stroked the gold chain round his neck—"we still mean to get it back, and to bring our curses home to Smaug—if we can.

"I have often wondered about my father's and my grandfather's escape. I see now they must have had a private Sidedoor which only they knew about. But apparently they made a map, and I should like to know how Gandalf got hold of it, and why it did not come down to me, the rightful heir."

"I did not 'get hold of it,' I was given it," said the wizard. "Your grandfather Thror was killed, you remember, in the mines of Moria by Azog the Goblin."

"Curse his name, yes," said Thorin.

"And Thrain your father went away on the twenty-first of April, a hundred years ago last Thursday, and has never been seen by you since—"

"True, true," said Thorin.

"Well, your father gave me this to give to you; and if I have chosen my own time and way for handing it over, you can hardly blame me, considering the trouble I had to find you. Your father could not remember his own name when he gave me the paper, and he never told me yours; so on the whole I think I ought to be praised and thanked! Here it is," said he handing the map to Thorin.

"I don't understand," said Thorin, and Bilbo felt he would have liked to say the same. The explanation did not seem to explain.

"Your grandfather," said the wizard slowly and grimly, "gave the map to his son for safety before he went to the

mines of Moria. Your father went away to try his luck with the
map after your grandfather was killed; and lots of adventures
of a most unpleasant sort he had, but he never got near the
Mountain. How he got there I don't know, but I found him
a prisoner in the dungeons of the Necromancer."

"Whatever were you doing there?" asked Thorin with a
shudder, and all the dwarves shivered.

"Never you mind. I was finding things out, as usual; and a
nasty dangerous business it was. Even I, Gandalf, only just
escaped. I tried to save your father, but it was too late. He was
witless and wandering, and had forgotten almost everything
except the map and the key."

"We have long ago paid the goblins of Moria," said Thorin;
"we must give a thought to the Necromancer."

"Don't be absurd! He is an enemy far beyond the powers of
all the dwarves put together, if they could all be collected
again from the four corners of the world. The one thing your
father wished was for his son to read the map and use the key.
The dragon and the Mountain are more than big enough tasks
for you!"

"Hear, hear!" said Bilbo, and accidentally said it aloud.

"Hear what?" they all said turning suddenly towards him,
and he was so flustered that he answered "Hear what I have
got to say!"

"What's that?" they asked.

"Well, I should say that you ought to go East and have a
look round. After all there is the Side-door, and dragons must
sleep sometimes, I suppose. If you sit on the door-step long
enough, I daresay you will think of something. And well,
don't you know, I think we have talked long enough for one
night, if you see what I mean. What about bed, and an early
start, and all that? I will give you a good breakfast before
you go."

"Before *we* go, I suppose you mean," said Thorin. "Aren't you the burglar? And isn't sitting on the door-step your job, not to speak of getting inside the door? But I agree about bed and breakfast. I like six eggs with my ham, when starting on a journey: fried not poached, and mind you don't break 'em."

After all the others had ordered their breakfasts without so much as a please (which annoyed Bilbo very much), they all got up. The hobbit had to find room for them all, and filled all his spare-rooms and made beds on chairs and sofas, before he got them all stowed and went to his own little bed very tired and not altogether happy. One thing he did make his mind up about was not to bother to get up very early and cook everybody else's wretched breakfast. The Tookishness was wearing off, and he was not now quite so sure that he was going on any journey in the morning.

As he lay in bed he could hear Thorin still humming to himself in the best bedroom next to him:

> *Far over the misty mountains cold*
> *To dungeons deep and caverns old*
> *We must away, ere break of day,*
> *To find our long-forgotten gold.*

Bilbo went to sleep with that in his ears, and it gave him very uncomfortable dreams. It was long after the break of day, when he woke up.

## Chapter II

# ROAST MUTTON

Up jumped Bilbo, and putting on his dressing-gown went into the dining-room. There he saw nobody, but all the signs of a large and hurried breakfast. There was a fearful mess in the room, and piles of unwashed crocks in the kitchen. Nearly every pot and pan he possessed seemed to have been used. The washing-up was so dismally real that Bilbo was forced to believe the party of the night before had not been part of his bad dreams, as he had rather hoped. Indeed he was really relieved after all to think that they had all gone without him, and without bothering to wake him up ("but with never a thank-you" he thought); and yet in a way he could not help feeling just a trifle disappointed. The feeling surprised him.

"Don't be a fool, Bilbo Baggins!" he said to himself, "thinking of dragons and all that outlandish nonsense at your age!" So he put on an apron, lit fires, boiled water, and washed up. Then he had a nice little breakfast in the kitchen before turning out the dining-room. By that time the sun was shining; and the front door was open, letting in a warm spring breeze. Bilbo began to whistle loudly and to forget about the night before. In fact he was just sitting down to a nice little second breakfast in the dining-room by the open window, when in walked Gandalf.

"My dear fellow," said he, "whenever *are* you going to

come? What about *an early start?*—and here you are having breakfast, or whatever you call it, at half past ten! They left you the message, because they could not wait."

"What message?" said poor Mr Baggins all in a fluster.

"Great elephants!" said Gandalf, "you are not at all yourself this morning—you have never dusted the mantelpiece!"

"What's that got to do with it? I have had enough to do with washing up for fourteen!"

"If you had dusted the mantelpiece, you would have found this just under the clock," said Gandalf, handing Bilbo a note (written, of course, on his own note-paper).

This is what he read:

"Thorin and Company to Burglar Bilbo greeting! For your hospitality our sincerest thanks, and for your offer of professional assistance our grateful acceptance. Terms: cash on delivery, up to and not exceeding one fourteenth of total profits (if any); all travelling expenses guaranteed in any event; funeral expenses to be defrayed by us or our representatives, if occasion arises and the matter is not otherwise arranged for.

"Thinking it unnecessary to disturb your esteemed repose, we have proceeded in advance to make requisite preparations, and shall await your respected person at the Green Dragon Inn, Bywater, at 11 a.m. sharp. Trusting that you will be *punctual*,

> "*We have the honour to remain*
> "*Yours deeply*
> > "*Thorin & Co.*"

"That leaves you just ten minutes. You will have to run," said Gandalf.

"But—," said Bilbo.

"No time for that either! Off you go!"

To the end of his days Bilbo could never remember how he found himself outside, without a hat, a walking-stick or any money, or anything that he usually took when he went out; leaving his second breakfast half-finished and quite unwashed-up, pushing his keys into Gandalf's hands, and running as fast as his furry feet could carry him down the lane, past the great Mill, across The Water, and then on for a mile or more.

Very puffed he was, when he got to Bywater just on the stroke of eleven, and found he had come without a pocket-handkerchief!

"Bravo!" said Balin who was standing at the inn door looking out for him.

Just then all the others came round the corner of the road from the village. They were on ponies, and each pony was slung about with all kinds of baggages, packages, parcels, and paraphernalia. There was a very small pony, apparently for Bilbo.

"Up you two get, and off we go!" said Thorin.

"I'm awfully sorry," said Bilbo, "but I have come without my hat, and I have left my pocket-handkerchief behind, and I haven't got any money. I didn't get your note until after 10.45 to be precise."

"Don't be precise," said Dwalin, "and don't worry! You will have to manage without pocket-handkerchiefs, and a good many other things, before you get to the journey's end. As for a hat, I have got a spare hood and cloak in my luggage."

That's how they all came to start, jogging off from the inn one fine morning just before May, on laden ponies; and Bilbo was wearing a dark-green hood (a little weather-stained) and a dark-green cloak borrowed from Dwalin. They were too large for him, and he looked rather comic. What his father Bungo would have thought of him, I daren't think. His only comfort was he couldn't be mistaken for a dwarf, as he had no beard.

They had not been riding very long, when up came Gandalf very splendid on a white horse. He had brought a lot of pocket-handkerchiefs, and Bilbo's pipe and tobacco. So after that the party went along very merrily, and they told stories or sang songs as they rode forward all day, except of course when they stopped for meals. These didn't come quite as often as Bilbo would have liked them, but still he began to feel that adventures were not so bad after all.

At first they had passed through hobbit-lands, a wide respectable country inhabited by decent folk, with good roads, an inn or two, and now and then a dwarf or a farmer ambling by on business. Then they came to lands where people spoke strangely, and sang songs Bilbo had never heard before. Now they had gone on far into the Lone-lands, where there were no people left, no inns, and the roads grew steadily worse. Not far ahead were dreary hills, rising higher and higher, dark with trees. On some of them were old castles with an evil look, as if they had been built by wicked people. Everything seemed gloomy, for the weather that day had taken a nasty turn. Mostly it had been as good as May can be, even in merry tales, but now it was cold and wet. In the Lone-lands they had been obliged to camp when they could, but at least it had been dry.

"To think it will soon be June," grumbled Bilbo, as he splashed along behind the others in a very muddy track. It was after tea-time; it was pouring with rain, and had been all day; his hood was dripping into his eyes, his cloak was full of water; the pony was tired and stumbled on stones; the others were too grumpy to talk. "And I'm sure the rain has got into the dry clothes and into the food-bags," thought Bilbo. "Bother burgling and everything to do with it! I wish I was at

home in my nice hole by the fire, with the kettle just beginning to sing!" It was not the last time that he wished that!

Still the dwarves jogged on, never turning round or taking
any notice of the hobbit. Somewhere behind the grey clouds
the sun must have gone down, for it began to get dark as they
went down into a deep valley with a river at the bottom. Wind
got up, and willows along its banks bent and sighed. Fortunately the road went over an ancient stone bridge, for the
river, swollen with the rains, came rushing down from the
hills and mountains in the north.

It was nearly night when they had crossed over. The wind
broke up the grey clouds, and a wandering moon appeared
above the hills between the flying rags. Then they stopped,
and Thorin muttered something about supper, "and where
shall we get a dry patch to sleep on?"

Not until then did they notice that Gandalf was missing. So
far he had come all the way with them, never saying if he was
in the adventure or merely keeping them company for a
while. He had eaten most, talked most, and laughed most. But
now he simply was not there at all!

"Just when a wizard would have been most useful, too,"
groaned Dori and Nori (who shared the hobbit's views about
regular meals, plenty and often).

They decided in the end that they would have to camp
where they were. They moved to a clump of trees, and though
it was drier under them, the wind shook the rain off the
leaves, and the drip, drip, was most annoying. Also the mischief seemed to have got into the fire. Dwarves can make a
fire almost anywhere out of almost anything, wind or no
wind; but they could not do it that night, not even Oin and
Gloin, who were specially good at it.

Then one of the ponies took fright at nothing and bolted.
He got into the river before they could catch him; and before

they could get him out again, Fili and Kili were nearly drowned, and all the baggage that he carried was washed away off him. Of course it was mostly food, and there was mighty little left for supper, and less for breakfast.

There they all sat glum and wet and muttering, while Oin and Gloin went on trying to light the fire, and quarrelling about it. Bilbo was sadly reflecting that adventures are not all pony-rides in May-sunshine, when Balin, who was always their look-out man, said: "There's a light over there!" There was a hill some way off with trees on it, pretty thick in parts. Out of the dark mass of the trees they could now see a light shining, a reddish comfortable-looking light, as it might be a fire or torches twinkling.

When they had looked at if for some while, they fell to arguing. Some said "no" and some said "yes." Some said they could but go and see, and anything was better than little supper, less breakfast, and wet clothes all the night.

Others said: "These parts are none too well known, and are too near the mountains. Travellers seldom come this way now. The old maps are no use: things have changed for the worse and the road is unguarded. They have seldom even heard of the king round here, and the less inquisitive you are as you go along, the less trouble you are likely to find." Some said: "After all there are fourteen of us." Others said: "Where has Gandalf got to?" This remark was repeated by everybody. Then the rain began to pour down worse than ever, and Oin and Gloin began to fight.

That settled it. "After all we have got a burglar with us," they said; and so they made off, leading their ponies (with all due and proper caution) in the direction of the light. They came to the hill and were soon in the wood. Up the hill they went; but there was no proper path to be seen, such as might lead to a house or a farm; and do what they could they made a deal of rustling and crackling and creaking (and a good deal of grumbling and dratting), as they went through the trees in the pitch dark.

Suddenly the red light shone out very bright through the tree-trunks not far ahead.

"Now it is the burglar's turn," they said, meaning Bilbo. "You must go on and find out all about that light, and what it is for, and if all is perfectly safe and canny," said Thorin to the hobbit. "Now scuttle off, and come back quick, if all is well. If not, come back if you can! If you can't, hoot twice like a barn-owl and once like a screech-owl, and we will do what we can."

Off Bilbo had to go, before he could explain that he could not hoot even once like any kind of owl any more than fly like a bat. But at any rate hobbits can move quietly in woods, absolutely quietly. They take a pride in it, and Bilbo had sniffed more than once at what he called "all this dwarvish racket," as they went along, though I don't suppose you or I would have noticed anything at all on a windy night, not if the whole cavalcade had passed two feet off. As for Bilbo walking primly towards the red light, I don't suppose even a weasel would have stirred a whisker at it. So, naturally, he got right up to the fire—for fire it was—without disturbing anyone. And this is what he saw.

Three very large persons sitting round a very large fire of beech-logs. They were toasting mutton on long spits of wood, and licking the gravy off their fingers. There was a fine toothsome smell. Also there was a barrel of good drink at hand, and they were drinking out of jugs. But they were trolls. Obviously trolls. Even Bilbo, in spite of his sheltered life, could see that: from the great heavy faces of them, and their size, and the shape of their legs, not to mention their language, which was not drawing-room fashion at all, at all.

"Mutton yesterday, mutton today, and blimey, if it don't look like mutton again tomorrer," said one of the trolls.

"Never a blinking bit of manflesh have we had for long enough," said a second. "What the 'ell William was a-thinkin' of to bring us into these parts at all, beats me—and the drink runnin' short, what's more," he said jogging the elbow of William, who was taking a pull at his jug.

William choked. "Shut yer mouth!" he said as soon as he could. "Yer can't expect folk to stop here for ever just to be et by you and Bert. You've et a village and a half between yer, since we come down from the mountains. How much more d'yer want? And time's been up our way, when yer'd have said 'thank yer Bill' for a nice bit o' fat valley mutton like what this is." He took a big bite off a sheep's leg he was roasting, and wiped his lips on his sleeve.

Yes, I am afraid trolls do behave like that, even those with only one head each. After hearing all this Bilbo ought to have done something at once. Either he should have gone back quietly and warned his friends that there were three fair-sized trolls at hand in a nasty mood, quite likely to try roasted dwarf, or even pony, for a change; or else he should have done a bit of good quick burgling. A really first-class and legendary burglar would at this point have picked the trolls' pockets—it is nearly always worth while, if you can manage it—, pinched the very mutton off the spits, purloined the beer, and walked off without their noticing him. Others more practical but with less professional pride would perhaps have stuck a dagger into each of them before they observed it. Then the night could have been spent cheerily.

Bilbo knew it. He had read of a good many things he had never seen or done. He was very much alarmed, as well as disgusted; he wished himself a hundred miles away, and yet—and yet somehow he could not go straight back to

Thorin and Company emptyhanded. So he stood and hesitated in the shadows. Of the various burglarious proceedings he had heard of picking the trolls' pockets seemed the least difficult, so at last he crept behind a tree just behind William.

Bert and Tom went off to the barrel. William was having another drink. Then Bilbo plucked up courage and put his little hand in William's enormous pocket. There was a purse in it, as big as a bag to Bilbo. "Ha!" thought he, warming to his new work as he lifted it carefully out, "this is a beginning!"

It was! Trolls' purses are the mischief, and this was no exception. " 'Ere, 'oo are you?" it squeaked, as it left the pocket; and William turned round at once and grabbed Bilbo by the neck, before he could duck behind the tree.

"Blimey, Bert, look what I've copped!" said William.

"What is it?" said the others coming up.

"Lumme, if I knows! What are yer?"

"Bilbo Baggins, a bur—a hobbit," said poor Bilbo, shaking all over, and wondering how to make owl-noises before they throttled him.

"A burrahobbit?" said they a bit startled. Trolls are slow in the uptake, and mighty suspicious about anything new to them.

"What's a burrahobbit got to do with my pocket, anyways?" said William.

"And can yer cook 'em?" said Tom.

"Yer can try," said Bert, picking up a skewer.

"He wouldn't make above a mouthful," said William, who had already had a fine supper, "not when he was skinned and boned."

"P'raps there are more like him round about, and we might make a pie," said Bert. "Here you, are there any more of your sort a-sneakin' in these here woods, yer nasty little rabbit," said he looking at the hobbit's furry feet; and he picked him up by the toes and shook him.

"Yes, lots," said Bilbo, before he remembered not to give his friends away. "No none at all, not one," he said immediately afterwards.

"What d'yer mean?" said Bert, holding him right way up, by the hair this time.

"What I say," said Bilbo gasping. "And please don't cook me, kind sirs! I am a good cook myself, and cook better than I cook, if you see what I mean. I'll cook beautifully for you, a perfectly beautiful breakfast for you, if only you won't have me for supper."

"Poor little blighter," said William. He had already had as much supper as he could hold; also he had had lots of beer. "Poor little blighter! Let him go!"

"Not till he says what he means by *lots* and *none at all*," said Bert. "I don't want to have me throat cut in me sleep! Hold his toes in the fire, till he talks!"

"I won't have it," said William. "I caught him anyway."

"You're a fat fool, William," said Bert, "as I've said afore this evening."

"And you're a lout!"

"And I won't take that from you, Bill Huggins," says Bert, and puts his fist in William's eye.

Then there was a gorgeous row. Bilbo had just enough wits left, when Bert dropped him on the ground, to scramble out of the way of their feet, before they were fighting like dogs, and calling one another all sorts of perfectly true and applicable names in very loud voices. Soon they were locked in one another's arms, and rolling nearly into the fire kicking and thumping, while Tom whacked at them both with a branch to bring them to their senses—and that of course only made them madder than ever.

That would have been the time for Bilbo to have left. But his poor little feet had been very squashed in Bert's big paw, and he had no breath in his body, and his head was going round; so there he lay for a while panting, just outside the circle of firelight.

Right in the middle of the fight up came Balin. The dwarves had heard noises from a distance, and after waiting for some time for Bilbo to come back, or to hoot like an owl, they started off one by one to creep towards the light as quietly as they could. No sooner did Tom see Balin come into the light than he gave an awful howl. Trolls simply detest the very sight of dwarves (uncooked). Bert and Bill stopped fighting immediately, and "a sack, Tom quick!" they said. Before Balin, who was wondering where in all this commotion Bilbo was, knew what was happening, a sack was over his head, and he was down.

"There's more to come yet," said Tom, "or I'm mighty mistook. Lots and none at all, it is," said he. "No burrahobbits, but lots of these here dwarves. That's about the shape of it!"

"I reckon you're right," said Bert, "and we'd best get out of the light."

And so they did. With sacks in their hands, that they used for carrying off mutton and other plunder, they waited in the shadows. As each dwarf came up and looked at the fire, and the spilled jugs, and the gnawed mutton, in surprise, pop! went a nasty smelly sack over his head, and he was down. Soon Dwalin lay by Balin, and Fili and Kili together, and Dori and Nori and Ori all in a heap, and Oin and Gloin and Bifur and Bofur and Bombur piled uncomfortably near the fire.

"That'll teach 'em," said Tom; for Bifur and Bombur had given a lot of trouble, and fought like mad, as dwarves will when cornered.

Thorin came last—and he was not caught unawares. He came expecting mischief, and didn't need to see his friends' legs sticking out of sacks to tell him that things were not all well. He stood outside in the shadows some way off, and said: "What's all this trouble? Who has been knocking my people about?"

"It's trolls!" said Bilbo from behind a tree. They had forgotten all about him. "They're hiding in the bushes with sacks," said he.

"O! are they?" said Thorin, and he jumped forward to the fire, before they could leap on him. He caught up a big branch all on fire at one end; and Bert got that end in his eye before he could step aside. That put him out of the battle for a bit. Bilbo did his best. He caught hold of Tom's leg—as well as he could, it was thick as a young tree-trunk—but he was sent spinning up into the top of some bushes, when Tom kicked the sparks up in Thorin's face.

Tom got the branch in his teeth for that, and lost one of the front ones. It made him howl, I can tell you. But just at that moment William came up behind and popped a sack right over Thorin's head and down to his toes. And so the fight ended. A nice pickle they were all in now: all neatly tied up in sacks, with three angry trolls (and two with burns and bashes to remember) sitting by them, arguing whether they should roast them slowly, or mince them fine and boil them, or just sit on them one by one and squash them into jelly; and Bilbo up in a bush, with his clothes and his skin torn, not daring to move for fear they should hear him.

It was just then that Gandalf came back. But no one saw him. The trolls had just decided to roast the dwarves now and eat them later—that was Bert's idea, and after a lot of argument they had all agreed to it.

"No good roasting 'em now, it'd take all night," said a voice. Bert thought it was William's.

"Don't start the argument all over again, Bill," he said, "or it *will* take all night."

"Who's a-arguing?" said William, who thought it was Bert that had spoken.

"You are," said Bert.

"You're a liar," said William; and so the argument began all over again. In the end they decided to mince them fine and boil them. So they got a great black pot, and they took out their knives.

"No good boiling 'em! We ain't got no water, and it's a long way to the well and all," said a voice. Bert and William thought it was Tom's.

"Shut up!" said they, "or we'll never have done. And yer can fetch the water yerself, if yer say any more."

"Shut up yerself!" said Tom, who thought it was William's voice. "Who's arguing but you, I'd like to know."

"You're a booby," said William.

"Booby yerself!" said Tom.

And so the argument began all over again, and went on hotter than ever, until at last they decided to sit on the sacks one by one and squash them, and boil them next time.

"Who shall we sit on first?" said the voice.

"Better sit on the last fellow first," said Bert, whose eye had been damaged by Thorin. He thought Tom was talking.

"Don't talk to yerself!" said Tom. "But if you wants to sit on the last one, sit on him. Which is he?"

"The one with the yellow stockings," said Bert.

"Nonsense, the one with the grey stockings," said a voice like William's.

"I made sure it was yellow," said Bert.

"Yellow it was," said William.

"Then what did yer say it was grey for?" said Bert.

"I never did. Tom said it."

"That I never did!" said Tom, "It was you."

"Two to one, so shut yer mouth!" said Bert.

"Who are you a-talkin' to?" said William.

"Now stop it!" said Tom and Bert together. "The night's gettin' on, and dawn comes early. Let's get on with it!"

"Dawn take you all, and be stone to you!" said a voice that sounded like William's. But it wasn't. For just at that moment the light came over the hill, and there was a mighty twitter in the branches. William never spoke for he stood turned to stone as he stooped; and Bert and Tom were stuck like rocks as they looked at him. And there they stand to this day, all alone, unless the birds perch on them; for trolls, as you probably know, must be underground before dawn, or they go back to the stuff of the mountains they are made of, and never move again. That is what had happened to Bert and Tom and William.

"Excellent!" said Gandalf, as he stepped from behind a tree, and helped Bilbo to climb down out of a thorn-bush. Then Bilbo understood. It was the wizard's voice that had kept the trolls bickering and quarrelling, until the light came and made an end of them.

The next thing was to untie the sacks and let out the dwarves. They were nearly suffocated, and very annoyed: they had not at all enjoyed lying there listening to the trolls making plans for roasting them and squashing them and mincing them. They had to hear Bilbo's account of what had happened to him twice over, before they were satisfied.

"Silly time to go practising pinching and pocket-picking," said Bombur, "when what we wanted was fire and food!"

"And that's just what you wouldn't have got of those fellows without a struggle, in any case," said Gandalf. "Anyhow

you are wasting time now. Don't you realize that the trolls
must have a cave or a hole dug somewhere near to hide from
the sun in? We must look into it!"

They searched about, and soon found the marks of trolls'
stony boots going away through the trees. They followed the
tracks up the hill, until hidden by bushes they came on a
big door of stone leading to a cave. But they could not open
it, not though they all pushed while Gandalf tried various
incantations.

"Would this be any good?" asked Bilbo, when they were
getting tired and angry. "I found it on the ground where the
trolls had their fight." He held out a largish key, though no
doubt William had thought it very small and secret. It must
have fallen out of his pocket, very luckily, before he was
turned to stone.

"Why on earth didn't you mention it before?" they cried.
Gandalf grabbed it and fitted it into the key-hole. Then the
stone door swung back with one big push, and they all went
inside. There were bones on the floor and a nasty smell was in
the air; but there was a good deal of food jumbled carelessly
on shelves and on the ground, among an untidy litter of
plunder, of all sorts from brass buttons to pots full of gold
coins standing in a corner. There were lots of clothes, too,
hanging on the walls—too small for trolls, I am afraid they
belonged to victims—and among them were several swords
of various makes, shapes, and sizes. Two caught their eyes
particularly, because of their beautiful scabbards and jewelled hilts.

Gandalf and Thorin each took one of these; and Bilbo took
a knife in a leather sheath. It would have made only a tiny
pocket-knife for a troll, but it was as good as a short sword for
the hobbit.

"These look like good blades," said the wizard, half drawing them and looking at them curiously. "They were not made by any troll, nor by any smith among men in these parts and days; but when we can read the runes on them, we shall know more about them."

"Let's get out of this horrible smell!" said Fili. So they carried out the pots of coins, and such food as was untouched and looked fit to eat, also one barrel of ale which was still full. By that time they felt like breakfast, and being very hungry they did not turn their noses up at what they had got from the trolls' larder. Their own provisions were very scanty. Now they had bread and cheese, and plenty of ale, and bacon to toast in the embers of the fire.

After that they slept, for their night had been disturbed; and they did nothing more till the afternoon. Then they brought up their ponies, and carried away the pots of gold, and buried them very secretly not far from the track by the river, putting a great many spells over them, just in case they ever had the chance to come back and recover them. When that was done, they all mounted once more, and jogged along again on the path towards the East.

"Where did you go to, if I may ask?" said Thorin to Gandalf as they rode along.

"To look ahead," said he.

"And what brought you back in the nick of time?"

"Looking behind," said he.

"Exactly!" said Thorin; "but could you be more plain?"

"I went on to spy out our road. It will soon become dangerous and difficult. Also I was anxious about replenishing our small stock of provisions. I had not gone very far, however, when I met a couple of friends of mine from Rivendell."

"Where's that?" asked Bilbo.

"Don't interrupt!" said Gandalf. "You will get there in a few days now, if we're lucky, and find out all about it. As I was saying I met two of Elrond's people. They were hurrying along for fear of the trolls. It was they who told me that three of them had come down from the mountains and settled in the woods not far from the road: they had frightened everyone away from the district, and they waylaid strangers.

"I immediately had a feeling that I was wanted back. Looking behind I saw a fire in the distance and made for it. So now you know. Please be more careful, next time, or we shall never get anywhere!"

"Thank you!" said Thorin.

*Chapter III*

# A SHORT REST

They did not sing or tell stories that day, even though the weather improved; nor the next day, nor the day after. They had begun to feel that danger was not far away on either side. They camped under the stars, and their horses had more to eat than they had; for there was plenty of grass, but there was not much in their bags, even with what they had got from the trolls. One morning they forded a river at a wide shallow place full of the noise of stones and foam. The far bank was steep and slippery. When they got to the top of it, leading their ponies, they saw that the great mountains had marched down very near to them. Already they seemed only a day's easy journey from the feet of the nearest. Dark and drear it looked, though there were patches of sunlight on its brown sides, and behind its shoulders the tips of snow-peaks gleamed.

"Is that *The* Mountain?" asked Bilbo in a solemn voice, looking at it with round eyes. He had never seen a thing that looked so big before.

"Of course not!" said Balin. "That is only the beginning of the Misty Mountains, and we have got to get through, or over, or under those somehow, before we can come into Wilderland beyond. And it is a deal of a way even from the other side of them to the Lonely Mountain in the East where Smaug lies on our treasure."

"O!" said Bilbo, and just at that moment he felt more tired than he ever remembered feeling before. He was thinking once again of his comfortable chair before the fire in his favourite sitting-room in his hobbit-hole, and of the kettle singing. Not for the last time!

Now Gandalf led the way. "We must not miss the road, or we shall be done for," he said. "We need food, for one thing, *and* rest in reasonable safety—also it is very necessary to tackle the Misty Mountains by the proper path, or else you will get lost in them, and have to come back and start at the beginning again (if you ever get back at all)."

They asked him where he was making for, and he answered: "You are come to the very edge of the Wild, as some of you may know. Hidden somewhere ahead of us is the fair valley of Rivendell where Elrond lives in the Last Homely House. I sent a message by my friends, and we are expected."

That sounded nice and comforting, but they had not got there yet, and it was not so easy as it sounds to find the Last Homely House west of the Mountains. There seemed to be no trees and no valleys and no hills to break the ground in front of them, only one vast slope going slowly up and up to meet the feet of the nearest mountain, a wide land the colour of heather and crumbling rock, with patches and slashes of grass-green and moss-green showing where water might be.

Morning passed, afternoon came; but in all the silent waste there was no sign of any dwelling. They were growing anxious, for they saw now that the house might be hidden almost anywhere between them and the mountains. They came on unexpected valleys, narrow with steep sides, that opened suddenly at their feet, and they looked down surprised to see trees below them and running water at the bottom. There were gullies that they could almost leap over, but very deep with waterfalls in them. There were dark ravines that one could neither jump over nor climb into. There were bogs, some of them green pleasant places to look at, with flowers growing bright and tall; but a pony that walked there with a pack on its back would never have come out again.

It was indeed a much wider land from the ford to the mountains than ever you would have guessed. Bilbo was astonished. The only path was marked with white stones, some of which were small, and others were half covered with moss or heather. Altogether it was a very slow business following the track, even guided by Gandalf, who seemed to know his way about pretty well.

His head and beard wagged this way and that as he looked for the stones, and they followed his lead, but they seemed no nearer to the end of the search when the day began to fail. Tea-time had long gone by, and it seemed supper-time would soon do the same. There were moths fluttering about, and the light became very dim, for the moon had not risen. Bilbo's pony began to stumble over roots and stones. They came to the edge of a steep fall in the ground so suddenly that Gandalf's horse nearly slipped down the slope.

"Here it is at last!" he called, and the others gathered round him and looked over the edge. They saw a valley far below. They could hear the voice of hurrying water in a rocky bed at the bottom; the scent of trees was in the air; and there was a light on the valley-side across the water.

Bilbo never forgot the way they slithered and slipped in the dusk down the steep zig-zag path into the secret valley of Rivendell. The air grew warmer as they got lower, and the smell of the pine-trees made him drowsy, so that every now and again he nodded and nearly fell off, or bumped his nose on the pony's neck. Their spirits rose as they went down and down. The trees changed to beech and oak, and there was a comfortable feeling in the twilight. The last green had almost faded out of the grass, when they came at length to an open glade not far above the banks of the stream.

"Hmmm! it smells like elves!" thought Bilbo, and he looked up at the stars. They were burning bright and blue. Just then there came a burst of song like laughter in the trees:

> *O! What are you doing,*
> *And where are you going?*
> *Your ponies need shoeing!*
> *The river is flowing!*
>   *O! tra-la-la-lally*
>     *here down in the valley!*
>
> *O! What are you seeking,*
> *And where are you making?*
> *The faggots are reeking,*
> *The bannocks are baking!*
>   *O! tril-lil-lil-lolly*
>     *the valley is jolly,*
>       *ha! ha!*
>
> *O! Where are you going*
> *With beards all a-wagging?*
> *No knowing, no knowing*
> *What brings Mister Baggins*
>   *And Balin and Dwalin*
>     *down into the valley*
>       *in June*
>       *ha! ha!*

> *O! Will you be staying,*
> *Or will you be flying?*
> *Your ponies are straying!*
> *The daylight is dying!*
> *To fly would be folly,*
> *To stay would be jolly*
>    *And listen and hark*
>    *Till the end of the dark*
>      *to our tune*
>      *ha! ha!*

So they laughed and sang in the trees; and pretty fair nonsense I daresay you think it. Not that they would care; they would only laugh all the more if you told them so. They were elves of course. Soon Bilbo caught glimpses of them as the darkness deepened. He loved elves, though he seldom met them; but he was a little frightened of them too. Dwarves don't get on well with them. Even decent enough dwarves like Thorin and his friends think them foolish (which is a very foolish thing to think), or get annoyed with them. For some elves tease them and laugh at them, and most of all at their beards.

"Well, well!" said a voice. "Just look! Bilbo the hobbit on a pony, my dear! Isn't it delicious!"

Then off they went into another song as ridiculous as the one I have written down in full. At last one, a tall young fellow, came out from the trees and bowed to Gandalf and to Thorin.

"Welcome to the valley!" he said.

"Thank you!" said Thorin a bit gruffly; but Gandalf was already off his horse and among the elves, talking merrily with them.

"You are a little out of your way," said the elf: "that is, if you are making for the only path across the water and to the house beyond. We will set you right, but you had best get on foot, until you are over the bridge. Are you going to stay a bit and sing with us, or will you go straight on? Supper is preparing over there," he said. "I can smell the wood-fires for the cooking."

Tired as he was, Bilbo would have liked to stay a while. Elvish singing is not a thing to miss, in June under the stars, not if you care for such things. Also he would have liked to have a few private words with these people that seemed to know his names and all about him, although he had never seen them before. He thought their opinion of his adventure might be interesting. Elves know a lot and are wondrous folk for news, and know what is going on among the peoples of the land, as quick as water flows, or quicker.

But the dwarves were all for supper as soon as possible just then, and would not stay. On they all went, leading their ponies, till they were brought to a good path and so at last to the very brink of the river. It was flowing fast and noisily, as mountain-streams do of a summer evening, when sun has been all day on the snow far up above. There was only a narrow bridge of stone without a parapet, as narrow as a pony could well walk on; and over that they had to go, slow and careful, one by one, each leading his pony by the bridle. The elves had brought bright lanterns to the shore, and they sang a merry song as the party went across.

"Don't dip your beard in the foam, father!" they cried to Thorin, who was bent almost on to his hands and knees. "It is long enough without watering it."

"Mind Bilbo doesn't eat all the cakes!" they called. "He is too fat to get through key-holes yet!"

"Hush, hush! Good People! and good night!" said Gandalf, who came last. "Valleys have ears, and some elves have over merry tongues. Good night!"

And so at last they all came to the Last Homely House, and found its doors flung wide.

Now it is a strange thing, but things that are good to have and days that are good to spend are soon told about, and not much to listen to; while things that are uncomfortable, palpitating, and even gruesome, may make a good tale, and take a deal of telling anyway. They stayed long in that good house, fourteen days at least, and they found it hard to leave. Bilbo would gladly have stopped there for ever and ever—even supposing a wish would have taken him right back to his hobbit-hole without trouble. Yet there is little to tell about their stay.

The master of the house was an elf-friend—one of those people whose fathers came into the strange stories before the beginning of History, the wars of the evil goblins and the elves and the first men in the North. In those days of our tale there were still some people who had both elves and heroes of the North for ancestors, and Elrond the master of the house was their chief.

He was as noble and as fair in face as an elf-lord, as strong as a warrior, as wise as a wizard, as venerable as a king of dwarves, and as kind as summer. He comes into many tales, but his part in the story of Bilbo's great adventure is only a small one, though important, as you will see, if we ever get to the end of it. His house was perfect, whether you liked food, or sleep, or work, or story-telling, or singing, or just sitting and thinking best, or a pleasant mixture of them all. Evil things did not come into that valley.

I wish I had time to tell you even a few of the tales or one or two of the songs that they heard in that house. All of them, the ponies as well, grew refreshed and strong in a few days there.

Their clothes were mended as well as their bruises, their tempers and their hopes. Their bags were filled with food and provisions light to carry but strong to bring them over the mountain passes. Their plans were improved with the best advice. So the time came to midsummer eve, and they were to go on again with the early sun on midsummer morning.

Elrond knew all about runes of every kind. That day he looked at the swords they had brought from the trolls' lair, and he said: "These are not troll-make. They are old swords, very old swords of the High Elves of the West, my kin. They were made in Gondolin for the Goblin-wars. They must have come from a dragon's hoard or goblin plunder, for dragons and goblins destroyed that city many ages ago. This, Thorin, the runes name Orcrist, the Goblin-cleaver in the ancient tongue of Gondolin; it was a famous blade. This, Gandalf, was Glamdring, Foehammer that the king of Gondolin once wore. Keep them well!"

"Whence did the trolls get them, I wonder?" said Thorin looking at his sword with new interest.

"I could not say," said Elrond, "but one may guess that your trolls had plundered other plunderers, or come on the remnants of old robberies in some hold in the mountains. I have heard that there are still forgotten treasures of old to be found in the deserted caverns of the mines of Moria, since the dwarf and goblin war."

Thorin pondered these words. "I will keep this sword in honour," he said. "May it soon cleave goblins once again!"

"A wish that is likely to be granted soon enough in the mountains!" said Elrond. "But show me now your map!"

He took it and gazed long at it, and he shook his head; for if he did not altogether approve of dwarves and their love of gold, he hated dragons and their cruel wickedness, and he grieved to remember the ruin of the town of Dale and its merry bells, and the burned banks of the bright River Running. The moon was shining in a broad silver crescent. He held up the map and the white light shone through it. "What is this?" he said. "There are moon-letters here, beside the plain runes which say 'five feet high the door and three may walk abreast.' "

"What are moon-letters?" asked the hobbit full of excitement. He loved maps, as I have told you before; and he also liked runes and letters and cunning handwriting, though when he wrote himself it was a bit thin and spidery.

"Moon-letters are rune-letters, but you cannot see them," said Elrond, "not when you look straight at them. They can only be seen when the moon shines behind them, and what is more, with the more cunning sort it must be a moon of the same shape and season as the day when they were written. The dwarves invented them and wrote them with silver pens, as your friends could tell you. These must have been written on a midsummer's eve in a crescent moon, a long while ago."

"What do they say?" asked Gandalf and Thorin together, a bit vexed perhaps that even Elrond should have found this out first, though really there had not been a chance before, and there would not have been another until goodness knows when.

"Stand by the grey stone when the thrush knocks," read Elrond, "and the setting sun with the last light of Durin's Day will shine upon the key-hole."

"Durin, Durin!" said Thorin. "He was the father of the fathers of the eldest race of Dwarves, the Longbeards, and my first ancestor: I am his heir."

"Then what is Durin's Day?" asked Elrond.

"The first day of the dwarves' New Year," said Thorin, "is as all should know the first day of the last moon of Autumn on the threshold of Winter. We still call it Durin's Day when the last moon of Autumn and the sun are in the sky together. But this will not help us much, I fear, for it passes our skill in these days to guess when such a time will come again."

"That remains to be seen," said Gandalf. "Is there any more writing?"

"None to be seen by this moon," said Elrond, and he gave the map back to Thorin; and then they went down to the water to see the elves dance and sing upon the midsummer's eve.

The next morning was a midsummer's morning as fair and fresh as could be dreamed: blue sky and never a cloud, and the sun dancing on the water. Now they rode away amid songs of farewell and good speed, with their hearts ready for more adventure, and with a knowledge of the road they must follow over the Misty Mountains to the land beyond.

*Chapter IV*

# OVER HILL AND UNDER HILL

There were many paths that led up into those mountains, and many passes over them. But most of the paths were cheats and deceptions and led nowhere or to bad ends; and most of the passes were infested by evil things and dreadful dangers. The dwarves and the hobbit, helped by the wise advice of El-rond and the knowledge and memory of Gandalf, took the right road to the right pass.

Long days after they had climbed out of the valley and left the Last Homely House miles behind, they were still going up and up and up. It was a hard path and a dangerous path, a crooked way and a lonely and a long. Now they could look back over the lands they had left, laid out behind them far below. Far, far away in the West, where things were blue and faint, Bilbo knew there lay his own country of safe and comfortable things, and his little hobbit-hole. He shivered. It was getting bitter cold up here, and the wind came shrill among the rocks. Boulders, too, at times came galloping down the mountainsides, let loose by mid-day sun upon the snow, and passed among them (which was lucky), or over their heads (which was alarming). The nights were comfortless and chill, and they did not dare to sing or talk too loud, for the echoes were uncanny, and the silence seemed to dislike being

broken—except by the noise of water and the wail of wind
and the crack of stone.

"The summer is getting on down below," thought Bilbo,
"and haymaking is going on and picnics. They will be har-
vesting and blackberrying, before we even begin to go down
the other side at this rate." And the others were thinking
equally gloomy thoughts, although when they had said good-
bye to Elrond in the high hope of a midsummer morning, they
had spoken gaily of the passage of the mountains, and of
riding swift across the lands beyond. They had thought of
coming to the secret door in the Lonely Mountain, perhaps
that very next last moon of Autumn—"and perhaps it will be
Durin's Day" they had said. Only Gandalf had shaken his
head and said nothing. Dwarves had not passed that way for
many years, but Gandalf had, and he knew how evil and
danger had grown and thriven in the Wild, since the dragons
had driven men from the lands, and the goblins had spread in
secret after the battle of the Mines of Moria. Even the good
plans of wise wizards like Gandalf and of good friends like
Elrond go astray sometimes when you are off on dangerous
adventures over the Edge of the Wild; and Gandalf was a wise
enough wizard to know it.

He knew that something unexpected might happen, and he
hardly dared to hope that they would pass without fearful adventure over those great tall mountains with lonely peaks and
valleys where no king ruled. They did not. All was well, until
one day they met a thunderstorm—more than a thunderstorm, a thunder-battle. You know how terrific a really big
thunderstorm can be down in the land and in a river-valley;
especially at times when two great thunderstorms meet and
clash. More terrible still are thunder and lightning in the
mountains at night, when storms come up from East and West

and make war. The lightning splinters on the peaks, and rocks shiver, and great crashes split the air and go rolling and tumbling into every cave and hollow; and the darkness is filled with overwhelming noise and sudden light.

Bilbo had never seen or imagined anything of the kind. They were high up in a narrow place, with a dreadful fall into a dim valley at one side of them. There they were sheltering under a hanging rock for the night, and he lay beneath a blanket and shook from head to toe. When he peeped out in the lightning-flashes, he saw that across the valley the stone-giants were out, and were hurling rocks at one another for a game, and catching them, and tossing them down into the darkness where they smashed among the trees far below, or splintered into little bits with a bang. Then came a wind and a rain, and the wind whipped the rain and the hail about in every direction, so that an overhanging rock was no protection at all. Soon they were getting drenched and their ponies were standing with their heads down and their tails between their legs, and some of them were whinnying with fright. They could hear the giants guffawing and shouting all over the mountainsides.

"This won't do at all!" said Thorin, "If we don't get blown off, or drowned, or struck by lightning, we shall be picked up by some giant and kicked sky-high for a football."

"Well, if you know of anywhere better, take us there!" said Gandalf, who was feeling very grumpy, and was far from happy about the giants himself.

The end of their argument was that they sent Fili and Kili to look for a better shelter. They had very sharp eyes, and being the youngest of the dwarves by some fifty years they usually got these sort of jobs (when everybody could see that it was absolutely no use sending Bilbo). There is nothing like looking, if you want to find something (or so Thorin said to the young dwarves). You certainly usually find something, if you look, but it is not always quite the something you were after. So it proved on this occasion.

Soon Fili and Kili came crawling back, holding on to the rocks in the wind. "We have found a dry cave," they said, "not far round the next corner; and ponies and all could get inside."

"Have you *thoroughly* explored it?" said the wizard, who knew that caves up in the mountains were seldom unoccupied.

"Yes, yes!" they said, though everybody knew they could not have been long about it; they had come back too quick. "It isn't all that big, and it does not go far back."

That, of course, is the dangerous part about caves: you don't know how far they go back, sometimes, or where a passage behind may lead to, or what is waiting for you inside. But now Fili and Kili's news seemed good enough. So they all got up and prepared to move. The wind was howling and the thunder still growling, and they had a business getting themselves and their ponies along. Still it was not very far to go, and before long they came to a big rock standing out into the path. If you stepped behind, you found a low arch in the side of the mountain. There was just room to get the ponies through with a squeeze, when they had been unpacked and unsaddled. As they passed under the arch, it was good to hear the wind and the rain outside instead of all about them, and to feel safe from the giants and their rocks. But the wizard was taking no risks. He lit up his wand—as he did that day in Bilbo's dining-room that seemed so long ago, if you remember—and by its light they explored the cave from end to end.

It seemed quite a fair size, but not too large and mysterious. It had a dry floor and some comfortable nooks. At one end there was room for the ponies; and there they stood (mighty glad of the change) steaming, and champing in their nosebags. Oin and Gloin wanted to light a fire at the door to dry their clothes, but Gandalf would not hear of it. So they spread out their wet things on the floor, and got dry ones out of their bundles; then they made their blankets comfortable, got out their pipes and blew smoke rings, which Gandalf turned into different colours and set dancing up by the roof to amuse them. They talked and talked, and forgot about the storm, and discussed what each would do with his share of the treasure (when they got it, which at the moment did not seem so impossible); and so they dropped off to sleep one by one. And that was the last time that they used the ponies, packages, baggages, tools and paraphernalia that they had brought with them.

It turned out a good thing that night that they had brought little Bilbo with them, after all. For, somehow, he could not go to sleep for a long while; and when he did sleep, he had very nasty dreams. He dreamed that a crack in the wall at the back of the cave got bigger and bigger, and opened wider and wider, and he was very afraid but could not call out or do anything but lie and look. Then he dreamed that the floor of the cave was giving way, and he was slipping—beginning to fall down, down, goodness knows where to.

At that he woke up with a horrible start, and found that part of his dream was true. A crack had opened at the back of the cave, and was already a wide passage. He was just in time to see the last of the ponies' tails disappearing into it. Of course he gave a very loud yell, as loud a yell as a hobbit can give, which is surprising for their size.

Out jumped the goblins, big goblins, great ugly-looking goblins, lots of goblins, before you could say *rocks and blocks*. There were six to each dwarf, at least, and two even for Bilbo;

and they were all grabbed and carried through the crack, before you could say *tinder and flint*. But not Gandalf. Bilbo's yell had done that much good. It had wakened him up wide in a splintered second, and when goblins came to grab him, there was a terrific flash like lightning in the cave, a smell like gunpowder, and several of them fell dead.

The crack closed with a snap, and Bilbo and the dwarves were on the wrong side of it! Where was Gandalf? Of that neither they nor the goblins had any idea, and the goblins did not wait to find out. They seized Bilbo and the dwarves and hurried them along. It was deep, deep, dark, such as only goblins that have taken to living in the heart of the mountains can see through. The passages there were crossed and tangled in all directions, but the goblins knew their way, as well as you do to the nearest post-office; and the way went down and down, and it was most horribly stuffy. The goblins were very rough, and pinched unmercifully, and chuckled and laughed in their horrible stony voices; and Bilbo was more unhappy even than when the troll had picked him up by his toes. He wished again and again for his nice bright hobbit-hole. Not for the last time.

Now there came a glimmer of a red light before them. The goblins began to sing, or croak, keeping time with the flap of their flat feet on the stone, and shaking their prisoners as well.

> *Clap! Snap! the black crack!*
> *Grip, grab! Pinch, nab!*
> *And down down to Goblin-town*
>    *You go, my lad!*
> *Clash, crash! Crush, smash!*
> *Hammer and tongs! Knocker and gongs!*
> *Pound, pound, far underground!*
>    *Ho, ho! my lad!*

*Swish, smack! Whip crack!*
*Batter and beat! Yammer and bleat!*
*Work, work! Nor dare to shirk,*
*While Goblins quaff, and Goblins laugh,*
*Round and round far underground*
*    Below, my lad!*

It sounded truly terrifying. The walls echoed to the *clap,*
*snap!* and the *crush, smash!* and to the ugly laughter of their
*ho, ho! my lad!* The general meaning of the song was only too
plain; for now the goblins took out whips and whipped them
with a *swish, smack!*, and set them running as fast as they
could in front of them; and more than one of the dwarves
were already yammering and bleating like anything, when
they stumbled into a big cavern.

It was lit by a great red fire in the middle, and by torches
along the walls, and it was full of goblins. They all laughed
and stamped and clapped their hands, when the dwarves (with
poor little Bilbo at the back and nearest to the whips) came
running in, while the goblin-drivers whooped and cracked
their whips behind. The ponies were already there huddled in
a corner; and there were all the baggages and packages lying broken open, and being rummaged by goblins, and smelt
by goblins, and fingered by goblins, and quarrelled over by
goblins.

I am afraid that was the last they ever saw of those excellent little ponies, including a jolly sturdy little white fellow
that Elrond had lent to Gandalf, since his horse was not suit-
able for the mountain-paths. For goblins eat horses and ponies
and donkeys (and other much more dreadful things), and
they are always hungry. Just now however the prisoners were
thinking only of themselves. The goblins chained their hands
behind their backs and linked them all together in a line, and

dragged them to the far end of the cavern with little Bilbo tugging at the end of the row.

There in the shadows on a large flat stone sat a tremendous goblin with a huge head, and armed goblins were standing round him carrying the axes and the bent swords that they use. Now goblins are cruel, wicked, and bad-hearted. They make no beautiful things, but they make many clever ones. They can tunnel and mine as well as any but the most skilled dwarves, when they take the trouble, though they are usually untidy and dirty. Hammers, axes, swords, daggers, pickaxes, tongs, and also instruments of torture, they make very well, or get other people to make to their design, prisoners and slaves that have to work till they die for want of air and light. It is not unlikely that they invented some of the machines that have since troubled the world, especially the ingenious devices for killing large numbers of people at once, for wheels and engines and explosions always delighted them, and also not working with their own hands more than they could help; but in those days and those wild parts they had not advanced (as it is called) so far. They did not hate dwarves especially, no more than they hated everybody and everything, and particularly the orderly and prosperous; in some parts wicked dwarves had even made alliances with them. But they had a special grudge against Thorin's people, because of the war which you have heard mentioned, but which does not come into this tale; and anyway goblins don't care who they catch, as long as it is done smart and secret, and the prisoners are not able to defend themselves.

"Who are these miserable persons?" said the Great Goblin.

"Dwarves, and this!" said one of the drivers, pulling at Bilbo's chain so that he fell forward onto his knees. "We found them sheltering in our Front Porch."

"What do you mean by it?" said the Great Goblin turning

to Thorin. "Up to no good, I'll warrant! Spying on the private business of my people, I guess! Thieves, I shouldn't be surprised to learn! Murderers and friends of Elves, not unlikely! Come! What have you got to say?"

"Thorin the dwarf at your service!" he replied—it was merely a polite nothing. "Of the things which you suspect and imagine we had no idea at all. We sheltered from a storm in what seemed a convenient cave and unused; nothing was further from our thoughts than inconveniencing goblins in any way whatever." That was true enough!

"Um!" said the Great Goblin. "So you say! Might I ask what you were doing up in the mountains at all, and where you were coming from, and where you were going to? In fact I should like to know all about you. Not that it will do you much good, Thorin Oakenshield, I know too much about your folk already; but let's have the truth, or I will prepare something particularly uncomfortable for you!"

"We were on a journey to visit our relatives, our nephews and nieces, and first, second, and third cousins, and the other descendants of our grandfathers, who live on the East side of these truly hospitable mountains," said Thorin, not quite knowing what to say all at once in a moment, when obviously the exact truth would not do at all.

"He is a liar, O truly tremendous one!" said one of the drivers. "Several of our people were struck by lightning in the cave, when we invited these creatures to come below; and they are as dead as stones. Also he has not explained this!" He held out the sword which Thorin had worn, the sword which came from the Trolls' lair.

The Great Goblin gave a truly awful howl of rage when he looked at it, and all his soldiers gnashed their teeth, clashed their shields, and stamped. They knew the sword at once. It had killed hundreds of goblins in its time, when the fair elves of Gondolin hunted them in the hills or did battle before their walls. They had called it Orcrist, Goblin-cleaver, but the goblins called it simply Biter. They hated it and hated worse any one that carried it.

"Murderers and elf-friends!" the Great Goblin shouted. "Slash them! Beat them! Bite them! Gnash them! Take them away to dark holes full of snakes, and never let them see the light again!" He was in such a rage that he jumped off his seat and himself rushed at Thorin with his mouth open.

Just at that moment all the lights in the cavern went out, and the great fire went off poof! into a tower of blue glowing smoke, right up to the roof, that scattered piercing white sparks all among the goblins.

The yells and yammering, croaking, jibbering and jabbering; howls, growls and curses; shrieking and skriking, that followed were beyond description. Several hundred wild cats and wolves being roasted slowly alive together would not have compared with it. The sparks were burning holes in the goblins, and the smoke that now fell from the roof made the air too thick for even their eyes to see through. Soon they were falling over one another and rolling in heaps on the floor, biting and kicking and fighting as if they had all gone mad.

Suddenly a sword flashed in its own light. Bilbo saw it go right through the Great Goblin as he stood dumbfounded in the middle of his rage. He fell dead, and the goblin soldiers fled before the sword shrieking into the darkness.

The sword went back into its sheath. "Follow me quick!" said a voice fierce and quiet; and before Bilbo understood what had happened he was trotting along again, as fast as he could trot, at the end of the line, down more dark passages with the yells of the goblin-hall growing fainter behind him. A pale light was leading them on.

"Quicker, quicker!" said the voice. "The torches will soon be relit."

"Half a minute!" said Dori, who was at the back next to Bilbo, and a decent fellow. He made the hobbit scramble on his shoulders as best he could with his tied hands, and then off they all went at a run, with a clink-clink of chains, and many a stumble, since they had no hands to steady themselves with. Not for a long while did they stop, and by that time they must have been right down in the very mountain's heart.

Then Gandalf lit up his wand. Of course it was Gandalf; but just then they were too busy to ask how he got there. He took out his sword again, and again it flashed in the dark by itself. It burned with a rage that made it gleam if goblins were about; now it was bright as blue flame for delight in the killing of the great lord of the cave. It made no trouble whatever of cutting through the goblin-chains and setting all the prisoners free as quickly as possible. This sword's name was Glamdring the Foe-hammer, if you remember. The goblins just called it Beater, and hated it worse than Biter if possible. Orcrist, too, had been saved; for Gandalf had brought it along as well, snatching it from one of the terrified guards. Gandalf thought of most things; and though he could not do everything, he could do a great deal for friends in a tight corner.

"Are we all here?" said he, handing his sword back to Thorin with a bow. "Let me see: one—that's Thorin; two, three, four, five, six, seven, eight, nine, ten, eleven; where are Fili and Kili? Here they are! twelve, thirteen—and here's Mr Baggins: fourteen! Well, well! it might be worse, and then again it might be a good deal better. No ponies, and no food, and no knowing quite where we are, and hordes of angry goblins just behind! On we go!"

On they went. Gandalf was quite right: they began to hear

goblin noises and horrible cries far behind in the passages they had come through. That sent them on faster than ever, and as poor Bilbo could not possibly go half as fast—for dwarves can roll along at a tremendous pace, I can tell you, when they have to—they took it in turn to carry him on their backs.

Still goblins go faster than dwarves, and these goblins knew the way better (they had made the paths themselves), and were madly angry; so that do what they could the dwarves heard the cries and howls getting closer and closer. Soon they could hear even the flap of the goblin feet, many many feet which seemed only just round the last corner. The blink of red torches could be seen behind them in the tunnel they were following; and they were getting deadly tired.

"Why, O why did I ever leave my hobbit-hole!" said poor Mr Baggins bumping up and down on Bombur's back.

"Why, O why did I ever bring a wretched little hobbit on a treasure hunt!" said poor Bombur, who was fat, and staggered along with the sweat dripping down his nose in his heat and terror.

At this point Gandalf fell behind, and Thorin with him. They turned a sharp corner. "About turn!" he shouted. "Draw your sword Thorin!"

There was nothing else to be done; and the goblins did not like it. They came scurrying round the corner in full cry, and found Goblin-cleaver, and Foe-hammer shining cold and bright right in their astonished eyes. The ones in front dropped their torches and gave one yell before they were killed. The ones behind yelled still more, and leaped back knocking over those that were running after them. "Biter and Beater!" they shrieked; and soon they were all in confusion, and most of them were hustling back the way they had come.

It was quite a long while before any of them dared to turn

that corner. By that time the dwarves had gone on again, a long, long, way on into the dark tunnels of the goblins' realm. When the goblins discovered that, they put out their torches and they slipped on soft shoes, and they chose out their very quickest runners with the sharpest ears and eyes. These ran forward, as swift as weasels in the dark, and with hardly any more noise than bats.

That is why neither Bilbo, nor the dwarves, nor even Gandalf heard them coming. Nor did they see them. But they were seen by the goblins that ran silently up behind, for Gandalf was letting his wand give out a faint light to help the dwarves as they went along.

Quite suddenly Dori, now at the back again carrying Bilbo, was grabbed from behind in the dark. He shouted and fell; and the hobbit rolled off his shoulders into the blackness, bumped his head on hard rock, and remembered nothing more.

*Chapter V*

# RIDDLES IN THE DARK

When Bilbo opened his eyes, he wondered if he had; for it was just as dark as with them shut. No one was anywhere near him. Just imagine his fright! He could hear nothing, see nothing, and he could feel nothing except the stone of the floor.

Very slowly he got up and groped about on all fours, till he touched the wall of the tunnel; but neither up nor down it could he find anything: nothing at all, no sign of goblins, no sign of dwarves. His head was swimming, and he was far from certain even of the direction they had been going in when he had his fall. He guessed as well as he could, and crawled along for a good way, till suddenly his hand met what felt like a tiny ring of cold metal lying on the floor of the tunnel. It was a turning point in his career, but he did not know it. He put the ring in his pocket almost without thinking; certainly it did not seem of any particular use at the moment. He did not go much further, but sat down on the cold floor and gave himself up to complete miserableness, for a long while. He thought of himself frying bacon and eggs in his own kitchen at home—for he could feel inside that it was high time for some meal or other; but that only made him miserabler.

He could not think what to do; nor could he think what had happened; or why he had been left behind; or why, if he had been left behind, the goblins had not caught him; or even why his head was so sore. The truth was he had been lying quiet, out of sight and out of mind, in a very dark corner for a long while.

After some time he felt for his pipe. It was not broken, and that was something. Then he felt for his pouch, and there was some tobacco in it, and that was something more. Then he felt for matches and he could not find any at all, and that shattered his hopes completely. Just as well for him, as he agreed when he came to his senses. Goodness knows what the striking of matches and the smell of tobacco would have brought on him out of dark holes in that horrible place. Still at the moment he felt very crushed. But in slapping all his pockets and feeling all round himself for matches his hand came on the hilt of his little sword—the little dagger that he got from the trolls, and that he had quite forgotten; nor fortunately had the goblins noticed it, as he wore it inside his breeches.

Now he drew it out. It shone pale and dim before his eyes. "So it is an elvish blade, too," he thought; "and goblins are not very near, and yet not far enough."

But somehow he was comforted. It was rather splendid to be wearing a blade made in Gondolin for the goblin-wars of which so many songs had sung; and also he had noticed that such weapons made a great impression on goblins that came upon them suddenly.

"Go back?" he thought. "No good at all! Go sideways? Impossible! Go forward? Only thing to do! On we go!" So up he got, and trotted along with his little sword held in front of him and one hand feeling the wall, and his heart all of a patter and a pitter.

\* \* \*

Now certainly Bilbo was in what is called a tight place. But
you must remember it was not quite so tight for him as it would
have been for me or for you. Hobbits are not quite like ordinary
people; and after all if their holes are nice cheery places and
properly aired, quite different from the tunnels of the goblins,
still they are more used to tunnelling than we are, and they do
not easily lose their sense of direction underground—not when
their heads have recovered from being bumped. Also they can
move very quietly, and hide easily, and recover wonderfully
from falls and bruises, and they have a fund of wisdom and
wise sayings that men have mostly never heard or have forgotten long ago.

I should not have liked to have been in Mr Baggins' place,
all the same. The tunnel seemed to have no end. All he knew
was that it was still going down pretty steadily and keeping in
the same direction in spite of a twist and a turn or two. There
were passages leading off to the side every now and then, as
he knew by the glimmer of his sword, or could feel with his
hand on the wall. Of these he took no notice, except to hurry
past for fear of goblins or half-imagined dark things coming
out of them. On and on he went, and down and down; and still
he heard no sound of anything except the occasional whirr of
a bat by his ears, which startled him at first, till it became too
frequent to bother about. I do not know how long he kept on
like this, hating to go on, not daring to stop, on, on, until he
was tireder than tired. It seemed like all the way to tomorrow
and over it to the days beyond.

Suddenly without any warning he trotted splash into water!
Ugh! it was icy cold. That pulled him up sharp and short. He
did not know whether it was just a pool in the path, or the
edge of an underground stream that crossed the passage, or
the brink of a deep dark subterranean lake. The sword was

hardly shining at all. He stopped, and he could hear, when he listened hard, drops drip-drip-dripping from an unseen roof into the water below; but there seemed no other sort of sound.

"So it is a pool or a lake, and not an underground river," he thought. Still he did not dare to wade out into the darkness. He could not swim; and he thought, too, of nasty slimy things, with big bulging blind eyes, wriggling in the water. There are strange things living in the pools and lakes in the hearts of mountains: fish whose fathers swam in, goodness only knows how many years ago, and never swam out again, while their eyes grew bigger and bigger and bigger from trying to see in the blackness; also there are other things more slimy than fish. Even in the tunnels and caves the goblins have made for themselves there are other things living unbeknown to them that have sneaked in from outside to lie up in the dark. Some of these caves, too, go back in their beginnings to ages before the goblins, who only widened them and joined them up with passages, and the original owners are still there in odd corners, slinking and nosing about.

Deep down here by the dark water lived old Gollum, a small slimy creature. I don't know where he came from, nor who or what he was. He was Gollum—as dark as darkness, except for two big round pale eyes in his thin face. He had a little boat, and he rowed about quite quietly on the lake; for lake it was, wide and deep and deadly cold. He paddled it with large feet dangling over the side, but never a ripple did he make. Not he. He was looking out of his pale lamp-like eyes for blind fish, which he grabbed with his long fingers as quick as thinking. He liked meat too. Goblin he thought good, when he could get it; but he took care they never found him out. He just throttled them from behind, if they ever came down alone anywhere near the edge of the water, while he was prowling about. They very seldom did, for they had a feeling that something unpleasant was lurking down there, down at the very roots of the mountain. They had come on the lake, when they were tunnelling down long ago, and they found they could go no further; so there their road ended in that direction, and there was no reason to go that way— unless the Great Goblin sent them. Sometimes he took a fancy for fish from the lake, and sometimes neither goblin nor fish came back.

Actually Gollum lived on a slimy island of rock in the middle of the lake. He was watching Bilbo now from the distance with his pale eyes like telescopes. Bilbo could not see him, but he was wondering a lot about Bilbo, for he could see that he was no goblin at all.

Gollum got into his boat and shot off from the island, while Bilbo was sitting on the brink altogether flummoxed and at the end of his way and his wits. Suddenly up came Gollum and whispered and hissed:

"Bless us and splash us, my precioussss! I guess it's a choice feast; at least a tasty morsel it'd make us, gollum!" And when he said *gollum* he made a horrible swallowing noise in his throat. That is how he got his name, though he always called himself "my precious."

The hobbit jumped nearly out of his skin when the hiss came in his ears, and he suddenly saw the pale eyes sticking out at him.

"Who are you?" he said, thrusting his dagger in front of him.

"What iss he, my preciouss?" whispered Gollum (who always spoke to himself through never having anyone else to speak to). This is what he had come to find out, for he was not really very hungry at the moment, only curious; otherwise he would have grabbed first and whispered afterwards.

"I am Mr Bilbo Baggins. I have lost the dwarves and I have lost the wizard, and I don't know where I am and I don't want to know, if only I can get away."

"What's he got in his handses?" said Gollum, looking at the sword, which he did not quite like.

"A sword, a blade which came out of Gondolin!"

"Sssss" said Gollum, and became quite polite. "Praps we sits here and chats with it a bitsy, my preciousss. It likes riddles, praps it does, does it?" He was anxious to appear friendly, at any rate for the moment, and until he found out more about the sword and the hobbit, whether he was quite alone really, whether he was good to eat, and whether Gollum was really hungry. Riddles were all he could think of. Asking them, and sometimes guessing them, had been the only game he had ever played with other funny creatures sitting in their holes in the long, long ago, before he lost all his friends and was driven away, alone, and crept down, down, into the dark under the mountains.

"Very well," said Bilbo, who was anxious to agree, until he found out more about the creature, whether he was quite alone, whether he was fierce or hungry, and whether he was a friend of the goblins.

"You ask first," he said, because he had not had time to think of a riddle.

So Gollum hissed:

> *What has roots as nobody sees,*
> *Is taller than trees,*
> *Up, up it goes,*
> *And yet never grows?*

"Easy!" said Bilbo. "Mountain, I suppose."

"Does it guess easy? It must have a competition with us,

my preciouss! If precious asks, and it doesn't answer, we eats it, my preciousss. If it asks us, and we doesn't answer, then we does what it wants, eh? We shows it the way out, yes!"

"All right!" said Bilbo, not daring to disagree, and nearly bursting his brain to think of riddles that could save him from being eaten.

> *Thirty white horses on a red hill,*
> *First they champ,*
> *Then they stamp,*
> *Then they stand still.*

That was all he could think of to ask—the idea of eating was rather on his mind. It was rather an old one, too, and Gollum knew the answer as well as you do.

"Chestnuts, chestnuts," he hissed. "Teeth! teeth! my preciousss; but we has only six!" Then he asked his second:

> *Voiceless it cries,*
> *Wingless flutters,*
> *Toothless bites,*
> *Mouthless mutters.*

"Half a moment!" cried Bilbo, who was still thinking uncomfortably about eating. Fortunately he had once heard something rather like this before, and getting his wits back he thought of the answer. "Wind, wind of course," he said, and he was so pleased that he made up one on the spot. "This'll puzzle the nasty little underground creature," he thought:

> *An eye in a blue face*
> *Saw an eye in a green face.*
> *"That eye is like to this eye"*

> *Said the first eye,*
> *"But in low place*
> *Not in high place."*

"Ss, ss, ss," said Gollum. He had been underground a long long time, and was forgetting this sort of thing. But just as Bilbo was beginning to hope that the wretch would not be able to answer, Gollum brought up memories of ages and ages and ages before, when he lived with his grandmother in a hole in a bank by a river, "Sss, sss, my preciouss," he said. "Sun on the daisies it means, it does."

But these ordinary above ground everyday sort of riddles were tiring for him. Also they reminded him of days when he had been less lonely and sneaky and nasty, and that put him out of temper. What is more they made him hungry; so this time he tried something a bit more difficult and more unpleasant:

> *It cannot be seen, cannot be felt,*
> *Cannot be heard, cannot be smelt.*
> *It lies behind stars and under hills,*
> *And empty holes it fills.*
> *It comes first and follows after,*
> *Ends life, kills laughter.*

Unfortunately for Gollum Bilbo had heard that sort of thing before; and the answer was all round him any way. "Dark!" he said without even scratching his head or putting on his thinking cap.

> *A box without hinges, key, or lid,*
> *Yet golden treasure inside is hid,*

he asked to gain time, until he could think of a really hard one. This he thought a dreadfully easy chestnut, though he had not asked it in the usual words. But it proved a nasty poser for Gollum. He hissed to himself, and still he did not answer; he whispered and spluttered.

After some while Bilbo became impatient. "Well, what is it?" he said. "The answer's not a kettle boiling over, as you seem to think from the noise you are making."

"Give us a chance; let it give us a chance, my preciouss—ss—ss."

"Well," said Bilbo after giving him a long chance, "what about your guess?"

But suddenly Gollum remembered thieving from nests long ago, and sitting under the river bank teaching his grandmother, teaching his grandmother to suck—"Eggses!" he hissed. "Eggses it is!" Then he asked:

> *Alive without breath,*
> *As cold as death;*
> *Never thirsty, ever drinking,*
> *All in mail never clinking.*

He also in his turn thought this was a dreadfully easy one, because he was always thinking of the answer. But he could not remember anything better at the moment, he was so flustered by the egg-question. All the same it was a poser for poor Bilbo, who never had anything to do with the water if he could help it. I imagine you know the answer, of course, or can guess it as easy as winking, since you are sitting comfortably at home and have not the danger of being eaten to disturb your thinking. Bilbo sat and cleared his throat once or twice, but no answer came.

After a while Gollum began to hiss with pleasure to himself: "Is it nice, my preciousss? Is it juicy? Is it scrumptiously crunchable?" He began to peer at Bilbo out of the darkness.

"Half a moment," said the hobbit shivering. "I gave you a good long chance just now."

"It must make haste, haste!" said Gollum, beginning to climb out of his boat on to the shore to get at Bilbo. But when he put his long webby foot in the water, a fish jumped out in a fright and fell on Bilbo's toes.

"Ugh!" he said, "it is cold and clammy!"—and so he guessed. "Fish! fish!" he cried. "It is fish!"

Gollum was dreadfully disappointed; but Bilbo asked another riddle as quick as ever he could, so that Gollum had to get back into his boat and think.

*No-legs lay on one-leg, two-legs sat near on three-legs, four-legs got some.*

It was not really the right time for this riddle, but Bilbo was in a hurry. Gollum might have had some trouble guessing it, if he had asked it at another time. As it was, talking of fish, "no-legs" was not so very difficult, and after that the rest was easy. "Fish on a little table, man at table sitting on a stool, the cat has the bones," that of course is the answer, and Gollum soon gave it. Then he thought the time had come to ask something hard and horrible. This is what he said:

> *This thing all things devours:*
> *Birds, beasts, trees, flowers;*
> *Gnaws iron, bites steel;*
> *Grinds hard stones to meal;*
> *Slays king, ruins town,*
> *And beats high mountain down.*

Poor Bilbo sat in the dark thinking of all the horrible names of all the giants and ogres he had ever heard told of in tales, but not one of them had done all these things. He had a feeling that the answer was quite different and that he ought to know it, but he could not think of it. He began to get frightened, and that is bad for thinking. Gollum began to get out of his boat. He flapped into the water and paddled to the bank; Bilbo could see his eyes coming towards him. His tongue seemed to stick in his mouth; he wanted to shout out: "Give me more time! Give me time!" But all that came out with a sudden squeal was:

"Time! Time!"

Bilbo was saved by pure luck. For that of course was the answer.

Gollum was disappointed once more; and now he was getting angry, and also tired of the game. It had made him very hungry indeed. This time he did not go back to the boat. He sat down in the dark by Bilbo. That made the hobbit most dreadfully uncomfortable and scattered his wits.

"It's got to ask uss a quesstion, my preciouss, yes, yess, yesss. Jusst one more question to guess, yes, yess," said Gollum.

But Bilbo simply could not think of any question with that nasty wet cold thing sitting next to him, and pawing and poking him. He scratched himself, he pinched himself; still he could not think of anything.

"Ask us! ask us!" said Gollum.

Bilbo pinched himself and slapped himself; he gripped on his little sword; he even felt in his pocket with his other hand. There he found the ring he had picked up in the passage and forgotten about.

"What have I got in my pocket?" he said aloud. He was

talking to himself, but Gollum thought it was a riddle, and he was frightfully upset.

"Not fair! not fair!" he hissed. "It isn't fair, my precious, is it, to ask us what it's got in its nassty little pocketses?"

Bilbo seeing what had happened and having nothing better to ask stuck to his question, "What have I got in my pocket?" he said louder.

"S-s-s-s-s," hissed Gollum. "It must give us three guess-eses, my preciouss, three guesseses."

"Very well! Guess away!" said Bilbo.

"Handses!" said Gollum.

"Wrong," said Bilbo, who had luckily just taken his hand out again. "Guess again!"

"S-s-s-s-s," said Gollum more upset than ever. He thought of all the things he kept in his own pockets: fish-bones, gob-lins' teeth, wet shells, a bit of bat-wing, a sharp stone to sharpen his fangs on, and other nasty things. He tried to think what other people kept in their pockets.

"Knife!" he said at last.

"Wrong!" said Bilbo, who had lost his some time ago. "Last guess!"

Now Gollum was in a much worse state than when Bilbo had asked him the egg-question. He hissed and spluttered and rocked himself backwards and forwards, and slapped his feet on the floor, and wriggled and squirmed; but still he did not dare to waste his last guess.

"Come on!" said Bilbo. "I am waiting!" He tried to sound bold and cheerful, but he did not feel at all sure how the game was going to end, whether Gollum guessed right or not.

"Time's up!" he said.

"String, or nothing!" shrieked Gollum, which was not quite fair—working in two guesses at once.

"Both wrong," cried Bilbo very much relieved; and he

jumped at once to his feet, put his back to the nearest wall, and held out his little sword. He knew, of course, that the riddle-game was sacred and of immense antiquity, and even wicked creatures were afraid to cheat when they played at it. But he felt he could not trust this slimy thing to keep any promise at a pinch. Any excuse would do for him to slide out of it. And after all that last question had not been a genuine riddle according to the ancient laws.

But at any rate Gollum did not at once attack him. He could see the sword in Bilbo's hand. He sat still, shivering and whispering. At last Bilbo could wait no longer.

"Well?" he said. "What about your promise? I want to go. You must show me the way."

"Did we say so, precious? Show the nassty little Baggins the way out, yes, yes. But what has it got in its pocketses, eh? Not string, precious, but not nothing. Oh no! gollum!"

"Never you mind," said Bilbo. "A promise is a promise."

"Cross it is, impatient, precious," hissed Gollum. "But it must wait, yes it must. We can't go up the tunnels so hasty. We must go and get some things first, yes, things to help us."

"Well, hurry up!" said Bilbo, relieved to think of Gollum going away. He thought he was just making an excuse and did not mean to come back. What was Gollum talking about? What useful thing could he keep out on the dark lake? But he was wrong. Gollum did mean to come back. He was angry now and hungry. And he was a miserable wicked creature, and already he had a plan.

Not far away was his island, of which Bilbo knew nothing, and there in his hiding-place he kept a few wretched oddments, and one very beautiful thing, very beautiful, very wonderful. He had a ring, a golden ring, a precious ring.

"My birthday-present!" he whispered to himself, as he had

ften done in the endless dark days. "That's what we wants
ow, yes; we wants it!"

He wanted it because it was a ring of power, and if you
lipped that ring on your finger, you were invisible; only in
he full sunlight could you be seen, and then only by your
hadow, and that would be shaky and faint.

"My birthday-present! It came to me on my birthday, my
precious." So he had always said to himself. But who knows
ow Gollum came by that present, ages ago in the old days
vhen such rings were still at large in the world? Perhaps even
he Master who ruled them could not have said. Gollum used
o wear it at first, till it tired him; and then he kept it in a pouch
ext his skin, till it galled him; and now usually he hid it in a
ole in the rock on his island, and was always going back to
ook at it. And still sometimes he put it on, when he could not
ear to be parted from it any longer, or when he was very,
ery hungry, and tired of fish. Then he would creep along
lark passages looking for stray goblins. He might even ven-
ure into places where the torches were lit and made his eyes
link and smart; for he would be safe. Oh yes, quite safe. No
ne would see him, no one would notice him, till he had his
ingers on their throat. Only a few hours ago he had worn it,
nd caught a small goblin-imp. How it squeaked! He still had
bone or two left to gnaw, but he wanted something softer.

"Quite safe, yes," he whispered to himself. "It won't see
s, will it, my precious? No. It won't see us, and its nassty
ittle sword will be useless, yes quite."

That is what was in his wicked little mind, as he slipped
suddenly from Bilbo's side, and flapped back to his boat, and
vent off into the dark. Bilbo thought he had heard the last of
im. Still he waited a while; for he had no idea how to find his
vay out alone.

Suddenly he heard a screech. It sent a shiver down his

back. Gollum was cursing and wailing away in the gloom, no
very far off by the sound of it. He was on his island, scrab
bling here and there, searching and seeking in vain.

"Where iss it? Where iss it?" Bilbo heard him crying
"Losst it is, my precious, lost, lost! Curse us and crush us, m
precious is lost!"

"What's the matter?" Bilbo called. "What have you lost?

"It mustn't ask us," shrieked Gollum. "Not its business
no, gollum! It's losst, gollum, gollum, gollum."

"Well, so am I," cried Bilbo, "and I want to get unlost. An
I won the game, and you promised. So come along! Com
and let me out, and then go on with your looking!" Utterly
miserable as Gollum sounded, Bilbo could not find much pit
in his heart, and he had a feeling that anything Gollun
wanted so much could hardly be something good. "Com
along!" he shouted.

"No, not yet, precious!" Gollum answered. "We mus
search for it, it's lost, gollum."

"But you never guessed my last question, and you prom
ised," said Bilbo.

"Never guessed!" said Gollum. Then suddenly out of th
gloom came a sharp hiss. "What has it got in its pocketses
Tell us that. It must tell first."

As far as Bilbo knew, there was no particular reason why
he should not tell. Gollum's mind had jumped to a gues
quicker than his; naturally, for Gollum had brooded for age
on this one thing, and he was always afraid of its being stolen
But Bilbo was annoyed at the delay. After all, he had won th
game, pretty fairly, at a horrible risk. "Answers were to b
guessed not given," he said.

"But it wasn't a fair question," said Gollum. "Not a riddle
precious, no."

"Oh well, if it's a matter of ordinary questions," Bilb

eplied, "then I asked one first. What have you lost? Tell me
hat!"

"What has it got in its pocketses?" The sound came hissing
ouder and sharper, and as he looked towards it, to his alarm
Bilbo now saw two small points of light peering at him. As
suspicion grew in Gollum's mind, the light of his eyes burned
with a pale flame.

"What have you lost?" Bilbo persisted.

But now the light in Gollum's eyes had become a green
fire, and it was coming swiftly nearer. Gollum was in his boat
again, paddling wildly back to the dark shore; and such a rage
of loss and suspicion was in his heart that no sword had any
more terror for him.

Bilbo could not guess what had maddened the wretched
creature, but he saw that all was up, and that Gollum meant to
murder him at any rate. Just in time he turned and ran blindly
back up the dark passage down which he had come, keeping
close to the wall and feeling it with his left hand.

"What has it got in its pocketses?" he heard the hiss loud
behind him, and the splash as Gollum leapt from his boat.
"What have I, I wonder?" he said to himself, as he panted
and stumbled along. He put his left hand in his pocket. The
ring felt very cold as it quietly slipped on to his groping
forefinger.

The hiss was close behind him. He turned now and saw
Gollum's eyes like small green lamps coming up the slope.
Terrified he tried to run faster, but suddenly he struck his
toes on a snag in the floor, and fell flat with his little sword
under him.

In a moment Gollum was on him. But before Bilbo could
do anything, recover his breath, pick himself up, or wave his
sword, Gollum passed by, taking no notice of him, cursing
and whispering as he ran.

What could it mean? Gollum could see in the dark. Bilbo could see the light of his eyes palely shining even from behind. Painfully he got up, and sheathed his sword, which was now glowing faintly again, then very cautiously he followed. There seemed nothing else to do. It was no good crawling back down to Gollum's water. Perhaps if he followed him, Gollum might lead him to some way of escape without meaning to.

"Curse it! curse it! curse it!" hissed Gollum. "Curse the Baggins! It's gone! What has it got in its pocketses? Oh we guess, we guess, my precious. He's found it, yes he must have. My birthday-present."

Bilbo pricked up his ears. He was at last beginning to guess himself. He hurried a little, getting as close as he dared behind Gollum, who was still going quickly, not looking back but turning his head from side to side, as Bilbo could see from the faint glimmer on the walls.

"My birthday-present! Curse it! How did we lose it, my precious? Yes, that's it. When we came this way last, when we twisted that nassty young squeaker. That's it. Curse it! It slipped from us, after all these ages and ages! It's gone, gollum."

Suddenly Gollum sat down and began to weep, a whistling and gurgling sound horrible to listen to. Bilbo halted and flattened himself against the tunnel-wall. After a while Gollum stopped weeping and began to talk. He seemed to be having an argument with himself.

"It's no good going back there to search, no. We doesn't remember all the places we've visited. And it's no use. The Baggins has got it in its pocketses; the nassty noser has found it, we says.

"We guesses, precious, only guesses. We can't know till we find the nassty creature and squeezes it. But it doesn't know what the present can do, does it? It'll just keep it in its pock-etses. It doesn't know, and it can't go far. It's lost itself, the nassty nosey thing. It doesn't know the way out. It said so.

"It said so, yes; but it's tricksy. It doesn't say what it means. It won't say what it's got in its pocketses. It knows. It knows a way in, it must know a way out, yes. It's off to the back-door. To the back-door, that's it.

"The goblinses will catch it then. It can't get out that way, precious.

"Ssss, sss, gollum! Goblinses! Yes, but if it's got the pres-ent, our precious present, then goblinses will get it, gollum! They'll find it, they'll find out what it does. We shan't ever be safe again, never, gollum! One of the goblinses will put it on, and then no one will see him. He'll be there but not seen. Not even our clever eyeses will notice him; and he'll come creepsy and tricksy and catch us, gollum, gollum!

"Then let's stop talking, precious, and make haste. If the Baggins has gone that way, we must go quick and see. Go! Not far now. Make haste!

With a spring Gollum got up and started shambling off at a great pace. Bilbo hurried after him, still cautiously, though his chief fear now was of tripping on another snag and falling with a noise. His head was in a whirl of hope and wonder. It seemed that the ring he had was a magic ring: it made you in-visible! He had heard of such things, of course, in old old tales; but it was hard to believe that he really had found one, by accident. Still there it was: Gollum with his bright eyes had passed him by, only a yard to one side.

On they went, Gollum flip-flapping ahead, hissing and cursing; Bilbo behind going as softly as a hobbit can. Soon they came to places where, as Bilbo had noticed on the way down, side-passages opened, this way and that. Gollum began at once to count them.

"One left, yes. One right, yes. Two right, yes, yes. Two left, yes, yes." And so on and on.

As the count grew he slowed down, and he began to get shaky and weepy; for he was leaving the water further and further behind, and he was getting afraid. Goblins might be about, and he had lost his ring. At last he stopped by a low opening, on their left as they went up.

"Seven right, yes. Six left, yes!" he whispered. "This is it. This is the way to the back-door, yes. Here's the passage!"

He peered in, and shrank back. "But we dursn't go in, precious, no we dursn't. Goblinses down there. Lots of goblinses. We smells them. Ssss!

"What shall we do? Curse them and crush them! We must wait here, precious, wait a bit and see."

So they came to a dead stop. Gollum had brought Bilbo to the way out after all, but Bilbo could not get in! There was Gollum sitting humped up right in the opening, and his eyes gleamed cold in his head, as he swayed it from side to side between his knees.

Bilbo crept away from the wall more quietly than a mouse; but Gollum stiffened at once, and sniffed, and his eyes went green. He hissed softly but menacingly. He could not see the hobbit, but now he was on the alert, and he had other senses that the darkness had sharpened: hearing and smell. He seemed to be crouched right down with his flat hands splayed on the floor, and his head thrust out, nose almost to the stone. Though he was only a black shadow in the gleam of his own eyes, Bilbo could see or feel that he was tense as a bowstring, gathered for a spring.

Bilbo almost stopped breathing, and went stiff himself. He was desperate. He must get away, out of this horrible darkness, while he had any strength left. He must fight. He must stab the foul thing, put its eyes out, kill it. It meant to kill him.

No, not a fair fight. He was invisible now. Gollum had no sword. Gollum had not actually threatened to kill him, or tried to yet. And he was miserable, alone, lost. A sudden understanding, a pity mixed with horror, welled up in Bilbo's heart: a glimpse of endless unmarked days without light or hope of betterment, hard stone, cold fish, sneaking and whispering. All these thoughts passed in a flash of a second. He trembled. And then quite suddenly in another flash, as if lifted by a new strength and resolve, he leaped.

No great leap for a man, but a leap in the dark. Straight over Gollum's head he jumped, seven feet forward and three in the air; indeed, had he known it, he only just missed cracking his skull on the low arch of the passage.

Gollum threw himself backwards, and grabbed as the hobbit flew over him, but too late: his hands snapped on thin air, and Bilbo, falling fair on his sturdy feet, sped off down the new tunnel. He did not turn to see what Gollum was doing. There was a hissing and cursing almost at his heels at first, then it stopped. All at once there came a blood-curdling shriek, filled with hatred and despair. Gollum was defeated. He dared go no further. He had lost: lost his prey, and lost, too, the only thing he had ever cared for, his precious. The cry brought Bilbo's heart to his mouth, but still he held on. Now faint as an echo, but menacing, the voice came behind:

"Thief, thief, thief! Baggins! We hates it, we hates it, we hates it for ever!"

Then there was a silence. But that too seemed menacing to Bilbo. "If goblins are so near that he smelt them," he thought, "then they'll have heard his shrieking and cursing. Careful now, or this way will lead you to worse things."

The passage was low and roughly made. It was not too difficult for the hobbit, except when, in spite of all care, he stubbed his poor toes again, several times, on nasty jagged stones in the floor. "A bit low for goblins, at least for the big ones," thought Bilbo, not knowing that even the big ones, the orcs of the mountains, go along at a great speed stooping low with their hands almost on the ground.

Soon the passage that had been sloping down began to go up again, and after a while it climbed steeply. That slowed Bilbo down. But at last the slope stopped, the passage turned a corner and dipped down again, and there, at the bottom of a short incline, he saw, filtering round another corner—a glimpse of light. Not red light, as of fire or lantern, but a pale out-of-doors sort of light. Then Bilbo began to run.

Scuttling as fast as his legs would carry him he turned the last corner and came suddenly right into an open space, where the light, after all that time in the dark, seemed dazzlingly bright. Really it was only a leak of sunshine in through a doorway, where a great door, a stone door, was left standing open.

Bilbo blinked, and then suddenly he saw the goblins: goblins in full armour with drawn swords sitting just inside the door, and watching it with wide eyes, and watching the passage that led to it. They were aroused, alert, ready for anything.

They saw him sooner than he saw them. Yes, they saw him. Whether it was an accident, or a last trick of the ring before it took a new master, it was not on his finger. With yells of delight the goblins rushed upon him.

A pang of fear and loss, like an echo of Gollum's misery, smote Bilbo, and forgetting even to draw his sword he struck his hands into his pockets. And there was the ring still, in his left pocket, and it slipped on his finger. The goblins stopped short. They could not see a sign of him. He had vanished. They yelled twice as loud as before, but not so delightedly.

"Where is it?" they cried.

"Go back up the passage!" some shouted.

"This way!" some yelled. "That way!" others yelled.

"Look out for the door," bellowed the captain.

Whistles blew, armour clashed, swords rattled, goblins cursed and swore and ran hither and thither, falling over one another and getting very angry. There was a terrible outcry, to-do, and disturbance.

Bilbo was dreadfully frightened, but he had the sense to understand what had happened and to sneak behind a big barrel which held drink for the goblin-guards, and so get out of the way and avoid being bumped into, trampled to death, or caught by feel.

"I must get to the door, I must get to the door!" he kept on saying to himself, but it was a long time before he ventured to try. Then it was like a horrible game of blind-man's-buff. The place was full of goblins running about, and the poor little hobbit dodged this way and that, was knocked over by a goblin who could not make out what he had bumped into, scrambled again on all fours, slipped between the legs of the captain just in time, got up, and ran for the door.

It was still ajar, but a goblin had pushed it nearly to. Bilbo struggled but he could not move it. He tried to squeeze through the crack. He squeezed and squeezed, and he stuck! It was awful. His buttons had got wedged on the edge of the door and the door-post. He could see outside into the open air: there were a few steps running down into a narrow valley between tall mountains; the sun came out from behind a cloud and shone bright on the outside of the door—but he could not get through.

Suddenly one of the goblins inside shouted: "There is a shadow by the door. Something is outside!"

Bilbo's heart jumped into his mouth. He gave a terrific squirm. Buttons burst off in all directions. He was through, with a torn coat and waistcoat, leaping down the steps like a goat, while bewildered goblins were still picking up his nice brass buttons on the doorstep.

Of course they soon came down after him, hooting and hallooing, and hunting among the trees. But they don't like the sun: it makes their legs wobble and their heads giddy. They could not find Bilbo with the ring on, slipping in and out of the shadow of the trees, running quick and quiet, and keeping out of the sun; so soon they went back grumbling and cursing to guard the door. Bilbo had escaped.

## Chapter VI

# OUT OF THE FRYING-PAN
# INTO THE FIRE

Bilbo had escaped the goblins, but he did not know where he was. He had lost hood, cloak, food, pony, his buttons and his friends. He wandered on and on, till the sun began to sink westwards—*behind the mountains*. Their shadows fell across Bilbo's path, and he looked back. Then he looked forward and could see before him only ridges and slopes falling towards lowlands and plains glimpsed occasionally between the trees.

"Good heavens!" he exclaimed. "I seem to have got right to the other side of the Misty Mountains, right to the edge of the Land Beyond! Where and O where can Gandalf and the dwarves have got to? I only hope to goodness they are not still back there in the power of the goblins!"

He still wandered on, out of the little high valley, over its edge, and down the slopes beyond; but all the while a very uncomfortable thought was growing inside him. He wondered whether he ought not, now he had the magic ring, to go back into the horrible, horrible, tunnels and look for his friends. He had just made up his mind that it was his duty, that he must turn back—and very miserable he felt about it—when he heard voices.

He stopped and listened. It did not sound like goblins; so he crept forward carefully. He was on a stony path winding downwards with a rocky wall on the left hand; on the other side the ground sloped away and there were dells below the level of the path overhung with bushes and low trees. In one of these dells under the bushes people were talking.

He crept still nearer, and suddenly he saw peering between two big boulders a head with a red hood on: it was Balin doing look-out. He could have clapped and shouted for joy, but he did not. He had still got the ring on, for fear of meeting something unexpected and unpleasant, and he saw that Balin was looking straight at him without noticing him.

"I will give them all a surprise," he thought, as he crawled into the bushes at the edge of the dell. Gandalf was arguing with the dwarves. They were discussing all that had happened to them in the tunnels, and wondering and debating what they were to do now. The dwarves were grumbling, and Gandalf was saying that they could not possibly go on with their journey leaving Mr Baggins in the hands of the goblins, without trying to find out if he was alive or dead, and without trying to rescue him.

"After all he is my friend," said the wizard, "and not a bad little chap. I feel responsible for him. I wish to goodness you had not lost him."

The dwarves wanted to know why he had ever been brought at all, why he could not stick to his friends and come along with them, and why the wizard had not chosen some-one with more sense. "He has been more trouble than use so far," said one. "If we have got to go back now into those abominable tunnels to look for him, then drat him, I say."

Gandalf answered angrily: "I brought him, and I don't bring things that are of no use. Either you help me to look for him, or I go and leave you here to get out of the mess as best you can yourselves. If we can only find him again, you will thank me before all is over. Whatever did you want to go and drop him for, Dori?"

"You would have dropped him," said Dori, "if a goblin had suddenly grabbed your legs from behind in the dark, tripped up your feet, and kicked you in the back!"

"Then why didn't you pick him up again?"

"Good heavens! Can you ask! Goblins fighting and biting in the dark, everybody falling over bodies and hitting one another! You nearly chopped off my head with Glamdring, and Thorin was stabbing here there and everywhere with Orcrist. All of a sudden you gave one of your blinding flashes, and we saw the goblins running back yelping. You shouted 'follow me everybody!' and everybody ought to have followed. We thought everybody had. There was no time to count, as you know quite well, till we had dashed through the gate-guards, out of the lower door, and helter-skelter down here. And here we are—without the burglar, confusticate him!"

"And here's the burglar!" said Bilbo stepping down into the middle of them, and slipping off the ring.

Bless me, how they jumped! Then they shouted with surprise and delight. Gandalf was as astonished as any of them, but probably more pleased than all the others. He called to Balin and told him what he thought of a look-out man who let people walk right into them like that without warning. It is a fact that Bilbo's reputation went up a very great deal with the dwarves after this. If they had still doubted that he was really a first-class burglar, in spite of Gandalf's words, they doubted no longer. Balin was the most puzzled of all; but everyone said it was a very clever bit of work.

Indeed Bilbo was so pleased with their praise that he just chuckled inside and said nothing whatever about the ring; and when they asked him how he did it, he said: "Oh, just crept along, you know—very carefully and quietly."

"Well, it is the first time that even a mouse has crept along carefully and quietly under my very nose and not been spotted," said Balin, "and I take off my hood to you." Which he did.

"Balin at your service," said he.

"Your servant, Mr Baggins," said Bilbo.

Then they wanted to know all about his adventures after they had lost him, and he sat down and told them everything—except about the finding of the ring ("not just now" he thought). They were particularly interested in the riddle-competition, and shuddered most appreciatively at his description of Gollum.

"And then I couldn't think of any other question with him sitting beside me," ended Bilbo; "so I said 'what's in my pocket?' And he couldn't guess in three goes. So I said: 'what about your promise? Show me the way out!' But he came at me to kill me, and I ran, and fell over, and he missed me in the dark. Then I followed him, because I heard him talking to himself. He thought I really knew the way out, and so he was making for it. And then he sat down in the entrance, and I could not get by. So I jumped over him and escaped, and ran down to the gate."

"What about the guards?" they asked. "Weren't there any?"

"O yes! lots of them; but I dodged 'em. I got stuck in the door, which was only open a crack, and I lost lots of buttons," he said sadly looking at his torn clothes. "But I squeezed through all right—and here I am."

The dwarves looked at him with quite a new respect, when he talked about dodging guards, jumping over Gollum, and squeezing through, as if it was not very difficult or very alarming.

"What did I tell you?" said Gandalf laughing. "Mr Baggins has more about him than you guess." He gave Bilbo a queer look from under his bushy eyebrows, as he said this, and the hobbit wondered if he guessed at the part of his tale that he had left out.

Then he had questions of his own to ask, for if Gandalf had explained it all by now to the dwarves, Bilbo had not heard it. He wanted to know how the wizard had turned up again, and where they had all got to now.

The wizard, to tell the truth, never minded explaining his cleverness more than once, so now he told Bilbo that both he and Elrond had been well aware of the presence of evil goblins in that part of the mountains. But their main gate used to come out on a different pass, one more easy to travel by, so that they often caught people benighted near their gates. Evidently people had given up going that way, and the goblins must have opened their new entrance at the top of the pass the dwarves had taken, quite recently, because it had been found quite safe up to now.

"I must see if I can't find a more or less decent giant to block it up again," said Gandalf, "or soon there will be no getting over the mountains at all."

As soon as Gandalf had heard Bilbo's yell he realized what had happened. In the flash which killed the goblins that were grabbing him he had nipped inside the crack, just as it snapped to. He followed after the drivers and prisoners right to the edge of the great hall, and there he sat down and worked up the best magic he could in the shadows.

"A very ticklish business, it was," he said. "Touch and go!"

But, of course, Gandalf had made a special study of bewitchments with fire and lights (even the hobbit had never forgotten the magic fireworks at Old Took's midsummer-eve parties, as you remember). The rest we all know—except that Gandalf knew all about the back-door, as the goblins called the lower gate, where Bilbo lost his buttons. As a matter of fact it was well known to anybody who was acquainted with this part of the mountains; but it took a wizard to keep his head in the tunnels and guide them in the right direction.

"They made that gate ages ago," he said, "partly for a way of escape, if they needed one; partly as a way out into the lands beyond, where they still come in the dark and do great damage. They guard it always and no one has ever managed to block it up. They will guard it doubly after this," he laughed.

All the others laughed too. After all they had lost a good deal, but they had killed the Great Goblin and a great many others besides, and they had all escaped, so they might be said to have had the best of it so far.

But the wizard called them to their senses. "We must be getting on at once, now we are a little rested," he said. "They will be out after us in hundreds when night comes on; and already shadows are lengthening. They can smell our footsteps for hours and hours after we have passed. We must be miles on before dusk. There will be a bit of moon, if it keeps fine, and that is lucky. Not that they mind the moon much, but it will give us a little light to steer by."

"O yes!" he said in answer to more questions from the hobbit. "You lose track of time inside goblin-tunnels. Today's Thursday, and it was Monday night or Tuesday morning that we were captured. We have gone miles and miles, and come right down through the heart of the mountains, and are now on the other side—quite a short cut. But we are not at the point to which our pass would have brought us; we are too far to the North, and have some awkward country ahead. And we are still pretty high up. Let's get on!"

"I am dreadfully hungry," groaned Bilbo, who was suddenly aware that he had not had a meal since the night before the night before last. Just think of that for a hobbit! His

stomach felt all empty and loose and his legs all wobbly, now
that the excitement was over.

"Can't help it," said Gandalf, "unless you like to go back
and ask the goblins nicely to let you have your pony back and
your luggage."

"No thank you!" said Bilbo.

"Very well then, we must just tighten our belts and trudge
on—or we shall be made into supper, and that will be much
worse than having none ourselves."

As they went on Bilbo looked from side to side for something to eat; but the blackberries were still only in flower, and
of course there were no nuts, not even hawthorn-berries. He
nibbled a bit of sorrel, and he drank from a small mountain-
stream that crossed the path, and he ate three wild straw-
berries that he found on its bank, but it was not much good.

They still went on and on. The rough path disappeared. The
bushes, and the long grasses between the boulders, the patches
of rabbit-cropped turf, the thyme and the sage and the mar-
joram, and the yellow rockroses all vanished, and they found
themselves at the top of a wide steep slope of fallen stones,
the remains of a landslide. When they began to go down this,
rubbish and small pebbles rolled away from their feet; soon
larger bits of split stone went clattering down and started
other pieces below them slithering and rolling; then lumps of
rock were disturbed and bounded off, crashing down with a
dust and a noise. Before long the whole slope above them and
below them seemed on the move, and they were sliding away,
huddled all together, in a fearful confusion of slipping, rattling,
cracking slabs and stones.

It was the trees at the bottom that saved them. They slid
into the edge of a climbing wood of pines that here stood right
up the mountain slope from the deeper darker forests of the
valleys below. Some caught hold of the trunks and swung

themselves into lower branches, some (like the little hobbit) got behind a tree to shelter from the onslaught of the rocks. Soon the danger was over, the slide had stopped, and the last faint crashes could be heard as the largest of the disturbed stones went bounding and spinning among the bracken and the pine-roots far below.

"Well! that has got us on a bit," said Gandalf; "and even goblins tracking us will have a job to come down here quietly."

"I daresay," grumbled Bombur; "but they won't find it difficult to send stones bouncing down on our heads." The dwarves (and Bilbo) were feeling far from happy, and were rubbing their bruised and damaged legs and feet.

"Nonsense! We are going to turn aside here out of the path of the slide. We must be quick! Look at the light!"

The sun had long gone behind the mountains. Already the shadows were deepening about them, though far away through the trees and over the black tops of those growing lower down they could still see the evening lights on the plains beyond. They limped along now as fast as they were able down the gentle slopes of a pine forest in a slanting path leading steadily southwards. At times they were pushing through a sea of bracken with tall fronds rising right above the hobbit's head; at times they were marching along quiet as quiet over a floor of pine-needles; and all the while the forest-gloom got heavier and the forest-silence deeper. There was no wind that evening to bring even a sea-sighing into the branches of the trees.

"Must we go any further?" asked Bilbo, when it was so dark that he could only just see Thorin's beard wagging beside him, and so quiet that he could hear the dwarves' breathing like a loud noise. "My toes are all bruised and bent, and my legs ache, and my stomach is wagging like an empty sack."

"A bit further," said Gandalf.

After what seemed ages further they came suddenly to an opening where no trees grew. The moon was up and was shining into the clearing. Somehow it struck all of them as not at all a nice place, although there was nothing wrong to see.

All of a sudden they heard a howl away down hill, a long shuddering howl. It was answered by another away to the right and a good deal nearer to them; then by another not far away to the left. It was wolves howling at the moon, wolves gathering together!

There were no wolves living near Mr Baggins' hole at home, but he knew that noise. He had had it described to him often enough in tales. One of his elder cousins (on the Took side), who had been a great traveller, used to imitate it to frighten him. To hear it out in the forest under the moon was too much for Bilbo. Even magic rings are not much use against wolves—especially against the evil packs that lived under the shadow of the goblin-infested mountains, over the Edge of the Wild on the borders of the unknown. Wolves of that sort smell keener than goblins, and do not need to see you to catch you!

"What shall we do, what shall we do!" he cried. "Escaping goblins to be caught by wolves!" he said, and it became a proverb, though we now say "out of the frying-pan into the fire" in the same sort of uncomfortable situations.

"Up the trees quick!" cried Gandalf; and they ran to the trees at the edge of the glade, hunting for those that had branches fairly low, or were slender enough to swarm up. They found them as quick as ever they could, you can guess; and up they went as high as ever they could trust the branches. You would have laughed (from a safe distance), if you had seen the dwarves sitting up in the trees with their beards dangling down, like old gentlemen gone cracked and playing at being boys. Fili and Kili were at the top of a tall larch like an enormous Christmas tree. Dori, Nori, Ori, Oin, and Gloin were more comfortable in a huge pine with regular branches sticking out at intervals like the spokes of a wheel. Bifur, Bofur, Bombur, and Thorin were in another. Dwalin and Balin had swarmed up a tall slender fir with few branches and were trying to find a place to sit in the greenery of the topmost boughs. Gandalf, who was a good deal taller than the others, had found a tree into which they could not climb, a large pine standing at the very edge of the glade. He was quite hidden in its boughs, but you could see his eyes gleaming in the moon as he peeped out.

And Bilbo? He could not get into any tree, and was scuttling about from trunk to trunk, like a rabbit that has lost its hole and has a dog after it.

"You've left the burglar behind again!" said Nori to Dori looking down.

"I can't be always carrying burglars on my back," said Dori, "down tunnels and up trees! What do you think I am? A porter?"

"He'll be eaten if we don't do something," said Thorin, for there were howls all round them now, getting nearer and nearer. "Dori!" he called, for Dori was lowest down in the easiest tree, "be quick, and give Mr Baggins a hand up!"

Dori was really a decent fellow in spite of his grumbling. Poor Bilbo could not reach his hand even when he climbed down to the bottom branch and hung his arm down as far as ever he could. So Dori actually climbed out of the tree and let Bilbo scramble up and stand on his back.

Just at that moment the wolves trotted howling into the clearing. All of a sudden there were hundreds of eyes looking at them. Still Dori did not let Bilbo down. He waited till he had clambered off his shoulders into the branches, and then he jumped for the branches himself. Only just in time! A wolf snapped at his cloak as he swung up, and nearly got him. In a minute there was a whole pack of them yelping all round the tree and leaping up at the trunk, with eyes blazing and tongues hanging out.

But even the wild Wargs (for so the evil wolves over the Edge of the Wild were named) cannot climb trees. For a time they were safe. Luckily it was warm and not windy. Trees are not very comfortable to sit in for long at any time; but in the cold and the wind, with wolves all round below waiting for you, they can be perfectly miserable places.

This glade in the ring of trees was evidently a meeting-place of the wolves. More and more kept coming in. They left guards at the foot of the tree in which Dori and Bilbo were, and then went snuffling about till they had smelt out every tree that had anyone in it. These they guarded too, while all the rest (hundreds and hundreds it seemed) went and sat in a great circle in the glade; and in the middle of the circle was a great grey wolf. He spoke to them in the dreadful language of the Wargs. Gandalf understood it. Bilbo did not, but it sounded terrible to him, and as if all their talk was about cruel and wicked things, as it was. Every now and then all the Wargs in the circle would answer their grey chief all together, and their dreadful clamour almost made the hobbit fall out of his pine-tree.

I will tell you what Gandalf heard, though Bilbo did not understand it. The Wargs and the goblins often helped one an-other in wicked deeds. Goblins do not usually venture very far from their mountains, unless they are driven out and are looking for new homes, or are marching to war (which I am glad to say has not happened for a long while). But in those days they sometimes used to go on raids, especially to get food or slaves to work for them. Then they often got the Wargs to help and shared the plunder with them. Sometimes they rode on wolves like men do on horses. Now it seemed that a great goblin-raid had been planned for that very night. The Wargs had come to meet the goblins and the goblins were late. The reason, no doubt, was the death of the Great Goblin, and all the excitement caused by the dwarves and Bilbo and the wizard, for whom they were probably still hunting.

In spite of the dangers of this far land bold men had of late been making their way back into it from the South, cutting down trees, and building themselves places to live in among the more pleasant woods in the valleys and along the river-shores. There were many of them, and they were brave and well-armed, and even the Wargs dared not attack them if there were many together, or in the bright day. But now they had planned with the goblins' help to come by night upon some of the villages nearest the mountains. If their plan had been carried out, there would have been none left there next day; all would have been killed except the few the goblins kept from the wolves and carried back as prisoners to their caves.

This was dreadful talk to listen to, not only because of the brave woodmen and their wives and children, but also because of the danger which now threatened Gandalf and his friends. The Wargs were angry and puzzled at finding them here in their very meeting-place. They thought they were friends of the woodmen, and were come to spy on them, and would take news of their plans down into the valleys, and then the goblins and the wolves would have to fight a terrible battle instead of capturing prisoners and devouring people waked suddenly from their sleep. So the Wargs had no intention of going away and letting the people up the trees escape, at any rate not until morning. And long before that, they said, goblin soldiers would be coming down from the mountains; and goblins can climb trees, or cut them down.

Now you can understand why Gandalf, listening to their growling and yelping, began to be dreadfully afraid, wizard though he was, and to feel that they were in a very bad place, and had not yet escaped at all. All the same he was not going to let them have it all their own way, though he could not do very much stuck up in a tall tree with wolves all round on the ground below. He gathered the huge pine-cones from the branches of the tree. Then he set one alight with bright blue fire, and threw it whizzing down among the circle of the wolves. It struck one on the back, and immediately his shaggy coat caught fire, and he was leaping to and fro yelping horribly. Then another came and another, one in blue flames, one in red, another in green. They burst on the ground in the middle of the circle and went off in coloured sparks and smoke. A specially large one hit the chief wolf on the nose, and he leaped in the air ten feet, and then rushed round and round the circle biting and snapping even at the other wolves in his anger and fright.

The dwarves and Bilbo shouted and cheered. The rage of the wolves was terrible to see, and the commotion they made filled all the forest. Wolves are afraid of fire at all times, but this was a most horrible and uncanny fire. If a spark got in their coats it stuck and burned into them, and unless they rolled over quick they were soon all in flames. Very soon all about the glade wolves were rolling over and over to put out the sparks on their backs, while those that were burning were running about howling and setting others alight, till their own friends chased them away and they fled off down the slopes crying and yammering and looking for water.

\*   \*   \*

"What is all this uproar in the forest tonight?" said the Lord of the Eagles. He was sitting, black in the moonlight, on the top of a lonely pinnacle of rock at the eastern edge of the mountains. "I hear wolves' voices! Are the goblins at mischief in the woods?"

He swept up into the air, and immediately two of his guards from the rocks at either hand leaped up to follow him. They circled up in the sky and looked down upon the ring of the Wargs, a tiny spot far far below. But eagles have keen eyes and can see small things at a great distance. The Lord of the Eagles of the Misty Mountains had eyes that could look at the sun unblinking, and could see a rabbit moving on the ground a mile below even in the moonlight. So though he could not see the people in the trees, he could make out the commotion among the wolves and see the tiny flashes of fire, and hear the howling and yelping come up faint from far beneath him. Also he could see the glint of the moon on goblin spears and helmets, as long lines of the wicked folk crept down the hillsides from their gate and wound into the wood.

Eagles are not kindly birds. Some are cowardly and cruel. But the ancient race of the northern mountains were the greatest of all birds; they were proud and strong and noble-hearted. They did not love goblins, or fear them. When they took any notice of them at all (which was seldom, for they did not eat such creatures), they swooped on them and drove them shrieking back to their caves, and stopped whatever wickedness they were doing. The goblins hated the eagles and feared them, but could not reach their lofty seats, or drive them from the mountains.

Tonight the Lord of the Eagles was filled with curiosity to know what was afoot; so he summoned many other eagles to him, and they flew away from the mountains, and slowly circling ever round and round they came down, down, down towards the ring of the wolves and the meeting-place of the goblins.

A very good thing too! Dreadful things had been going on down there. The wolves that had caught fire and fled into the forest had set it alight in several places. It was high summer, and on this eastern side of the mountains there had been little rain for some time. Yellowing bracken, fallen branches, deep-piled pine-needles, and here and there dead trees, were soon in flames. All round the clearing of the Wargs fire was leaping. But the wolf-guards did not leave the trees. Maddened and angry they were leaping and howling round the trunks, and cursing the dwarves in their horrible language, with their tongues hanging out, and their eyes shining as red and fierce as the flames.

Then suddenly goblins came running up yelling. They thought a battle with the woodmen was going on; but they soon learned what had really happened. Some of them actually sat down and laughed. Others waved their spears and clashed the shafts against their shields. Goblins are not afraid of fire, and they soon had a plan which seemed to them most amusing.

Some got all the wolves together in a pack. Some stacked fern and brushwood round the tree-trunks. Others rushed round and stamped and beat, and beat and stamped, until nearly all the flames were put out—but they did not put out the fire nearest to the trees where the dwarves were. That fire they fed with leaves and dead branches and bracken. Soon they had a ring of smoke and flame all round the dwarves, a ring which they kept from spreading outwards; but it closed slowly in, till the running fire was licking the fuel piled under the trees. Smoke was in Bilbo's eyes, he could feel the heat of the flames; and through the reek he could see the goblins dancing round and round in a circle like people round a mid-summer bonfire. Outside the ring of dancing warriors with spears and axes stood the wolves at a respectful distance, watching and waiting.

He could hear the goblins beginning a horrible song:

> *Fifteen birds in five firtrees,*
> *their feathers were fanned in a fiery breeze!*
> *But, funny little birds, they had no wings!*
> *O what shall we do with the funny little things?*
> *Roast 'em alive, or stew them in a pot;*
> *fry them, boil them and eat them hot?*

Then they stopped and shouted out: "Fly away little birds! Fly away if you can! Come down little birds, or you will get roasted in your nests! Sing, sing little birds! Why don't you sing?"

"Go away! little boys!" shouted Gandalf in answer. "It isn't bird-nesting time. Also naughty little boys that play with fire get punished." He said it to make them angry, and to show them he was not frightened of them—though of course he was, wizard though he was. But they took no notice, and they went on singing.

> *Burn, burn tree and fern!*
> *Shrivel and scorch! A fizzling torch*
> *To light the night for our delight,*
>    *Ya hey!*

> *Bake and toast 'em, fry and roast 'em!*
> *till beards blaze, and eyes glaze;*
> *till hair smells and skins crack,*
> *fat melts, and bones black*

> *in cinders lie*
> *beneath the sky!*
> *So dwarves shall die,*
> *and light the night for our delight,*
> *Ya hey!*
> *Ya-harri-hey!*
> *Ya hoy!*

And with that *Ya hoy!* the flames were under Gandalf's tree. In a moment it spread to the others. The bark caught fire, the lower branches cracked.

Then Gandalf climbed to the top of his tree. The sudden splendour flashed from his wand like lightning, as he got ready to spring down from on high right among the spears of the goblins. That would have been the end of him, though he would probably have killed many of them as he came hurtling down like a thunderbolt. But he never leaped.

Just at that moment the Lord of the Eagles swept down from above, seized him in his talons, and was gone.

There was a howl of anger and surprise from the goblins. Loud cried the Lord of the Eagles, to whom Gandalf had now spoken. Back swept the great birds that were with him, and down they came like huge black shadows. The wolves yammered and gnashed their teeth; the goblins yelled and stamped with rage, and flung their heavy spears in the air in vain. Over them swooped the eagles; the dark rush of their beating wings smote them to the floor or drove them far away; their talons tore at goblin faces. Other birds flew to the tree-tops and seized the dwarves, who were scrambling up now as far as they ever dared to go.

Poor little Bilbo was very nearly left behind again! He just managed to catch hold of Dori's legs, as Dori was borne off last of all; and up they went together above the tumult and the burning, Bilbo swinging in the air with his arms nearly breaking.

Now far below the goblins and the wolves were scattering far and wide in the woods. A few eagles were still circling and sweeping above the battle-ground. The flames about the trees sprang suddenly up above the highest branches. They went up in crackling fire. There was a sudden flurry of sparks and smoke. Bilbo had escaped only just in time!

Soon the light of the burning was faint below, a red twinkle on the black floor; and they were high up in the sky, rising all the time in strong sweeping circles. Bilbo never forgot that flight, clinging onto Dori's ankles. He moaned "my arms, my arms!"; but Dori groaned "my poor legs, my poor legs!"

At the best of times heights made Bilbo giddy. He used to turn queer if he looked over the edge of quite a little cliff; and he had never liked ladders, let alone trees (never having had to escape from wolves before). So you can imagine how his head swam now, when he looked down between his dangling toes and saw the dark lands opening wide underneath him, touched here and there with the light of the moon on a hill-side rock or a stream in the plains.

The pale peaks of the mountains were coming nearer, moonlit spikes of rock sticking out of black shadows. Summer or not, it seemed very cold. He shut his eyes and wondered if he could hold on any longer. Then he imagined what would happen if he did not. He felt sick.

The flight ended only just in time for him, just before his arms gave way. He loosed Dori's ankles with a gasp and fell onto the rough platform of an eagle's eyrie. There he lay without speaking, and his thoughts were a mixture of surprise at being saved from the fire, and fear lest he fall off that narrow place into the deep shadows on either side. He was feeling very queer indeed in his head by this time after the dreadful adventures of the last three days with next to nothing to eat, and he found himself saying aloud: "Now I know what a piece of bacon feels like when it is suddenly picked out of the pan on a fork and put back on the shelf!"

"No you don't!" he heard Dori answering, "because the bacon knows that it will get back in the pan sooner or later; and it is to be hoped we shan't. Also eagles aren't forks!"

"O no! Not a bit like storks—forks, I mean," said Bilbo sitting up and looking anxiously at the eagle who was perched close by. He wondered what other nonsense he had been saying, and if the eagle would think it rude. You ought not to be rude to an eagle, when you are only the size of a hobbit, and are up in his eyrie at night!

The eagle only sharpened his beak on a stone and trimmed his feathers and took no notice.

Soon another eagle flew up. "The Lord of the Eagles bids you to bring your prisoners to the Great Shelf," he cried and was off again. The other seized Dori in his claws and flew away with him into the night leaving Bilbo all alone. He had just strength to wonder what the messenger had meant by "prisoners," and to begin to think of being torn up for supper like a rabbit, when his own turn came.

The eagle came back, seized him in his talons by the back of his coat, and swooped off. This time he flew only a short way. Very soon Bilbo was laid down, trembling with fear, on a wide shelf of rock on the mountain-side. There was no path down on to it save by flying; and no path down off it except by jumping over a precipice. There he found all the others sitting with their backs to the mountain wall. The Lord of the Eagles also was there and was speaking to Gandalf.

It seems that Bilbo was not going to be eaten after all. The wizard and the eagle-lord appeared to know one another slightly, and even to be on friendly terms. As a matter of fact Gandalf, who had often been in the mountains, had once rendered a service to the eagles and healed their lord from an arrow-wound. So you see "prisoners" had meant "prisoners rescued from the goblins" only, and not captives of the eagles. As Bilbo listened to the talk of Gandalf he realized that at last they were going to escape really and truly from the dreadful mountains. He was discussing plans with the Great Eagle for carrying the dwarves and himself and Bilbo far away and setting them down well on their journey across the plains below.

The Lord of the Eagles would not take them anywhere near where men lived. "They would shoot at us with their great bows of yew," he said, "for they would think we were after their sheep. And at other times they would be right. No! we are glad to cheat the goblins of their sport, and glad to repay our thanks to you, but we will not risk ourselves for dwarves in the southward plains."

"Very well," said Gandalf. "Take us where and as far as you will! We are already deeply obliged to you. But in the meantime we are famished with hunger."

"I am nearly dead of it," said Bilbo in a weak little voice that nobody heard.

"That can perhaps be mended," said the Lord of the Eagles.

Later on you might have seen a bright fire on the shelf of rock and the figures of the dwarves round it cooking and making a fine roasting smell. The eagles had brought up dry boughs for fuel, and they had brought rabbits, hares, and a small sheep. The dwarves managed all the preparations. Bilbo was too weak to help, and anyway he was not much good at skinning rabbits or cutting up meat, being used to having it delivered by the butcher all ready to cook. Gandalf, too, was lying down after doing his part in setting the fire going, since

Oin and Gloin had lost their tinder-boxes. (Dwarves have never taken to matches even yet.)

So ended the adventures of the Misty Mountains. Soon Bilbo's stomach was feeling full and comfortable again, and he felt he could sleep contentedly, though really he would have liked a loaf and butter better than bits of meat toasted on sticks. He slept curled up on the hard rock more soundly than ever he had done on his feather-bed in his own little hole at home. But all night he dreamed of his own house and wandered in his sleep into all his different rooms looking for something that he could not find nor remember what it looked like.

## Chapter VII

# QUEER LODGINGS

The next morning Bilbo woke up with the early sun in his eyes. He jumped up to look at the time and to go and put his kettle on—and found he was not home at all. So he sat down and wished in vain for a wash and a brush. He did not get either, nor tea nor toast nor bacon for his breakfast, only cold mutton and rabbit. And after that he had to get ready for a fresh start.

This time he was allowed to climb on to an eagle's back and cling between his wings. The air rushed over him and he shut his eyes. The dwarves were crying farewells and promising to repay the Lord of the Eagles if ever they could, as off rose fifteen great birds from the mountain's side. The sun was still close to the eastern edge of things. The morning was cool, and mists were in the valleys and hollows and twined here and there about the peaks and pinnacles of the hills. Bilbo opened an eye to peep and saw that the birds were already high up and the world was far away, and the mountains were falling back behind them into the distance. He shut his eyes again and held on tighter.

"Don't pinch!" said his eagle. "You need not be frightened like a rabbit, even if you look rather like one. It is a fair morning with little wind. What is finer than flying?"

Bilbo would have liked to say: "A warm bath and late

breakfast on the lawn afterwards;" but he thought it better to say nothing at all, and to let go his clutch just a tiny bit.

After a good while the eagles must have seen the point they were making for, even from their great height, for they began to go down circling round in great spirals. They did this for a long while, and at last the hobbit opened his eyes again. The earth was much nearer, and below them were trees that looked like oaks and elms, and wide grass lands, and a river running through it all. But cropping out of the ground, right in the path of the stream which looped itself about it, was a great rock, almost a hill of stone, like a last outpost of the distant mountains, or a huge piece cast miles into the plain by some giant among giants.

Quickly now to the top of this rock the eagles swooped one by one and set down their passengers.

"Farewell!" they cried, "wherever you fare, till your eyries receive you at the journey's end!" That is the polite thing to say among eagles.

"May the wind under your wings bear you where the sun sails and the moon walks," answered Gandalf, who knew the correct reply.

And so they parted. And though the Lord of the Eagles became in after days the King of All Birds and wore a golden crown, and his fifteen chieftains golden collars (made of the gold that the dwarves gave them), Bilbo never saw them again—except high and far off in the battle of Five Armies. But as that comes in at the end of this tale we will say no more about it just now.

There was a flat space on the top of the hill of stone and a well worn path with many steps leading down it to the river, across which a ford of huge flat stones led to the grass-land beyond the stream. There was a little cave (a wholesome one with a pebbly floor) at the foot of the steps and near the end of the stony ford. Here the party gathered and discussed what was to be done.

"I always meant to see you all safe (if possible) over the mountains," said the wizard, "and now by good management *and* good luck I have done it. Indeed we are now a good deal further east than I ever meant to come with you, for after all this is not my adventure. I may look in on it again before it is all over, but in the meanwhile I have some other pressing business to attend to."

The dwarves groaned and looked most distressed, and Bilbo wept. They had begun to think Gandalf was going to come all the way and would always be there to help them out of difficulties. "I am not going to disappear this very instant," said he. "I can give you a day or two more. Probably I can help you out of your present plight, and I need a little help myself. We have no food, and no baggage, and no ponies to ride; and you don't know where you are. Now I can tell you that. You are still some miles north of the path which we should have been following, if we had not left the mountain pass in a hurry. Very few people live in these parts, unless they have come here since I was last down this way, which is some years ago. But there is *somebody* that I know of, who lives not far away. That Somebody made the steps on the great rock—the Carrock I believe he calls it. He does not come here often, certainly not in the daytime, and it is no good waiting for him. In fact it would be very dangerous. We must go and find him; and if all goes well at our meeting, I think I shall be off and wish you like the eagles "farewell wherever you fare!"

They begged him not to leave them. They offered him dragon-gold and silver and jewels, but he would not change his mind. "We shall see, we shall see!" he said, "and I think I

have earned already some of your dragon-gold—when you
have got it."

After that they stopped pleading. Then they took off their
clothes and bathed in the river, which was shallow and clear
and stony at the ford. When they had dried in the sun, which
was now strong and warm, they were refreshed, if still sore
and a little hungry. Soon they crossed the ford (carrying the
hobbit), and then began to march through the long green
grass and down the lines of the wide-armed oaks and the
tall elms.

"And why is it called the Carrock?" asked Bilbo as he went
along at the wizard's side.

"He called it the Carrock, because carrock is his word for
it. He calls things like that carrocks, and this one is *the* Carrock because it is the only one near his home and he knows it
well."

"Who calls it? Who knows it?"

"The Somebody I spoke of—a very great person. You must
all be very polite when I introduce you. I shall introduce you
slowly, two by two, I think; and you *must* be careful not to
annoy him, or heaven knows what will happen. He can be ap-
palling when he is angry, though he is kind enough if hu-
moured. Still I warn you he gets angry easily."

The dwarves all gathered round when they heard the
wizard talking like this to Bilbo. "Is that the person you are
taking us to now?" they asked. "Couldn't you find someone
more easy-tempered? Hadn't you better explain it all a bit
clearer?"—and so on.

"Yes it certainly is! No I could not! And I was explaining
very carefully," answered the wizard crossly. "If you must
know more, his name is Beorn. He is very strong, and he is a
skin-changer."

"What! a furrier, a man that calls rabbits conies, when he doesn't turn their skins into squirrels?" asked Bilbo.

"Good gracious heavens, no, no, NO, NO!" said Gandalf. "Don't be a fool Mr Baggins if you can help it; and in the name of all wonder don't mention the word furrier again as long as you are within a hundred miles of his house, nor rug, cape, tippet, muff, nor any other such unfortunate word! He is a skin-changer. He changes his skin: sometimes he is a huge black bear, sometimes he is a great strong black-haired man with huge arms and a great beard. I cannot tell you much more, though that ought to be enough. Some say that he is a bear descended from the great and ancient bears of the mountains that lived there before the giants came. Others say that he is a man descended from the first men who lived before Smaug or the other dragons came into this part of the world, and before the goblins came into the hills out of the North. I cannot say, though I fancy the last is the true tale. He is not the sort of person to ask questions of.

"At any rate he is under no enchantment but his own. He lives in an oak-wood and has a great wooden house; and as a man he keeps cattle and horses which are nearly as marvellous as himself. They work for him and talk to him. He does not eat them; neither does he hunt or eat wild animals. He keeps hives and hives of great fierce bees, and lives most on cream and honey. As a bear he ranges far and wide. I once saw him sitting all alone on the top of the Carrock at night watching the moon sinking towards the Misty Mountains, and I heard him growl in the tongue of bears: 'The day will come when they will perish and I shall go back!' That is why I believe he once came from the mountains himself."

Bilbo and the dwarves had now plenty to think about, and they asked no more questions. They still had a long way to walk before them. Up slope and down dale they plodded. It grew very hot. Sometimes they rested under the trees, and then Bilbo felt so hungry that he would have eaten acorns, if any had been ripe enough yet to have fallen to the ground.

It was the middle of the afternoon before they noticed that great patches of flowers had begun to spring up, all the same kinds growing together as if they had been planted. Especially there was clover, waving patches of cockscomb clover, and purple clover, and wide stretches of short white sweet honey-smelling clover. There was a buzzing and a whirring and a droning in the air. Bees were busy everywhere. And such bees! Bilbo had never seen anything like them.

"If one was to sting me," he thought, "I should swell up as big again as I am!"

They were bigger than hornets. The drones were bigger than your thumb, a good deal, and the bands of yellow on their deep black bodies shone like fiery gold.

"We are getting near," said Gandalf. "We are on the edge of his bee-pastures."

After a while they came to a belt of tall and very ancient oaks, and beyond these to a high thorn-hedge through which you could neither see nor scramble.

"You had better wait here," said the wizard to the dwarves; "and when I call or whistle begin to come after me—you will see the way I go—but only in pairs, mind, about five minutes between each pair of you. Bombur is fattest and will do for two, he had better come alone and last. Come on Mr Baggins! There is a gate somewhere round this way." And with that he went off along the hedge taking the frightened hobbit with him.

They soon came to a wooden gate, high and broad, beyond which they could see gardens and a cluster of low wooden

buildings, some thatched and made of unshaped logs: barns,
stables, sheds, and a long low wooden house. Inside on the
southward side of the great hedge were rows and rows of
hives with bell-shaped tops made of straw. The noise of the
giant bees flying to and fro and crawling in and out filled all
the air.

The wizard and the hobbit pushed open the heavy creaking
gate and went down a wide track towards the house. Some
horses, very sleek and well-groomed, trotted up across the
grass and looked at them intently with very intelligent faces,
then off they galloped to the buildings.

"They have gone to tell him of the arrival of strangers,"
said Gandalf.

Soon they reached a courtyard, three walls of which were
formed by the wooden house and its two long wings. In the
middle there was lying a great oak-trunk with many lopped
branches beside it. Standing near was a huge man with a thick
black beard and hair, and great bare arms and legs with
knotted muscles. He was clothed in a tunic of wool down to
his knees, and was leaning on a large axe. The horses were
standing by him with their noses at his shoulder.

"Ugh! here they are!" he said to the horses. "They don't
look dangerous. You can be off!" He laughed a great rolling
laugh, put down his axe and came forward.

"Who are you and what do you want?" he asked gruffly,
standing in front of them and towering tall above Gandalf. As
for Bilbo he could easily have trotted through his legs without
ducking his head to miss the fringe of the man's brown tunic.

"I am Gandalf," said the wizard.

"Never heard of him," growled the man, "And what's this
little fellow?" he said stooping down to frown at the hobbit
with his bushy black eyebrows.

"That is Mr Baggins, a hobbit of good family and unimreachable reputation," said Gandalf. Bilbo bowed. He had no hat to take off, and was painfully conscious of his many missing buttons. "I am a wizard," continued Gandalf. "I have heard of you, if you have not heard of me; but perhaps you have heard of my good cousin Radagast who lives near the Southern borders of Mirkwood?"

"Yes; not a bad fellow as wizards go, I believe. I used to see him now and again," said Beorn. "Well, now I know who you are, or who you say you are. What do you want?"

"To tell you the truth, we have lost our luggage and nearly lost our way, and are rather in need of help, or at least of advice. I may say we have had rather a bad time with goblins in the mountains."

"Goblins?" said the big man less gruffly. "O ho, so you've been having trouble with *them* have you? What did you go near them for?"

"We did not mean to. They surprised us at night in a pass which we had to cross, we were coming out of the Lands over West into these countries—it is a long tale."

"Then you had better come inside and tell me some of it, if it won't take all day," said the man leading the way through a dark door that opened out of the courtyard into the house.

Following him they found themselves in a wide hall with a fire-place in the middle. Though it was summer there was a wood-fire burning and the smoke was rising to the blackened rafters in search of the way out through an opening in the roof. They passed through this dim hall, lit only by the fire and the hole above it, and came through another smaller door into a sort of veranda propped on wooden posts made of single tree-trunks. It faced south and was still warm and filled with the light of the westering sun which slanted into it, and fell golden on the garden full of flowers that came right up to the steps.

Here they sat on wooden benches while Gandalf began h
tale, and Bilbo swung his dangling legs and looked at t
flowers in the garden, wondering what their names could b
as he had never seen half of them before.

"I was coming over the mountains with a friend or two . .
said the wizard.

"Or two? I can only see one, and a little one at that," sa
Beorn.

"Well to tell you the truth, I did not like to bother you wi
a lot of us, until I found out if you were busy. I will give a cal
if I may."

"Go on, call away!"

So Gandalf gave a long shrill whistle, and presently Thor
and Dori came round the house by the garden path and stoc
bowing low before them.

"One or three you meant, I see!" said Beorn. "But the
aren't hobbits, they are dwarves!"

"Thorin Oakenshield, at your service! Dori at your se
vice!" said the two dwarves bowing again.

"I don't need your service, thank you," said Beorn, "but
expect you need mine. I am not over fond of dwarves; but if
is true you are Thorin (son of Thrain, son of Thror, I believe
and that your companion is respectable, and that you are ene
mies of goblins and are not up to any mischief in my lands–
what are you up to, by the way?"

"They are on their way to visit the land of their father
away east beyond Mirkwood," put in Gandalf, "and it is er
tirely an accident that we are in your lands at all. We wei
crossing by the High Pass that should have brought us to th
road that lies to the south of your country, when we were a
tacked by the evil goblins—as I was about to tell you."

"Go on telling, then!" said Beorn, who was never ver
polite.

"There was a terrible storm; the stone-giants were out hurling rocks, and at the head of the pass we took refuge in a cave, the hobbit and I and several of our companions . . ."

"Do you call two several?"

"Well, no. As a matter of fact there were more than two."

"Where are they? Killed, eaten, gone home?"

"Well, no. They don't seem all to have come when I whistled. Shy, I expect. You see, we are very much afraid that we are rather a lot for you to entertain."

"Go on, whistle again! I am in for a party, it seems, and one or two more won't make much difference," growled Beorn.

Gandalf whistled again; but Nori and Ori were there almost before he had stopped, for, if you remember, Gandalf had told them to come in pairs every five minutes.

"Hullo!" said Beorn. "You came pretty quick—where were you hiding? Come on my jack-in-the-boxes!"

"Nori at your service, Ori at . . ." they began; but Beorn interrupted them.

"Thank you! When I want your help I will ask for it. Sit down, and let's get on with this tale, or it will be supper-time before it is ended."

"As soon as we were asleep," went on Gandalf, "a crack at the back of the cave opened; goblins came out and grabbed the hobbit and the dwarves and our troop of ponies—"

"Troop of ponies? What were you—a travelling circus? Or were you carrying lots of goods? Or do you always call six a troop?"

"O no! As a matter of fact there were more than six ponies, for there were more than six of us—and well, here are two more!" Just at that moment Balin and Dwalin appeared and bowed so low that their beards swept the stone floor. The big man was frowning at first, but they did their best to be frightfully polite, and kept on nodding and bending and bowing and waving their hoods before their knees (in proper dwarf fashion), till he stopped frowning and burst into a chuckling laugh: they looked so comical.

"Troop, was right," he said. "A fine comic one. Come in my merry men, and what are *your* names? I don't want your service just now, only your names; and then sit down and stop wagging!"

"Balin and Dwalin," they said not daring to be offended, and sat flop on the floor looking rather surprised.

"Now go on again!" said Beorn to the wizard.

"Where was I? O yes—I was *not* grabbed. I killed a goblin or two with a flash—"

"Good!" growled Beorn, "It is some good being a wizard then."

"—and slipped inside the crack before it closed. I followed down into the main hall, which was crowded with goblins. The Great Goblin was there with thirty or forty armed guards. I thought to myself 'even if they were not all chained together, what can a dozen do against so many?' "

"A dozen! That's the first time I've heard eight called a dozen. Or have you still got some more jacks that haven't yet come out of their boxes?"

"Well, yes, there seem to be a couple more here now—Fili and Kili, I believe," said Gandalf, as these two now appeared and stood smiling and bowing.

"That's enough!" said Beorn. "Sit down and be quiet! Now go on, Gandalf!"

So Gandalf went on with the tale, until he came to the fight in the dark, the discovery of the lower gate, and their horror when they found that Mr Baggins had been mislaid. "We counted ourselves and found that there was no hobbit. There were only fourteen of us left!"

"Fourteen! That's the first time I've heard one from ten

leave fourteen. You mean nine, or else you haven't told me yet all the names of your party."

"Well, of course you haven't seen Oin and Gloin yet. And, bless me! here they are. I hope you will forgive them for bothering you."

"O let 'em all come! Hurry up! Come along, you two, and sit down! But look here, Gandalf, even now we have only got yourself and ten dwarves and the hobbit that was lost. That only makes eleven (plus one mislaid) and not fourteen, unless wizards count differently to other people. But now please get on with the tale." Beorn did not show it more than he could help, but really he had begun to get very interested. You see, in the old days he had known the very part of the mountains that Gandalf was describing. He nodded and he growled, when he heard of the hobbit's reappearance and of their scramble down the stone-slide and of the wolf-ring in the woods.

When Gandalf came to their climbing into trees with the wolves all underneath, he got up and strode about and muttered: "I wish I had been there! I would have given them more than fireworks!"

"Well," said Gandalf very glad to see that his tale was making a good impression, "I did the best I could. There we were with the wolves going mad underneath us and the forest beginning to blaze in places, when the goblins came down from the hills and discovered us. They yelled with delight and sang songs making fun of us. *Fifteen birds in five fir-trees . . .*"

"Good heavens!" growled Beorn. "Don't pretend that goblins can't count. They can. Twelve isn't fifteen and they know it."

"And so do I. There were Bifur and Bofur as well. I haven't ventured to introduce them before, but here they are."

In came Bifur and Bofur. "And me!" gasped Bombur puffing up behind. He was fat, and also angry at being left till last. He refused to wait five minutes, and followed immediately after the other two.

"Well, now there *are* fifteen of you; and since goblins can count, I suppose that is all that there were up the trees. Now perhaps we can finish this story without any more interruptions." Mr Baggins saw then how clever Gandalf had been. The interruptions had really made Beorn more interested in the story, and the story had kept him from sending the dwarves off at once like suspicious beggars. He never invited people into his house, if he could help it. He had very few friends and they lived a good way away; and he never invited more than a couple of these to his house at a time. Now he had got fifteen strangers sitting in his porch!

By the time the wizard had finished his tale and had told of the eagles' rescue and of how they had all been brought to the Carrock, the sun had fallen behind the peaks of the Misty Mountains and the shadows were long in Beorn's garden.

"A very good tale!" said he. "The best I have heard for a long while. If all beggars could tell such a good one, they might find me kinder. You may be making it all up, of course, but you deserve a supper for the story all the same. Let's have something to eat!"

"Yes please!" they all said together. "Thank you very much!"

Inside the hall it was now quite dark. Beorn clapped his hands, and in trotted four beautiful white ponies and several large long-bodied grey dogs. Beorn said something to them in a queer language like animal noises turned into talk. They went out again and soon came back carrying torches in their mouths, which they lit at the fire and stuck in low brackets on the pillars of the hall about the central hearth. The dogs could stand on their hind-legs when they wished, and carry things with their fore-feet. Quickly they got out boards and trestles from the side walls and set them up near the fire.

Then baa—baa—baa! was heard, and in came some snow-white sheep led by a large coal-black ram. One bore a white cloth embroidered at the edges with figures of animals; others bore on their broad backs trays with bowls and platters and knives and wooden spoons, which the dogs took and quickly laid on the trestle-tables. These were very low, low enough even for Bilbo to sit at comfortably. Beside them a pony pushed two low-seated benches with wide rush-bottoms and little short thick legs for Gandalf and Thorin, while at the far end he put Beorn's big black chair of the same sort (in which he sat with his great legs stuck far out under the table). These were all the chairs he had in his hall, and he probably had them low like the tables for the convenience of the wonderful animals that waited on him. What did the rest sit on? They were not forgotten. The other ponies came in rolling round drum-shaped sections of logs, smoothed and polished, and low enough even for Bilbo; so soon they were all seated at Beorn's table, and the hall had not seen such a gathering for many a year.

There they had a supper, or a dinner, such as they had not had since they left the Last Homely House in the West and said good-bye to Elrond. The light of the torches and the fire flickered about them, and on the table were two tall red beeswax candles. All the time they ate, Beorn in his deep rolling voice told tales of the wild lands on this side of the mountains, and especially of the dark and dangerous wood, that lay outstretched far to North and South a day's ride before them, barring their way to the East, the terrible forest of Mirkwood.

The dwarves listened and shook their beards, for they knew that they must soon venture into that forest and that

after the mountains it was the worst of the perils they had to
pass before they came to the dragon's stronghold. When dinner was over they began to tell tales of their own, but Beorn
seemed to be growing drowsy and paid little heed to them.
They spoke most of gold and silver and jewels and the
making of things by smith-craft, and Beorn did not appear to
care for such things: there were no things of gold or silver in
his hall, and few save the knives were made of metal at all.

They sat long at the table with their wooden drinking-
bowls filled with mead. The dark night came on outside. The
fires in the middle of the hall were built with fresh logs and
the torches were put out, and still they sat in the light of the
dancing flames with the pillars of the house standing tall behind them, and dark at the top like trees of the forest. Whether
it was magic or not, it seemed to Bilbo that he heard a sound
like wind in the branches stirring in the rafters, and the hoot
of owls. Soon he began to nod with sleep and the voices
seemed to grow far away, until he woke with a start.

The great door had creaked and slammed. Beorn was
gone. The dwarves were sitting cross-legged on the floor
round the fire, and presently they began to sing. Some of the
verses were like this, but there were many more, and their
singing went on for a long while:

> The wind was on the withered heath,
> but in the forest stirred no leaf:
> there shadows lay by night and day,
> and dark things silent crept beneath.
>
> The wind came down from mountains cold,
> and like a tide it roared and rolled;
> the branches groaned, the forest moaned,
> and leaves were laid upon the mould.

*The wind went on from West to East;*
*all movement in the forest ceased,*
*but shrill and harsh across the marsh*
*its whistling voices were released.*

*The grasses hissed, their tassels bent,*
*the reeds were rattling—on it went*
*o'er shaken pool under heavens cool*
*where racing clouds were torn and rent.*

*It passed the lonely Mountain bare*
*and swept above the dragon's lair:*
*there black and dark lay boulders stark*
*and flying smoke was in the air.*

*It left the world and took its flight*
*over the wide seas of the night.*
*The moon set sail upon the gale,*
*and stars were fanned to leaping light.*

Bilbo began to nod again. Suddenly up stood Gandalf.

"It is time for us to sleep," he said, "—for us, but not I think
for Beorn. In this hall we can rest sound and safe, but I warn
you all not to forget what Beorn said before he left us: you
must not stray outside until the sun is up, on your peril."

Bilbo found that beds had already been laid at the side of
the hall, on a sort of raised platform between the pillars and
the outer wall. For him there was a little mattress of straw and
woollen blankets. He snuggled into them very gladly, sum-
mertime though it was. The fire burned low and he fell asleep.
Yet in the night he woke: the fire had now sunk to a few embers; the dwarves and Gandalf were all asleep, to judge by
their breathing; a splash of white on the floor came from the

high moon, which was peering down through the smoke-hole in the roof.

There was a growling sound outside, and a noise as of some great animal scuffling at the door. Bilbo wondered what it was, and whether it could be Beorn in enchanted shape, and if he would come in as a bear and kill them. He dived under the blankets and hid his head, and fell asleep again at last in spite of his fears.

It was full morning when he awoke. One of the dwarves had fallen over him in the shadows where he lay, and had rolled down with a bump from the platform on to the floor. It was Bofur, and he was grumbling about it, when Bilbo opened his eyes.

"Get up lazybones," he said, "or there will be no breakfast left for you."

Up jumped Bilbo. "Breakfast!" he cried. "Where is breakfast?"

"Mostly inside us," answered the other dwarves who were moving about the hall; "but what is left is out on the veranda. We have been about looking for Beorn ever since the sun got up; but there is no sign of him anywhere, though we found breakfast laid as soon as we went out."

"Where is Gandalf?" asked Bilbo, moving off to find something to eat as quick as he could.

"O! out and about somewhere," they told him. But he saw no sign of the wizard all that day until the evening. Just before sunset he walked into the hall, where the hobbit and the dwarves were having supper, waited on by Beorn's wonderful animals, as they had been all day. Of Beorn they had seen and heard nothing since the night before, and they were getting puzzled.

"Where is our host, and where have *you* been all day yourself?" they all cried.

"One question at a time—and none till after supper! I haven't had a bite since breakfast."

At last Gandalf pushed away his plate and jug—he had eaten two whole loaves (with masses of butter and honey and clotted cream) and drunk at least a quart of mead—and he took out his pipe. "I will answer the second question first," he said, "—but bless me! this is a splendid place for smoke rings!" Indeed for a long time they could get nothing more out of him, he was so busy sending smoke-rings dodging round the pillars of the hall, changing them into all sorts of different shapes and colours, and setting them at last chasing one another out of the hole in the roof. They must have looked very queer from outside, popping out into the air one after another, green, blue, red, silver-grey, yellow, white; big ones, little ones; little ones dodging through big ones and joining into figure-eights, and going off like a flock of birds into the distance.

"I have been picking out bear-tracks," he said at last. "There must have been a regular bears' meeting outside here last night. I soon saw that Beorn could not have made them all: there were far too many of them, and they were of various sizes too. I should say there were little bears, large bears, ordinary bears, and gigantic big bears, all dancing outside from dark to nearly dawn. They came from almost every direction, except from the west over the river, from the Mountains. In that direction only one set of footprints led—none coming, only ones going away from here. I followed these as far as the Carrock. There they disappeared into the river, but the water was too deep and strong beyond the rock for me to cross. It is easy enough, as you remember, to get from this bank to the Carrock by the ford, but on the other side is a cliff standing up from a swirling channel. I had to walk miles before I found a place where the river was wide and shallow enough for me to wade and swim, and then miles back again to pick up the tracks again. By that time it was too late for me to follow them far. They went straight off in the direction of the pine-woods on the east side of the Misty Mountains, where we had our pleasant little party with the Wargs the night before last. And now I think I have answered your first question, too," ended Gandalf, and he sat a long while silent.

Bilbo thought he knew what the wizard meant. "What shall we do," he cried, "if he leads all the Wargs and the goblins down here? We shall all be caught and killed! I thought you said he was not a friend of theirs."

"So I did. And don't be silly! You had better go to bed, your wits are sleepy."

The hobbit felt quite crushed, and as there seemed nothing else to do he did go to bed; and while the dwarves were still singing songs he dropped asleep, still puzzling his little head about Beorn, till he dreamed a dream of hundreds of black bears dancing slow heavy dances round and round in the moonlight in the courtyard. Then he woke up when everyone else was asleep, and he heard the same scraping, scuffling, snuffling, and growling as before.

Next morning they were all wakened by Beorn himself. "So here you all are still!" he said. He picked up the hobbit and laughed: "Not eaten up by Wargs or goblins or wicked bears yet I see"; and he poked Mr Baggins' waistcoat most disrespectfully. "Little bunny is getting nice and fat again on bread and honey," he chuckled. "Come and have some more!"

So they all went to breakfast with him. Beorn was most jolly for a change; indeed he seemed to be in a splendidly good humour and set them all laughing with his funny stories; nor did they have to wonder long where he had been or why he was so nice to them, for he told them himself. He had been over the river and right back up into the mountains—from which you can guess that he could travel quickly, in bear's shape at any rate. From the burnt wolf-glade he had soon found out that part of their story was true; but he had found more than that: he had caught a Warg and a goblin wandering in the woods. From these he had got news: the goblin patrols were still hunting with Wargs for the dwarves, and they were fiercely angry because of the death of the Great Goblin, and also because of the burning of the chief wolf's nose and the death from the wizard's fire of many of his chief servants. So much they told him when he forced them, but he guessed there was more wickedness than this afoot, and that a great raid of the whole goblin army with their wolf-allies into the lands shadowed by the mountains might soon be made to find the dwarves, or to take vengeance on the men and creatures that lived there, and who they thought must be sheltering them.

"It was a good story, that of yours," said Beorn, "but I like it still better now I am sure it is true. You must forgive my not taking your word. If you lived near the edge of Mirkwood, you would take the word of no one that you did not know as well as your brother or better. As it is, I can only say that I have hurried home as fast as I could to see that you were safe, and to offer you any help that I can. I shall think more kindly of dwarves after this. Killed the Great Goblin, killed the Great Goblin!" he chuckled fiercely to himself.

"What did you do with the goblin and the Warg?" asked Bilbo suddenly.

"Come and see!" said Beorn, and they followed round the house. A goblin's head was stuck outside the gate and a warg-skin was nailed to a tree just beyond. Beorn was a fierce enemy. But now he was their friend, and Gandalf thought it wise to tell him their whole story and the reason of their journey, so that they could get the most help he could offer.

This is what he promised to do for them. He would provide ponies for each of them, and a horse for Gandalf, for their journey to the forest, and he would lade them with food to last them for weeks with care, and packed so as to be as easy as possible to carry—nuts, flour, sealed jars of dried fruits, and red earthenware pots of honey, and twice-baked cakes that would keep good a long time, and on a little of which they could march far. The making of these was one of his secrets; but honey was in them, as in most of his foods, and they were good to eat, though they made one thirsty. Water, he said, they would not need to carry this side of the forest, for there were streams and springs along the road. "But your way through Mirkwood is dark, dangerous and difficult," he said. "Water is not easy to find there, nor food. The time is not yet come for nuts (though it may be past and gone indeed before you get to the other side), and nuts are about all that grows there fit for food; in there the wild things are dark, queer, and savage. I will provide you with skins for carrying water, and I will give you some bows and arrows. But I doubt very much whether anything you find in Mirkwood will be wholesome to eat or to drink. There is one stream there, I know, black and strong which crosses the path. That you should neither drink of, nor bathe in; for I have heard that it carries enchantment and a great drowsiness and forgetfulness. And in the dim shadows of that place I don't think you will shoot anything, wholesome or unwholesome, without straying from the path. That you MUST NOT do, for any reason.

"That is all the advice I can give you. Beyond the edge of the forest I cannot help you much; you must depend on your luck and your courage and the food I send with you. At the gate of the forest I must ask you to send back my horse and my ponies. But I wish you all speed, and my house is open to you, if ever you come back this way again."

They thanked him, of course, with many bows and sweepings of their hoods and with many an "at your service, O master of the wide wooden halls!" But their spirits sank at his grave words, and they all felt that the adventure was far more dangerous than they had thought, while all the time, even if they passed all the perils of the road, the dragon was waiting at the end.

All that morning they were busy with preparations. Soon after midday they ate with Beorn for the last time, and after the meal they mounted the steeds he was lending them, and bidding him many farewells they rode off through his gate at a good pace.

As soon as they left his high hedges at the east of his fenced lands they turned north and then bore to the northwest. By his advice they were no longer making for the main forest-road to the south of his land. Had they followed the pass, their path would have led them down a stream from the mountains that joined the great river miles south of the Carrock. At that point there was a deep ford which they might have passed, if they had still had their ponies, and beyond that a track led to the skirts of the wood and to the entrance of the old forest road. But Beorn had warned them that that way was now often used by the goblins, while the forest-road itself, he had heard, was overgrown and disused at the eastern end and led to impassable marshes where the paths had long been lost. Its eastern opening had also always been far to the south of the Lonely Mountain, and would have left them still with a long and difficult northward march when they got to the other side. North of the Carrock the edge of Mirkwood drew closer to the borders of the Great River, and though here the Mountains too drew down nearer, Beorn advised them to take this way; for at a place a few days' ride due north of the Carrock was the gate of a little-known pathway through Mirkwood that led almost straight towards the Lonely Mountains.

"The goblins," Beorn had said, "will not dare to cross the Great River for a hundred miles north of the Carrock nor to come near my house—it is well protected at night!—but I should ride fast; for if they make their raid soon they will cross the river to the south and scour all the edge of the forest so as to cut you off, and Wargs run swifter than ponies. Still you are safer going north, even though you seem to be going back nearer to their strongholds; for that is what they will least expect, and they will have the longer ride to catch you. Be off now as quick as you may!"

That is why they were now riding in silence, galloping wherever the ground was grassy and smooth, with the mountains dark on their left, and in the distance the line of the river with its trees drawing ever closer. The sun had only just turned west when they started, and till evening it lay golden on the land about them. It was difficult to think of pursuing goblins behind, and when they had put many miles between them and Beorn's house they began to talk and to sing again and to forget the dark forest-path that lay in front. But in the evening when the dusk came on and the peaks of the mountains glowered against the sunset they made a camp and set a guard, and most of them slept uneasily with dreams in which there came the howl of hunting wolves and the cries of goblins.

Still the next morning dawned bright and fair again. There was an autumn-like mist white upon the ground and the air was chill, but soon the sun rose red in the East and the mists vanished, and while the shadows were still long they were off again. So they rode now for two more days, and all the while they saw nothing save grass and flowers and birds and scattered trees, and occasionally small herds of red deer browsing or sitting at noon in the shade. Sometimes Bilbo saw the horns of the harts sticking up out of the long grass, and at first he thought they were the dead branches of trees. That third evening they were so eager to press on, for Beorn had said that they should reach the forest-gate early on the fourth day, that they rode still forward after dusk and into the night beneath the moon. As the light faded Bilbo thought he saw away to the right, or to the left, the shadowy form of a great bear prowling along in the same direction. But if he dared to mention it to Gandalf, the wizard only said: "Hush! Take no notice!"

Next day they started before dawn, though their night had been short. As soon as it was light they could see the forest coming as it were to meet them, or waiting for them like a black and frowning wall before them. The land began to slope up and up, and it seemed to the hobbit that a silence began to draw in upon them. Birds began to sing less. There were no more deer; not even rabbits were to be seen. By the afternoon they had reached the eaves of Mirkwood, and were resting almost beneath the great overhanging boughs of its outer trees. Their trunks were huge and gnarled, their branches twisted, their leaves were dark and long. Ivy grew on them and trailed along the ground.

"Well, here is Mirkwood!" said Gandalf. "The greatest of the forests of the Northern world. I hope you like the look of it. Now you must send back these excellent ponies you have borrowed."

The dwarves were inclined to grumble at this, but the wizard told them they were fools. "Beorn is not as far off as you seem to think, and you had better keep your promises

anyway, for he is a bad enemy. Mr Baggins' eyes are sharper
than yours, if you have not seen each night after dark a great
bear going along with us or sitting far off in the moon
watching our camps. Not only to guard you and guide you,
but to keep an eye on the ponies too. Beorn may be your
friend, but he loves his animals as his children. You do not
guess what kindness he has shown you in letting dwarves ride
them so far and so fast, nor what would happen to you, if you
tried to take them into the forest."

"What about the horse, then?" said Thorin. "You don't
mention sending that back."

"I don't, because I am not sending it."

"What about *your* promise then?"

"I will look after that. I am not sending the horse back, I
am riding it!"

Then they knew that Gandalf was going to leave them at
the very edge of Mirkwood, and they were in despair. But
nothing they could say would change his mind.

"Now we had this all out before, when we landed on the
Carrock," he said. "It is no use arguing. I have, as I told you,
some pressing business away south; and I am already late
through bothering with you people. We may meet again before all is over, and then again of course we may not. That depends on your luck and on your courage and sense; and I am
sending Mr Baggins with you. I have told you before that he
has more about him than you guess, and you will find that out
before long. So cheer up Bilbo and don't look so glum. Cheer
up Thorin and Company! This is your expedition after all.
Think of the treasure at the end, and forget the forest and the
dragon, at any rate until tomorrow morning!"

When tomorrow morning came he still said the same. So
now there was nothing left to do but to fill their water-skins at

a clear spring they found close to the forest-gate, and unpack the ponies. They distributed the packages as fairly as they could, though Bilbo thought his lot was wearisomely heavy, and did not at all like the idea of trudging for miles and miles with all that on his back.

"Don't you worry!" said Thorin. "It will get lighter all too soon. Before long I expect we shall all wish our packs heavier, when the food begins to run short."

Then at last they said good-bye to their ponies and turned their heads for home. Off they trotted gaily, seeming very glad to put their tails towards the shadow of Mirkwood. As they went away Bilbo could have sworn that a thing like a bear left the shadow of the trees and shambled off quickly after them.

Now Gandalf too said farewell. Bilbo sat on the ground feeling very unhappy and wishing he was beside the wizard on his tall horse. He had gone just inside the forest after breakfast (a very poor one), and it had seemed as dark in there in the morning as at night, and very secret: "a sort of watching and waiting feeling," he said to himself.

"Good-bye!" said Gandalf to Thorin. "And good-bye to you all, good-bye! Straight through the forest is your way now. Don't stray off the track!—if you do, it is a thousand to one you will never find it again and never get out of Mirkwood; and then I don't suppose I, or any one else, will ever see you again."

"Do we really have to go through?" groaned the hobbit.

"Yes, you do!" said the wizard, "if you want to get to the other side. You must either go through or give up your quest. And I am not going to allow you to back out now, Mr Baggins. I am ashamed of you for thinking of it. You have got to look after all these dwarves for me," he laughed.

"No! no!" said Bilbo. "I didn't mean that. I meant, is there no way round?"

"There is, if you care to go two hundred miles or so out of your way north, and twice that south. But you wouldn't get a safe path even then. There are no safe paths in this part of the world. Remember you are over the Edge of the Wild now, and in for all sorts of fun wherever you go. Before you could get round Mirkwood in the North you would be right among the slopes of the Grey Mountains, and they are simply stiff with goblins, hobgoblins, and orcs of the worst description. Before you could get round it in the South, you would get into the land of the Necromancer; and even you, Bilbo, won't need me to tell you tales of that black sorcerer. I don't advise you to go anywhere near the places overlooked by his dark tower! Stick to the forest-track, keep your spirits up, hope for the best, and with a tremendous slice of luck you *may* come out one day and see the Long Marshes lying below you, and beyond them, high in the East, the Lonely Mountain where dear old Smaug lives, though I hope he is not expecting you."

"Very comforting you are to be sure," growled Thorin. "Good-bye! If you won't come with us, you had better get off without any more talk!"

"Good-bye then, and really good-bye!" said Gandalf, and he turned his horse and rode down into the West. But he could not resist the temptation to have the last word. Before he had passed quite out of hearing he turned and put his hands to his mouth and called to them. They heard his voice come faintly: "Good-bye! Be good, take care of yourselves—and DON'T LEAVE THE PATH!"

Then he galloped away and was soon lost to sight. "O good-bye and go away!" grunted the dwarves, all the more angry because they were really filled with dismay at losing him. Now began the most dangerous part of all the journey. They each shouldered the heavy pack and the water-skin which was their share, and turned from the light that lay on the lands outside and plunged into the forest.

## Chapter VIII

# FLIES AND SPIDERS

They walked in single file. The entrance to the path was like a sort of arch leading into a gloomy tunnel made by two great trees that leant together, too old and strangled with ivy and hung with lichen to bear more than a few blackened leaves. The path itself was narrow and wound in and out among the trunks. Soon the light at the gate was like a little bright hole far behind, and the quiet was so deep that their feet seemed to thump along while all the trees leaned over them and listened.

As their eyes became used to the dimness they could see a little way to either side in a sort of darkened green glimmer. Occasionally a slender beam of sun that had the luck to slip in through some opening in the leaves far above, and still more luck in not being caught in the tangled boughs and matted twigs beneath, stabbed down thin and bright before them. But this was seldom, and it soon ceased altogether.

There were black squirrels in the wood. As Bilbo's sharp inquisitive eyes got used to seeing things he could catch glimpses of them whisking off the path and scuttling behind tree-trunks. There were queer noises too, grunts, scufflings, and hurryings in the undergrowth, and among the leaves that lay piled endlessly thick in places on the forest-floor; but what made the noises he could not see. The nastiest things they saw were the cobwebs: dark dense cobwebs with threads extraordinarily thick, often stretched from tree to tree, or tangled in the lower branches on either side of them. There were none stretched across the path, but whether because some magic kept it clear, or for what other reason they could not guess.

It was not long before they grew to hate the forest as heartily as they had hated the tunnels of the goblins, and it seemed to offer even less hope of any ending. But they had to go on and on, long after they were sick for a sight of the sun and of the sky, and longed for the feel of wind on their faces. There was no movement of air down under the forest-roof, and it was everlastingly still and dark and stuffy. Even the dwarves felt it, who were used to tunnelling, and lived at times for long whiles without the light of the sun; but the hobbit, who liked holes to make a house in but not to spend summer days in, felt that he was being slowly suffocated.

The nights were the worst. It then became pitch-dark—not what you call pitch-dark, but really pitch: so black that you really could see nothing. Bilbo tried flapping his hand in front of his nose, but he could not see it at all. Well, perhaps it is not true to say that they could see nothing: they could see eyes. They slept all closely huddled together, and took it in turns to watch; and when it was Bilbo's turn he would see gleams in the darkness round them, and sometimes pairs of yellow or red or green eyes would stare at him from a little distance, and then slowly fade and disappear and slowly shine out again in another place. And sometimes they would gleam down from the branches just above him; and that was most terrifying. But the eyes that he liked the least were horrible pale bulbous sort of eyes. "Insect eyes," he thought, "not animal eyes, only they are much too big."

Although it was not yet very cold, they tried lighting watch-fires at night, but they soon gave that up. It seemed to bring hundreds and hundreds of eyes all round them, though the creatures, whatever they were, were careful never to let their bodies show in the little flicker of the flames. Worse still it brought thousands of dark-grey and black moths, some nearly as big as your hand, flapping and whirring round their ears. They could not stand that, nor the huge bats, black as a top-hat, either; so they gave up fires and sat at night and dozed in the enormous uncanny darkness.

All this went on for what seemed to the hobbit ages upon ages; and he was always hungry, for they were extremely careful with their provisions. Even so, as days followed days, and still the forest seemed just the same, they began to get anxious. The food would not last for ever: it was in fact already beginning to get low. They tried shooting at the squirrels, and they wasted many arrows before they managed to bring one down on the path. But when they roasted it, it proved horrible to taste, and they shot no more squirrels.

They were thirsty too, for they had none too much water, and in all the time they had seen neither spring nor stream. This was their state when one day they found their path blocked by a running water. It flowed fast and strong but not very wide right across the way, and it was black, or looked it in the gloom. It was well that Beorn had warned them against it, or they would have drunk from it, whatever its colour, and filled some of their emptied skins at its bank. As it was they only thought of how to cross it without wetting themselves in its water. There had been a bridge of wood across, but it had rotted and fallen leaving only the broken posts near the bank.

Bilbo kneeling on the brink and peering forward cried: "There is a boat against the far bank! Now why couldn't it have been this side!"

"How far away do you think it is?" asked Thorin, for by now they knew Bilbo had the sharpest eyes among them.

"Not at all far. I shouldn't think above twelve yards."

"Twelve yards! I should have thought it was thirty at least, but my eyes don't see as well as they used a hundred years ago. Still twelve yards is as good as a mile. We can't jump it, and we daren't try to wade or swim."

"Can any of you throw a rope?"

"What's the good of that? The boat is sure to be tied up, even if we could hook it, which I doubt."

"I don't believe it is tied," said Bilbo, "though of course I can't be sure in this light; but it looks to me as if it was just drawn up on the bank, which is low just there where the path goes down into the water."

"Dori is the strongest, but Fili is the youngest and still has the best sight," said Thorin. "Come here Fili, and see if you can see the boat Mr Baggins is talking about."

Fili thought he could; so when he had stared a long while to get an idea of the direction, the others brought him a rope. They had several with them, and on the end of the longest they fastened one of the large iron hooks they had used for catching their packs to the straps about their shoulders. Fili took this in his hand, balanced it for a moment, and then flung it across the stream.

Splash it fell in the water! "Not far enough!" said Bilbo who was peering forward. "A couple of feet and you would have dropped it on to the boat. Try again. I don't suppose the magic is strong enough to hurt you, if you just touch a bit of wet rope."

Fili picked up the hook when he had drawn it back, rather doubtfully all the same. This time he threw it with great strength.

"Steady!" said Bilbo, "you have thrown it right into the wood on the other side now. Draw it back gently." Fili hauled the rope back slowly, and after a while Bilbo said: "Carefully! It is lying on the boat; let's hope the hook will catch."

It did. The rope went taut, and Fili pulled in vain. Kili came to his help, and then Oin and Gloin. They tugged and tugged, and suddenly they all fell over on their backs. Bilbo was on the look out, however, caught the rope, and with a piece of stick fended off the little black boat as it came rushing across the stream. "Help!" he shouted, and Balin was just in time to seize the boat before it floated off down the current.

"It was tied after all," said he, looking at the snapped painter that was still dangling from it. "That was a good pull, my lads; and a good job that our rope was the stronger."

"Who'll cross first?" asked Bilbo.

"I shall," said Thorin, "and you will come with me, and Fili and Balin. That's as many as the boat will hold at a time. After that Kili and Oin and Gloin and Dori; next Ori and Nori, Bifur and Bofur; and last Dwalin and Bombur."

"I'm always last and I don't like it," said Bombur. "It's somebody else's turn today."

"You should not be so fat. As you are, you must be with the last and lightest boatload. Don't start grumbling against orders, or something bad will happen to you."

"There aren't any oars. How are you going to push the boat back to the far bank?" asked the hobbit.

"Give me another length of rope and another hook," said Fili, and when they had got it ready, he cast it into the darkness ahead and as high as he could throw it. Since it did not fall down again, they saw that it must have stuck in the branches. "Get in now," said Fili, "and one of you haul on the rope that is stuck in a tree on the other side. One of the others must keep hold of the hook we used at first, and when we are safe on the other side he can hook it on, and you can draw the boat back."

In this way they were all soon on the far bank safe across the enchanted stream. Dwalin had just scrambled out with the coiled rope on his arm, and Bombur (still grumbling) was getting ready to follow, when something bad did happen. There was a flying sound of hooves on the path ahead. Out of the gloom came suddenly the shape of a flying deer. It charged into the dwarves and bowled them over, then gathered itself for a leap. High it sprang and cleared the water with a mighty jump. But it did not reach the other side in safety. Thorin was the only one who had kept his feet and his wits. As soon as they had landed he had bent his bow and fitted an arrow in case any hidden guardian of the boat appeared. Now he sent a swift and sure shot into the leaping beast. As it reached the further bank it stumbled. The shadows swallowed it up, but they heard the sound of hooves quickly falter and then go still.

Before they could shout in praise of the shot, however, a dreadful wail from Bilbo put all thoughts of venison out of their minds. "Bombur has fallen in! Bombur is drowning!" he cried. It was only too true. Bombur had only one foot on the land when the hart bore down on him, and sprang over him. He had stumbled, thrusting the boat away from the bank, and then toppled back into the dark water, his hands slipping off the slimy roots at the edge, while the boat span slowly off and disappeared.

They could still see his hood above the water when they ran to the bank. Quickly, they flung a rope with a hook towards him. His hand caught it, and they pulled him to the shore. He was drenched from hair to boots, of course, but that was not the worst. When they laid him on the bank he was already fast asleep, with one hand clutching the rope so tight that they could not get it from his grasp; and fast asleep he remained in spite of all they could do.

They were still standing over him, cursing their ill luck, and Bombur's clumsiness, and lamenting the loss of the boat which made it impossible for them to go back and look for the hart, when they became aware of the dim blowing of horns in the wood and the sound as of dogs baying far off. Then they all fell silent; and as they sat it seemed they could hear the noise of a great hunt going by to the north of the path, though they saw no sign of it.

There they sat for a long while and did not dare to make a move. Bombur slept on with a smile on his fat face, as if he no longer cared for all the troubles that vexed them. Suddenly on the path ahead appeared some white deer, a hind and fawns as snowy white as the hart had been dark. They glimmered in the shadows. Before Thorin could cry out three of the dwarves had leaped to their feet and loosed off arrows from their bows. None seemed to find their mark. The deer turned and vanished in the trees as silently as they had come, and in vain the dwarves shot their arrows after them.

"Stop! stop!" shouted Thorin; but it was too late, the excited dwarves had wasted their last arrows, and now the bows that Beorn had given them were useless.

They were a gloomy party that night, and the gloom gathered still deeper on them in the following days. They had crossed the enchanted stream; but beyond it the path seemed to straggle on just as before, and in the forest they could see no change. Yet if they had known more about it and considered the meaning of the hunt and the white deer that had appeared upon their path, they would have known that they were at last drawing towards the eastern edge, and would soon have come, if they could have kept up their courage and their hope, to thinner trees and places where the sunlight came again.

But they did not know this, and they were burdened with the heavy body of Bombur, which they had to carry along with them as best they could, taking the wearisome task in turns of four each while the others shared their packs. If these had not become all too light in the last few days, they would never have managed it; but a slumbering and smiling Bombur was a poor exchange for packs filled with food however heavy. In a few days a time came when there was practically nothing left to eat or to drink. Nothing wholesome could they see growing in the wood, only funguses and herbs with pale leaves and unpleasant smell.

About four days from the enchanted stream they came to a part where most of the trees were beeches. They were at first inclined to be cheered by the change, for here there was no undergrowth and the shadow was not so deep. There was a greenish light about them, and in places they could see some distance to either side of the path. Yet the light only showed them endless lines of straight grey trunks like the pillars of some huge twilight hall. There was a breath of air and a noise of wind, but it had a sad sound. A few leaves came rustling down to remind them that outside autumn was coming on. Their feet ruffled among the dead leaves of countless other autumns that drifted over the banks of the path from the deep red carpets of the forest.

Still Bombur slept and they grew very weary. At times they heard disquieting laughter. Sometimes there was singing in the distance too. The laughter was the laughter of fair voices not of goblins, and the singing was beautiful, but it sounded eerie and strange, and they were not comforted, rather they hurried on from those parts with what strength they had left.

Two days later they found their path going downwards, and before long they were in a valley filled almost entirely with a mighty growth of oaks.

"Is there no end to this accursed forest?" said Thorin. "Somebody must climb a tree and see if he can get his head above the roof and have a look round. The only way is to choose the tallest tree that overhangs the path."

Of course "somebody" meant Bilbo. They chose him, because to be of any use the climber must get his head above the topmost leaves, and so he must be light enough for the highest and slenderest branches to bear him. Poor Mr Baggins had never had much practice in climbing trees, but they hoisted him up into the lowest branches of an enormous oak that grew right out into the path, and up he had to go as best he could. He pushed his way through the tangled twigs with many a slap in the eye; he was greened and grimed from the old bark of the greater boughs; more than once he slipped and caught himself just in time; and at last, after a dreadful struggle in a difficult place where there seemed to be no convenient branches at all, he got near the top. All the time he was wondering whether there were spiders in the tree, and how he was going to get down again (except by falling).

In the end he poked his head above the roof of leaves, and then he found spiders all right. But they were only small ones of ordinary size, and they were after the butterflies. Bilbo's eyes were nearly blinded by the light. He could hear the dwarves shouting up at him from far below, but he could not answer, only hold on and blink. The sun was shining brilliantly, and it was a long while before he could bear it. When he could, he saw all round him a sea of dark green, ruffled here and there by the breeze; and there were everywhere hundreds of butterflies. I expect they were a kind of "purple emperor", a butterfly that loves the tops of oak-woods, but these were not purple at all, they were a dark dark velvety black without any markings to be seen.

He looked at the "black emperors" for a long time, and enjoyed the feel of the breeze in his hair and on his face; but at length the cries of the dwarves, who were now simply stamping with impatience down below, reminded him of his real business. It was no good. Gaze as much as he might, he could see no end to the trees and the leaves in any direction. His heart, that had been lightened by the sight of the sun and the feel of the wind, sank back into his toes: there was no food to go back to down below.

Actually, as I have told you, they were not far off the edge of the forest; and if Bilbo had had the sense to see it, the tree that he had climbed, though it was tall in itself, was standing near the bottom of a wide valley, so that from its top the trees seemed to swell up all round like the edges of a great bowl, and he could not expect to see how far the forest lasted. Still he did not see this, and he climbed down full of despair. He got to the bottom again at last, scratched, hot, and miserable, and he could not see anything in the gloom below when he got there. His report soon made the others as miserable as he was.

"The forest goes on for ever and ever and ever in all directions! Whatever shall we do? And what is the use of sending a hobbit!" they cried, as if it was his fault. They did not care tuppence about the butterflies, and were only made more angry when he told them of the beautiful breeze, which they were too heavy to climb up and feel.

That night they ate their very last scraps and crumbs of food; and next morning when they woke the first thing they noticed was that they were still gnawingly hungry, and the next thing was that it was raining and that here and there the drip of it was dropping heavily on the forest floor. That only reminded them that they were also parchingly thirsty, without doing anything to relieve them: you cannot quench a terrible thirst by standing under giant oaks and waiting for a chance drip to fall on your tongue. The only scrap of comfort there was came unexpectedly from Bombur.

He woke up suddenly and sat up scratching his head. He could not make out where he was at all, nor why he felt so hungry; for he had forgotten everything that had happened since they started their journey that May morning long ago. The last thing that he remembered was the party at the hobbit's house, and they had great difficulty in making him believe their tale of all the many adventures they had had since.

When he heard that there was nothing to eat, he sat down and wept, for he felt very weak and wobbly in the legs. "Why ever did I wake up!" he cried. "I was having such beautiful dreams. I dreamed I was walking in a forest rather like this one, only lit with torches on the trees and lamps swinging from the branches and fires burning on the ground; and there was a great feast going on, going on for ever. A woodland king was there with a crown of leaves, and there was a merry singing, and I could not count or describe the things there were to eat and drink."

"You need not try," said Thorin. "In fact if you can't talk about something else, you had better be silent. We are quite annoyed enough with you as it is. If you hadn't waked up, we should have left you to your idiotic dreams in the forest; you are no joke to carry even after weeks of short commons."

There was nothing now to be done but to tighten the belts round their empty stomachs, and hoist their empty sacks and packs, and trudge along the track without any great hope of ever getting to the end before they lay down and died of starvation. This they did all that day, going very slowly and wearily; while Bombur kept on wailing that his legs would not carry him and that he wanted to lie down and sleep.

"No you don't!" they said. "Let your legs take their share, we have carried you far enough."

All the same he suddenly refused to go a step further and flung himself on the ground. "Go on, if you must," he said. "I'm just going to lie here and sleep and dream of food, if I can't get it any other way. I hope I never wake up again."

At that very moment Balin, who was a little way ahead, called out: "What was that? I thought I saw a twinkle of light in the forest."

They all looked, and a longish way off, it seemed, they saw a red twinkle in the dark; then another and another sprang out beside it. Even Bombur got up, and they hurried along then, not caring if it was trolls or goblins. The light was in front of them and to the left of the path, and when at last they had drawn level with it, it seemed plain that torches and fires were burning under the trees, but a good way off their track.

"It looks as if my dreams were coming true," gasped Bombur puffing up behind. He wanted to rush straight off into the wood after the lights. But the others remembered only too well the warnings of the wizard and of Beorn.

"A feast would be no good, if we never got back alive from it," said Thorin.

"But without a feast we shan't remain alive much longer anyway," said Bombur, and Bilbo heartily agreed with him. They argued about it backwards and forwards for a long while, until they agreed at length to send out a couple of spies, to creep near the lights and find out more about them. But then they could not agree on who was to be sent: no one seemed anxious to run the chance of being lost and never finding his friends again. In the end, in spite of warnings, hunger decided them, because Bombur kept on describing all the good things that were being eaten, according to his dream, in the woodland feast; so they all left the path and plunged into the forest together.

After a good deal of creeping and crawling they peered round the trunks and looked into a clearing where some trees had been felled and the ground levelled. There were many people there, elvish-looking folk, all dressed in green and brown and sitting on sawn rings of the felled trees in a great circle. There was a fire in their midst and there were torches fastened to some of the trees round about; but most splendid sight of all: they were eating and drinking and laughing merrily.

The smell of the roast meats was so enchanting that, without waiting to consult one another, every one of them got up and scrambled forwards into the ring with the one idea of begging for some food. No sooner had the first stepped into the clearing than all the lights went out as if by magic. Somebody kicked the fire and it went up in rockets of glittering sparks and vanished. They were lost in a completely lightless dark and they could not even find one another, not for a long time at any rate. After blundering frantically in the gloom, falling over logs, bumping crash into trees, and shouting and calling till they must have waked everything in the forest for miles, at last they managed to gather themselves in a bundle and count themselves by touch. By that time they had, of course, quite forgotten in what direction the path lay, and they were all hopelessly lost, at least till morning.

There was nothing for it but to settle down for the night where they were; they did not even dare to search on the ground for scraps of food for fear of becoming separated again. But they had not been lying long, and Bilbo was only ust getting drowsy, when Dori, whose turn it was to watch first, said in a loud whisper:

"The lights are coming out again over there, and there are more than ever of them."

Up they all jumped. There, sure enough, not far away were scores of twinkling lights, and they heard the voices and the laughter quite plainly. They crept slowly towards them, in a single line, each touching the back of the one in front. When they got near Thorin said: "No rushing forward this time! No one is to stir from hiding till I say. I shall send Mr Baggins alone first to talk to them. They won't be frightened of him— ('What about me of them?' thought Bilbo)—and any way I hope they won't do anything nasty to him."

When they got to the edge of the circle of lights they pushed Bilbo suddenly from behind. Before he had time to slip on his ring, he stumbled forward into the full blaze of the fire and torches. It was no good. Out went all the lights again and complete darkness fell.

If it had been difficult collecting themselves before, it was far worse this time. And they simply could not find the hobbit. Every time they counted themselves it only made thirteen. They shouted and called: "Bilbo Baggins! Hobbit! You dratted hobbit! Hi! hobbit!, confusticate you, where are you?" and other things of that sort, but there was no answer.

They were just giving up hope, when Dori stumbled across him by sheer luck. In the dark he fell over what he thought was a log, and he found it was the hobbit curled up fast asleep. It took a deal of shaking to wake him, and when he was awake he was not pleased at all.

"I was having such a lovely dream," he grumbled, "all about having a most gorgeous dinner."

"Good heavens! he has gone like Bombur," they said.

"Don't tell us about dreams. Dream-dinners aren't any good, and we can't share them."

"They are the best I am likely to get in this beastly place," he muttered, as he lay down beside the dwarves and tried to go back to sleep and find his dream again.

But that was not the last of the lights in the forest. Later when the night must have been getting old, Kili who was watching then, came and roused them all again, saying:

"There's a regular blaze of light begun not far away— hundreds of torches and many fires must have been lit suddenly and by magic. And hark to the singing and the harps!"

After lying and listening for a while, they found they could not resist the desire to go nearer and try once more to get help. Up they got again; and this time the result was disastrous. The feast that they now saw was greater and more magnificent than before; and at the head of a long line of feasters sat a woodland king with a crown of leaves upon his golden hair, very much as Bombur had described the figure in his dream. The elvish folk were passing bowls from hand to hand and across the fires, and some were harping and many were singing. Their gleaming hair was twined with flowers; green and white gems glinted on their collars and their belts; and their faces and their songs were filled with mirth. Loud and clear and fair were those songs, and out stepped Thorin in to their midst.

Dead silence fell in the middle of a word. Out went all light. The fires leaped up in black smokes. Ashes and cinders were in the eyes of the dwarves, and the wood was filled again with their clamour and their cries.

Bilbo found himself running round and round (as he thought) and calling and calling: "Dori, Nori, Ori, Oin, Gloin, Fili, Kili, Bombur, Bifur, Bofur, Dwalin, Balin, Thorin Oakenshield," while people he could not see or feel were doing the same all round him (with an occasional "Bilbo!" thrown in). But the cries of the others got steadily further and fainter, and though after a while it seemed to him they changed to yells and cries for help in the far distance, all noise at last died right away, and he was left alone in complete silence and darkness.

That was one of his most miserable moments. But he soon made up his mind that it was no good trying to do anything till day came with some little light, and quite useless to go blundering about tiring himself out with no hope of any breakfast to revive him. So he sat himself down with his back to a tree, and not for the last time fell to thinking of his far-distant hobbit-hole with its beautiful pantries. He was deep in thoughts of bacon and eggs and toast and butter when he felt something touch him. Something like a strong sticky string was against his left hand, and when he tried to move he found that his legs were already wrapped in the same stuff, so that when he got up he fell over.

Then the great spider, who had been busy tying him up while he dozed, came from behind him and came at him. He could only see the thing's eyes, but he could feel its hairy legs as it struggled to wind its abominable threads round and round him. It was lucky that he had come to his senses in time. Soon he would not have been able to move at all. As it was, he had a desperate fight before he got free. He beat the creature off with his hands—it was trying to poison him to keep him quiet, as small spiders do to flies—until he remembered his sword and drew it out. Then the spider jumped back, and he had time to cut his legs loose. After that it was his turn to attack. The spider evidently was not used to things that carried such stings at their sides, or it would have hurried away quicker. Bilbo came at it before it could disappear and stuck it with his sword right in the eyes. Then it went mad and leaped and danced and flung out its legs in horrible jerks, until he killed it with another stroke; and then he fell down and remembered nothing more for a long while.

There was the usual dim grey light of the forest-day about him when he came to his senses. The spider lay dead beside him, and his sword-blade was stained black. Somehow the killing of the giant spider, all alone by himself in the dark without the help of the wizard or the dwarves or of anyone else, made a great difference to Mr Baggins. He felt a different person, and much fiercer and bolder in spite of an empty stomach, as he wiped his sword on the grass and put it back into its sheath.

"I will give you a name," he said to it, "and I shall call you *Sting*."

After that he set out to explore. The forest was grim and silent, but obviously he had first of all to look for his friends, who were not likely to be very far off, unless they had been made prisoners by the elves (or worse things). Bilbo felt that it was unsafe to shout, and he stood a long while wondering in what direction the path lay, and in what direction he should go first to look for the dwarves.

"O! why did we not remember Beorn's advice, and Gandalf's!" he lamented. "What a mess we are in now! We! I only wish it was *we*: it is horrible being all alone."

In the end he made as good a guess as he could at the direction from which the cries for help had come in the night—and by luck (he was born with a good share of it) he guessed more or less right, as you will see. Having made up his mind he crept along as cleverly as he could. Hobbits are clever at quietness, especially in woods, as I have already told you; also Bilbo had slipped on his ring before he started. That is why the spiders neither saw nor heard him coming.

He had picked his way stealthily for some distance, when

he noticed a place of dense black shadow ahead of him, black
even for that forest, like a patch of midnight that had never
been cleared away. As he drew nearer, he saw that it was made
by spider-webs one behind and over and tangled with another. Suddenly he saw, too, that there were spiders huge and
horrible sitting in the branches above him, and ring or no ring
he trembled with fear lest they should discover him. Standing behind a tree he watched a group of them for some time,
and then in the silence and stillness of the wood he realised
that these loathsome creatures were speaking one to another.
Their voices were a sort of thin creaking and hissing, but he
could make out many of the words that they said. They were
talking about the dwarves!

"It was a sharp struggle, but worth it," said one. "What
nasty thick skins they have to be sure, but I'll wager there is
good juice inside."

"Aye, they'll make fine eating, when they've hung a bit,"
said another.

"Don't hang 'em too long," said a third. "They're not as fat
as they might be. Been feeding none too well of late, I should
guess."

"Kill 'em, I say," hissed a fourth; "kill 'em now and hang
'em dead for a while."

"They're dead now, I'll warrant," said the first.

"That they are not. I saw one a-struggling just now. Just
coming round again, I should say, after a bee-autiful sleep.
I'll show you."

With that one of the fat spiders ran along a rope till it came
to a dozen bundles hanging in a row from a high branch. Bilbo
was horrified, now that he noticed them for the first time dangling in the shadows, to see a dwarvish foot sticking out of
the bottoms of some of the bundles, or here and there the tip
of a nose, or a bit of beard or of a hood.

To the fattest of these bundles the spider went—"It is poor old Bombur, I'll bet," thought Bilbo—and nipped hard at the nose that stuck out. There was a muffled yelp inside, and a toe shot up and kicked the spider straight and hard. There was life in Bombur still. There was a noise like the kicking of a flabby football, and the enraged spider fell off the branch, only catching itself with its own thread just in time.

The others laughed. "You were quite right," they said, "the meat's alive and kicking!"

"I'll soon put an end to that," hissed the angry spider climbing back onto the branch.

Bilbo saw that the moment had come when he must do something. He could not get up at the brutes and he had nothing to shoot with; but looking about he saw that in this place there were many stones lying in what appeared to be a now dry little watercourse. Bilbo was a pretty fair shot with a stone, and it did not take him long to find a nice smooth egg-shaped one that fitted his hand cosily. As a boy he used to practise throwing stones at things, until rabbits and squirrels, and even birds, got out of his way as quick as lightning if they saw him stoop; and even grown-up he had still spent a deal of his time at quoits, dart-throwing, shooting at the wand, bowls, ninepins and other quiet games of the aiming and throwing sort—indeed he could do lots of things, besides blowing smoke-rings, asking riddles and cooking, that I haven't had time to tell you about. There is no time now. While he was picking up stones, the spider had reached Bombur, and soon he would have been dead. At that moment Bilbo threw. The stone struck the spider plunk on the head, and it dropped senseless off the tree, flop to the ground, with all its legs curled up.

The next stone went whizzing through a big web, snapping

its cords, and taking off the spider sitting in the middle of it, whack, dead. After that there was a deal of commotion in the spider-colony, and they forgot the dwarves for a bit, I can tell you. They could not see Bilbo, but they could make a good guess at the direction from which the stones were coming. As quick as lightning they came running and swinging towards the hobbit, flinging out their long threads in all directions, till the air seemed full of waving snares.

Bilbo, however, soon slipped away to a different place. The idea came to him to lead the furious spiders further and further away from the dwarves, if he could; to make them curious, excited and angry all at once. When about fifty had gone off to the place where he had stood before, he threw some more stones at these, and at others that had stopped behind; then dancing among the trees he began to sing a song to infuriate them and bring them all after him, and also to let the dwarves hear his voice.

This is what he sang:

> *Old fat spider spinning in a tree!*
> *Old fat spider can't see me!*
> *Attercop! Attercop!*
> *Won't you stop,*
> *Stop your spinning and look for me?*

> *Old Tomnoddy, all big body,*
> *Old Tomnoddy can't spy me!*
> *Attercop! Attercop!*
> *Down you drop!*
> *You'll never catch me up your tree!*

Not very good perhaps, but then you must remember that he had to make it up himself, on the spur of a very awkward moment. It did what he wanted any way. As he sang he threw some more stones and stamped. Practically all the spiders in the place came after him: some dropped to the ground, others raced along the branches, swung from tree to tree, or cast new ropes across the dark spaces. They made for his noise far quicker than he had expected. They were frightfully angry. Quite apart from the stones no spider has ever liked being called Attercop, and Tomnoddy of course is insulting to anybody.

Off Bilbo scuttled to a fresh place, but several of the spiders had run now to different points in the glade where they lived, and were busy spinning webs across all the spaces between the tree-stems. Very soon the hobbit would be caught in a thick fence of them all round him—that at least was the spiders' idea. Standing now in the middle of the hunting and spinning insects Bilbo plucked up his courage and began a new song:

> *Lazy Lob and crazy Cob*
> *are weaving webs to wind me,*
> *I am far more sweet than other meat,*
> *but still they cannot find me!*
>
> *Here am I, naughty little fly;*
> *you are fat and lazy.*
> *You cannot trap me, though you try,*
> *in your cobwebs crazy.*

With that he turned and found that the last space between two tall trees had been closed with a web—but luckily not a proper web, only great strands of double-thick spider-rope run hastily backwards and forwards from trunk to trunk. Out came his little sword. He slashed the threads to pieces and went off singing.

The spiders saw the sword, though I don't suppose they knew what it was, and at once the whole lot of them came hurrying after the hobbit along the ground and the branches, hairy legs waving, nippers and spinners snapping, eyes popping, full of froth and rage. They followed him into the forest until Bilbo had gone as far as he dared. Then quieter than a mouse he stole back.

He had precious little time, he knew, before the spiders were disgusted and came back to their trees where the dwarves were hung. In the meanwhile he had to rescue them. The worst part of the job was getting up on to the long branch where the bundles were dangling. I don't suppose he would have managed it, if a spider had not luckily left a rope hanging down; with its help, though it stuck to his hand and hurt him, he scrambled up—only to meet an old slow wicked fat-bodied spider who had remained behind to guard the prisoners, and had been busy pinching them to see which was the juiciest to eat. It had thought of starting the feast while the others were away, but Mr Baggins was in a hurry, and before the spider knew what was happening it felt his sting and rolled off the branch dead.

Bilbo's next job was to loose a dwarf. What was he to do? If he cut the string which hung him up, the wretched dwarf would tumble thump to the ground a good way below. Wriggling along the branch (which made all the poor dwarves dance and dangle like ripe fruit) he reached the first bundle.

"Fili or Kili," he thought by the tip of a blue hood sticking out at the top. "Most likely Fili," he thought by the tip of a long nose poking out of the winding threads. He managed by leaning over to cut most of the strong sticky threads that bound him round, and then, sure enough, with a kick and a struggle most of Fili emerged. I am afraid Bilbo actually laughed at the sight of him jerking his stiff arms and legs as he danced on the spider-string under his armpits, just like one of those funny toys bobbing on a wire.

Somehow or other Fili was got on to the branch, and then he did his best to help the hobbit, although he was feeling very sick and ill from spider-poison, and from hanging most of the night and the next day wound round and round with only his nose to breathe through. It took him ages to get the beastly stuff out of his eyes and eyebrows, and as for his beard, he had to cut most of it off. Well, between them they started to haul up first one dwarf and then another and slash them free. None of them were better off than Fili, and some of them were worse. Some had hardly been able to breathe at all (long noses are sometimes useful you see) and some had been more poisoned.

In this way they rescued Kili, Bifur, Bofur, Dori and Nori. Poor old Bombur was so exhausted—he was the fattest and had been constantly pinched and poked—that he just rolled off the branch and fell plop on to the ground, fortunately on to leaves, and lay there. But there were still five dwarves hanging at the end of the branch when the spiders began to come back, more full of rage than ever.

Bilbo immediately went to the end of the branch nearest the tree-trunk and kept back those that crawled up. He had taken off his ring when he rescued Fili and forgotten to put it on again, so now they all began to splutter and hiss:

"Now we see you, you nasty little creature! We will eat you and leave your bones and skin hanging on a tree. Ugh! he's got a sting has he? Well, we'll get him all the same, and then we'll hang him head downwards for a day or two."

While this was going on, the other dwarves were working

at the rest of the captives, and cutting at the threads with their knives. Soon all would be free, though it was not clear what would happen after that. The spiders had caught them pretty easily the night before, but that had been unawares and in the dark. This time there looked like being a horrible battle.

Suddenly Bilbo noticed that some of the spiders had gathered round old Bombur on the floor, and had tied him up again and were dragging him away. He gave a shout and slashed at the spiders in front of him. They quickly gave way, and he scrambled and fell down the tree right into the middle of those on the ground. His little sword was something new in the way of stings for them. How it darted to and fro! It shone with delight as he stabbed at them. Half a dozen were killed before the rest drew off and left Bombur to Bilbo.

"Come down! Come down!" he shouted to the dwarves on the branch. "Don't stay up there and be netted!" For he saw spiders swarming up all the neighbouring trees, and crawling along the boughs above the heads of the dwarves.

Down the dwarves scrambled or jumped or dropped, eleven all in a heap, most of them very shaky and little use on their legs. There they were at last, twelve of them counting poor old Bombur, who was being propped up on either side by his cousin Bifur, and his brother Bofur; and Bilbo was dancing about and waving his Sting; and hundreds of angry spiders were goggling at them all round and about and above. It looked pretty hopeless.

Then the battle began. Some of the dwarves had knives, and some had sticks, and all of them could get at stones; and Bilbo had his elvish dagger. Again and again the spiders were beaten off, and many of them were killed. But it could not go on for long. Bilbo was nearly tired out; only four of the dwarves were able to stand firmly, and soon they would all be

overpowered like weary flies. Already the spiders were beginning to weave their webs all round them again from tree
to tree.

In the end Bilbo could think of no plan except to let the
dwarves into the secret of his ring. He was rather sorry about
it, but it could not be helped.

"I am going to disappear," he said. "I shall draw the spiders
off, if I can; and you must keep together and make in the opposite direction. To the left there, that is more or less the way
towards the place where we last saw the elf-fires."

It was difficult to get them to understand, what with their
dizzy heads, and the shouts, and the whacking of sticks and
the throwing of stones; but at last Bilbo felt he could delay no
longer—the spiders were drawing their circle ever closer. He
suddenly slipped on his ring, and to the great astonishment of
the dwarves he vanished.

Soon there came the sound of "Lazy Lob" and "Attercop"
from among the trees away on the right. That upset the spiders greatly. They stopped advancing, and some went off in
the direction of the voice. "Attercop" made them so angry
that they lost their wits. Then Balin, who had grasped Bilbo's
plan better than the rest, led an attack. The dwarves huddled
together in a knot, and sending a shower of stones they drove
at the spiders on the left, and burst through the ring. Away behind them now the shouting and singing suddenly stopped.

Hoping desperately that Bilbo had not been caught the
dwarves went on. Not fast enough, though. They were sick
and weary, and they could not go much better than a hobble
and a wobble, though many of the spiders were close behind.
Every now and then they had to turn and fight the creatures
that were overtaking them; and already some spiders were in
the trees above them and throwing down their long clinging
threads.

Things were looking pretty bad again, when suddenly Bilbo reappeared, and charged into the astonished spiders unexpectedly from the side.

"Go on! Go on!" he shouted. "I will do the stinging!"

And he did. He darted backwards and forwards, slashing at spider-threads, hacking at their legs, and stabbing at their fat bodies if they came too near. The spiders swelled with rage, and spluttered and frothed, and hissed out horrible curses; but they had become mortally afraid of Sting, and dared not come very near, now that it had come back. So curse as they would, their prey moved slowly but steadily away. It was a most terrible business, and seemed to take hours. But at last, just when Bilbo felt that he could not lift his hand for a single stroke more, the spiders suddenly gave it up, and followed them no more, but went back disappointed to their dark colony.

The dwarves then noticed that they had come to the edge of a ring where elf-fires had been. Whether it was one of those they had seen the night before, they could not tell. But it seemed that some good magic lingered in such spots, which the spiders did not like. At any rate here the light was greener, and the boughs less thick and threatening, and they had a chance to rest and draw breath.

There they lay for some time, puffing and panting. But very soon they began to ask questions. They had to have the whole vanishing business carefully explained, and the finding of the ring interested them so much that for a while they forgot their own troubles. Balin in particular insisted on having the Gollum story, riddles and all, told all over again, with the ring in its proper place. But after a time the light began to fail, and then other questions were asked. Where were they, and where was their path, and where was there any food, and what were they going to do next? These questions they asked over

and over again, and it was from little Bilbo that they seemed
to expect to get the answers. From which you can see that
they had changed their opinion of Mr Baggins very much,
and had begun to have a great respect for him (as Gandalf had
said they would). Indeed they really expected him to think of
some wonderful plan for helping them, and were not merely
grumbling. They knew only too well that they would soon all
have been dead, if it had not been for the hobbit; and they
thanked him many times. Some of them even got up and
bowed right to the ground before him, though they fell over
with the effort, and could not get on their legs again for some
time. Knowing the truth about the vanishing did not lessen
their opinion of Bilbo at all; for they saw that he had some
wits, as well as luck and a magic ring—and all three are very
useful possessions. In fact they praised him so much that
Bilbo began to feel there really was something of a bold ad-
venturer about himself after all, though he would have felt a
lot bolder still, if there had been anything to eat.

But there was nothing, nothing at all; and none of them
were fit to go and look for anything, or to search for the lost
path. The lost path! No other idea would come into Bilbo's
tired head. He just sat staring in front of him at the endless
trees; and after a while they all fell silent again. All except
Balin. Long after the others had stopped talking and shut
their eyes, he kept on muttering and chuckling to himself.

"Gollum! Well I'm blest! So that's how he sneaked past
me, is it? Now I know! Just crept quietly along did you, Mr
Baggins? Buttons all over the doorstep! Good old Bilbo—
Bilbo—Bilbo—bo—bo—bo—" And then he fell asleep, and
there was complete silence for a long while.

All of a sudden Dwalin opened an eye, and looked round at
them. "Where is Thorin?" he asked.

It was a terrible shock. Of course there were only thirteen

of them, twelve dwarves and the hobbit. Where indeed was Thorin? They wondered what evil fate had befallen him, magic or dark monsters; and shuddered as they lay lost in the forest. There they dropped off one by one into uncomfortable sleep full of horrible dreams, as evening wore to black night; and there we must leave them for the present, too sick and weary to set guards or to take turns at watching.

Thorin had been caught much faster than they had. You remember Bilbo falling like a log into sleep, as he stepped into a circle of light? The next time it had been Thorin who stepped forward, and as the lights went out he fell like a stone enchanted. All the noise of the dwarves lost in the night, their cries as the spiders caught them and bound them, and all the sounds of the battle next day, had passed over him unheard. Then the Wood-elves had come to him, and bound him, and carried him away.

The feasting people were Wood-elves, of course. These are not wicked folk. If they have a fault it is distrust of strangers. Though their magic was strong, even in those days they were wary. They differed from the High Elves of the West, and were more dangerous and less wise. For most of them (together with their scattered relations in the hills and mountains) were descended from the ancient tribes that never went to Faerie in the West. There the Light-elves and the Deep-elves and the Sea-elves went and lived for ages, and grew fairer and wiser and more learned, and invented their magic and their cunning craft in the making of beautiful and marvellous things, before some came back into the Wide World. In the Wide World the Wood-elves lingered in the twilight of our Sun and Moon, but loved best the stars; and they wandered in the great forests that grew tall in lands that are now lost. They dwelt most often by the edges of the woods, from which they could escape at times to hunt, or to ride and run over the open lands by moonlight or starlight; and after the coming of Men they took ever more and more to the gloaming and the dusk. Still elves they were and remain, and that is Good People.

In a great cave some miles within the edge of Mirkwood on its eastern side there lived at this time their greatest king. Before his huge doors of stone a river ran out of the heights of the forest and flowed on and out into the marshes at the feet of the high wooded lands. This great cave, from which countless smaller ones opened out on every side, wound far underground and had many passages and wide halls; but it was lighter and more wholesome than any goblin-dwelling, and neither so deep nor so dangerous. In fact the subjects of the king mostly lived and hunted in the open woods, and had houses or huts on the ground and in the branches. The beeches were their favourite trees. The king's cave was his palace, and the strong place of his treasure, and the fortress of his people against their enemies.

It was also the dungeon of his prisoners. So to the cave they dragged Thorin—not too gently, for they did not love dwarves, and thought he was an enemy. In ancient days they had had wars with some of the dwarves, whom they accused of stealing their treasure. It is only fair to say that the dwarves gave a different account, and said that they only took what was their due, for the elf-king had bargained with them to shape his raw gold and silver, and had afterwards refused to give them their pay. If the elf-king had a weakness it was for treasure, especially for silver and white gems; and though his hoard was rich, he was ever eager for more, since he had not yet as great a treasure as other elf-lords of old. His people neither mined nor worked metals or jewels, nor did they bother much with trade or with tilling the earth. All this was well known to every dwarf, though Thorin's family had had nothing to do

with the old quarrel I have spoken of. Consequently Thorin
was angry at their treatment of him, when they took their
spell off him and he came to his senses; and also he was determined that no word of gold or jewels should be dragged out
of him.

The king looked sternly on Thorin, when he was brought
before him, and asked him many questions. But Thorin
would only say that he was starving.

"Why did you and your folk three times try to attack my
people at their merrymaking?" asked the king.

"We did not attack them," answered Thorin; "we came to
beg, because we were starving."

"Where are your friends now, and what are they doing?"

"I don't know, but I expect starving in the forest."

"What were you doing in the forest?"

"Looking for food and drink, because we were starving."

"But what brought you into the forest at all?" asked the
king angrily.

At that Thorin shut his mouth and would not say another word.

"Very well!" said the king. "Take him away and keep him
safe, until he feels inclined to tell the truth, even if he waits a
hundred years."

Then the elves put thongs on him, and shut him in one of
the inmost caves with strong wooden doors, and left him.
They gave him food and drink, plenty of both, if not very fine;
for Wood-elves were not goblins, and were reasonably well-
behaved even to their worst enemies, when they captured
them. The giant spiders were the only living things that they
had no mercy upon.

There in the king's dungeon poor Thorin lay; and after he
had got over his thankfulness for bread and meat and water,
he began to wonder what had become of his unfortunate

friends. It was not very long before he discovered; but that belongs to the next chapter and the beginning of another adventure in which the hobbit again showed his usefulness.

*Chapter IX*

# BARRELS OUT OF BOND

The day after the battle with the spiders Bilbo and the dwarves made one last despairing effort to find a way out before they died of hunger and thirst. They got up and staggered on in the direction which eight out of the thirteen of them guessed to be the one in which the path lay; but they never found out if they were right. Such day as there ever was in the forest was fading once more into the blackness of night, when suddenly out sprang the light of many torches all round them, like hundreds of red stars. Out leaped Wood-elves with their bows and spears and called the dwarves to halt.

There was no thought of a fight. Even if the dwarves had not been in such a state that they were actually glad to be captured, their small knives, the only weapons they had, would have been of no use against the arrows of the elves that could hit a bird's eye in the dark. So they simply stopped dead and sat down and waited—all except Bilbo, who popped on his ring and slipped quickly to one side. That is why, when the elves bound the dwarves in a long line, one behind the other, and counted them, they never found or counted the hobbit.

Nor did they hear or feel him trotting along well behind their torch-light as they led off their prisoners into the forest. Each dwarf was blindfolded, but that did not make much difference, for even Bilbo with the use of his eyes could not see where they were going, and neither he nor the others knew where they had started from anyway. Bilbo had all he could do to keep up with the torches, for the elves were making the dwarves go as fast as ever they could, sick and weary as they were. The king had ordered them to make haste. Suddenly the torches stopped, and the hobbit had just time to catch them up before they began to cross the bridge. This was the bridge that led across the river to the king's doors. The water flowed dark and swift and strong beneath; and at the far end were gates before the mouth of a huge cave that ran into the side of a steep slope covered with trees. There the great beeches came right down to the bank, till their feet were in the stream.

Across the bridge the elves thrust their prisoners, but Bilbo hesitated in the rear. He did not at all like the look of the cavern-mouth, and he only made up his mind not to desert his friends just in time to scuttle over at the heels of the last elves, before the great gates of the king closed behind them with a clang.

Inside the passages were lit with red torch-light, and the elf-guards sang as they marched along the twisting, crossing, and echoing paths. These were not like those of the goblin-cities; they were smaller, less deep underground, and filled with a cleaner air. In a great hall with pillars hewn out of the living stone sat the Elvenking on a chair of carven wood. On his head was a crown of berries and red leaves, for the autumn was come again. In the spring he wore a crown of woodland flowers. In his hand he held a carven staff of oak.

The prisoners were brought before him; and though he looked grimly at them, he told his men to unbind them, for they were ragged and weary. "Besides they need no ropes in here," said he. "There is no escape from my magic doors for those who are once brought inside."

Long and searchingly he questioned the dwarves about their doings, and where they were going to, and where they were coming from; but he got little more news out of them than out of Thorin. They were surly and angry and did not even pretend to be polite.

"What have we done, O king?" said Balin, who was the eldest left. "Is it a crime to be lost in the forest, to be hungry and thirsty, to be trapped by spiders? Are the spiders your tame beasts or your pets, if killing them makes you angry?"

Such a question of course made the king angrier than ever, and he answered: "It is a crime to wander in my realm without leave. Do you forget that you were in my kingdom, using the road that my people made? Did you not three times pursue and trouble my people in the forest and rouse the spiders with your riot and clamour? After all the disturbance you have made I have a right to know what brings you here, and if you will not tell me now, I will keep you all in prison until you have learned sense and manners!"

Then he ordered the dwarves each to be put in a separate cell and to be given food and drink, but not to be allowed to pass the doors of their little prisons, until one at least of them was willing to tell him all he wanted to know. But he did not tell them that Thorin was also a prisoner with him. It was Bilbo who found that out.

Poor Mr Baggins—it was a weary long time that he lived in that place all alone, and always in hiding, never daring to take off his ring, hardly daring to sleep, even tucked away in the darkest and remotest corners he could find. For something to do he took to wandering about the Elvenking's palace. Magic shut the gates, but he could sometimes get out, if he was quick. Companies of the Wood-elves, sometimes with the king at their head, would from time to time ride out to hunt, or

to other business in the woods and in the lands to the East.
Then if Bilbo was very nimble, he could slip out just behind
them; though it was a dangerous thing to do. More than once
he was nearly caught in the doors, as they clashed together
when the last elf passed; yet he did not dare to march among
them because of his shadow (altogether thin and wobbly as it
was in torchlight), or for fear of being bumped into and discovered. And when he did go out, which was not very often,
he did no good. He did not wish to desert the dwarves, and indeed he did not know where in the world to go without them.
He could not keep up with the hunting elves all the time they
were out, so he never discovered the ways out of the wood,
and was left to wander miserably in the forest, terrified of
losing himself, until a chance came of returning. He was
hungry too outside, for he was no hunter; but inside the caves
he could pick up a living of some sort by stealing food from
store or table when no one was at hand.

"I am like a burglar that can't get away, but must go on miserably burgling the same house day after day," he thought.
"This is the dreariest and dullest part of all this wretched,
tiresome, uncomfortable adventure! I wish I was back in my
hobbit-hole by my own warm fireside with the lamp shining!"
He often wished, too, that he could get a message for help
sent to the wizard, but that of course was quite impossible;
and he soon realized that if anything was to be done, it would
have to be done by Mr Baggins, alone and unaided.

Eventually, after a week or two of this sneaking sort of life,
by watching and following the guards and taking what chances
he could, he managed to find out where each dwarf was kept.
He found all their twelve cells in different parts of the palace,
and after a time he got to know his way about very well. What
was his surprise one day to overhear some of the guards

alking and to learn that there was another dwarf in prison
oo, in a specially deep dark place. He guessed at once, of
ourse, that that was Thorin; and after a while he found that
iis guess was right. At last after many difficulties he managed
o find the place when no one was about, and to have a word
vith the chief of the dwarves.

Thorin was too wretched to be angry any longer at his mis-
ortunes, and was even beginning to think of telling the king
ll about his treasure and his quest (which shows how low-
pirited he had become), when he heard Bilbo's little voice at
iis keyhole. He could hardly believe his ears. Soon however
ie made up his mind that he could not be mistaken, and he
:ame to the door and had a long whispered talk with the
iobbit on the other side.

So it was that Bilbo was able to take secretly Thorin's mes-
age to each of the other imprisoned dwarves, telling them
hat Thorin their chief was also in prison close at hand, and
hat no one was to reveal their errand to the king, not yet, nor
iefore Thorin gave the word. For Thorin had taken heart
igain hearing how the hobbit had rescued his companions
rom the spiders, and was determined once more not to ran-
iom himself with promises to the king of a share in the
reasure, until all hope of escaping in any other way had dis-
ippeared; until in fact the remarkable Mr Invisible Baggins
of whom he began to have a very high opinion indeed) had
iltogether failed to think of something clever.

The other dwarves quite agreed when they got the mes-
iage. They all thought their own shares in the treasure (which
hey quite regarded as theirs, in spite of their plight and the
itill unconquered dragon) would suffer seriously if the Wood-
:lves claimed part of it, and they all trusted Bilbo. Just what
Gandalf had said would happen, you see. Perhaps that was
iart of his reason for going off and leaving them.

Bilbo, however, did not feel nearly so hopeful as they did. He did not like being depended on by everyone, and he wished he had the wizard at hand. But that was no use: probably all the dark distance of Mirkwood lay between them. He sat and thought and thought, until his head nearly burst, but no bright idea would come. One invisible ring was a very fine thing, but it was not much good among fourteen. But of course, as you have guessed, he did rescue his friends in the end, and this is how it happened.

One day, nosing and wandering about, Bilbo discovered a very interesting thing: the great gates were *not* the only entrance to the caves. A stream flowed under part of the lowest regions of the palace, and joined the Forest River some way further to the east, beyond the steep slope out of which the main mouth opened. Where this underground watercourse came forth from the hillside there was a water-gate. There the rocky roof came down close to the surface of the stream, and from it a portcullis could be dropped right to the bed of the river to prevent anyone coming in or out that way. But the portcullis was often open, for a good deal of traffic went out and in by the water-gate. If anyone had come in that way, he would have found himself in a dark rough tunnel leading deep into the heart of the hill; but at one point where it passed under the caves the roof had been cut away and covered with great oaken trapdoors. These opened upwards into the king's cellars. There stood barrels, and barrels, and barrels; for the Wood-elves, and especially their king, were very fond of wine, though no vines grew in those parts. The wine, and other goods, were brought from far away, from their kinsfolk in the South, or from the vineyards of Men in distant lands.

Hiding behind one of the largest barrels Bilbo discovered the trapdoors and their use, and lurking there, listening to the

alk of the king's servants, he learned how the wine and other
goods came up the rivers, or over land, to the Long Lake. It
seemed a town of Men still throve there, built out on bridges
far into the water as a protection against enemies of all sorts,
and especially against the dragon of the Mountain. From
Lake-town the barrels were brought up the Forest River.
Often they were just tied together like big rafts and poled or
rowed up the stream; sometimes they were loaded on to flat
boats.

When the barrels were empty the elves cast them through
the trapdoors, opened the water-gate, and out the barrels
floated on the stream, bobbing along, until they were carried
by the current to a place far down the river where the bank
jutted out, near to the very eastern edge of Mirkwood. There
they were collected and tied together and floated back to
Lake-town, which stood close to the point where the Forest
River flowed into the Long Lake.

For some time Bilbo sat and thought about this water-gate,
and wondered if it could be used for the escape of his friends,
and at last he had the desperate beginnings of a plan.

The evening meal had been taken to the prisoners. The
guards were tramping away down the passages taking the
torchlight with them and leaving everything in darkness.
Then Bilbo heard the king's butler bidding the chief of the
guards goodnight.

"Now come with me," he said, "and taste the new wine that
has just come in. I shall be hard at work tonight clearing the
cellars of the empty wood, so let us have a drink first to help
the labour."

"Very good," laughed the chief of the guards. "I'll taste
with you, and see if it is fit for the king's table. There is a feast
tonight and it would not do to send up poor stuff!"

* * *

When he heard this Bilbo was all in a flutter, for he saw th
luck was with him and he had a chance at once to try his de
perate plan. He followed the two elves, until they entered
small cellar and sat down at a table on which two larg
flagons were set. Soon they began to drink and laugh merril
Luck of an unusual kind was with Bilbo then. It must be po
tent wine to make a wood-elf drowsy; but this wine, it wou
seem, was the heady vintage of the great gardens of Do
winion, not meant for his soldiers or his servants, but for th
king's feasts only, and for smaller bowls not for the butler
great flagons.

Very soon the chief guard nodded his head, then he laid
on the table and fell fast asleep. The butler went on talkin
and laughing to himself for a while without seeming to no
tice, but soon his head too nodded to the table, and he fe
asleep and snored beside his friend. Then in crept the hobbi
Very soon the chief guard had no keys, but Bilbo was trottin
as fast as he could along the passages towards the cells. Th
great bunch seemed very heavy to his arms, and his heart wa
often in his mouth, in spite of his ring, for he could not pre
vent the keys from making every now and then a loud clin
and clank, which put him all in a tremble.

First he unlocked Balin's door, and locked it again care
fully as soon as the dwarf was outside. Balin was most sur
prised, as you can imagine; but glad as he was to get out of hi
wearisome little stone room, he wanted to stop and ask ques
tions, and know what Bilbo was going to do, and all about it

"No time now!" said the hobbit. "You just follow me! W
must all keep together and not risk getting separated. All of u
must escape or none, and this is our last chance. If this i
found out, goodness knows where the king will put you nex

with chains on your hands and feet too, I expect. Don't argue, there's a good fellow!"

Then off he went from door to door, until his following had grown to twelve—none of them any too nimble, what with the dark, and what with their long imprisonment. Bilbo's heart thumped every time one of them bumped into another, or grunted or whispered in the dark. "Drat this dwarvish racket!" he said to himself. But all went well, and they met no guards. As a matter of fact there was a great autumn feast in the woods that night, and in the halls above. Nearly all the king's folk were merry-making.

At last after much blundering they came to Thorin's dungeon, far down in a deep place and fortunately not far from the cellars.

"Upon my word!" said Thorin, when Bilbo whispered to him to come out and join his friends, "Gandalf spoke true, as usual! A pretty fine burglar you make, it seems, when the time comes. I am sure we are all for ever at your service, whatever happens after this. But what comes next?"

Bilbo saw that the time had come to explain his idea, as far as he could; but he did not feel at all sure how the dwarves would take it. His fears were quite justified, for they did not like it a bit, and started grumbling loudly in spite of their danger.

"We shall be bruised and battered to pieces, and drowned too, for certain!" they muttered. "We thought you had got some sensible notion, when you managed to get hold of the keys. This is a mad idea!"

"Very well!" said Bilbo very downcast, and also rather annoyed. "Come along back to your nice cells, and I will lock you all in again, and you can sit there comfortably and think of a better plan—but I don't suppose I shall ever get hold of the keys again, even if I feel inclined to try."

That was too much for them, and they calmed down. In the
end, of course, they had to do just what Bilbo suggested, because it was obviously impossible for them to try and find
their way into the upper halls, or to fight their way out of gates
that closed by magic; and it was no good grumbling in the
passages until they were caught again. So following the hobbit, down into the lowest cellars they crept. They passed a
door through which the chief guard and the butler could be
seen still happily snoring with smiles upon their faces. The
wine of Dorwinion brings deep and pleasant dreams. There
would be a different expression on the face of the chief guard
next day, even though Bilbo, before they went on, stole in and
kindheartedly put the keys back on his belt.

"That will save him some of the trouble he is in for," said
Mr Baggins to himself. "He wasn't a bad fellow, and quite decent to the prisoners. It will puzzle them all too. They will
think we had a very strong magic to pass through all those
locked doors and disappear. Disappear! We have got to get
busy very quick, if that is to happen!"

Balin was told off to watch the guard and the butler and
give warning if they stirred. The rest went into the adjoining
cellar with the trapdoors. There was little time to lose. Before
long, as Bilbo knew, some elves were under orders to come
down and help the butler get the empty barrels through the
doors into the stream. These were in fact already standing in
rows in the middle of the floor waiting to be pushed off. Some
of them were wine-barrels, and these were not much use, as
they could not easily be opened at the end without a deal of
noise, nor could they easily be secured again. But among
them were several others, which had been used for bringing
other stuffs, butter, apples, and all sorts of things, to the
king's palace.

They soon found thirteen with room enough for a dwarf in each. In fact some were too roomy, and as they climbed in the dwarves thought anxiously of the shaking and the bumping they would get inside, though Bilbo did his best to find straw and other stuff to pack them in as cosily as could be managed in a short time. At last twelve dwarves were stowed. Thorin had given a lot of trouble, and turned and twisted in his tub and grumbled like a large dog in a small kennel; while Balin, who came last, made a great fuss about his air-holes and said he was stifling, even before his lid was on. Bilbo had done what he could to close holes in the sides of the barrels, and to fix on all the lids as safely as could be managed, and now he was left alone again, running round putting the finishing touches to the packing, and hoping against hope that his plan would come off.

It had not been done a bit too soon. Only a minute or two after Balin's lid had been fitted on there came the sound of voices and the flicker of lights. A number of elves came laughing and talking into the cellars and singing snatches of song. They had left a merry feast in one of the halls and were bent on returning as soon as they could.

"Where's old Galion, the butler?" said one. "I haven't seen him at the tables tonight. He ought to be here now to show us what is to be done."

"I shall be angry if the old slowcoach is late," said another. "I have no wish to waste time down here while the song is up!"

"Ha, ha!" came a cry. "Here's the old villain with his head on a jug! He's been having a little feast all to himself and his friend the captain."

"Shake him! Wake him!" shouted the others impatiently.

Galion was not at all pleased at being shaken or wakened, and still less at being laughed at. "You're all late," he grumbled. "Here am I waiting and waiting down here, while you fellows drink and make merry and forget your tasks. Small wonder if I fall asleep from weariness!"

"Small wonder," said they, "when the explanation stands close at hand in a jug! Come give us a taste of your sleeping-draught before we fall to! No need to wake the turnkey yonder. He has had his share by the looks of it."

Then they drank once round and became mighty merry all of a sudden. But they did not quite lose their wits. "Save us, Galion!" cried some, "you began your feasting early and muddled your wits! You have stacked some full casks here instead of the empty ones, if there is anything in weight."

"Get on with the work!" growled the butler. "There is nothing in the feeling of weight in an idle toss-pot's arms. These are the ones to go and no others. Do as I say!"

"Very well, very well," they answered rolling the barrels to the opening. "On your head be it, if the king's full buttertubs and his best wine is pushed into the river for the Lake-men to feast on for nothing!"

> Roll—roll—roll—roll,
> roll-roll-rolling down the hole!
> Heave ho! Splash plump!
> Down they go, down they bump!

So they sang as first one barrel and then another rumbled to the dark opening and was pushed over into the cold water some feet below. Some were barrels really empty, some were tubs neatly packed with a dwarf each; but down they all went, one after another, with many a clash and a bump, thudding on top of ones below, smacking into the water, jostling against the walls of the tunnel, knocking into one another, and bobbing away down the current.

It was just at this moment that Bilbo suddenly discovered

the weak point in his plan. Most likely you saw it some time ago and have been laughing at him; but I don't suppose you would have done half as well yourselves in his place. Of course he was not in a barrel himself, nor was there anyone to pack him in, even if there had been a chance! It looked as if he would certainly lose his friends this time (nearly all of them had already disappeared through the dark trapdoor), and get utterly left behind and have to stay lurking as a permanent burglar in the elf-caves for ever. For even if he could have escaped through the upper gates at once, he had precious small chance of ever finding the dwarves again. He did not know the way by land to the place where the barrels were collected. He wondered what on earth would happen to them without him; for he had not had time to tell the dwarves all that he had learned, or what he had meant to do, once they were out of the wood.

While all these thoughts were passing through his mind, the elves being very merry began to sing a song round the river-door. Some had already gone to haul on the ropes which pulled up the portcullis at the water-gate so as to let out the barrels as soon as they were all afloat below.

> *Down the swift dark stream you go*
> *Back to lands you once did know!*
> *Leave the halls and caverns deep,*
> *Leave the northern mountains steep,*
> *Where the forest wide and dim*
> *Stoops in shadow grey and grim!*
> *Float beyond the world of trees*
> *Out into the whispering breeze,*
> *Past the rushes, past the reeds,*
> *Past the marsh's waving weeds,*
> *Through the mist that riseth white*

*Up from mere and pool at night!*
*Follow, follow stars that leap*
*Up the heavens cold and steep;*
*Turn when dawn comes over land,*
*Over rapid, over sand,*
*South away! and South away!*
*Seek the sunlight and the day,*
*Back to pasture, back to mead,*
*Where the kine and oxen feed!*
*Back to gardens on the hills*
*Where the berry swells and fills*
*Under sunlight, under day!*
*South away! and South away!*
*Down the swift dark stream you go*
*Back to lands you once did know!*

Now the very last barrel was being rolled to the doors! In despair and not knowing what else to do, poor little Bilbo caught hold of it and was pushed over the edge with it. Down into the water he fell, splash! into the cold dark water with the barrel on top of him.

He came up again spluttering and clinging to the wood like a rat, but for all his efforts he could not scramble on top. Every time he tried, the barrel rolled round and ducked him under again. It was really empty, and floated light as a cork. Though his ears were full of water, he could hear the elves still singing in the cellar above. Then suddenly the trapdoors fell to with a boom and their voices faded away. He was in the dark tunnel floating in icy water, all alone—for you cannot count friends that are all packed up in barrels.

Very soon a grey patch came in the darkness ahead. He heard the creak of the water-gate being hauled up, and he found that he was in the midst of a bobbing and bumping

mass of casks and tubs all pressing together to pass under the
arch and get out into the open stream. He had as much as he
could do to prevent himself from being hustled and battered
to bits; but at last the jostling crowd began to break up and
swing off, one by one, under the stony arch and away. Then he
saw that it would have been no good even if he had managed
to get astride his barrel, for there was no room to spare, not
even for a hobbit, between its top and the suddenly stooping
roof where the gate was.

Out they went under the overhanging branches of the trees
on either bank. Bilbo wondered what the dwarves were
feeling and whether a lot of water was getting into their tubs.
Some of those that bobbed along by him in the gloom seemed
pretty low in the water, and he guessed that these had dwarves
inside.

"I do hope I put the lids on tight enough!" he thought, but
before long he was worrying too much about himself to remember the dwarves. He managed to keep his head above the
water, but he was shivering with the cold, and he wondered if
he would die of it before the luck turned, and how much
longer he would be able to hang on, and whether he should
risk the chance of letting go and trying to swim to the bank.

The luck turned all right before long: the eddying current
carried several barrels close ashore at one point and there for
a while they stuck against some hidden root. Then Bilbo took
the opportunity of scrambling up the side of his barrel while
it was held steady against another. Up he crawled like a
drowned rat, and lay on the top spread out to keep the balance
as best he could. The breeze was cold but better than the
water, and he hoped he would not suddenly roll off again
when they started off once more.

Before long the barrels broke free again and turned and

twisted off down the stream, and out into the main current.
Then he found it quite as difficult to stick on as he had feared,
but he managed it somehow, though it was miserably uncomfortable. Luckily he was very light, and the barrel was a good
big one and being rather leaky had now shipped a small
amount of water. All the same it was like trying to ride,
without bridle or stirrups, a round-bellied pony that was always thinking of rolling on the grass.

In this way at last Mr Baggins came to a place where the
trees on either hand grew thinner. He could see the paler sky
between them. The dark river opened suddenly wide, and
there it was joined to the main water of the Forest River
flowing down in haste from the king's great doors. There was
a dim sheet of water no longer overshadowed, and on its
sliding surface there were dancing and broken reflections of
clouds and of stars. Then the hurrying water of the Forest
River swept all the company of casks and tubs away to the
north bank, in which it had eaten out a wide bay. This had a
shingly shore under hanging banks and was walled at the
eastern end by a little jutting cape of hard rock. On the
shallow shore most of the barrels ran aground, though a few
went on to bump against the stony pier.

There were people on the look-out on the banks. They
quickly poled and pushed all the barrels together into the
shadows, and when they had counted them they roped them
together and left them till the morning. Poor dwarves! Bilbo
was not badly off now. He slipped from his barrel and waded
ashore, and then sneaked along to some huts that he could see
near the water's edge. He no longer thought twice about
picking up a supper uninvited if he got the chance, he had
been obliged to do it for so long, and he knew now only too
well what it was to be really hungry, not merely politely interested in the dainties of a well-filled larder. Also he had caught

glimpse of a fire through the trees, and that appealed to him with his dripping and ragged clothes clinging to him cold and clammy.

There is no need to tell you much of his adventures that night, for now we are drawing near the end of the eastward journey and coming to the last and greatest adventure, so we must hurry on. Of course helped by his magic ring he got on very well at first, but he was given away in the end by his wet footsteps and the trail of drippings that he left wherever he went or sat; and also he began to snivel, and wherever he tried to hide he was found out by the terrific explosions of his suppressed sneezes. Very soon there was a fine commotion in the village by the riverside; but Bilbo escaped into the woods carrying a loaf and a leather bottle of wine and a pie that did not belong to him. The rest of the night he had to pass wet as he was and far from a fire, but the bottle helped him to do that, and he actually dozed a little on some dry leaves, even though the year was getting late and the air was chilly.

He woke again with a specially loud sneeze. It was already grey morning, and there was a merry racket down by the river. They were making up a raft of barrels, and the raft-elves would soon be steering it off down the stream to Lake-town. Bilbo sneezed again. He was no longer dripping but he felt cold all over. He scrambled down as fast as his stiff legs would take him and managed just in time to get on to the mass of casks without being noticed in the general bustle. Luckily there was no sun at the time to cast an awkward shadow, and for a mercy he did not sneeze again for a good while.

There was a mighty pushing of poles. The elves that were standing in the shallow water heaved and shoved. The barrels now all lashed together creaked and fretted.

"This is a heavy load!" some grumbled. "They float too

deep—some of these are never empty. If they had come ashor
in the daylight, we might have had a look inside," they said.

"No time now!" cried the raftman. "Shove off!"

And off they went at last, slowly at first, until they had passe
the point of rock where other elves stood to fend them off wit
poles, and then quicker and quicker as they caught the mai
stream and went sailing away down, down towards the Lake.

They had escaped the dungeons of the king and wer
through the wood, but whether alive or dead still remains t
be seen.

*Chapter X*

# A WARM WELCOME

The day grew lighter and warmer as they floated along. After a while the river rounded a steep shoulder of land that came down upon their left. Under its rocky feet like an inland cliff the deepest stream had flowed lapping and bubbling. Suddenly the cliff fell away. The shores sank. The trees ended. Then Bilbo saw a sight:

The lands opened wide about him, filled with the waters of the river which broke up and wandered in a hundred winding courses, or halted in marshes and pools dotted with isles on every side; but still a strong water flowed on steadily through the midst. And far away, its dark head in a torn cloud, there loomed the Mountain! Its nearest neighbours to the North-East and the tumbled land that joined it to them could not be seen. All alone it rose and looked across the marshes to the forest. The Lonely Mountain! Bilbo had come far and through many adventures to see it, and now he did not like the look of it in the least.

As he listened to the talk of the raftmen and pieced together the scraps of information they let fall, he soon realized that he was very fortunate ever to have seen it at all, even from this distance. Dreary as had been his imprisonment and unpleasant as was his position (to say nothing of the poor dwarves underneath him) still, he had been more lucky than

he had guessed. The talk was all of the trade that came and
went on the waterways and the growth of the traffic on the
river, as the roads out of the East towards Mirkwood vanished
or fell into disuse; and of the bickerings of the Lake-men and
the Wood-elves about the upkeep of the Forest River and the
care of the banks.

Those lands had changed much since the days when
dwarves dwelt in the Mountain, days which most people now
remembered only as a very shadowy tradition. They had
changed even in recent years, and since the last news that
Gandalf had had of them. Great floods and rains had swollen
the waters that flowed east; and there had been an earthquake
or two (which some were inclined to attribute to the dragon—
alluding to him chiefly with a curse and an ominous nod in
the direction of the Mountain). The marshes and bogs had
spread wider and wider on either side. Paths had vanished,
and many a rider and wanderer too, if they had tried to find
the lost ways across. The elf-road through the wood which the
dwarves had followed on the advice of Beorn now came to a
doubtful and little used end at the eastern edge of the forest;
only the river offered any longer a safe way from the skirts of
Mirkwood in the North to the mountain-shadowed plains beyond, and the river was guarded by the Wood-elves' king.

So you see Bilbo had come in the end by the only road that
was any good. It might have been some comfort to Mr Baggins shivering on the barrels, if he had known that news of
this had reached Gandalf far away and given him great anxi-
ety, and that he was in fact finishing his other business (which
does not come into this tale) and getting ready to come in
search of Thorin's company. But Bilbo did not know it.

All he knew was that the river seemed to go on and on and
on for ever, and he was hungry, and had a nasty cold in the
nose, and did not like the way the Mountain seemed to frown

at him and threaten him as it drew ever nearer. After a while, however, the river took a more southerly course and the Mountain receded again, and at last, late in the day the shores grew rocky, the river gathered all its wandering waters together into a deep and rapid flood, and they swept along at great speed.

The sun had set when turning with another sweep towards the East the forest-river rushed into the Long Lake. There it had a wide mouth with stony clifflike gates at either side whose feet were piled with shingles. The Long Lake! Bilbo had never imagined that any water that was not the sea could look so big. It was so wide that the opposite shores looked small and far, but it was so long that its northerly end, which pointed towards the Mountain, could not be seen at all. Only from the map did Bilbo know that away up there, where the stars of the Wain were already twinkling, the Running River came down into the lake from Dale and with the Forest River filled with deep waters what must once have been a great deep rocky valley. At the southern end the doubled waters poured out again over high waterfalls and ran away hurriedly to unknown lands. In the still evening air the noise of the falls could be heard like a distant roar.

Not far from the mouth of the Forest River was the strange town he heard the elves speak of in the king's cellars. It was not built on the shore, though there were a few huts and buildings there, but right out on the surface of the lake, protected from the swirl of the entering river by a promontory of rock which formed a calm bay. A great bridge made of wood ran out to where on huge piles made of forest trees was built a busy wooden town, not a town of elves but of Men, who still dared to dwell here under the shadow of the distant dragon-mountain. They still throve on the trade that came up the great river from the South and was carted past the falls to their town; but in the great days of old, when Dale in the North was rich and prosperous, they had been wealthy and powerful, and there had been fleets of boats on the water, and some were filled with gold and some with warriors in armour, and there had been wars and deeds which were now only a legend. The rotting piles of a greater town could still be seen along the shores when the waters sank in a drought.

But men remembered little of all that, though some still sang old songs of the dwarf-kings of the Mountain, Thror and Thrain of the race of Durin, and of the coming of the Dragon and the fall of the lords of Dale. Some sang too that Thror and Thrain would come back one day and gold would flow in rivers, through the mountain-gates, and all that land would be filled with new song and new laughter. But this pleasant legend did not much affect their daily business.

As soon as the raft of barrels came in sight boats rowed out from the piles of the town, and voices hailed the raft-steerers. Then ropes were cast and oars were pulled, and soon the raft was drawn out of the current of the Forest River and towed away round the high shoulder of rock into the little bay of Lake-town. There it was moored not far from the shoreward head of the great bridge. Soon men would come up from the South and take some of the casks away, and others they would fill with goods they had brought to be taken back up the stream to the Wood-elves' home. In the meanwhile the barrels were left afloat while the elves of the raft and the boatmen went to feast in Lake-town.

They would have been surprised, if they could have seen what happened down by the shore, after they had gone and the shades of night had fallen. First of all a barrel was cut loose by Bilbo and pushed to the shore and opened. Groans came from inside, and out crept a most unhappy dwarf. Wet straw was in his draggled beard; he was so sore and stiff, so bruised and buffeted he could hardly stand or stumble through the shallow water to lie groaning on the shore. He had a famished and a savage look like a dog that has been chained and forgotten in a kennel for a week. It was Thorin, but you could only have told it by his golden chain, and by the colour of his now dirty and tattered sky-blue hood with its tarnished silver tassel. It was some time before he would be even polite to the hobbit.

"Well, are you alive or are you dead?" asked Bilbo quite crossly. Perhaps he had forgotten that he had had at least one good meal more than the dwarves, and also the use of his arms and legs, not to speak of a greater allowance of air. "Are you still in prison, or are you free? If you want food, and if you want to go on with this silly adventure—it's yours after all and not mine—you had better slap your arms and rub your legs and try and help me get the others out while there is a chance!"

Thorin of course saw the sense of this, so after a few more groans he got up and helped the hobbit as well as he could. In the darkness floundering in the cold water they had a difficult and very nasty job finding which were the right barrels. Knocking outside and calling only discovered about six dwarves that could answer. These were unpacked and helped ashore where they sat or lay muttering and moaning; they were so soaked and bruised and cramped that they could hardly yet realize their release or be properly thankful for it.

Dwalin and Balin were two of the most unhappy, and it was no good asking them to help. Bifur and Bofur were less knocked about and drier, but they lay down and would do nothing. Fili and Kili, however, who were young (for dwarves) and had also been packed more neatly with plenty of straw into smaller casks, came out more or less smiling, with only a bruise or two and a stiffness that soon wore off.

"I hope I never smell the smell of apples again!" said Fili. "My tub was full of it. To smell apples everlastingly when you can scarcely move and are cold and sick with hunger is maddening. I could eat anything in the wide world now, for hours on end—but not an apple!"

With the willing help of Fili and Kili, Thorin and Bilbo at last discovered the remainder of the company and got them out. Poor fat Bombur was asleep or senseless; Dori, Nori, Ori, Oin and Gloin were waterlogged and seemed only half alive; they all had to be carried one by one and laid helpless on the shore.

"Well! Here we are!" said Thorin. "And I suppose we ought to thank our stars and Mr Baggins. I am sure he has a right to expect it, though I wish he could have arranged a more comfortable journey. Still—all very much at your service once more, Mr Baggins. No doubt we shall feel properly grateful, when we are fed and recovered. In the meanwhile what next?"

"I suggest Lake-town," said Bilbo. "What else is there?"

Nothing else could, of course, be suggested; so leaving the others Thorin and Fili and Kili and the hobbit went along the shore to the great bridge. There were guards at the head of it, but they were not keeping very careful watch, for it was so long since there had been any real need. Except for occasional squabbles about river-tolls they were friends with the Wood-elves. Other folk were far away; and some of the younger people in the town openly doubted the existence of any dragon in the mountain, and laughed at the greybeards and gammers who said that they had seen him flying in the sky in their young days. That being so it is not surprising that the guards were drinking and laughing by a fire in their hut, and did not hear the noise of the unpacking of the dwarves or the footsteps of the four scouts. Their astonishment was enormous when Thorin Oakenshield stepped in through the door.

"Who are you and what do you want?" they shouted leaping to their feet and groping for weapons.

"Thorin son of Thrain son of Thror King under the Mountain!" said the dwarf in a loud voice, and he looked it, in spite of his torn clothes and draggled hood. The gold gleamed on his neck and waist; his eyes were dark and deep. "I have come back. I wish to see the Master of your town!"

Then there was tremendous excitement. Some of the more foolish ran out of the hut as if they expected the Mountain to go golden in the night and all the waters of the lake turn yellow right away. The captain of the guard came forward.

"And who are these?" he asked, pointing to Fili and Kili and Bilbo.

"The sons of my father's daughter," answered Thorin, "Fili and Kili of the race of Durin, and Mr Baggins who has travelled with us out of the West."

"If you come in peace lay down your arms!" said the captain.

"We have none," said Thorin, and it was true enough: their knives had been taken from them by the wood-elves, and the great sword Orcrist too. Bilbo had his short sword, hidden as usual, but he said nothing about that. "We have no need of weapons, who return at last to our own as spoken of old. Nor could we fight against so many. Take us to your master!"

"He is at feast," said the captain.

"Then all the more reason for taking us to him," burst in Fili, who was getting impatient at these solemnities. "We are worn and famished after our long road and we have sick comrades. Now make haste and let us have no more words, or your master may have something to say to you."

"Follow me then," said the captain, and with six men about them he led them over the bridge through the gates and into the market-place of the town. This was a wide circle of quiet water surrounded by the tall piles on which were built the greater houses, and by long wooden quays with many steps and ladders going down to the surface of the lake. From one great hall shone many lights and there came the sound of many voices. They passed its doors and stood blinking in the light looking at long tables filled with folk.

"I am Thorin son of Thrain son of Thror King under the Mountain! I return!" cried Thorin in a loud voice from the door, before the captain could say anything.

All leaped to their feet. The Master of the town sprang from his great chair. But none rose in greater surprise than the raft-men of the elves who were sitting at the lower end of the hall. Pressing forward before the Master's table they cried:

"These are prisoners of our king that have escaped, wandering vagabond dwarves that could not give any good account of themselves, sneaking through the woods and molesting our people!"

"Is this true?" asked the Master. As a matter of fact he thought it far more likely than the return of the King under the Mountain, if any such person had ever existed.

"It is true that we were wrongfully waylaid by the Elven-king and imprisoned without cause as we journeyed back to our own land," answered Thorin. "But lock nor bar may hinder the homecoming spoken of old. Nor is this town in the Wood-elves' realm. I speak to the Master of the town of the Men of the Lake, not to the raft-men of the king."

Then the Master hesitated and looked from one to the other. The Elvenking was very powerful in those parts and the

Master wished for no enmity with him, nor did he think much of old songs, giving his mind to trade and tolls, to cargoes and gold, to which habit he owed his position. Others were of different mind, however, and quickly the matter was settled without him. The news had spread from the doors of the hall like fire through all the town. People were shouting inside the hall and outside it. The quays were thronged with hurrying feet. Some began to sing snatches of old songs concerning the return of the King under the Mountain; that it was Thror's grandson not Thror himself that had come back did not bother them at all. Others took up the song and it rolled loud and high over the lake.

> *The King beneath the mountains,*
> *The King of carven stone,*
> *The lord of silver fountains*
> *Shall come into his own!*
>
> *His crown shall be upholden,*
> *His harp shall be restrung,*
> *His halls shall echo golden*
> *To songs of yore re-sung.*
>
> *The woods shall wave on mountains*
> *And grass beneath the sun;*
> *His wealth shall flow in fountains*
> *And the rivers golden run.*
>
> *The streams shall run in gladness,*
> *The lakes shall shine and burn,*
> *All sorrow fail and sadness*
> *At the Mountain-king's return!*

So they sang, or very like that, only there was a great deal more of it, and there was much shouting as well as the music of harps and of fiddles mixed up with it. Indeed such excitement had not been known in the town in the memory of the oldest grandfather. The Wood-elves themselves began to wonder greatly and even to be afraid. They did not know of course how Thorin had escaped, and they began to think their king might have made a serious mistake. As for the Master he saw there was nothing else for it but to obey the general clamour, for the moment at any rate, and to pretend to believe that Thorin was what he said. So he gave up to him his own great chair and set Fili and Kili beside him in places of honour. Even Bilbo was given a seat at the high table, and no explanation of where he came in—no songs had alluded to him even in the obscurest way—was asked for in the general bustle.

Soon afterwards the other dwarves were brought into the town amid scenes of astonishing enthusiasm. They were all doctored and fed and housed and pampered in the most delightful and satisfactory fashion. A large house was given up to Thorin and his company; boats and rowers were put at their service; and crowds sat outside and sang songs all day, or cheered if any dwarf showed so much as his nose.

Some of the songs were old ones; but some of them were quite new and spoke confidently of the sudden death of the dragon and of cargoes of rich presents coming down the river to Lake-town. These were inspired largely by the Master and they did not particularly please the dwarves but in the meantime they were well contented and they quickly grew fat and strong again. Indeed within a week they were quite recovered, fitted out in fine cloth of their proper colours, with beards combed and trimmed, and proud steps. Thorin looked and walked as if his kingdom was already regained and Smaug chopped up into little pieces.

Then, as he had said, the dwarves' good feeling towards the little hobbit grew stronger every day. There were no more groans or grumbles. They drank his health, and they patted him on the back, and they made a great fuss of him; which was just as well, for he was not feeling particularly cheerful. He had not forgotten the look of the Mountain, nor the thought of the dragon, and he had beside a shocking cold. For three days he sneezed and coughed, and he could not go out, and even after that his speeches at banquets were limited to "Thag you very buch."

In the meanwhile the Wood-elves had gone back up the Forest River with their cargoes, and there was great excitement in the king's palace. I have never heard what happened to the chief of the guards and the butler. Nothing of course was ever said about keys or barrels while the dwarves stayed in Lake-town, and Bilbo was careful never to become invisible. Still, I daresay, more was guessed than was known, though doubtless Mr Baggins remained a bit of a mystery. In any case the king knew now the dwarves' errand, or thought he did, and he said to himself:

"Very well! We'll see! No treasure will come back through Mirkwood without my having something to say in the matter. But I expect they will all come to a bad end, and serve them right!" He at any rate did not believe in dwarves fighting and killing dragons like Smaug, and he strongly suspected attempted burglary or something like it—which shows he was a wise elf and wiser than the men of the town, though not quite right, as we shall see in the end. He sent out his spies about the shores of the lake and as far northward towards the Mountain as they would go, and waited.

At the end of a fortnight Thorin began to think of departure. While the enthusiasm still lasted in the town was the time to get help. It would not do to let everything cool down with delay. So he spoke to the Master and his councillors and said that soon he and his company must go on towards the Mountain.

Then for the first time the Master was surprised and a little frightened; and he wondered if Thorin was after all really a descendant of the old kings. He had never thought that the dwarves would actually dare to approach Smaug, but believed they were frauds who would sooner or later be discovered and be turned out. He was wrong. Thorin, of course, was really the grandson of the King under the Mountain, and there is no knowing what a dwarf will not dare and do for revenge or the recovery of his own.

But the Master was not sorry at all to let them go. They were expensive to keep, and their arrival had turned things into a long holiday in which business was at a standstill. "Let them go and bother Smaug, and see how he welcomes them!" he thought. "Certainly, O Thorin Thrain's son Thror's son!" was what he said. "You must claim your own. The hour is at hand, spoken of old. What help we can offer shall be yours, and we trust to your gratitude when your kingdom is regained."

So one day, although autumn was now getting far on, and winds were cold, and leaves were falling fast, three large boats left Lake-town, laden with rowers, dwarves, Mr Baggins, and many provisions. Horses and ponies had been sent round by circuitous paths to meet them at their appointed landing-place. The Master and his councillors bade them farewell from the great steps of the town-hall that went down to the lake. People sang on the quays and out of windows. The white oars dipped and splashed, and off they went north up the lake on the last stage of their long journey. The only person thoroughly unhappy was Bilbo.

*Chapter XI*

# ON THE DOORSTEP

In two days going they rowed right up the Long Lake and passed out into the River Running, and now they could all see the Lonely Mountain towering grim and tall before them. The stream was strong and their going slow. At the end of the third day, some miles up the river, they drew in to the left or western bank and disembarked. Here they were joined by the horses with other provisions and necessaries and the ponies for their own use that had been sent to meet them. They packed what they could on the ponies and the rest was made into a store under a tent, but none of the men of the town would stay with them even for the night so near the shadow of the Mountain.

"Not at any rate until the songs have come true!" said they. It was easier to believe in the Dragon and less easy to believe in Thorin in these wild parts. Indeed their stores had no need of any guard, for all the land was desolate and empty. So their escort left them, making off swiftly down the river and the shoreward paths, although the night was already drawing on.

They spent a cold and lonely night and their spirits fell. The next day they set out again. Balin and Bilbo rode behind, each leading another pony heavily laden beside him; the others were some way ahead picking out a slow road, for there were no paths. They made north-west, slanting away from the River Running, and drawing ever nearer and nearer to a great spur of the Mountain that was flung out southwards towards them.

It was a weary journey, and a quiet and stealthy one. There was no laughter or song or sound of harps, and the pride and hopes which had stirred in their hearts at the singing of old songs by the lake died away to a plodding gloom. They knew that they were drawing near to the end of their journey, and that it might be a very horrible end. The land about them grew bleak and barren, though once, as Thorin told them, it had been green and fair. There was little grass, and before long there was neither bush nor tree, and only broken and blackened stumps to speak of ones long vanished. They were come to the Desolation of the Dragon, and they were come at the waning of the year.

They reached the skirts of the Mountain all the same without meeting any danger or any sign of the Dragon other than the wilderness he had made about his lair. The Mountain lay dark and silent before them and ever higher above them. They made their first camp on the western side of the great southern spur, which ended in a height called Ravenhill. On this there had been an old watch-post; but they dared not climb it yet, it was too exposed.

Before setting out to search the western spurs of the Mountain for the hidden door, on which all their hopes rested, Thorin sent out a scouting expedition to spy out the land to the South where the Front Gate stood. For this purpose he chose Balin and Fili and Kili, and with them went Bilbo. They marched under the grey and silent cliffs to the feet of Ravenhill. There the river, after winding a wide loop over the valley of Dale, turned from the Mountain on its road to the Lake, flowing swift and noisily. Its bank was bare and rocky, tall and steep above the stream; and gazing out from it over the narrow water, foaming and splashing among many boulders, they could see in the wide valley shadowed by the Mountain's arms the grey ruins of ancient houses, towers, and walls.

"There lies all that is left of Dale," said Balin. "The mountain's sides were green with woods and all the sheltered valley rich and pleasant in the days when the bells rang in that town." He looked both sad and grim as he said this: he had been one of Thorin's companions on the day the Dragon came.

They did not dare to follow the river much further towards the Gate; but they went on beyond the end of the southern spur, until lying hidden behind a rock they could look out and see the dark cavernous opening in a great cliff-wall between the arms of the Mountain. Out of it the waters of the Running River sprang; and out of it too there came a steam and a dark smoke. Nothing moved in the waste, save the vapour and the water, and every now and again a black and ominous crow. The only sound was the sound of the stony water, and every now and again the harsh croak of a bird. Balin shuddered.

"Let us return!" he said. "We can do no good here! And I don't like these dark birds, they look like spies of evil."

"The dragon is still alive and in the halls under the Mountain then—or I imagine so from the smoke," said the hobbit.

"That does not prove it," said Balin, "though I don't doubt you are right. But he might be gone away some time, or he might be lying out on the mountain-side keeping watch, and still I expect smokes and steams would come out of the gates: all the halls within must be filled with his foul reek."

*  *  *

With such gloomy thoughts, followed ever by croaking crows above them, they made their weary way back to the camp. Only in June they had been guests in the fair house of Elrond, and though autumn was now crawling towards winter that pleasant time now seemed years ago. They were alone in the perilous waste without hope of further help. They were at the end of their journey, but as far as ever, it seemed, from the end of their quest. None of them had much spirit left.

Now strange to say Mr Baggins had more than the others. He would often borrow Thorin's map and gaze at it, pondering over the runes and the message of the moon-letters Elrond had read. It was he that made the dwarves begin the dangerous search on the western slopes for the secret door. They moved their camp then to a long valley, narrower than the great dale in the South where the Gates of the river stood, and walled with lower spurs of the Mountain. Two of these were thrust forward west from the main mass in long steep-sided ridges that fell ever downwards towards the plain. On this western side there were fewer signs of the dragon's marauding feet, and there was some grass for their ponies. From this western camp, shadowed all day by cliff and wall until the sun began to sink towards the forest, day by day they toiled in parties searching for paths up the mountain-side. If the map was true, somewhere high above the cliff at the valley's head must stand the secret door. Day by day they came back to their camp without success.

But at last unexpectedly they found what they were seeking. Fili and Kili and the hobbit went back one day down the valley and scrambled among the tumbled rocks at its southern corner. About midday, creeping behind a great stone that stood alone like a pillar, Bilbo came on what looked like rough steps going upwards. Following these excitedly he and the dwarves found traces of a narrow track, often lost, often

rediscovered, that wandered on to the top of the southern
ridge and brought them at last to a still narrower ledge, which
turned north across the face of the Mountain. Looking down
they saw that they were at the top of the cliff at the valley'
head and were gazing down on to their own camp below
Silently, clinging to the rocky wall on their right, they wen
in single file along the ledge, till the wall opened and the
turned into a little steep-walled bay, grassy-floored, still and
quiet. Its entrance which they had found could not be seen
from below because of the overhang of the cliff, nor from fur
ther off because it was so small that it looked like a dark crack
and no more. It was not a cave and was open to the sky above
but at its inner end a flat wall rose up that in the lower part
close to the ground, was as smooth and upright as masons
work, but without a joint or crevice to be seen. No sign was
there of post or lintel or threshold, nor any sign of bar or bol
or key-hole; yet they did not doubt that they had found the
door at last.

They beat on it, they thrust and pushed at it, they implored
it to move, they spoke fragments of broken spells of opening
and nothing stirred. At last tired out they rested on the grass a
its feet, and then at evening began their long climb down.

There was excitement in the camp that night. In the morn
ing they prepared to move once more. Only Bofur and Bom
bur were left behind to guard the ponies and such stores a
they had brought with them from the river. The others wen
down the valley and up the newly found path, and so to the
narrow ledge. Along this they could carry no bundles o
packs, so narrow and breathless was it, with a fall of a hun
dred and fifty feet beside them on to sharp rocks below; bu
each of them took a good coil of rope wound tight about his

aist, and so at last without mishap they reached the little
grassy bay.

There they made their third camp, hauling up what they
needed from below with their ropes. Down the same way they
were able occasionally to lower one of the more active dwarves,
such as Kili, to exchange such news as there was, or to take a
share in the guard below, while Bofur was hauled up to the
higher camp. Bombur would not come up either the rope or
the path.

"I am too fat for such fly-walks," he said. "I should turn
dizzy and tread on my beard, and then you would be thirteen
again. And the knotted ropes are too slender for my weight."
Luckily for him that was not true, as you will see.

In the meanwhile some of them explored the ledge beyond
the opening and found a path that led higher and higher on to
the mountain; but they did not dare to venture very far that
way, nor was there much use in it. Out up there a silence
reigned, broken by no bird or sound except that of the wind in
the crannies of stone. They spoke low and never called or
sang, for danger brooded in every rock. The others who were
busy with the secret of the door had no more success. They
were too eager to trouble about the runes or the moon-letters,
but tried without resting to discover where exactly in the
smooth face of the rock the door was hidden. They had
brought picks and tools of many sorts from Lake-town, and at
first they tried to use these. But when they struck the stone the
handles splintered and jarred their arms cruelly, and the steel
heads broke or bent like lead. Mining work, they saw clearly,
was no good against the magic that had shut this door; and
they grew terrified, too, of the echoing noise.

Bilbo found sitting on the doorstep lonesome and
wearisome—there was not a doorstep, of course, really, but

they used to call the little grassy space between the wall a
the opening the "doorstep" in fun, remembering Bilbe
words long ago at the unexpected party in his hobbit-ho
when he said they could sit on the doorstep till they thoug
of something. And sit and think they did, or wandered ai
lessly about, and glummer and glummer they became.

Their spirits had risen a little at the discovery of the pa
but now they sank into their boots; and yet they would n
give it up and go away. The hobbit was no longer mu
brighter than the dwarves. He would do nothing but sit wi
his back to the rock-face and stare away west through t
opening, over the cliff, over the wide lands to the black w
of Mirkwood, and to the distances beyond, in which he som
times thought he could catch glimpses of the Misty Mou
tains small and far. If the dwarves asked him what he w
doing he answered:

"You said sitting on the doorstep and thinking would
my job, not to mention getting inside, so I am sitting a
thinking." But I am afraid he was not thinking much of t
job, but of what lay beyond the blue distance, the quiet We
ern Land and the Hill and his hobbit-hole under it.

A large grey stone lay in the centre of the grass and
stared moodily at it or watched the great snails. They seeme
to love the little shut-in bay with its walls of cool rock, a
there were many of them of huge size crawling slowly a
stickily along its sides.

"Tomorrow begins the last week of autumn," said Thor
one day.

"And winter comes after autumn," said Bifur.

"And next year after that," said Dwalin, "and our bear
will grow till they hang down the cliff to the valley befo
anything happens here. What is our burglar doing for u

ince he has got an invisible ring, and ought to be a specially
xcellent performer now, I am beginning to think he might go
through the Front Gate and spy things out a bit!"

Bilbo heard this—the dwarves were on the rocks just
above the enclosure where he was sitting—and "Good Gracious!" he thought, "so that is what they are beginning to
think, is it? It is always poor me that has to get them out of
their difficulties, at least since the wizard left. Whatever am I
going to do? I might have known that something dreadful
would happen to me in the end. I don't think I could bear to
see the unhappy valley of Dale again, and as for that steaming
gate!!!"

That night he was very miserable and hardly slept. Next
day the dwarves all went wandering off in various directions;
some were exercising the ponies down below, some were
moving about the mountain-side. All day Bilbo sat gloomily in
the grassy bay gazing at the stone, or out west through the
narrow opening. He had a queer feeling that he was waiting
for something. "Perhaps the wizard will suddenly come back
today," he thought.

If he lifted his head he could see a glimpse of the distant
forest. As the sun turned west there was a gleam of yellow
upon its far roof, as if the light caught the last pale leaves.
Soon he saw the orange ball of the sun sinking towards the
level of his eyes. He went to the opening and there pale and
faint was a thin new moon above the rim of Earth.

At that very moment he heard a sharp crack behind him.
There on the grey stone in the grass was an enormous thrush,
nearly coal black, its pale yellow breast freckled with dark
spots. Crack! It had caught a snail and was knocking it on the
stone. Crack! Crack!

Suddenly Bilbo understood. Forgetting all danger he stood
on the ledge and hailed the dwarves, shouting and waving.

Those that were nearest came tumbling over the rocks and
fast as they could along the ledge to him, wondering what
earth was the matter; the others shouted to be hauled up t
ropes (except Bombur, of course: he was asleep).

Quickly Bilbo explained. They all fell silent: the hobb
standing by the grey stone, and the dwarves with waggi
beards watching impatiently. The sun sank lower and lowe
and their hopes fell. It sank into a belt of reddened cloud a
disappeared. The dwarves groaned, but still Bilbo stood a
most without moving. The little moon was dipping to t
horizon. Evening was coming on. Then suddenly when the
hope was lowest a red ray of the sun escaped like a fing
through a rent in the cloud. A gleam of light came straig
through the opening into the bay and fell on the smooth roc
face. The old thrush, who had been watching from a hig
perch with beady eyes and head cocked on one side, gave
sudden trill. There was a loud crack. A flake of rock split fro
the wall and fell. A hole appeared suddenly about three fe
from the ground.

Quickly, trembling lest the chance should fade, the dwarv
rushed to the rock and pushed—in vain.

"The key! The key!" cried Bilbo. "Where is Thorin?"

Thorin hurried up.

"The key!" shouted Bilbo. "The key that went with t
map! Try it now while there is still time!"

Then Thorin stepped up and drew the key on its chain fro
round his neck. He put it to the hole. It fitted and it turne
Snap! The gleam went out, the sun sank, the moon was gon
and evening sprang into the sky.

Now they all pushed together, and slowly a part of t
rock-wall gave way. Long straight cracks appeared an
widened. A door five feet high and three broad was outline
and slowly without a sound swung inwards. It seemed

f darkness flowed out like a vapour from the hole in the
mountain-side, and deep darkness in which nothing could
be seen lay before their eyes, a yawning mouth leading in
and down.

*Chapter XII*

# INSIDE INFORMATION

For a long time the dwarves stood in the dark before the doc
and debated, until at last Thorin spoke:

"Now is the time for our esteemed Mr Baggins, who ha
proved himself a good companion on our long road, and
hobbit full of courage and resource far exceeding his size
and if I may say so possessed of good luck far exceeding th
usual allowance—now is the time for him to perform the ser
vice for which he was included in our Company; now is th
time for him to earn his Reward."

You are familiar with Thorin's style on important occa
sions, so I will not give you any more of it, though he went o
a good deal longer than this. It certainly was an important oc
casion, but Bilbo felt impatient. By now he was quite familia
with Thorin too, and he knew what he was driving at.

"If you mean you think it is my job to go into the secre
passage first, O Thorin Thrain's son Oakenshield, may you
beard grow ever longer," he said crossly, "say so at once an
have done! I might refuse. I have got you out of two messe
already, which were hardly in the original bargain, so that
am, I think, already owed some reward. But 'third time pay
for all' as my father used to say, and somehow I don't think
shall refuse. Perhaps I have begun to trust my luck more tha

I used to in the old days"—he meant last spring before he left his own house, but it seemed centuries ago—"but anyway I think I will go and have a peep at once and get it over. Now who is coming with me?"

He did not expect a chorus of volunteers, so he was not disappointed. Fili and Kili looked uncomfortable and stood on one leg, but the others made no pretence of offering—except old Balin, the look-out man, who was rather fond of the hobbit. He said he would come inside at least and perhaps a bit of the way too, ready to call for help if necessary.

The most that can be said for the dwarves is this: they intended to pay Bilbo really handsomely for his services; they had brought him to do a nasty job for them, and they did not mind the poor little fellow doing it if he would; but they would all have done their best to get him out of trouble, if he got into it, as they did in the case of the trolls at the beginning of their adventures before they had any particular reasons for being grateful to him. There it is: dwarves are not heroes, but calculating folk with a great idea of the value of money; some are tricky and treacherous and pretty bad lots; some are not, but are decent enough people like Thorin and Company, if you don't expect too much.

The stars were coming out behind him in a pale sky barred with black when the hobbit crept through the enchanted door and stole into the Mountain. It was far easier going than he expected. This was no goblin entrance, or rough wood-elves' cave. It was a passage made by dwarves, at the height of their wealth and skill: straight as a ruler, smooth-floored and smooth-sided, going with a gentle never-varying slope direct—to some distant end in the blackness below.

After a while Balin bade Bilbo "Good luck!" and stopped where he could still see the faint outline of the door, and by a

trick of the echoes of the tunnel hear the rustle of the whispering voices of the others just outside. Then the hobbit
slipped on his ring, and warned by the echoes to take more
than hobbit's care to make no sound, he crept noiselessly
down, down, down into the dark. He was trembling with fear,
but his little face was set and grim. Already he was a very different hobbit from the one that had run out without a pocket-
handkerchief from Bag-End long ago. He had not had a
pocket-handkerchief for ages. He loosened his dagger in its
sheath, tightened his belt, and went on.

"Now you are in for it at last, Bilbo Baggins," he said to
himself. "You went and put your foot right in it that night of
the party, and now you have got to pull it out and pay for it!
Dear me, what a fool I was and am!" said the least Tookish
part of him. "I have absolutely no use for dragon-guarded
treasures, and the whole lot could stay here for ever, if only I
could wake up and find this beastly tunnel was my own front-
hall at home!"

He did not wake up of course, but went still on and on, till
all sign of the door behind had faded away. He was altogether
alone. Soon he thought it was beginning to feel warm. "Is that
a kind of a glow I seem to see coming right ahead down
there?" he thought.

It was. As he went forward it grew and grew, till there was
no doubt about it. It was a red light steadily getting redder and
redder. Also it was now undoubtedly hot in the tunnel. Wisps
of vapour floated up and past him and he began to sweat. A
sound, too, began to throb in his ears, a sort of bubbling like
the noise of a large pot galloping on the fire, mixed with a
rumble as of a gigantic tom-cat purring. This grew to the un-
mistakable gurgling noise of some vast animal snoring in its
sleep down there in the red glow in front of him.

It was at this point that Bilbo stopped. Going on from there was the bravest thing he ever did. The tremendous things that happened afterwards were as nothing compared to it. He fought the real battle in the tunnel alone, before he ever saw the vast danger that lay in wait. At any rate after a short halt go on he did; and you can picture him coming to the end of the tunnel, an opening of much the same size and shape as the door above. Through it peeps the hobbit's little head. Before him lies the great bottom-most cellar or dungeon-hall of the ancient dwarves right at the Mountain's root. It is almost dark so that its vastness can only be dimly guessed, but rising from the near side of the rocky floor there is a great glow. The glow of Smaug!

There he lay, a vast red-golden dragon, fast asleep; a thrumming came from his jaws and nostrils, and wisps of smoke, but his fires were low in slumber. Beneath him, under all his limbs and his huge coiled tail, and about him on all sides stretching away across the unseen floors, lay countless piles of precious things, gold wrought and unwrought, gems and jewels, and silver red-stained in the ruddy light.

Smaug lay, with wings folded like an immeasurable bat, turned partly on one side, so that the hobbit could see his underparts and his long pale belly crusted with gems and fragments of gold from his long lying on his costly bed. Behind him where the walls were nearest could dimly be seen coats of mail, helms and axes, swords and spears hanging; and there in rows stood great jars and vessels filled with a wealth that could not be guessed.

To say that Bilbo's breath was taken away is no description at all. There are no words left to express his staggerment, since Men changed the language that they learned of elves in the days when all the world was wonderful. Bilbo had heard tell and sing of dragon-hoards before, but the splendour, the lust, the glory of such treasure had never yet come home to him. His heart was filled and pierced with enchantment and with the desire of dwarves; and he gazed motionless, almost forgetting the frightful guardian, at the gold beyond price and count.

He gazed for what seemed an age, before drawn almost against his will, he stole from the shadow of the doorway, across the floor to the nearest edge of the mounds of treasure. Above him the sleeping dragon lay, a dire menace even in his sleep. He grasped a great two-handled cup, as heavy as he could carry, and cast one fearful eye upwards. Smaug stirred a wing, opened a claw, the rumble of his snoring changed its note.

Then Bilbo fled. But the dragon did not wake—not yet—but shifted into other dreams of greed and violence, lying there in his stolen hall while the little hobbit toiled back up the long tunnel. His heart was beating and a more fevered shaking was in his legs than when he was going down, but still he clutched the cup, and his chief thought was: "I've done it! This will show them. 'More like a grocer than a burglar' indeed! Well, we'll hear no more of that."

Nor did he. Balin was overjoyed to see the hobbit again, and as delighted as he was surprised. He picked Bilbo up and carried him out into the open air. It was midnight and clouds had covered the stars, but Bilbo lay with his eyes shut, gasping and taking pleasure in the feel of the fresh air again, and hardly noticing the excitement of the dwarves, or how they praised him and patted him on the back and put themselves and all their families for generations to come at his service.

\* \* \*

The dwarves were still passing the cup from hand to hand and talking delightedly of the recovery of their treasure, when suddenly a vast rumbling woke in the mountain underneath as if it was an old volcano that had made up its mind to start eruptions once again. The door behind them was pulled nearly to, and blocked from closing with a stone, but up the long tunnel came the dreadful echoes, from far down in the depths, of a bellowing and a trampling that made the ground beneath them tremble.

Then the dwarves forgot their joy and their confident boasts of a moment before and cowered down in fright. Smaug was still to be reckoned with. It does not do to leave a live dragon out of your calculations, if you live near him. Dragons may not have much real use for all their wealth, but they know it to an ounce as a rule, especially after long possession; and Smaug was no exception. He had passed from an uneasy dream (in which a warrior, altogether insignificant in size but provided with a bitter sword and great courage, figured most unpleasantly) to a doze, and from a doze to wide waking. There was a breath of strange air in his cave. Could there be a draught from that little hole? He had never felt quite happy about it, though it was so small, and now he glared at it in suspicion and wondered why he had never blocked it up. Of late he had half fancied he had caught the dim echoes of a knocking sound from far above that came down through it to his lair. He stirred and stretched forth his neck to sniff. Then he missed the cup!

Thieves! Fire! Murder! Such a thing had not happened since first he came to the Mountain! His rage passes description— the sort of rage that is only seen when rich folk that have more than they can enjoy suddenly lose something that they have long had but have never before used or wanted. His fire belched forth, the hall smoked, he shook the mountain-roots. He thrust his head in vain at the little hole, and then coiling his length together, roaring like thunder underground, he sped from his deep lair through its great door, out into the huge passages of the mountain-palace and up towards the Front Gate.

To hunt the whole mountain till he had caught the thief and had torn and trampled him was his one thought. He issued from the Gate, the waters rose in fierce whistling steam, and up he soared blazing into the air and settled on the mountain-top in a spout of green and scarlet flame. The dwarves heard the awful rumour of his flight, and they crouched against the walls of the grassy terrace cringing under boulders, hoping somehow to escape the frightful eyes of the hunting dragon.

There they would have all been killed, if it had not been for Bilbo once again. "Quick! Quick!" he gasped. "The door! The tunnel! It's no good here."

Roused by these words they were just about to creep inside the tunnel when Bifur gave a cry: "My cousins! Bombur and Bofur—we have forgotten them, they are down in the valley!"

"They will be slain, and all our ponies too, and all our stores lost," moaned the others. "We can do nothing."

"Nonsense!" said Thorin, recovering his dignity. "We cannot leave them. Get inside Mr Baggins and Balin, and you two Fili and Kili—the dragon shan't have all of us. Now you others, where are the ropes? Be quick!"

Those were perhaps the worst moments they had been through yet. The horrible sounds of Smaug's anger were echoing in the stony hollows far above; at any moment he might come blazing down or fly whirling round and find them there near the perilous cliff's edge hauling madly on the ropes. Up came Bofur, and still all was safe. Up came Bombur, puffing and blowing while the ropes creaked, and still all was safe

Up came some tools and bundles of stores, and then danger was upon them.

A whirring noise was heard. A red light touched the points of standing rocks. The dragon came.

They had barely time to fly back to the tunnel, pulling and dragging in their bundles, when Smaug came hurtling from the North, licking the mountain-sides with flame, beating his great wings with a noise like a roaring wind. His hot breath shrivelled the grass before the door, and drove in through the crack they had left and scorched them as they lay hid. Flickering fires leaped up and black rock-shadows danced. Then darkness fell as he passed again. The ponies screamed with terror, burst their ropes and galloped wildly off. The dragon swooped and turned to pursue them, and was gone.

"That'll be the end of our poor beasts!" said Thorin. "Nothing can escape Smaug once he sees it. Here we are and here we shall have to stay, unless any one fancies tramping the long open miles back to the river with Smaug on the watch!"

It was not a pleasant thought! They crept further down the tunnel, and there they lay and shivered though it was warm and stuffy, until dawn came pale through the crack of the door. Every now and again through the night they could hear the roar of the flying dragon grow and then pass and fade, as he hunted round and round the mountain-sides.

He guessed from the ponies, and from the traces of the camps he had discovered, that men had come up from the river and the lake and had scaled the mountain-side from the valley where the ponies had been standing; but the door withstood his searching eye, and the little high-walled bay had kept out his fiercest flames. Long he had hunted in vain till the dawn chilled his wrath and he went back to his golden couch to sleep—and to gather new strength. He would not forget or forgive the theft, not if a thousand years turned him to smouldering stone, but he could afford to wait. Slow and silent he crept back to his lair and half closed his eyes.

When morning came the terror of the dwarves grew less. They realized that dangers of this kind were inevitable in dealing with such a guardian, and that it was no good giving up their quest yet. Nor could they get away just now, as Thorin had pointed out. Their ponies were lost or killed, and they would have to wait some time before Smaug relaxed his watch sufficiently for them to dare the long way on foot. Luckily they had saved enough of their stores to last them still for some time.

They debated long on what was to be done, but they could think of no way of getting rid of Smaug—which had always been a weak point in their plans, as Bilbo felt inclined to point out. Then as is the nature of folk that are thoroughly perplexed, they began to grumble at the hobbit, blaming him for what had at first so pleased them: for bringing away a cup and stirring up Smaug's wrath so soon.

"What else do you suppose a burglar is to do?" asked Bilbo angrily. "I was not engaged to kill dragons, that is warrior's work, but to steal treasure. I made the best beginning I could. Did you expect me to trot back with the whole hoard of Thror on my back? If there is any grumbling to be done, I think I might have a say. You ought to have brought five hundred burglars, not one. I am sure it reflects great credit on your grandfather, but you cannot pretend that you ever made the vast extent of his wealth clear to me. I should want hundreds of years to bring it all up, if I was fifty times as big, and Smaug as tame as a rabbit."

After that of course the dwarves begged his pardon. "What then do you propose we should do, Mr Baggins?" asked Thorin politely.

"I have no idea at the moment—if you mean about removing the treasure. That obviously depends entirely on some new turn of luck and the getting rid of Smaug. Getting rid of dragons is not at all in my line, but I will do my best to think about it. Personally I have no hopes at all, and wish I was safe back at home."

"Never mind that for the moment! What are we to do now, to-day?"

"Well, if you really want my advice, I should say we can do nothing but stay where we are. By day we can no doubt creep out safely enough to take the air. Perhaps before long one or two could be chosen to go back to the store by the river and replenish our supplies. But in the meanwhile everyone ought to be well inside the tunnel by night.

"Now I will make you an offer. I have got my ring and will creep down this very noon—then if ever Smaug ought to be napping—and see what he is up to. Perhaps something will turn up. 'Every worm has his weak spot,' as my father used to say, though I am sure it was not from personal experience."

Naturally the dwarves accepted the offer eagerly. Already they had come to respect little Bilbo. Now he had become the real leader in their adventure. He had begun to have ideas and plans of his own. When midday came he got ready for another journey down into the Mountain. He did not like it of course, but it was not so bad now he knew, more or less, what was in front of him. Had he known more about dragons and their wily ways, he might have been more frightened and less hopeful of catching this one napping.

The sun was shining when he started, but it was as dark as night in the tunnel. The light from the door, almost closed, soon faded as he went down. So silent was his going that smoke on a gentle wind could hardly have surpassed it, and he was inclined to feel a bit proud of himself as he drew near the lower door. There was only the very faintest glow to be seen.

"Old Smaug is weary and asleep," he thought. "He can't see me and he won't hear me. Cheer up Bilbo!" He had forgotten or had never heard about dragons' sense of smell. It is also an awkward fact that they can keep half an eye open watching while they sleep, if they are suspicious.

Smaug certainly looked fast asleep, almost dead and dark, with scarcely a snore more than a whiff of unseen steam, when Bilbo peeped once more from the entrance. He was just about to step out on to the floor when he caught a sudden thin and piercing ray of red from under the drooping lid of Smaug's left eye. He was only pretending to sleep! He was watching the tunnel entrance! Hurriedly Bilbo stepped back and blessed the luck of his ring. Then Smaug spoke.

"Well, thief! I smell you and I feel your air. I hear your breath. Come along! Help yourself again, there is plenty and to spare!"

But Bilbo was not quite so unlearned in dragon-lore as all that, and if Smaug hoped to get him to come nearer so easily he was disappointed. "No thank you, O Smaug the Tremendous!" he replied. "I did not come for presents. I only wished to have a look at you and see if you were truly as great as tales say. I did not believe them."

"Do you now?" said the dragon somewhat flattered, even though he did not believe a word of it.

"Truly songs and tales fall utterly short of the reality, O Smaug the Chiefest and Greatest of Calamities," replied Bilbo.

"You have nice manners for a thief and a liar," said the dragon. "You seem familiar with my name, but I don't seem to remember smelling you before. Who are you and where do you come from, may I ask?"

"You may indeed! I come from under the hill, and under

the hills and over the hills my paths led. And through the air. I am he that walks unseen."

"So I can well believe," said Smaug, "but that is hardly your usual name."

"I am the clue-finder, the web-cutter, the stinging fly. I was chosen for the lucky number."

"Lovely titles!" sneered the dragon. "But lucky numbers don't always come off."

"I am he that buries his friends alive and drowns them and draws them alive again from the water. I came from the end of a bag, but no bag went over me."

"These don't sound so creditable," scoffed Smaug.

"I am the friend of bears and the guest of eagles. I am Ringwinner and Luckwearer; and I am Barrel-rider," went on Bilbo beginning to be pleased with his riddling.

"That's better!" said Smaug. "But don't let your imagination run away with you!"

This of course is the way to talk to dragons, if you don't want to reveal your proper name (which is wise), and don't want to infuriate them by a flat refusal (which is also very wise). No dragon can resist the fascination of riddling talk and of wasting time trying to understand it. There was a lot here which Smaug did not understand at all (though I expect you do, since you know all about Bilbo's adventures to which he was referring), but he thought he understood enough, and he chuckled in his wicked inside.

"I thought so last night," he smiled to himself. "Lake-men, some nasty scheme of those miserable tub-trading Lake-men, or I'm a lizard. I haven't been down that way for an age and an age; but I will soon alter that!"

"Very well, O Barrel-rider!" he said aloud. "Maybe Barrel was your pony's name; and maybe not, though it was fat enough. You may walk unseen, but you did not walk all the way. Let me tell you I ate six ponies last night and I shall catch and eat all the others before long. In return for the excellent meal I will give you one piece of advice for your good: don't have more to do with dwarves than you can help!"

"Dwarves!" said Bilbo in pretended surprise.

"Don't talk to me!" said Smaug. "I know the smell (and taste) of dwarf—no one better. Don't tell me that I can eat a dwarf-ridden pony and not know it! You'll come to a bad end, if you go with such friends, Thief Barrel-rider. I don't mind if you go back and tell them so from me." But he did not tell Bilbo that there was one smell he could not make out at all, hobbit-smell; it was quite outside his experience and puzzled him mightily.

"I suppose you got a fair price for that cup last night?" he went on. "Come now, did you? Nothing at all! Well, that's just like them. And I suppose they are skulking outside, and your job is to do all the dangerous work and get what you can when I'm not looking—for them? And you will get a fair share? Don't you believe it! If you get off alive, you will be lucky."

Bilbo was now beginning to feel really uncomfortable. Whenever Smaug's roving eye, seeking for him in the shadows, flashed across him, he trembled, and an unaccountable desire seized hold of him to rush out and reveal himself and tell all the truth to Smaug. In fact he was in grievous danger of coming under the dragon-spell. But plucking up courage he spoke again.

"You don't know everything, O Smaug the Mighty," said he. "Not gold alone brought us hither."

"Ha! Ha! You admit the 'us' " laughed Smaug. "Why not say 'us fourteen' and be done with it, Mr Lucky Number? I am pleased to hear that you had other business in these parts besides my gold. In that case you may, perhaps, not altogether waste your time.

"I don't know if it has occurred to you that, even if you could steal the gold bit by bit—a matter of a hundred years or so—you could not get it very far? Not much use on the mountain side? Not much use in the forest? Bless me! Had you never thought of the catch? A fourteenth share, I suppose, or something like it, those were the terms, eh? But what about delivery? What about cartage? What about armed guards and tolls?" And Smaug laughed aloud. He had a wicked and a wily heart, and he knew his guesses were not far out, though he suspected that the Lake-men were at the back of the plans, and that most of the plunder was meant to stop there in the town by the shore that in his young days had been called Esgaroth.

You will hardly believe it, but poor Bilbo was really very taken aback. So far all his thoughts and energies had been concentrated on getting to the Mountain and finding the entrance. He had never bothered to wonder how the treasure was to be removed, certainly never how any part of it that might fall to his share was to be brought back all the way to Bag-End Under-Hill.

Now a nasty suspicion began to grow in his mind—had the dwarves forgotten this important point too, or were they laughing in their sleeves at him all the time? That is the effect that dragon-talk has on the inexperienced. Bilbo of course ought to have been on his guard; but Smaug had rather an overwhelming personality.

"I tell you," he said, in an effort to remain loyal to his friends and to keep his end up, "that gold was only an afterthought with us. We came over hill and under hill, by wave and wind, for *Revenge*. Surely, O Smaug the unassessably wealthy, you must realize that your success has made you some bitter enemies?"

Then Smaug really did laugh—a devastating sound which shook Bilbo to the floor, while far up in the tunnel the dwarves huddled together and imagined that the hobbit had come to a sudden and a nasty end.

"Revenge!" he snorted, and the light of his eyes lit the hall from floor to ceiling like scarlet lightning. "Revenge! The King under the Mountain is dead and where are his kin that dare seek revenge? Girion Lord of Dale is dead, and I have eaten his people like a wolf among sheep, and where are his sons' sons that dare approach me? I kill where I wish and none dare resist. I laid low the warriors of old and their like is not in the world today. Then I was but young and tender. Now I am old and strong, strong, strong, Thief in the Shadows!" he gloated. "My armour is like tenfold shields, my teeth are swords, my claws spears, the shock of my tail a thunderbolt, my wings a hurricane, and my breath death!"

"I have always understood," said Bilbo in a frightened squeak, "that dragons were softer underneath, especially in the region of the—er—chest; but doubtless one so fortified has thought of that."

The dragon stopped short in his boasting. "Your information is antiquated," he snapped. "I am armoured above and below with iron scales and hard gems. No blade can pierce me."

"I might have guessed it," said Bilbo. "Truly there can nowhere be found the equal of Lord Smaug the Impenetrable. What magnificence to possess a waistcoat of fine diamonds!"

"Yes, it is rare and wonderful, indeed," said Smaug absurdly pleased. He did not know that the hobbit had already caught a glimpse of his peculiar under-covering on his previous visit, and was itching for a closer view for reasons of his own. The dragon rolled over. "Look!" he said. "What do you say to that?"

"Dazzlingly marvellous! Perfect! Flawless! Staggering!" exclaimed Bilbo aloud, but what he thought inside was: "Old fool! Why there is a large patch in the hollow of his left breast as bare as a snail out of its shell!"

After he had seen that Mr Baggins' one idea was to get away. "Well, I really must not detain Your Magnificence any longer," he said, "or keep you from much needed rest. Ponies take some catching, I believe, after a long start. And so do burglars," he added as a parting shot, as he darted back and fled up the tunnel.

It was an unfortunate remark, for the dragon spouted terrific flames after him, and fast though he sped up the slope, he had not gone nearly far enough to be comfortable before the ghastly head of Smaug was thrust against the opening behind. Luckily the whole head and jaws could not squeeze in, but the nostrils sent forth fire and vapour to pursue him, and he was nearly overcome, and stumbled blindly on in great pain and fear. He had been feeling rather pleased with the cleverness of his conversation with Smaug, but his mistake at the end shook him into better sense.

"Never laugh at live dragons, Bilbo you fool!" he said to himself, and it became a favourite saying of his later, and passed into a proverb. "You aren't nearly through this adventure yet," he added, and that was pretty true as well.

The afternoon was turning into evening when he came out again and stumbled and fell in a faint on the "door-step". The dwarves revived him, and doctored his scorches as well as they could; but it was a long time before the hair on the back of his head and his heels grew properly again: it had all been singed and frizzled right down to the skin. In the meanwhile

his friends did their best to cheer him up; and they were eage
for his story, especially wanting to know why the dragon ha
made such an awful noise, and how Bilbo had escaped.

But the hobbit was worried and uncomfortable, and the
had difficulty in getting anything out of him. On thinkin
things over he was now regretting some of the things he ha
said to the dragon, and was not eager to repeat them. The ol
thrush was sitting on a rock near by with his head cocked o
one side, listening to all that was said. It shows what an il
temper Bilbo was in: he picked up a stone and threw it at th
thrush, which merely fluttered aside and came back.

"Drat the bird!" said Bilbo crossly. "I believe he is lis
tening, and I don't like the look of him."

"Leave him alone!" said Thorin. "The thrushes are goo
and friendly—this is a very old bird indeed, and is maybe th
last left of the ancient breed that used to live about here, tam
to the hands of my father and grandfather. They were a long
lived and magical race, and this might even be one of thos
that were alive then, a couple of hundreds of years or mor
ago. The Men of Dale used to have the trick of understandin
their language, and used them for messengers to fly to th
Men of the Lake and elsewhere."

"Well, he'll have news to take to Lake-town all right, if tha
is what he is after," said Bilbo; "though I don't suppose ther
are any people left there that trouble with thrush-language."

"Why what has happened?" cried the dwarves. "Do get or
with your tale!"

So Bilbo told them all he could remember, and he con
fessed that he had a nasty feeling that the dragon guessed to
much from his riddles added to the camps and the ponies. "
am sure he knows we came from Lake-town and had hel
from there; and I have a horrible feeling that his next mov
may be in that direction. I wish to goodness I had never sai

that about Barrel-rider; it would make even a blind rabbit in these parts think of the Lake-men."

"Well, well! It cannot be helped, and it is difficult not to slip in talking to a dragon, or so I have always heard," said Balin anxious to comfort him. "I think you did very well, if you ask me—you found out one very useful thing at any rate, and got home alive, and that is more than most can say who have had words with the likes of Smaug. It may be a mercy and a blessing yet to know of the bare patch in the old Worm's diamond waistcoat."

That turned the conversation, and they all began discussing dragon-slayings historical, dubious, and mythical, and the various sorts of stabs and jabs and undercuts, and the different arts devices and stratagems by which they had been accomplished. The general opinion was that catching a dragon napping was not as easy as it sounded, and the attempt to stick one or prod one asleep was more likely to end in disaster than a bold frontal attack. All the while they talked the thrush listened, till at last when the stars began to peep forth, it silently spread its wings and flew away. And all the while they talked and the shadows lengthened Bilbo became more and more unhappy and his foreboding grew.

At last he interrupted them. "I am sure we are very unsafe here," he said, "and I don't see the point of sitting here. The dragon has withered all the pleasant green, and anyway the night has come and it is cold. But I feel it in my bones that this place will be attacked again. Smaug knows now how I came down to his hall, and you can trust him to guess where the other end of the tunnel is. He will break all this side of the Mountain to bits, if necessary, to stop up our entrance, and if we are smashed with it the better he will like it."

"You are very gloomy, Mr Baggins!" said Thorin. "Why

has not Smaug blocked the lower end, then, if he is so eager to keep us out? He has not, or we should have heard him."

"I don't know, I don't know—because at first he wanted to try and lure me in again, I suppose, and now perhaps because he is waiting till after tonight's hunt, or because he does not want to damage his bedroom if he can help it—but I wish you would not argue. Smaug will be coming out at any minute now, and our only hope is to get well in the tunnel and shut the door."

He seemed so much in earnest that the dwarves at last did as he said, though they delayed shutting the door—it seemed a desperate plan, for no one knew whether or how they could get it open again from the inside, and the thought of being shut in a place from which the only way out led through the dragon's lair was not one they liked. Also everything seemed quite quiet, both outside and down the tunnel. So for a long-ish while they sat inside not far down from the half-open door and went on talking.

The talk turned to the dragon's wicked words about the dwarves. Bilbo wished he had never heard them, or at least that he could feel quite certain that the dwarves now were ab-solutely honest when they declared that they had never thought at all about what would happen after the treasure had been won. "We knew it would be a desperate venture," said Thorin, "and we know that still; and I still think that when we have won it will be time enough to think what to do about it. As for your share, Mr Baggins, I assure you we are more than grate-ful and you shall choose your own fourteenth, as soon as we have anything to divide. I am sorry if you are worried about transport, and I admit the difficulties are great—the lands have not become less wild with the passing of time, rather the reverse—but we will do whatever we can for you, and take our share of the cost when the time comes. Believe me or not as you like!"

From that the talk turned to the great hoard itself and to the things that Thorin and Balin remembered. They wondered if they were still lying there unharmed in the hall below: the spears that were made for the armies of the great King Bladorthin (long since dead), each had a thrice-forged head and their shafts were inlaid with cunning gold, but they were never delivered or paid for; shields made for warriors long dead; the great golden cup of Thror, two-handed, hammered and carven with birds and flowers whose eyes and petals were of jewels; coats of mail gilded and silvered and impenetrable; the necklace of Girion, Lord of Dale, made of five hundred emeralds green as grass, which he gave for the arming of his eldest son in a coat of dwarf-linked rings the like of which had never been made before, for it was wrought of pure silver to the power and strength of triple steel. But fairest of all was the great white gem, which the dwarves had found beneath the roots of the Mountain, the Heart of the Mountain, the Arkenstone of Thrain.

"The Arkenstone! The Arkenstone!" murmured Thorin in the dark, half dreaming with his chin upon his knees. "It was like a globe with a thousand facets; it shone like silver in the firelight, like water in the sun, like snow under the stars, like rain upon the Moon!"

But the enchanted desire of the hoard had fallen from Bilbo. All through their talk he was only half listening to them. He sat nearest to the door with one ear cocked for any beginnings of a sound without, his other was alert for echoes beyond the murmurs of the dwarves, for any whisper of a movement from far below.

Darkness grew deeper and he grew ever more uneasy. "Shut the door!" he begged them, "I fear that dragon in my marrow. I like this silence far less than the uproar of last night. Shut the door before it is too late!"

Something in his voice gave the dwarves an uncomfortable feeling. Slowly Thorin shook off his dreams and getting up he kicked away the stone that wedged the door. Then they thrust upon it, and it closed with a snap and a clang. No trace of a keyhole was there left on the inside. They were shut in the Mountain!

And not a moment too soon. They had hardly gone any distance down the tunnel when a blow smote the side of the Mountain like the crash of battering-rams made of forest oaks and swung by giants. The rock boomed, the walls cracked and stones fell from the roof on their heads. What would have happened if the door had still been open I don't like to think. They fled further down the tunnel glad to be still alive, while behind them outside they heard the roar and rumble of Smaug's fury. He was breaking rocks to pieces, smashing wall and cliff with the lashings of his huge tail, till their little lofty camping ground, the scorched grass, the thrush's stone, the snail-covered walls, the narrow ledge, and all disappeared in a jumble of smithereens, and an avalanche of splintered stones fell over the cliff into the valley below.

Smaug had left his lair in silent stealth, quietly soared into the air, and then floated heavy and slow in the dark like a monstrous crow, down the wind towards the west of the Mountain, in the hopes of catching unawares something or somebody there, and of spying the outlet to the passage which the thief had used. This was the outburst of his wrath when he could find nobody and see nothing, even where he guessed the outlet must actually be.

After he had left off his rage in this way he felt better and he thought in his heart that he would not be troubled again from that direction. In the meanwhile he had further vengeance to take. "Barrel-rider!" he snorted. "Your feet came from the waterside and up the water you came without a doubt. I don't know your smell, but if you are not one of those men of the Lake, you had their help. They shall see me and remember who is the real King under the Mountain!"

He rose in fire and went away south towards the Running River.

*Chapter XIII*

# NOT AT HOME

In the meanwhile, the dwarves sat in darkness, and utter silence fell about them. Little they ate and little they spoke. They could not count the passing of time; and they scarcely dared to move, for the whisper of their voices echoed and rustled in the tunnel. If they dozed, they woke still to darkness and to silence going on unbroken. At last after days and days of waiting, as it seemed, when they were becoming choked and dazed for want of air, they could bear it no longer. They would almost have welcomed sounds from below of the dragon's return. In the silence they feared some cunning devilry of his, but they could not sit there for ever.

Thorin spoke: "Let us try the door!" he said. "I must feel the wind on my face soon or die. I think I would rather be smashed by Smaug in the open than suffocate in here!" So several of the dwarves got up and groped back to where the door had been. But they found that the upper end of the tunnel had been shattered and blocked with broken rock. Neither key nor the magic it had once obeyed would ever open that door again.

"We are trapped!" they groaned. "This is the end. We shall die here."

But somehow, just when the dwarves were most despairing, Bilbo felt a strange lightening of the heart, as if a heavy weight had gone from under his waistcoat.

"Come, come!" he said. " 'While there's life there's hope!' as my father used to say, and 'Third time pays for all.' I am going *down* the tunnel once again. I have been that way twice, when I knew there was a dragon at the other end, so I will risk a third visit when I am no longer sure. Anyway the only way out is down. And I think this time you had better all come with me."

In desperation they agreed, and Thorin was the first to go forward by Bilbo's side.

"Now do be careful!" whispered the hobbit, "and as quiet as you can be! There may be no Smaug at the bottom, but then again there may be. Don't let us take any unnecessary risks!"

Down, down they went. The dwarves could not, of course, compare with the hobbit in real stealth, and they made a deal of puffing and shuffling which echoes magnified alarmingly; but though every now and again Bilbo in fear stopped and listened, not a sound stirred below. Near the bottom, as well as he could judge, Bilbo slipped on his ring and went ahead. But he did not need it: the darkness was complete, and they were all invisible, ring or no ring. In fact so black was it that the hobbit came to the opening unexpectedly, put his hand on air, stumbled forward, and rolled headlong into the hall!

There he lay face downwards on the floor and did not dare to get up, or hardly even to breathe. But nothing moved. There was not a gleam of light—unless, as it seemed to him, when at last he slowly raised his head, there was a pale white glint, above him and far off in the gloom. But certainly it was not a spark of dragon-fire, though the worm-stench was heavy in the place, and the taste of vapour was on his tongue.

At length Mr Baggins could bear it no longer. "Confound you, Smaug, you worm!" he squeaked aloud. "Stop playing hide-and-seek! Give me a light, and then eat me, if you can catch me!"

Faint echoes ran round the unseen hall, but there was no answer.

Bilbo got up, and found that he did not know in what direction to turn.

"Now I wonder what on earth Smaug is playing at," he said. "He is not at home today (or tonight, or whatever it is), I do believe. If Oin and Gloin have not lost their tinder-boxes, perhaps we can make a little light, and have a look round before the luck turns."

"Light!" he cried. "Can anybody make a light?"

The dwarves, of course, were very alarmed when Bilbo fell forward down the step with a bump into the hall, and they sat huddled just where he had left them at the end of the tunnel.

"Sh! sh!" they hissed, when they heard his voice; and though that helped the hobbit to find out where they were, it was some time before he could get anything else out of them. But in the end, when Bilbo actually began to stamp on the floor, and screamed out "light!" at the top of his shrill voice, Thorin gave way, and Oin and Gloin were sent back to their bundles at the top of the tunnel.

After a while a twinkling gleam showed them returning, Oin with a small pine-torch alight in his hand, and Gloin with a bundle of others under his arm. Quickly Bilbo trotted to the door and took the torch; but he could not persuade the dwarves to light the others or to come and join him yet. As Thorin carefully explained, Mr Baggins was still officially their expert burglar and investigator. If he liked to risk a light, that was his affair. They would wait in the tunnel for his report. So they sat near the door and watched.

They saw the little dark shape of the hobbit start across the floor holding his tiny light aloft. Every now and again, while he was still near enough, they caught a glint and a tinkle as he stumbled on some golden thing. The light grew smaller as he wandered away into the vast hall; then it began to rise dancing into the air. Bilbo was climbing the great mound of treasure. Soon he stood upon the top, and still went on. Then they saw him halt and stoop for a moment; but they did not know the reason.

It was the Arkenstone, the Heart of the Mountain. So Bilbo guessed from Thorin's description; but indeed there could not be two such gems, even in so marvellous a hoard, even in all the world. Ever as he climbed, the same white gleam had shone before him and drawn his feet towards it. Slowly it grew to a little globe of pallid light. Now as he came near, it was tinged with a flickering sparkle of many colours at the surface, reflected and splintered from the wavering light of his torch. At last he looked down upon it, and he caught his breath. The great jewel shone before his feet of its own inner light, and yet, cut and fashioned by the dwarves, who had dug it from the heart of the mountain long ago, it took all light that fell upon it and changed it into ten thousand sparks of white radiance shot with glints of the rainbow.

Suddenly Bilbo's arm went towards it drawn by its enchantment. His small hand would not close about it, for it was a large and heavy gem; but he lifted it, shut his eyes, and put it in his deepest pocket.

"Now I am a burglar indeed!" thought he. "But I suppose I must tell the dwarves about it—some time. They did say I could pick and choose my own share; and I think I would choose this, if they took all the rest!" All the same he had an uncomfortable feeling that the picking and choosing had not

really been meant to include this marvellous gem, and that
trouble would yet come of it.

Now he went on again. Down the other side of the great
mound he climbed, and the spark of his torch vanished from
the sight of the watching dwarves. But soon they saw it far
away in the distance again. Bilbo was crossing the floor of
the hall.

He went on, until he came to the great doors at the further
side, and there a draught of air refreshed him, but it almost
puffed out his light. He peeped timidly through, and caught a
glimpse of great passages and of the dim beginnings of wide
stairs going up into the gloom. And still there was no sight
nor sound of Smaug. He was just going to turn and go back
when a black shape swooped at him, and brushed his face. He
squeaked and started, stumbled backwards and fell. His torch
dropped head downwards and went out!

"Only a bat, I suppose and hope!" he said miserably. "But
now what am I to do? Which is East, South, North, or West?"

"Thorin! Balin! Oin! Gloin! Fili! Kili!" he cried as loud as
he could—it seemed a thin little noise in the wide blackness.
"The light's gone out! Someone come and find me and help
me!" For the moment his courage had failed altogether.

Faintly the dwarves heard his small cries, though the only
word they could catch was "help!"

"Now what on earth or under it has happened?" said
Thorin. "Certainly not the dragon, or he would not go on
squeaking."

They waited a moment or two, and still there were no
dragon-noises, no sound at all in fact but Bilbo's distant
voice. "Come, one of you, get another light or two!" Thorin
ordered. "It seems we have got to go and help our burglar."

"It is about our turn to help," said Balin, "and I am quite
willing to go. Anyway I expect it is safe for the moment."

Gloin lit several more torches, and then they all crept out, one by one, and went along the wall as hurriedly as they could. It was not long before they met Bilbo himself coming back towards them. His wits had quickly returned as soon as he saw the twinkle of their lights.

"Only a bat and a dropped torch, nothing worse!" he said in answer to their questions. Though they were much relieved, they were inclined to be grumpy at being frightened for nothing; but what they would have said, if he had told them at that moment about the Arkenstone, I don't know. The mere fleeting glimpses of treasure which they had caught as they went along had rekindled all the fire of their dwarvish hearts; and when the heart of a dwarf, even the most respectable, is wakened by gold and by jewels, he grows suddenly bold, and he may become fierce.

The dwarves indeed no longer needed any urging. All were now eager to explore the hall while they had the chance, and willing to believe that, for the present, Smaug was away from home. Each now gripped a lighted torch; and as they gazed, first on one side and then on another, they forgot fear and even caution. They spoke aloud, and cried out to one another, as they lifted old treasures from the mound or from the wall and held them in the light, caressing and fingering them.

Fili and Kili were almost in merry mood, and finding still hanging there many golden harps strung with silver they took them and struck them; and being magical (and also untouched by the dragon, who had small interest in music) they were still in tune. The dark hall was filled with a melody that had long been silent. But most of the dwarves were more practical: they gathered gems and stuffed their pockets, and let what they could not carry fall back through their fingers with a sigh. Thorin was not least among these; but always he searched from side to side for something which he could no find. It was the Arkenstone; but he spoke of it yet to no one.

Now the dwarves took down mail and weapons from the walls, and armed themselves. Royal indeed did Thorin look clad in a coat of gold-plated rings, with a silver-hafted axe in a belt crusted with scarlet stones.

"Mr Baggins!" he cried. "Here is the first payment of your reward! Cast off your old coat and put on this!"

With that he put on Bilbo a small coat of mail, wrought for some young elf-prince long ago. It was of silver-steel, which the elves call *mithril*, and with it went a belt of pearls and crystals. A light helm of figured leather strengthened beneath with hoops of steel, and studded about the brim with white gems, was set upon the hobbit's head.

"I feel magnificent," he thought; "but I expect I look rather absurd. How they would laugh on the Hill at home! Still I wish there was a looking-glass handy!"

All the same Mr Baggins kept his head more clear of the bewitchment of the hoard than the dwarves did. Long before the dwarves were tired of examining the treasures, he became weary of it and sat down on the floor; and he began to wonder nervously what the end of it all would be. "I would give a good many of these precious goblets," he thought, "for a drink of something cheering out of one of Beorn's wooden bowls!"

"Thorin!" he cried aloud. "What next? We are armed, but what good has any armour ever been before against Smaug the Dreadful? This treasure is not yet won back. We are not looking for gold yet, but for a way of escape; and we have tempted luck too long!"

"You speak the truth!" answered Thorin, recovering his wits. "Let us go! I will guide you. Not in a thousand years should I forget the ways of this palace." Then he hailed the others, and they gathered together, and holding their torches above their heads they passed through the gaping doors, not without many a backward glance of longing.

Their glittering mail they had covered again with their old cloaks and their bright helms with their tattered hoods, and one by one they walked behind Thorin, a line of little lights in the darkness that halted often, listening in fear once more for any rumour of the dragon's coming.

Though all the old adornments were long mouldered or destroyed, and though all was befouled and blasted with the comings and goings of the monster, Thorin knew every passage and every turn. They climbed long stairs, and turned and went down wide echoing ways, and turned again and climbed yet more stairs, and yet more stairs again. These were smooth, cut out of the living rock broad and fair; and up, up, the dwarves went, and they met no sign of any living thing, only furtive shadows that fled from the approach of their torches fluttering in the draughts.

The steps were not made, all the same, for hobbit-legs, and Bilbo was just feeling that he could go on no longer, when suddenly the roof sprang high and far beyond the reach of their torch-light. A white glimmer could be seen coming through some opening far above, and the air smelt sweeter. Before them light came dimly through great doors, that hung twisted on their hinges and half burnt.

"This is the great chamber of Thror," said Thorin; "the hall of feasting and of council. Not far off now is the Front Gate."

They passed through the ruined chamber. Tables were rotting there; chairs and benches were lying there overturned, charred and decaying. Skulls and bones were upon the floor among flagons and bowls and broken drinking-horns and dust. As they came through yet more doors at the further end, a sound of water fell upon their ears, and the grey light grew suddenly more full.

"There is the birth of the Running River," said Thorin. "From here it hastens to the Gate. Let us follow it!"

Out of a dark opening in a wall of rock there issued a boiling water, and it flowed swirling in a narrow channel carved and made straight and deep by the cunning of ancient hands. Beside it ran a stone-paved road, wide enough for many men abreast. Swiftly along this they ran, and round a wide-sweeping turn—and behold! before them stood the broad light of day. In front there rose a tall arch, still showing the fragments of old carven work within, worn and splintered and blackened though it was. A misty sun sent its pale light between the arms of the Mountain, and beams of gold fell on the pavement at the threshold.

A whirl of bats frightened from slumber by their smoking torches flurried over them; as they sprang forward their feet slithered on stones rubbed smooth and slimed by the passing of the dragon. Now before them the water fell noisily outward and foamed down towards the valley. They flung their pale torches to the ground, and stood gazing out with dazzled eyes. They were come to the Front Gate, and were looking out upon Dale.

"Well!" said Bilbo, "I never expected to be looking *out* of this door. And I never expected to be so pleased to see the sun again, and to feel the wind on my face. But, ow! this wind is cold!"

It was. A bitter easterly breeze blew with a threat of oncoming winter. It swirled over and round the arms of the Mountain into the valley, and sighed among the rocks. After their long time in the stewing depths of the dragon-haunted caverns, they shivered in the sun.

Suddenly Bilbo realized that he was not only tired but also

very hungry indeed. "It seems to be late morning," he said, "and so I suppose it is more or less breakfast-time—if there is any breakfast to have. But I don't feel that Smaug's front doorstep is the safest place for a meal. Do let's go somewhere where we can sit quiet for a bit!"

"Quite right!" said Balin. "And I think I know which way we should go: we ought to make for the old look-out post at the South-West corner of the Mountain."

"How far is that?" asked the hobbit.

"Five hours march, I should think. It will be rough going. The road from the Gate along the left edge of the stream seems all broken up. But look down there! The river loops suddenly east across Dale in front of the ruined town. At that point there was once a bridge, leading to steep stairs that climbed up the right bank, and so to a road running towards Ravenhill. There is (or was) a path that left the road and climbed up to the post. A hard climb, too, even if the old steps are still there."

"Dear me!" grumbled the hobbit. "More walking and more climbing without breakfast! I wonder how many breakfasts, and other meals, we have missed inside that nasty clockless, timeless hole?"

As a matter of fact two nights and the day between had gone by (and not altogether without food) since the dragon smashed the magic door, but Bilbo had quite lost count, and it might have been one night or a week of nights for all he could tell.

"Come, come!" said Thorin laughing—his spirits had begun to rise again, and he rattled the precious stones in his pockets. "Don't call my palace a nasty hole! You wait till it has been cleaned and redecorated!"

"That won't be till Smaug's dead," said Bilbo glumly. "In the meanwhile where is he? I would give a good breakfast to

know. I hope he is not up on the Mountain looking down
at us!"

That idea disturbed the dwarves mightily, and they quickly
decided that Bilbo and Balin were right.

"We must move away from here," said Dori. "I feel as if his
eyes were on the back of my head."

"It's a cold lonesome place," said Bombur. "There may be
drink, but I see no sign of food. A dragon would always be
hungry in such parts."

"Come on! Come on!" cried the others. "Let us follow
Balin's path!"

Under the rocky wall to the right there was no path, so on
they trudged among the stones on the left side of the river,
and the emptiness and desolation soon sobered even Thorin
again. The bridge that Balin had spoken of they found long
fallen, and most of its stones were now only boulders in the
shallow noisy stream; but they forded the water without
much difficulty, and found the ancient steps, and climbed the
high bank. After going a short way they struck the old road,
and before long came to a deep dell sheltered among the
rocks; there they rested for a while and had such a breakfast
as they could, chiefly *cram* and water. (If you want to know
what *cram* is, I can only say that I don't know the recipe; but it
is biscuitish, keeps good indefinitely, is supposed to be sus-
taining, and is certainly not entertaining, being in fact very
uninteresting except as a chewing exercise. It was made by
the Lake-men for long journeys.)

After that they went on again; and now the road struck
westwards and left the river, and the great shoulder of the
south-pointing mountain-spur drew ever nearer. At length
they reached the hill path. It scrambled steeply up, and they
plodded slowly one behind the other, till at last in the late

afternoon they came to the top of the ridge and saw the wintry sun going downwards to the West.

Here they found a flat place without a wall on three sides, but backed to the North by a rocky face in which there was an opening like a door. From that door there was a wide view East and South and West.

"Here," said Balin, "in the old days we used always to keep watchmen, and that door behind leads into a rock-hewn chamber that was made here as a guardroom. There were several places like it round the Mountain. But there seemed small need for watching in the days of our prosperity, and the guards were made over comfortable, perhaps—otherwise we might have had longer warning of the coming of the dragon, and things might have been different. Still, here we can now lie hid and sheltered for a while, and can see much without being seen."

"Not much use, if we have been seen coming here," said Dori, who was always looking up towards the Mountain's peak, as if he expected to see Smaug perched there like a bird on a steeple.

"We must take our chance of that," said Thorin. "We can go no further to-day."

"Hear, hear!" cried Bilbo, and flung himself on the ground. In the rock-chamber there would have been room for a hundred, and there was a small chamber further in, more removed from the cold outside. It was quite deserted; not even wild animals seemed to have used it in all the days of Smaug's dominion. There they laid their burdens; and some threw themselves down at once and slept, but the others sat near the outer door and discussed their plans. In all their talk they came perpetually back to one thing: where was Smaug? They looked West and there was nothing, and East there was nothing, and in the South there was no sign of the dragon, but there was a gathering of very many birds. At that they gazed and wondered; but they were no nearer understanding it, when the first cold stars came out.

## Chapter XIV

# FIRE AND WATER

Now if you wish, like the dwarves, to hear news of Smaug, you must go back again to the evening when he smashed the door and flew off in rage, two days before.

The men of the lake-town Esgaroth were mostly indoors, for the breeze was from the black East and chill, but a few were walking on the quays, and watching, as they were fond of doing, the stars shine out from the smooth patches of the lake as they opened in the sky. From their town the Lonely Mountain was mostly screened by the low hills at the far end of the lake, through a gap in which the Running River came down from the North. Only its high peak could they see in clear weather, and they looked seldom at it, for it was ominous and drear even in the light of morning. Now it was lost and gone, blotted in the dark.

Suddenly it flickered back to view; a brief glow touched it and faded.

"Look!" said one. "The lights again! Last night the watchmen saw them start and fade from midnight until dawn. Something is happening up there."

"Perhaps the King under the Mountain is forging gold," said another. "It is long since he went North. It is time the songs began to prove themselves again."

"Which king?" said another with a grim voice. "As like as

not it is the marauding fire of the Dragon, the only king under
the Mountain we have ever known."

"You are always foreboding gloomy things!" said the
others. "Anything from floods to poisoned fish. Think of
something cheerful!"

Then suddenly a great light appeared in the low place in
the hills and the northern end of the lake turned golden. "The
King beneath the Mountain!" they shouted. "His wealth is
like the Sun, his silver like a fountain, his rivers golden run!
The river is running gold from the Mountain!" they cried, and
everywhere windows were opening and feet were hurrying.

There was once more a tremendous excitement and enthusiasm. But the grim-voiced fellow ran hotfoot to the Master.
"The dragon is coming or I am a fool!" he cried. "Cut the
bridges! To arms! To arms!"

Then warning trumpets were suddenly sounded, and echoed
along the rocky shores. The cheering stopped and the joy was
turned to dread. So it was that the dragon did not find them
quite unprepared.

Before long, so great was his speed, they could see him as a
spark of fire rushing towards them and growing ever huger
and more bright, and not the most foolish doubted that the
prophecies had gone rather wrong. Still they had a little time.
Every vessel in the town was filled with water, every warrior
was armed, every arrow and dart was ready, and the bridge to
the land was thrown down and destroyed, before the roar of
Smaug's terrible approach grew loud, and the lake rippled red
as fire beneath the awful beating of his wings.

Amid shrieks and wailing and the shouts of men he came
over them, swept towards the bridge and was foiled! The
bridge was gone, and his enemies were on an island in deep
water—too deep and dark and cool for his liking. If he plunged
into it, a vapour and a steam would arise enough to cover all

the land with a mist for days; but the lake was mightier than he, it would quench him before he could pass through.

Roaring he swept back over the town. A hail of dark arrows leaped up and snapped and rattled on his scales and jewels, and their shafts fell back kindled by his breath burning and hissing into the lake. No fireworks you ever imagined equalled the sights that night. At the twanging of the bows and the shrilling of the trumpets the dragon's wrath blazed to its height, till he was blind and mad with it. No one had dared to give battle to him for many an age; nor would they have dared now, if it had not been for the grim-voiced man (Bard was his name), who ran to and fro cheering on the archers and urging the Master to order them to fight to the last arrow.

Fire leaped from the dragon's jaws. He circled for a while high in the air above them lighting all the lake; the trees by the shores shone like copper and like blood with leaping shadows of dense black at their feet. Then down he swooped straight through the arrow-storm, reckless in his rage, taking no heed to turn his scaly sides towards his foes, seeking only to set their town ablaze.

Fire leaped from thatched roofs and wooden beam-ends as he hurtled down and past and round again, though all had been drenched with water before he came. Once more water was flung by a hundred hands wherever a spark appeared. Back swirled the dragon. A sweep of his tail and the roof of the Great House crumbled and smashed down. Flames unquenchable sprang high into the night. Another swoop and another, and another house and then another sprang afire and fell; and still no arrow hindered Smaug or hurt him more than a fly from the marshes.

Already men were jumping into the water on every side. Women and children were being huddled into laden boats in the market-pool. Weapons were flung down. There was mourning and weeping, where but a little time ago the old songs of mirth to come had been sung about the dwarves. Now men cursed their names. The Master himself was turning to his great gilded boat, hoping to row away in the confusion and save himself. Soon all the town would be deserted and burned down to the surface of the lake.

That was the dragon's hope. They could all get into boats for all he cared. There he could have fine sport hunting them, or they could stop till they starved. Let them try to get to land and he would be ready. Soon he would set all the shoreland woods ablaze and wither every field and pasture. Just now he was enjoying the sport of town-baiting more than he had enjoyed anything for years.

But there was still a company of archers that held their ground among the burning houses. Their captain was Bard, grim-voiced and grim-faced, whose friends had accused him of prophesying floods and poisoned fish, though they knew his worth and courage. He was a descendant in long line of Girion, Lord of Dale, whose wife and child had escaped down the Running River from the ruin long ago. Now he shot with a great yew bow, till all his arrows but one were spent. The flames were near him. His companions were leaving him. He bent his bow for the last time.

Suddenly out of the dark something fluttered to his shoulder. He started—but it was only an old thrush. Unafraid it perched by his ear and it brought him news. Marvelling he found he could understand its tongue, for he was of the race of Dale.

"Wait! Wait!" it said to him. "The moon is rising. Look for the hollow of the left breast as he flies and turns above you!" And while Bard paused in wonder it told him of tidings up in the Mountain and of all that it had heard.

Then Bard drew his bow-string to his ear. The dragon was circling back, flying low, and as he came the moon rose above the eastern shore and silvered his great wings.

"Arrow!" said the bowman. "Black arrow! I have saved you to the last. You have never failed me and always I have recovered you. I had you from my father and he from of old. If ever you came from the forges of the true king under the Mountain, go now and speed well!"

The dragon swooped once more lower than ever, and as he turned and dived down his belly glittered white with sparkling fires of gems in the moon—but not in one place. The great bow twanged. The black arrow sped straight from the string, straight for the hollow by the left breast where the foreleg was flung wide. In it smote and vanished, barb, shaft and feather, so fierce was its flight. With a shriek that deafened men, felled trees and split stone, Smaug shot spouting into the air, turned over and crashed down from on high in ruin.

Full on the town he fell. His last throes splintered it to sparks and gledes. The lake roared in. A vast steam leaped up, white in the sudden dark under the moon. There was a hiss, a gushing whirl, and then silence. And that was the end of Smaug and Esgaroth, but not of Bard.

The waxing moon rose higher and higher and the wind grew loud and cold. It twisted the white fog into bending pillars and hurrying clouds and drove it off to the West to scatter in tattered shreds over the marshes before Mirkwood. Then the many boats could be seen dotted dark on the surface of the lake, and down the wind came the voices of the people of Esgaroth lamenting their lost town and goods and ruined houses. But they had really much to be thankful for, had they thought of it, though it could hardly be expected that they should just then: three quarters of the people of the town had at least escaped alive; their woods and fields and pastures and cattle and most of their boats remained undamaged; and the dragon was dead. What that meant they had not yet realized.

They gathered in mournful crowds upon the western shores, shivering in the cold wind, and their first complaints and anger were against the Master, who had left the town so soon, while some were still willing to defend it.

"He may have a good head for business—especially his own business," some murmured, "but he is no good when anything serious happens!" And they praised the courage of Bard and his last mighty shot. "If only he had not been killed," they all said, "we would make him a king. Bard the Dragon-shooter of the line of Girion! Alas that he is lost!"

And in the very midst of their talk a tall figure stepped from the shadows. He was drenched with water, his black hair hung wet over his face and shoulders, and a fierce light was in his eyes.

"Bard is not lost!" he cried. "He dived from Esgaroth, when the enemy was slain. I am Bard, of the line of Girion; I am the slayer of the dragon!"

"King Bard! King Bard!" they shouted; but the Master ground his chattering teeth.

"Girion was lord of Dale, not king of Esgaroth," he said. "In the Lake-town we have always elected masters from among the old and wise, and have not endured the rule of mere fighting men. Let 'King Bard' go back to his own kingdom—Dale is now freed by his valour, and nothing hinders his return. And any that wish can go with him, if they prefer the cold stones under the shadow of the Mountain to the green shores of the lake. The wise will stay here and hope to rebuild our town, and enjoy again in time its peace and riches."

"We will have King Bard!" the people near at hand shouted
in reply. "We have had enough of the old men and the money-
counters!" And people further off took up the cry: "Up the
Bowman, and down with Moneybags," till the clamour echoed
along the shore.

"I am the last man to undervalue Bard the Bowman," said
the Master warily (for Bard now stood close beside him). "He
has tonight earned an eminent place in the roll of the benefac-
tors of our town; and he is worthy of many imperishable
songs. But, why O People?"—and here the Master rose to his
feet and spoke very loud and clear—"Why do I get all your
blame? For what fault am I to be deposed? Who aroused the
dragon from his slumber, I might ask? Who obtained of us
rich gifts and ample help, and led us to believe that old songs
could come true? Who played on our soft hearts and our
pleasant fancies? What sort of gold have they sent down the
river to reward us? Dragon-fire and ruin! From whom should
we claim the recompense of our damage, and aid for our
widows and orphans?"

As you see, the Master had not got his position for nothing.
The result of his words was that for the moment the people
quite forgot their idea of a new king, and turned their angry
thoughts towards Thorin and his company. Wild and bitter
words were shouted from many sides; and some of those who
had before sung the old songs loudest, were now heard as
loudly crying that the dwarves had stirred the dragon up
against them deliberately!

"Fools!" said Bard. "Why waste words and wrath on those
unhappy creatures? Doubtless they perished first in fire, before Smaug came to us." Then even as he was speaking, the
thought came into his heart of the fabled treasure of the
Mountain lying without guard or owner, and he fell suddenly

silent. He thought of the Master's words, and of Dale rebuilt, and filled with golden bells, if he could but find the men.

At length he spoke again: "This is no time for angry words, Master, or for considering weighty plans of change. There is work to do. I serve you still—though after a while I may think again of your words and go North with any that will fol-low me."

Then he strode off to help in the ordering of the camps and in the care of the sick and the wounded. But the Master scowled at his back as he went, and remained sitting on the ground. He thought much but said little, unless it was to call loudly for men to bring him fire and food.

Now everywhere Bard went he found talk running like fire among the people concerning the vast treasure that was now unguarded. Men spoke of the recompense for all their harm that they would soon get from it, and wealth over and to spare with which to buy rich things from the South; and it cheered them greatly in their plight. That was as well, for the night was bitter and miserable. Shelters could be contrived for few (the Master had one) and there was little food (even the Master went short). Many took ill of wet and cold and sorrow that night, and afterwards died, who had escaped uninjured from the ruin of the town; and in the days that followed there was much sickness and great hunger.

Meanwhile Bard took the lead, and ordered things as he wished, though always in the Master's name, and he had a hard task to govern the people and direct the preparations for their protection and housing. Probably most of them would have perished in the winter that now hurried after autumn, if help had not been to hand. But help came swiftly; for Bard at once had speedy messengers sent up the river to the Forest to ask the aid of the King of the Elves of the Wood, and these messengers had found a host already on the move, although it was then only the third day after the fall of Smaug.

The Elvenking had received news from his own messengers and from the birds that loved his folk, and already knew much of what had happened. Very great indeed was the commotion among all things with wings that dwelt on the borders of the Desolation of the Dragon. The air was filled with circling flocks, and their swift-flying messengers flew here and there across the sky. Above the borders of the Forest there was whistling, crying and piping. Far over Mirkwood tidings spread: "Smaug is dead!" Leaves rustled and startled ears were lifted. Even before the Elvenking rode forth the news had passed west right to the pinewoods of the Misty Mountains; Beorn had heard it in his wooden house, and the goblins were at council in their caves.

"That will be the last we shall hear of Thorin Oakenshield, I fear," said the king. "He would have done better to have remained my guest. It is an ill wind, all the same," he added, "that blows no one any good." For he too had not forgotten the legend of the wealth of Thror. So it was that Bard's messengers found him now marching with many spearmen and bowmen; and crows were gathered thick above him, for they thought that war was awakening again, such as had not been in those parts for a long age.

But the king, when he received the prayers of Bard, had pity, for he was the lord of a good and kindly people; so turning his march, which had at first been direct towards the Mountain, he hastened now down the river to the Long Lake. He had not boats or rafts enough for his host, and they were forced to go the slower way by foot; but great store of goods he sent ahead by water. Still elves are lightfooted, and though they were not in these days much used to the marches and the treacherous lands between the Forest and the Lake, their

going was swift. Only five days after the death of the dragon
they came upon the shores and looked on the ruins of the
town. Their welcome was good, as may be expected, and the
men and their Master were ready to make any bargain for
the future in return for the Elvenking's aid.

Their plans were soon made. With the women and the chil
dren, the old and the unfit, the Master remained behind; and
with him were some men of crafts and many skilled elves;
and they busied themselves felling trees, and collecting the
timber sent down from the Forest. Then they set about raising
many huts by the shore against the oncoming winter; and also
under the Master's direction they began the planning of a new
town, designed more fair and large even than before, but not
in the same place. They removed northward higher up the
shore; for ever after they had a dread of the water where the
dragon lay. He would never again return to his golden bed,
but was stretched cold as stone, twisted upon the floor of the
shallows. There for ages his huge bones could be seen in calm
weather amid the ruined piles of the old town. But few dared
to cross the cursed spot, and none dared to dive into the shivering water or recover the precious stones that fell from his rotting carcase.

But all the men of arms who were still able, and the most of
the Elvenking's array, got ready to march north to the Mountain. It was thus that in eleven days from the ruin of the town
the head of their host passed the rock-gates at the end of the
lake and came into the desolate lands.

*Chapter XV*

# THE GATHERING
# OF THE CLOUDS

Now we will return to Bilbo and the dwarves. All night one of them had watched, but when morning came they had not heard or seen any sign of danger. But ever more thickly the birds were gathering. Their companies came flying from the South; and the crows that still lived about the Mountain were wheeling and crying unceasingly above.

"Something strange is happening," said Thorin. "The time has gone for the autumn wanderings; and these are birds that dwell always in the land; there are starlings and flocks of finches; and far off there are many carrion birds as if a battle were afoot!"

Suddenly Bilbo pointed: "There is that old thrush again!" he cried. "He seems to have escaped, when Smaug smashed the mountain-side, but I don't suppose the snails have!"

Sure enough the old thrush was there, and as Bilbo pointed, he flew towards them and perched on a stone near by. Then he fluttered his wings and sang; then he cocked his head on one side, as if to listen; and again he sang, and again he listened.

"I believe he is trying to tell us something," said Balin; "but I cannot follow the speech of such birds, it is very quick and difficult. Can you make it out, Baggins?"

"Not very well," said Bilbo (as a matter of fact, he could

make nothing of it at all); "but the old fellow seems very excited."

"I only wish he was a raven!" said Balin.

"I thought you did not like them! You seemed very shy of them, when we came this way before."

"Those were crows! And nasty suspicious-looking creatures at that, and rude as well. You must have heard the ugly names they were calling after us. But the ravens are different. There used to be great friendship between them and the people of Thror; and they often brought us secret news, and were rewarded with such bright things as they coveted to hide in their dwellings.

"They live many a year, and their memories are long, and they hand on their wisdom to their children. I knew many among the ravens of the rocks when I was a dwarf-lad. This very height was once named Ravenhill, because there was a wise and famous pair, old Carc and his wife, that lived here above the guard-chamber. But I don't suppose that any of that ancient breed linger here now."

No sooner had he finished speaking than the old thrush gave a loud call, and immediately flew away.

"We may not understand him, but that old bird understands us, I am sure," said Balin. "Keep watch now, and see what happens!"

Before long there was a fluttering of wings, and back came the thrush; and with him came a most decrepit old bird. He was getting blind, he could hardly fly, and the top of his head was bald. He was an aged raven of great size. He alighted stiffly on the ground before them, slowly flapped his wings, and bobbed towards Thorin.

"O Thorin son of Thrain, and Balin son of Fundin," he croaked (and Bilbo could understand what he said, for he used ordinary language and not bird-speech). "I am Roäc son of Carc. Carc is dead, but he was well known to you once. It is a hundred years and three and fifty since I came out of the egg, but I do not forget what my father told me. Now I am the chief of the great ravens of the Mountain. We are few, but we remember still the king that was of old. Most of my people are abroad, for there are great tidings in the South—some are tidings of joy to you, and some you will not think so good.

"Behold! the birds are gathering back again to the Mountain and to Dale from South and East and West, for word has gone out that Smaug is dead!"

"Dead! Dead?" shouted the dwarves. "Dead! Then we have been in needless fear—and the treasure is ours!" They all sprang up and began to caper about for joy.

"Yes, dead," said Roäc. "The thrush, may his feathers never fall, saw him die, and we may trust his words. He saw him fall in battle with the men of Esgaroth the third night back from now at the rising of the moon."

It was some time before Thorin could bring the dwarves to be silent and listen to the raven's news. At length when he had told all the tale of the battle he went on:

"So much for joy, Thorin Oakenshield. You may go back to your halls in safety; all the treasure is yours—for the moment. But many are gathering hither beside the birds. The news of the death of the guardian has already gone far and wide, and the legend of the wealth of Thror has not lost in the telling during many years; many are eager for a share of the spoil. Already a host of the elves is on the way, and carrion birds are with them hoping for battle and slaughter. By the lake men murmur that their sorrows are due to the dwarves; for they are homeless and many have died, and Smaug has destroyed their town. They too think to find amends from your treasure, whether you are alive or dead.

"Your own wisdom must decide your course; but thirteen

is small remnant of the great folk of Durin that once dwelt here, and now are scattered far. If you will listen to my counsel, you will not trust the Master of the Lake-men, but rather him that shot the dragon with his bow. Bard is he, of the race of Dale, of the line of Girion; he is a grim man but true. We would see peace once more among dwarves and men and elves after the long desolation; but it may cost you dear in gold. I have spoken."

Then Thorin burst forth in anger: "Our thanks, Roäc Carc's son. You and your people shall not be forgotten. But none of our gold shall thieves take or the violent carry off while we are alive. If you would earn our thanks still more, bring us news of any that draw near. Also I would beg of you, if any of you are still young and strong of wing, that you would send messengers to our kin in the mountains of the North, both west from here and east, and tell them of our plight. But go specially to my cousin Dain in the Iron Hills, for he has many people well-armed, and dwells nearest to this place. Bid him hasten!"

"I will not say if this counsel be good or bad," croaked Roäc, "but I will do what can be done." Then off he slowly flew.

"Back now to the Mountain!" cried Thorin. "We have little time to lose."

"And little food to use!" cried Bilbo, always practical on such points. In any case he felt that the adventure was, properly speaking, over with the death of the dragon—in which he was much mistaken—and he would have given most of his share of the profits for the peaceful winding up of these affairs.

"Back to the Mountain!" cried the dwarves as if they had not heard him; so back he had to go with them.

\* \* \*

As you have heard some of the events already, you will see that the dwarves still had some days before them. They explored the caverns once more, and found, as they expected, that only the Front Gate remained open; all the other gates (except, of course, the small secret door) had long ago been broken and blocked by Smaug, and no sign of them remained. So now they began to labour hard in fortifying the main entrance, and in making a new path that led from it. Tools were to be found in plenty that the miners and quarriers and builders of old had used; and at such work the dwarves were still very skilled.

As they worked the ravens brought them constant tidings. In this way they learned that the Elvenking had turned aside to the Lake, and they still had a breathing space. Better still, they heard that three of their ponies had escaped and were wandering wild far down the banks of the Running River, not far from where the rest of their stores had been left. So while the others went on with their work, Fili and Kili were sent, guided by a raven, to find the ponies and bring back all they could.

They were four days gone, and by that time they knew that the joined armies of the Lake-men and the Elves were hurrying toward the Mountain. But now their hopes were higher; for they had food for some weeks with care—chiefly *cram*, of course, and they were very tired of it; but *cram* is much better than nothing—and already the gate was blocked with a wall of squared stones laid dry, but very thick and high, across the opening. There were holes in the wall through which they could see (or shoot), but no entrance. They climbed in or out with ladders, and hauled stuff up with ropes. For the issuing of the stream they had contrived a small low arch under the new wall; but near the entrance they had so altered the narrow bed that a wide pool stretched from the mountain-wall to the head of the fall over which the stream went towards Dale. Approach to the Gate was now only possible, without swimming, along a narrow ledge of the cliff, to the right as one looked outwards from the wall. The ponies they had brought only to the head of the steps above the old bridge, and unloading them there had bidden them return to their masters and sent them back riderless to the South.

There came a night when suddenly there were many lights as of fires and torches away south in Dale before them.

"They have come!" called Balin. "And their camp is very great. They must have come into the valley under the cover of dusk along both banks of the river."

That night the dwarves slept little. The morning was still pale when they saw a company approaching. From behind their wall they watched them come up to the valley's head and climb slowly up. Before long they could see that both men of the lake armed as if for war and elvish bowmen were among them. At length the foremost of these climbed the tumbled rocks and appeared at the top of the falls; and very great was their surprise to see the pool before them and the Gate blocked with a wall of new-hewn stone.

As they stood pointing and speaking to one another Thorin hailed them: "Who are you," he called in a very loud voice, "that come as if in war to the gates of Thorin son of Thrain, King under the Mountain, and what do you desire?"

But they answered nothing. Some turned swiftly back, and the others after gazing for a while at the Gate and its defences soon followed them. That day the camp was moved to the east of the river, right between the arms of the Mountain. The rocks echoed then with voices and with song, as they had not done for many a day. There was the sound, too, of elven-harps and of sweet music; and as it echoed up towards them it seemed that the chill of the air was warmed, and they caught faintly the fragrance of woodland flowers blossoming in spring.

Then Bilbo longed to escape from the dark fortress and to go down and join in the mirth and feasting by the fires. Some of the younger dwarves were moved in their hearts, too, and they muttered that they wished things had fallen out otherwise and that they might welcome such folk as friends; but Thorin scowled.

Then the dwarves themselves brought forth harps and instruments regained from the hoard, and made music to soften his mood; but their song was not as elvish song, and was much like the song they had sung long before in Bilbo's little hobbit-hole.

> Under the Mountain dark and tall
> The King has come unto his hall!
> His foe is dead, the Worm of Dread,
> And ever so his foes shall fall.
>
> The sword is sharp, the spear is long,
> The arrow swift, the Gate is strong;
> The heart is bold that looks on gold;
> The dwarves no more shall suffer wrong.
>
> The dwarves of yore made mighty spells,
> While hammers fell like ringing bells
> In places deep, where dark things sleep,
> In hollow halls beneath the fells.
>
> On silver necklaces they strung
> The light of stars, on crowns they hung

*The dragon-fire, from twisted wire*
*The melody of harps they wrung.*

*The mountain throne once more is freed!*
*O! wandering folk, the summons heed!*
*Come haste! Come haste! across the waste!*
*The king of friend and kin has need.*

*Now call we over mountains cold,*
*"Come back unto the caverns old!"*
*Here at the Gates the king awaits,*
*His hands are rich with gems and gold.*

*The king is come unto his hall*
*Under the Mountain dark and tall.*
*The Worm of Dread is slain and dead,*
*And ever so our foes shall fall!*

This song appeared to please Thorin, and he smiled again
and grew merry; and he began reckoning the distance to the
Iron Hills and how long it would be before Dain could reach
the Lonely Mountain, if he had set out as soon as the message
reached him. But Bilbo's heart fell, both at the song and the
talk: they sounded much too warlike.

The next morning early a company of spearmen was seen
crossing the river, and marching up the valley. They bore with
them the green banner of the Elvenking and the blue banner
of the Lake, and they advanced until they stood right before
the wall at the Gate.

Again Thorin hailed them in a loud voice: "Who are you
that come armed for war to the gates of Thorin son of Thrain,
King under the Mountain?" This time he was answered.

A tall man stood forward, dark of hair and grim of face,

and he cried: "Hail Thorin! Why do you fence yourself like a robber in his hold? We are not yet foes, and we rejoice that you are alive beyond our hope. We came expecting to find none living here; yet now that we are met there is matter for a parley and a council."

"Who are you, and of what would you parley?"

"I am Bard, and by my hand was the dragon slain and your treasure delivered. Is that not a matter that concerns you? Moreover I am by right descent the heir of Girion of Dale, and in your hoard is mingled much of the wealth of his halls and towns, which of old Smaug stole. Is not that a matter of which we may speak? Further in his last battle Smaug destroyed the dwellings of the men of Esgaroth, and I am yet the servant of their Master. I would speak for him and ask whether you have no thought for the sorrow and misery of his people. They aided you in your distress, and in recompense you have thus far brought ruin only, though doubtless undesigned."

Now these were fair words and true, if proudly and grimly spoken; and Bilbo thought that Thorin would at once admit what justice was in them. He did not, of course, expect that any one would remember that it was he who discovered all by himself the dragon's weak spot; and that was just as well, for no one ever did. But also he did not reckon with the power that gold has upon which a dragon has long brooded, nor with dwarvish hearts. Long hours in the past days Thorin had spent in the treasury, and the lust of it was heavy on him. Though he had hunted chiefly for the Arkenstone, yet he had an eye for many another wonderful thing that was lying there, about which were wound old memories of the labours and the sorrows of his race.

"You put your worst cause last and in the chief place," Thorin answered. "To the treasure of my people no man has a claim, because Smaug who stole it from us also robbed him of life or home. The treasure was not his that his evil deeds should be amended with a share of it. The price of the goods and the assistance that we received of the Lake-men we will fairly pay—in due time. But *nothing* will we give, not even a loaf's worth, under threat of force. While an armed host lies before our doors, we look on you as foes and thieves.

"It is in my mind to ask what share of their inheritance you would have paid to our kindred, had you found the hoard unguarded and us slain."

"A just question," replied Bard. "But you are not dead, and we are not robbers. Moreover the wealthy may have pity beyond right on the needy that befriended them when they were in want. And still my other claims remain unanswered."

"I will not parley, as I have said, with armed men at my gate. Nor at all with the people of Elvenking, whom I remember with small kindness. In this debate they have no place. Begone now ere our arrows fly! And if you would speak with me again, first dismiss the elvish host to the woods where it belongs, and then return, laying down your arms before you approach the threshold."

"The Elvenking is my friend, and he has succoured the people of the Lake in their need, though they had no claim but friendship on him," answered Bard. "We will give you time to repent your words. Gather your wisdom ere we return!" Then he departed and went back to the camp.

Ere many hours were past, the banner-bearers returned, and trumpeters stood forth and blew a blast:

"In the name of Esgaroth and the Forest," one cried, "we speak unto Thorin Thrain's son Oakenshield, calling himself the King under the Mountain, and we bid him consider well the claims that have been urged, or be declared our foe. At the least he shall deliver one twelfth portion of the treasure unto

Bard, as the dragon-slayer, and as the heir of Girion. From that portion Bard will himself contribute to the aid of Esgaroth; but if Thorin would have the friendship and honour of the lands about, as his sires had of old, then he will give also somewhat of his own for the comfort of the men of the Lake."

Then Thorin seized a bow of horn and shot an arrow at the speaker. It smote into his shield and stuck there quivering.

"Since such is your answer," he called in return, "I declare the Mountain besieged. You shall not depart from it, until you call on your side for a truce and a parley. We will bear no weapons against you, but we leave you to your gold. You may eat that, if you will!"

With that the messengers departed swiftly, and the dwarves were left to consider their case. So grim had Thorin become, that even if they had wished, the others would not have dared to find fault with him; but indeed most of them seemed to share his mind—except perhaps old fat Bombur and Fili and Kili. Bilbo, of course, disapproved of the whole turn of affairs. He had by now had more than enough of the Mountain, and being besieged inside it was not at all to his taste.

"The whole place still stinks of dragon," he grumbled to himself, "and it makes me sick. And *cram* is beginning simply to stick in my throat."

*Chapter XVI*

# A THIEF IN THE NIGHT

Now the days passed slowly and wearily. Many of the dwarves spent their time piling and ordering the treasure; and now Thorin spoke of the Arkenstone of Thrain, and bade them eagerly to look for it in every corner.

"For the Arkenstone of my father," he said, "is worth more than a river of gold in itself, and to me it is beyond price. That stone of all the treasure I name unto myself, and I will be avenged on anyone who finds it and withholds it."

Bilbo heard these words and he grew afraid, wondering what would happen, if the stone was found—wrapped in an old bundle of tattered oddments that he used as a pillow. All the same he did not speak of it, for as the weariness of the days grew heavier, the beginnings of a plan had come into his little head.

Things had gone on like this for some time, when the ravens brought news that Dain and more than five hundred dwarves, hurrying from the Iron Hills, were now within about two days' march of Dale, coming from the North-East.

"But they cannot reach the Mountain unmarked," said Roäc, "and I fear lest there be battle in the valley. I do not call this counsel good. Though they are a grim folk, they are not likely to overcome the host that besets you; and even if they did so, what will you gain? Winter and snow is hastening be-

ind them. How shall you be fed without the friendship and
oodwill of the lands about you? The treasure is likely to be
our death, though the dragon is no more!"

But Thorin was not moved. "Winter and snow will bite
oth men and elves," he said, "and they may find their dwell-
ig in the waste grievous to bear. With my friends behind
1em and winter upon them, they will perhaps be in softer
1ood to parley with."

That night Bilbo made up his mind. The sky was black and
1oonless. As soon as it was full dark, he went to a corner of
n inner chamber just within the gate and drew from his
undle a rope, and also the Arkenstone wrapped in a rag.
hen he climbed to the top of the wall. Only Bombur was
1ere, for it was his turn to watch, and the dwarves kept only
ne watchman at a time.

"It is mighty cold!" said Bombur. "I wish we could have a
re up here as they have in the camp!"

"It is warm enough inside," said Bilbo.

"I daresay; but I am bound here till midnight," grumbled
1e fat dwarf. "A sorry business altogether. Not that I venture
) disagree with Thorin, may his beard grow ever longer; yet
e was ever a dwarf with a stiff neck."

"Not as stiff as my legs," said Bilbo. "I am tired of stairs
nd stone passages. I would give a good deal for the feel of
rass at my toes."

"I would give a good deal for the feel of a strong drink in
1y throat, and for a soft bed after a good supper!"

"I can't give you those, while the siege is going on. But it is
ong since I watched, and I will take your turn for you, if you
ke. There is no sleep in me tonight."

"You are a good fellow, Mr Baggins, and I will take your
ffer kindly. If there should be anything to note, rouse me

first, mind you! I will lie in the inner chamber to the left, no
far away."

"Off you go!" said Bilbo. "I will wake you at midnight
and you can wake the next watchman."

As soon as Bombur had gone, Bilbo put on his ring, fas
tened his rope, slipped down over the wall, and was gone. H
had about five hours before him. Bombur would sleep (h
could sleep at any time, and ever since the adventure i
the forest he was always trying to recapture the beautifu
dreams he had then); and all the others were busy wit
Thorin. It was unlikely that any, even Fili or Kili, would com
out on the wall until it was their turn.

It was very dark, and the road after a while, when he le
the newly made path and climbed down towards the lowe
course of the stream, was strange to him. At last he came to
the bend where he had to cross the water, if he was to mak
for the camp, as he wished. The bed of the stream was ther
shallow but already broad, and fording it in the dark was no
easy for the little hobbit. He was nearly across when h
missed his footing on a round stone and fell into the col
water with a splash. He had barely scrambled out on the fa
bank, shivering and spluttering, when up came elves in th
gloom with bright lanterns and searched for the cause of th
noise.

"That was no fish!" one said. "There is a spy about. Hid
your lights! They will help him more than us, if it is that quee
little creature that is said to be their servant."

"Servant, indeed!" snorted Bilbo; and in the middle of hi
snort he sneezed loudly, and the elves immediately gathere
towards the sound.

"Let's have a light!" he said. "I am here, if you want me!"
and he slipped off his ring, and popped from behind a rock.

They seized him quickly, in spite of their surprise. "Wh

re you? Are you the dwarves' hobbit? What are you doing?
low did you get so far past our sentinels?" they asked one
fter another.

"I am Mr Bilbo Baggins," he answered, "companion of
horin, if you want to know. I know your king well by sight,
ough perhaps he doesn't know me to look at. But Bard will
emember me, and it is Bard I particularly want to see."

"Indeed!" said they, "and what may be your business?"

"Whatever it is, it's my own, my good elves. But if you
vish ever to get back to your own woods from this cold
heerless place," he answered shivering, "you will take me
long quick to a fire, where I can dry—and then you will let
e speak to your chiefs as quick as may be. I have only an
our or two to spare."

That is how it came about that some two hours after his es-
ape from the Gate, Bilbo was sitting beside a warm fire in
ront of a large tent, and there sat too, gazing curiously at
im, both the Elvenking and Bard. A hobbit in elvish armour,
artly wrapped in an old blanket, was something new to them.

"Really you know," Bilbo was saying in his best business
nanner, "things are impossible. Personally I am tired of the
vhole affair. I wish I was back in the West in my own home,
vhere folk are more reasonable. But I have an interest in this
natter—one fourteenth share, to be precise, according to a
etter, which fortunately I believe I have kept." He drew from
 pocket in his old jacket (which he still wore over his mail),
 rumpled and much folded, Thorin's letter that had been put
 nder the clock on his mantelpiece in May!

"A share in the *profits*, mind you," he went on. "I am aware
f that. Personally I am only too ready to consider all your
laims carefully, and deduct what is right from the total be-
ore putting in my own claim. However you don't know

Thorin Oakenshield as well as I do now. I assure you, he
quite ready to sit on a heap of gold and starve, as long as y
sit here."

"Well, let him!" said Bard. "Such a fool deserves
starve."

"Quite so," said Bilbo. "I see your point of view. At t
same time winter is coming on fast. Before long you will
having snow and what not, and supplies will be difficult-
even for elves I imagine. Also there will be other difficultie
You have not heard of Dain and the dwarves of the Ir
Hills?"

"We have, a long time ago; but what has he got to do wi
us?" asked the king.

"I thought as much. I see I have some information y
have not got. Dain, I may tell you, is now less than two day
march off, and has at least five hundred grim dwarves wi
him—a good many of them have had experience in the drea
ful dwarf and goblin wars, of which you have no doubt hear
When they arrive there may be serious trouble."

"Why do you tell us this? Are you betraying your friend
or are you threatening us?" asked Bard grimly.

"My dear Bard!" squeaked Bilbo. "Don't be so hasty!
never met such suspicious folk! I am merely trying to avo
trouble for all concerned. Now I will make you an offer!!"

"Let us hear it!" they said.

"You may see it!" said he. "It is this!" and he drew forth t
Arkenstone, and threw away the wrapping.

The Elvenking himself, whose eyes were used to things
wonder and beauty, stood up in amazement. Even Bard gaze
marvelling at it in silence. It was as if a globe had been fille
with moonlight and hung before them in a net woven of t
glint of frosty stars.

"This is the Arkenstone of Thrain," said Bilbo, "the Hea

f the Mountain; and it is also the heart of Thorin. He values
t above a river of gold. I give it to you. It will aid you in your
bargaining." Then Bilbo, not without a shudder, not without a
glance of longing, handed the marvellous stone to Bard, and
he held it in his hand, as though dazed.

"But how is it yours to give?" he asked at last with an
effort.

"O well!" said the hobbit uncomfortably. "It isn't exactly;
but, well, I am willing to let it stand against all my claim,
don't you know. I may be a burglar—or so they say: personally I never really felt like one—but I am an honest one, I
hope, more or less. Anyway I am going back now, and the
dwarves can do what they like to me. I hope you will find it
useful."

The Elvenking looked at Bilbo with a new wonder. "Bilbo
Baggins!" he said. "You are more worthy to wear the armour
of elf-princes than many that have looked more comely in it.
But I wonder if Thorin Oakenshield will see it so. I have more
knowledge of dwarves in general than you have perhaps. I advise you to remain with us, and here you shall be honoured
and thrice welcome."

"Thank you very much I am sure," said Bilbo with a bow.
"But I don't think I ought to leave my friends like this, after
all we have gone through together. And I promised to wake
old Bombur at midnight, too! Really I must be going, and
quickly."

Nothing they could say would stop him; so an escort was
provided for him, and as he went both the king and Bard
saluted him with honour. As they passed through the camp an
old man, wrapped in a dark cloak, rose from a tent door
where he was sitting and came towards them.

"Well done! Mr Baggins!" he said, clapping Bilbo on the

back. "There is always more about you than anyone expects!"
It was Gandalf.

For the first time for many a day Bilbo was really delighted. But there was no time for all the questions that he immediately wished to ask.

"All in good time!" said Gandalf. "Things are drawing towards the end now, unless I am mistaken. There is an unpleasant time just in front of you; but keep your heart up! You *may* come through all right. There is news brewing that even the ravens have not heard. Good night!"

Puzzled but cheered, Bilbo hurried on. He was guided to a safe ford and set across dry, and then he said farewell to the elves and climbed carefully back towards the Gate. Great weariness began to come over him; but it was well before midnight when he clambered up the rope again—it was still where he had left it. He untied it and hid it, and then he sat down on the wall and wondered anxiously what would happen next.

At midnight he woke up Bombur; and then in turn rolled himself up in his corner, without listening to the old dwarf's thanks (which he felt he had hardly earned). He was soon fast asleep forgetting all his worries till the morning. As a matter of fact he was dreaming of eggs and bacon.

*Chapter XVII*

# THE CLOUDS BURST

Next day the trumpets rang early in the camp. Soon a single runner was seen hurrying along the narrow path. At a distance he stood and hailed them, asking whether Thorin would now listen to another embassy, since new tidings had come to hand, and matters were changed.

"That will be Dain!" said Thorin when he heard. "They will have got wind of his coming. I thought that would alter their mood! Bid them come few in number and weaponless, and I will hear," he called to the messenger.

About midday the banners of the Forest and the Lake were seen to be borne forth again. A company of twenty was approaching. At the beginning of the narrow way they laid aside sword and spear, and came on towards the Gate. Wondering, the dwarves saw that among them were both Bard and the Elvenking, before whom an old man wrapped in cloak and hood bore a strong casket of iron-bound wood.

"Hail Thorin!" said Bard. "Are you still of the same mind?"

"My mind does not change with the rising and setting of a few suns," answered Thorin. "Did you come to ask me idle questions? Still the elf-host has not departed as I bade! Till then you come in vain to bargain with me."

"Is there then nothing for which you would yield any o
your gold?"

"Nothing that you or your friends have to offer."

"What of the Arkenstone of Thrain?" said he, and at the
same moment the old man opened the casket and held aloft
the jewel. The light leapt from his hand, bright and white in
the morning.

Then Thorin was stricken dumb with amazement and con
fusion. No one spoke for a long while.

Thorin at length broke the silence, and his voice was thick
with wrath. "That stone was my father's, and is mine," he
said. "Why should I purchase my own?" But wonder over-
came him and he added: "But how came you by the heirloom
of my house—if there is need to ask such a question o
thieves?"

"We are not thieves," Bard answered. "Your own we wil
give back in return for our own."

"How came you by it?" shouted Thorin in gathering rage.

"I gave it to them!" squeaked Bilbo, who was peering over
the wall, by now in a dreadful fright.

"You! You!" cried Thorin, turning upon him and grasping
him with both hands. "You miserable hobbit! You undersized—
burglar!" he shouted at a loss for words, and he shook poor
Bilbo like a rabbit.

"By the beard of Durin! I wish I had Gandalf here! Curse
him for his choice of you! May his beard wither! As for you
I will throw you to the rocks!" he cried and lifted Bilbo in
his arms.

"Stay! Your wish is granted!" said a voice. The old man
with the casket threw aside his hood and cloak. "Here is Gandalf! And none too soon it seems. If you don't like my Burglar, please don't damage him. Put him down, and listen first
to what he has to say!"

"You all seem in league!" said Thorin dropping Bilbo on the top of the wall. "Never again will I have dealings with any wizard or his friends. What have you to say, you descendant of rats?"

"Dear me! Dear me!" said Bilbo. "I am sure this is all very uncomfortable. You may remember saying that I might choose my own fourteenth share? Perhaps I took it too literally—I have been told that dwarves are sometimes politer in word than in deed. The time was, all the same, when you seemed to think that I had been of some service. Descendant of rats, indeed! Is this all the service of you and your family that I was promised, Thorin? Take it that I have disposed of my share as I wished, and let it go at that!"

"I will," said Thorin grimly. "And I will let you go at that—and may we never meet again!" Then he turned and spoke over the wall. "I am betrayed," he said. "It was rightly guessed that I could not forbear to redeem the Arkenstone, the treasure of my house. For it I will give one fourteenth share of the hoard in silver and gold, setting aside the gems; but that shall be accounted the promised share of this traitor, and with that reward he shall depart, and you can divide it as you will. He will get little enough, I doubt not. Take him, if you wish him to live; and no friendship of mine goes with him.

"Get down now to your friends!" he said to Bilbo, "or I will throw you down."

"What about the gold and silver?" asked Bilbo.

"That shall follow after, as can be arranged," said he. "Get down!"

"Until then we keep the stone," cried Bard.

"You are not making a very splendid figure as King under the Mountain," said Gandalf. "But things may change yet."

"They may indeed," said Thorin. And already, so strong

was the bewilderment of the treasure upon him, he was pondering whether by the help of Dain he might not recapture the Arkenstone and withhold the share of the reward.

And so Bilbo was swung down from the wall, and departed with nothing for all his trouble, except the armour which Thorin had given him already. More than one of the dwarves in their hearts felt shame and pity at his going.

"Farewell!" he cried to them. "We may meet again as friends."

"Be off!" called Thorin. "You have mail upon you, which was made by my folk, and is too good for you. It cannot be pierced by arrows; but if you do not hasten, I will sting your miserable feet. So be swift!"

"Not so hasty!" said Bard. "We will give you until to-morrow. At noon we will return, and see if you have brought from the hoard the portion that is to be set against the stone. If that is done without deceit, then we will depart, and the elf-host will go back to the Forest. In the meanwhile farewell!"

With that they went back to the camp; but Thorin sent messengers by Roäc telling Dain of what had passed, and bidding him come with wary speed.

That day passed and the night. The next day the wind shifted west, and the air was dark and gloomy. The morning was still early when a cry was heard in the camp. Runners came in to report that a host of dwarves had appeared round the eastern spur of the Mountain and was now hastening to Dale. Dain had come. He had hurried on through the night, and so had come upon them sooner than they had expected. Each one of his folk was clad in a hauberk of steel mail that hung to his knees, and his legs were covered with hose of a fine and flexible metal mesh, the secret of whose making was possessed by Dain's people. The dwarves are exceedingly strong for their height, but most of these were strong even for dwarves. In battle they wielded heavy two-handed mattocks; but each of them had also a short broad sword at his side and a roundshield slung at his back. Their beards were forked and plaited and thrust into their belts. Their caps were of iron and they were shod with iron, and their faces were grim.

Trumpets called men and elves to arms. Before long the dwarves could be seen coming up the valley at a great pace. They halted between the river and the eastern spur; but a few held on their way, and crossing the river drew near the camp; and there they laid down their weapons and held up their hands in sign of peace. Bard went out to meet them, and with him went Bilbo.

"We are sent from Dain son of Nain," they said when questioned. "We are hastening to our kinsmen in the Mountain, since we learn that the kingdom of old is renewed. But who are you that sit in the plain as foes before defended walls?" This, of course, in the polite and rather old-fashioned language of such occasions, meant simply: "You have no business here. We are going on, so make way or we shall fight you!" They meant to push on between the Mountain and the loop of the river; for the narrow land there did not seem to be strongly guarded.

Bard, of course, refused to allow the dwarves to go straight on to the Mountain. He was determined to wait until the gold and silver had been brought out in exchange for the Arkenstone; for he did not believe that this would be done, if once the fortress was manned with so large and warlike a company. They had brought with them a great store of supplies; for the dwarves can carry very heavy burdens, and nearly all of Dain's folk, in spite of their rapid march, bore huge packs on their backs in addition to their weapons. They would stand a siege for weeks, and by that time yet more dwarves might come, and yet more, for Thorin had many relatives. Also they would be able to reopen and guard some other gate, so that the besiegers would have to encircle the whole mountain; and for that they had not sufficient numbers.

These were, in fact, precisely their plans (for the raven-messengers had been busy between Thorin and Dain); but for the moment the way was barred, so after angry words the dwarf-messengers retired muttering in their beards. Bard then sent messengers at once to the Gate; but they found no gold or payment. Arrows came forth as soon as they were within shot, and they hastened back in dismay. In the camp all was now astir, as if for battle; for the dwarves of Dain were advancing along the eastern bank.

"Fools!" laughed Bard, "to come thus beneath the Mountain's arm! They do not understand war above ground, whatever they may know of battle in the mines. There are many of our archers and spearmen now hidden in the rocks upon their right flank. Dwarf-mail may be good, but they will soon be hard put to it. Let us set on them now from both sides, before they are fully rested!"

But the Elvenking said: "Long will I tarry, ere I begin this war for gold. The dwarves cannot pass us, unless we will, or do anything that we cannot mark. Let us hope still for something that will bring reconciliation. Our advantage in numbers will be enough, if in the end it must come to unhappy blows."

But he reckoned without the dwarves. The knowledge that the Arkenstone was in the hands of the besiegers burned in their thoughts; also they guessed the hesitation of Bard and his friends, and resolved to strike while they debated.

Suddenly without a signal they sprang silently forward to attack. Bows twanged and arrows whistled; battle was about to be joined.

Still more suddenly a darkness came on with dreadful swiftness! A black cloud hurried over the sky. Winter thunder on a wild wind rolled roaring up and rumbled in the Mountain, and lightning lit its peak. And beneath the thunder another blackness could be seen whirling forward; but it did not come with the wind, it came from the North, like a vast cloud of birds, so dense that no light could be seen between their wings.

"Halt!" cried Gandalf, who appeared suddenly, and stood alone, with arms uplifted, between the advancing dwarves and the ranks awaiting them. "Halt!" he called in a voice like thunder, and his staff blazed forth with a flash like the lightning. "Dread has come upon you all! Alas! it has come more swiftly than I guessed. The Goblins are upon you! Bolg of the North is coming, O Dain! whose father you slew in Moria. Behold! the bats are above his army like a sea of locusts. They ride upon wolves and Wargs are in their train!"

Amazement and confusion fell upon them all. Even as Gandalf had been speaking the darkness grew. The dwarves halted and gazed at the sky. The elves cried out with many voices.

"Come!" called Gandalf. "There is yet time for council. Let Dain son of Nain come swiftly to us!"

So began a battle that none had expected; and it was called the Battle of Five Armies, and it was very terrible. Upon one side were the Goblins and the Wild Wolves, and upon the other were Elves and Men and Dwarves. This is how it fell out. Ever since the fall of the Great Goblin of the Misty

Mountains the hatred of their race for the dwarves had been
rekindled to fury. Messengers had passed to and fro between
all their cities, colonies and strongholds; for they resolved
now to win the dominion of the North. Tidings they had gath
ered in secret ways; and in all the mountains there was a
forging and an arming. Then they marched and gathered by
hill and valley, going ever by tunnel or under dark, until
around and beneath the great mountain Gundabad of the
North, where was their capital, a vast host was assembled
ready to sweep down in time of storm unawares upon the
South. Then they learned of the death of Smaug, and joy was
in their hearts; and they hastened night after night through the
mountains, and came thus at last on a sudden from the North
hard on the heels of Dain. Not even the ravens knew of their
coming until they came out in the broken lands which divided
the Lonely Mountain from the hills behind. How much Gan
dalf knew cannot be said, but it is plain that he had not ex
pected this sudden assault.

This is the plan that he made in council with the Elvenking
and with Bard; and with Dain, for the dwarf-lord now joined
them: the Goblins were the foes of all, and at their coming all
other quarrels were forgotten. Their only hope was to lure the
goblins into the valley between the arms of the Mountain;
and themselves to man the great spurs that struck south and
east. Yet this would be perilous, if the goblins were in sufficient numbers to overrun the Mountain itself, and so attack
them also from behind and above; but there was no time to
make any other plan, or to summon any help.

Soon the thunder passed, rolling away to the South-East;
but the bat-cloud came, flying lower, over the shoulder of the
Mountain, and whirled above them shutting out the light and
filling them with dread.

"To the Mountain!" called Bard. "To the Mountain! Let us take our places while there is yet time!"

On the Southern spur, in its lower slopes and in the rocks at its feet, the Elves were set; on the Eastern spur were men and dwarves. But Bard and some of the nimblest of men and elves climbed to the height of the Eastern shoulder to gain a view to the North. Soon they could see the lands before the Mountain's feet black with a hurrying multitude. Ere long the vanguard swirled round the spur's end and came rushing into Dale. These were the swiftest wolf-riders, and already their cries and howls rent the air afar. A few brave men were strung before them to make a feint of resistance, and many there fell before the rest drew back and fled to either side. As Gandalf had hoped, the goblin army had gathered behind the resisted vanguard, and poured now in rage into the valley, driving wildly up between the arms of the Mountain, seeking for the foe. Their banners were countless, black and red, and they came on like a tide in fury and disorder.

It was a terrible battle. The most dreadful of all Bilbo's experiences, and the one which at the time he hated most—which is to say it was the one he was most proud of, and most fond of recalling long afterwards, although he was quite unimportant in it. Actually I may say he put on his ring early in the business and vanished from sight, if not from all danger. A magic ring of that sort is not a complete protection in a goblin charge, nor does it stop flying arrows and wild spears; but it does help in getting out of the way, and it prevents your head from being specially chosen for a sweeping stroke by a goblin swordsman.

The elves were the first to charge. Their hatred for the goblins is cold and bitter. Their spears and swords shone in the gloom with a gleam of chill flame, so deadly was the wrath of the hands that held them. As soon as the host of their enemies was dense in the valley, they sent against it a shower of arrows, and each flickered as it fled as if with stinging fire. Behind the arrows a thousand of their spearmen leapt down and charged. The yells were deafening. The rocks were stained black with goblin blood.

Just as the goblins were recovering from the onslaught and the elf-charge was halted, there rose from across the valley a deep-throated roar. With cries of "Moria!" and "Dain, Dain!" the dwarves of the Iron Hills plunged in, wielding their mattocks, upon the other side; and beside them came the men of the Lake with long swords.

Panic came upon the Goblins; and even as they turned to meet this new attack, the elves charged again with renewed numbers. Already many of the goblins were flying back down the river to escape from the trap; and many of their own wolves were turning upon them and rending the dead and the wounded. Victory seemed at hand, when a cry rang out on the heights above.

Goblins had scaled the Mountain from the other side and already many were on the slopes above the Gate, and others were streaming down recklessly, heedless of those that fell screaming from cliff and precipice, to attack the spurs from above. Each of these could be reached by paths that ran down from the main mass of the Mountain in the centre; and the defenders had too few to bar the way for long. Victory now vanished from hope. They had only stemmed the first onslaught of the black tide.

Day drew on. The goblins gathered again in the valley. There a host of Wargs came ravening and with them came the bodyguard of Bolg, goblins of huge size with scimitars of steel. Soon actual darkness was coming into a stormy sky; while still the great bats swirled about the heads and ears of elves and men, or fastened vampire-like on the stricken. Now

Bard was fighting to defend the Eastern spur, and yet giving slowly back; and the elf-lords were at bay about their king upon the southern arm, near to the watch-post on Ravenhill.

Suddenly there was a great shout, and from the Gate came a trumpet call. They had forgotten Thorin! Part of the wall, moved by levers, fell outward with a crash into the pool. Out leapt the King under the Mountain, and his companions followed him. Hood and cloak were gone; they were in shining armour, and red light leapt from their eyes. In the gloom the great dwarf gleamed like gold in a dying fire.

Rocks were hurled down from on high by the goblins above; but they held on, leapt down to the falls' foot, and rushed forward to battle. Wolf and rider fell or fled before them. Thorin wielded his axe with mighty strokes, and nothing seemed to harm him.

"To me! To me! Elves and Men! To me! O my kinsfolk!" he cried, and his voice shook like a horn in the valley.

Down, heedless of order, rushed all the dwarves of Dain to his help. Down too came many of the Lake-men, for Bard could not restrain them; and out upon the other side came many of the spearmen of the elves. Once again the goblins were stricken in the valley; and they were piled in heaps till Dale was dark and hideous with their corpses. The Wargs were scattered and Thorin drove right against the bodyguard of Bolg. But he could not pierce their ranks.

Already behind him among the goblin dead lay many men and many dwarves, and many a fair elf that should have lived yet long ages merrily in the wood. And as the valley widened his onset grew ever slower. His numbers were too few. His flanks were unguarded. Soon the attackers were attacked, and they were forced into a great ring, facing every way, hemmed all about with goblins and wolves returning to the assault. The bodyguard of Bolg came howling against them, and drove in upon their ranks like waves upon cliffs of sand. Their friends could not help them, for the assault from the Mountain was renewed with redoubled force, and upon either side men and elves were being slowly beaten down.

On all this Bilbo looked with misery. He had taken his stand on Ravenhill among the Elves—partly because there was more chance of escape from that point, and partly (with the more Tookish part of his mind) because if he was going to be in a last desperate stand, he preferred on the whole to defend the Elvenking. Gandalf, too, I may say, was there, sitting on the ground as if in deep thought, preparing, I suppose, some last blast of magic before the end.

That did not seem far off. "It will not be long now," thought Bilbo, "before the goblins win the Gate, and we are all slaughtered or driven down and captured. Really it is enough to make one weep, after all one has gone through. I would rather old Smaug had been left with all the wretched treasure, than that these vile creatures should get it, and poor old Bombur, and Balin and Fili and Kili and all the rest come to a bad end; and Bard too, and the Lake-men and the merry elves. Misery me! I have heard songs of many battles, and I have always understood that defeat may be glorious. It seems very uncomfortable, not to say distressing. I wish I was well out of it."

The clouds were torn by the wind, and a red sunset slashed the West. Seeing the sudden gleam in the gloom Bilbo looked round. He gave a great cry: he had seen a sight that made his heart leap, dark shapes small yet majestic against the distant glow.

"The Eagles! The Eagles!" he shouted. "The Eagles are coming!"

Bilbo's eyes were seldom wrong. The eagles were coming

down the wind, line after line, in such a host as must have gathered from all the eyries of the North.

"The Eagles! the Eagles!" Bilbo cried, dancing and waving his arms. If the elves could not see him they could hear him. Soon they too took up the cry, and it echoed across the valley. Many wondering eyes looked up, though as yet nothing could be seen except from the southern shoulders of the Mountain.

"The Eagles!" cried Bilbo once more, but at that moment a stone hurtling from above smote heavily on his helm, and he fell with a crash and knew no more.

## Chapter XVIII

# THE RETURN JOURNEY

When Bilbo came to himself, he was literally by himself. He was lying on the flat stones of Ravenhill, and no one was near. A cloudless day, but cold, was broad above him. He was shaking, and as chilled as stone, but his head burned with fire.

"Now I wonder what has happened?" he said to himself. "At any rate I am not yet one of the fallen heroes; but I suppose there is still time enough for that!"

He sat up painfully. Looking into the valley he could see no living goblins. After a while as his head cleared a little, he thought he could see elves moving in the rocks below. He rubbed his eyes. Surely there was a camp still in the plain some distance off; and there was a coming and going about the Gate? Dwarves seemed to be busy removing the wall. But all was deadly still. There was no call and no echo of a song. Sorrow seemed to be in the air.

"Victory after all, I suppose!" he said, feeling his aching head. "Well, it seems a very gloomy business."

Suddenly he was aware of a man climbing up and coming towards him.

"Hullo there!" he called with a shaky voice. "Hullo there! What news?"

"What voice is it that speaks among the stones?" said

the man halting and peering about him not far from where
Bilbo sat.

Then Bilbo remembered his ring! "Well I'm blessed!" said
he. "This invisibility has its drawbacks after all. Otherwise I
suppose I might have spent a warm and comfortable night in
bed!"

"It's me, Bilbo Baggins, companion of Thorin!" he cried,
hurriedly taking off the ring.

"It is well that I have found you!" said the man striding forward. "You are needed and we have looked for you long. You
would have been numbered among the dead, who are many, if
Gandalf the wizard had not said that your voice was last
heard in this place. I have been sent to look here for the last
time. Are you much hurt?"

"A nasty knock on the head, I think," said Bilbo. "But I
have a helm and a hard skull. All the same I feel sick and my
legs are like straws."

"I will carry you down to the camp in the valley," said the
man, and picked him lightly up.

The man was swift and sure-footed. It was not long before
Bilbo was set down before a tent in Dale; and there stood
Gandalf, with his arm in a sling. Even the wizard had not escaped without a wound; and there were few unharmed in all
the host.

When Gandalf saw Bilbo, he was delighted. "Baggins!" he
exclaimed. "Well I never! Alive after all—I *am* glad! I began
to wonder if even your luck would see you through! A terrible
business, and it nearly was disastrous. But other news can
wait. Come!" he said more gravely. "You are called for;" and
leading the hobbit he took him within the tent.

"Hail! Thorin," he said as he entered. "I have brought
him."

There indeed lay Thorin Oakenshield, wounded with many

wounds, and his rent armour and notched axe were cast upon the floor. He looked up as Bilbo came beside him.

"Farewell, good thief," he said. "I go now to the halls of waiting to sit beside my fathers, until the world is renewed. Since I leave now all gold and silver, and go where it is of little worth, I wish to part in friendship from you, and I would take back my words and deeds at the Gate."

Bilbo knelt on one knee filled with sorrow. "Farewell, King under the Mountain!" he said. "This is a bitter adventure, if it must end so; and not a mountain of gold can amend it. Yet I am glad that I have shared in your perils—that has been more than any Baggins deserves."

"No!" said Thorin. "There is more in you of good than you know, child of the kindly West. Some courage and some wisdom, blended in measure. If more of us valued food and cheer and song above hoarded gold, it would be a merrier world. But sad or merry, I must leave it now. Farewell!"

Then Bilbo turned away, and he went by himself, and sat alone wrapped in a blanket, and, whether you believe it or not, he wept until his eyes were red and his voice was hoarse. He was a kindly little soul. Indeed it was long before he had the heart to make a joke again. "A mercy it is," he said at last to himself, "that I woke up when I did. I wish Thorin were living, but I am glad that we parted in kindness. You are a fool, Bilbo Baggins, and you made a great mess of that business with the stone; and there was a battle, in spite of all your efforts to buy peace and quiet, but I suppose you can hardly be blamed for that."

All that had happened after he was stunned, Bilbo learned later; but it gave him more sorrow than joy, and he was now weary of his adventure. He was aching in his bones for the homeward journey. That, however, was a little delayed, so in the meantime I will tell something of events. The Eagles had long had suspicion of the goblins' mustering; from their watchfulness the movements in the mountains could not be altogether hid. So they too had gathered in great numbers, under the great Eagle of the Misty Mountains; and at length smelling battle from afar they had come speeding down the gale in the nick of time. They it was who dislodged the goblins from the mountain-slopes, casting them over precipices, or driving them down shrieking and bewildered among their foes. It was not long before they had freed the Lonely Mountain, and elves and men on either side of the valley could come at last to the help of the battle below.

But even with the Eagles they were still outnumbered. In that last hour Beorn himself had appeared—no one knew how or from where. He came alone, and in bear's shape; and he seemed to have grown almost to giant-size in his wrath.

The roar of his voice was like drums and guns; and he tossed wolves and goblins from his path like straws and feathers. He fell upon their rear, and broke like a clap of thunder through the ring. The dwarves were making a stand still about their lords upon a low rounded hill. Then Beorn stooped and lifted Thorin, who had fallen pierced with spears, and bore him out of the fray.

Swiftly he returned and his wrath was redoubled, so that nothing could withstand him, and no weapon seemed to bite upon him. He scattered the bodyguard, and pulled down Bolg himself and crushed him. Then dismay fell on the Goblins and they fled in all directions. But weariness left their enemies with the coming of new hope, and they pursued them closely, and prevented most of them from escaping where they could. They drove many of them into the Running River, and such as fled south or west they hunted into the marshes about the Forest River; and there the greater part of the last fugitives perished, while those that came hardly to the Wood-elves' realm were there slain, or drawn in to die deep in the trackless dark of Mirkwood. Songs have said that three parts of the goblin warriors of the North perished on that day, and the mountains had peace for many a year.

Victory had been assured before the fall of night, but the pursuit was still on foot, when Bilbo returned to the camp; and not many were in the valley save the more grievously wounded.

"Where are the Eagles?" he asked Gandalf that evening, as he lay wrapped in many warm blankets.

"Some are in the hunt," said the wizard, "but most have gone back to their eyries. They would not stay here, and departed with the first light of morning. Dain has crowned their chief with gold, and sworn friendship with them for ever."

"I am sorry. I mean, I should have liked to see them again," said Bilbo sleepily; "perhaps I shall see them on the way home. I suppose I shall be going home soon?"

"As soon as you like," said the wizard.

Actually it was some days before Bilbo really set out. They buried Thorin deep beneath the Mountain, and Bard laid the Arkenstone upon his breast.

"There let it lie till the Mountain falls!" he said. "May it bring good fortune to all his folk that dwell here after!"

Upon his tomb the Elvenking then laid Orcrist, the elvish sword that had been taken from Thorin in captivity. It is said in songs that it gleamed ever in the dark if foes approached, and the fortress of the dwarves could not be taken by surprise. There now Dain son of Nain took up his abode, and he became King under the Mountain, and in time many other dwarves gathered to his throne in the ancient halls. Of the twelve companions of Thorin, ten remained. Fili and Kili had fallen defending him with shield and body, for he was their mother's elder brother. The others remained with Dain; for Dain dealt his treasure well.

There was, of course, no longer any question of dividing the hoard in such shares as had been planned, to Balin and Dwalin, and Dori and Nori and Ori, and Oin and Gloin, and Bifur and Bofur and Bombur—or to Bilbo. Yet a fourteenth share of all the silver and gold, wrought and unwrought, was given up to Bard; for Dain said: "We will honour the agreement of the dead, and he has now the Arkenstone in his keeping."

Even a fourteenth share was wealth exceedingly great, greater than that of many mortal kings. From that treasure Bard sent much gold to the Master of Lake-town; and he rewarded his followers and friends freely. To the Elvenking he gave the emeralds of Girion, such jewels as he most loved, which Dain had restored to him.

To Bilbo he said: "This treasure is as much yours as it is mine; though old agreements cannot stand, since so many have a claim in its winning and defence. Yet even though you were willing to lay aside all your claim, I should wish that the words of Thorin, of which he repented, should not prove true: that we should give you little. I would reward you most richly of all."

"Very kind of you," said Bilbo. "But really it is a relief to me. How on earth should I have got all that treasure home without war and murder all along the way, I don't know. And I don't know what I should have done with it when I got home. I am sure it is better in your hands."

In the end he would only take two small chests, one filled with silver, and the other with gold, such as one strong pony could carry. "That will be quite as much as I can manage," said he.

At last the time came for him to say good-bye to his

friends. "Farewell, Balin!" he said; "and farewell, Dwalin; and farewell Dori, Nori, Ori, Oin, Gloin, Bifur, Bofur, and Bombur! May your beards never grow thin!" And turning towards the Mountain he added: "Farewell Thorin Oakenshield! And Fili and Kili! May your memory never fade!"

Then the dwarves bowed low before their Gate, but words stuck in their throats. "Good-bye and good luck, wherever you fare!" said Balin at last. "If ever you visit us again, when our halls are made fair once more, then the feast shall indeed be splendid!"

"If ever you are passing my way," said Bilbo, "don't wait to knock! Tea is at four; but any of you are welcome at any time!"

Then he turned away.


The elf-host was on the march; and if it was sadly lessened, yet many were glad, for now the northern world would be merrier for many a long day. The dragon was dead, and the goblins overthrown, and their hearts looked forward after winter to a spring of joy.

Gandalf and Bilbo rode behind the Elvenking, and beside them strode Beorn, once again in man's shape, and he laughed and sang in a loud voice upon the road. So they went on until they drew near to the borders of Mirkwood, to the north of the place where the Forest River ran out. Then they halted, for the wizard and Bilbo would not enter the wood, even though the king bade them stay a while in his halls. They intended to go along the edge of the forest, and round its northern end in the waste that lay between it and the beginning of the Grey Mountains. It was a long and cheerless road, but now that the goblins were crushed, it seemed safer to them than the dreadful pathways under the trees. Moreover Beorn was going that way too.

"Farewell! O Elvenking!" said Gandalf. "Merry be the green-wood, while the world is yet young! And merry be all your folk!"

"Farewell! O Gandalf!" said the king. "May you ever appear where you are most needed and least expected! The oftener you appear in my halls the better shall I be pleased!"

"I beg of you," said Bilbo stammering and standing on one foot, "to accept this gift!" and he brought out a necklace of silver and pearls that Dain had given him at their parting.

"In what way have I earned such a gift, O hobbit?" said the king.

"Well, er, I thought, don't you know," said Bilbo rather confused, "that, er, some little return should be made for your, er, hospitality. I mean even a burglar has his feelings. I have drunk much of your wine and eaten much of your bread."

"I will take your gift, O Bilbo the Magnificent!" said the king gravely. "And I name you elf-friend and blessed. May your shadow never grow less (or stealing would be too easy)! Farewell!"

Then the elves turned towards the Forest, and Bilbo started on his long road home.

He had many hardships and adventures before he got back. The Wild was still the Wild, and there were many other things in it in those days beside goblins; but he was well guided and well guarded—the wizard was with him, and Beorn for much of the way—and he was never in great danger again. Anyway by mid-winter Gandalf and Bilbo had come all the way back, along both edges of the Forest, to the doors of Beorn's house; and there for a while they both stayed. Yule-tide was warm and merry there; and men came from far and wide to feast at Beorn's bidding. The goblins of the Misty Mountains were now few and terrified, and hidden in the deepest holes they could find; and the Wargs had vanished from the woods, so that men went abroad without fear. Beorn indeed became a great chief afterwards in those regions and ruled a wide land between the mountains and the wood; and it is said that for many generations the men of his line had the power of taking bear's shape, and some were grim men and bad, but most were in heart like Beorn, if less in size and strength. In their day the last goblins were hunted from the Misty Mountains and a new peace came over the edge of the Wild.

It was spring, and a fair one with mild weathers and a bright sun, before Bilbo and Gandalf took their leave at last of Beorn, and though he longed for home, Bilbo left with regret, for the flowers of the gardens of Beorn were in springtime no less marvellous than in high summer.

At last they came up the long road, and reached the very pass where the goblins had captured them before. But they came to that high point at morning, and looking backward they saw a white sun shining over the outstretched lands. There behind lay Mirkwood, blue in the distance, and darkly green at the nearer edge even in the spring. There far away was the Lonely Mountain on the edge of eyesight. On its highest peak snow yet unmelted was gleaming pale.

"So comes snow after fire, and even dragons have their ending!" said Bilbo, and he turned his back on his adventure. The Tookish part was getting very tired, and the Baggins was daily getting stronger. "I wish now only to be in my own armchair!" he said.

*Chapter XIX*

# THE LAST STAGE

It was on May the First that the two came back at last to the brink of the valley of Rivendell, where stood the Last (or the First) Homely House. Again it was evening, their ponies were tired, especially the one that carried the baggage; and they all felt in need of rest. As they rode down the steep path, Bilbo heard the elves still singing in the trees, as if they had not stopped since he left; and as soon as the riders came down into the lower glades of the wood they burst into a song of much the same kind as before. This is something like it:

> *The dragon is withered,*
> *His bones are now crumbled;*
> *His armour is shivered,*
> *His splendour is humbled!*
> *Though sword shall be rusted,*
> *And throne and crown perish*
> *With strength that men trusted*
> *And wealth that they cherish,*
> *Here grass is still growing,*
> *And leaves are yet swinging,*
> *The white water flowing,*
> *And elves are yet singing*

*Come! Tra-la-la-lally!*
*Come back to the Valley!*

*The stars are far brighter*
*Than gems without measure,*
*The moon is far whiter*
*Than silver in treasure:*
*The fire is more shining*
*On hearth in the gloaming*
*Than gold won by mining,*
*So why go a-roaming?*
   *O! Tra-la-la-lally*
   *Come back to the Valley.*

*O! Where are you going,*
*So late in returning?*
*The river is flowing,*
*The stars are all burning!*
*O! Whither so laden,*
*So sad and so dreary?*
*Here elf and elf-maiden*
*Now welcome the weary*
   *With Tra-la-la-lally*
   *Come back to the Valley,*
      *Tra-la-la-lally*
      *Fa-la-la-lally*
         *Fa-la!*

Then the elves of the valley came out and greeted them and led them across the water to the house of Elrond. There a warm welcome was made them, and there were many eager ears that evening to hear the tale of their adventures. Gandalf it was who spoke, for Bilbo was fallen quiet and drowsy. Most of the tale he knew, for he had been in it, and had himself told much of it to the wizard on their homeward way or in the house of Beorn; but every now and again he would open one eye, and listen, when a part of the story which he did not yet know came in.

It was in this way that he learned where Gandalf had been to; for he overheard the words of the wizard to Elrond. It appeared that Gandalf had been to a great council of the white wizards, masters of lore and good magic; and that they had at last driven the Necromancer from his dark hold in the south of Mirkwood.

"Ere long now," Gandalf was saying, "The Forest will grow somewhat more wholesome. The North will be freed from that horror for many long years, I hope. Yet I wish he were banished from the world!"

"It would be well indeed," said Elrond; "but I fear that will not come about in this age of the world, or for many after."

When the tale of their journeyings was told, there were other tales, and yet more tales, tales of long ago, and tales of new things, and tales of no time at all, till Bilbo's head fell forward on his chest, and he snored comfortably in a corner.

He woke to find himself in a white bed, and the moon shining through an open window. Below it many elves were singing loud and clear on the banks of the stream.

> *Sing all ye joyful, now sing all together!*
> *The wind's in the tree-top, the wind's in the heather;*
> *The stars are in blossom, the moon is in flower,*
> *And bright are the windows of Night in her tower.*
>
> *Dance all ye joyful, now dance all together!*
> *Soft is the grass, and let foot be like feather!*

*The river is silver, the shadows are fleeting;*
*Merry is May-time, and merry our meeting.*

*Sing we now softly, and dreams let us weave him!*
*Wind him in slumber and there let us leave him!*
*The wanderer sleepeth. Now soft be his pillow!*
*Lullaby! Lullaby! Alder and Willow!*

*Sigh no more Pine, till the wind of the morn!*
*Fall Moon! Dark be the land!*
*Hush! Hush! Oak, Ash, and Thorn!*
*Hushed be all water, till dawn is at hand!*

"Well, Merry People!" said Bilbo looking out. "What time by the moon is this? Your lullaby would waken a drunken goblin! Yet I thank you."

"And your snores would waken a stone dragon—yet we thank you," they answered with laughter. "It is drawing towards dawn, and you have slept now since the night's beginning. Tomorrow, perhaps, you will be cured of weariness."

"A little sleep does a great cure in the house of Elrond," said he; "but I will take all the cure I can get. A second good night, fair friends!" And with that he went back to bed and slept till late morning.

Weariness fell from him soon in that house, and he had many a merry jest and dance, early and late, with the elves of the valley. Yet even that place could not long delay him now, and he thought always of his own home. After a week, therefore, he said farewell to Elrond, and giving him such small gifts as he would accept, he rode away with Gandalf.

Even as they left the valley the sky darkened in the West before them, and wind and rain came up to meet them.

"Merry is May-time!" said Bilbo, as the rain beat into his

face. "But our back is to legends and we are coming home. I suppose this is the first taste of it."

"There is a long road yet," said Gandalf.

"But it is the last road," said Bilbo.

They came to the river that marked the very edge of the borderland of the Wild, and to the ford beneath the steep bank, which you may remember. The water was swollen both with the melting of the snows at the approach of summer, and with the daylong rain; but they crossed with some difficulty, and pressed forward, as evening fell, on the last stage of their journey.

This was much as it had been before, except that the company was smaller, and more silent; also this time there were no trolls. At each point on the road Bilbo recalled the happenings and the words of a year ago—it seemed to him more like ten—so that, of course, he quickly noted the place where the pony had fallen in the river, and they had turned aside for their nasty adventure with Tom and Bert and Bill.

Not far from the road they found the gold of the trolls, which they had buried, still hidden and untouched. "I have enough to last me my time," said Bilbo, when they had dug it up. "You had better take this, Gandalf. I daresay you can find a use for it."

"Indeed I can!" said the wizard. "But share and share alike! You may find you have more needs than you expect."

So they put the gold in bags and slung them on the ponies, who were not at all pleased about it. After that their going was slower, for most of the time they walked. But the land was green and there was much grass through which the hobbit strolled along contentedly. He mopped his face with a red silk handkerchief—no! not a single one of his own had survived, he had borrowed this one from Elrond—for now June had brought summer, and the weather was bright and hot again.

As all things come to an end, even this story, a day came at last when they were in sight of the country where Bilbo had been born and bred, where the shapes of the land and of the trees were as well known to him as his hands and toes. Coming to a rise he could see his own Hill in the distance, and he stopped suddenly and said:

> Roads go ever ever on,
>> Over rock and under tree,
> By caves where never sun has shone,
>> By streams that never find the sea;
> Over snow by winter sown,
>> And through the merry flowers of June,
> Over grass and over stone,
>> And under mountains in the moon.
>
> Roads go ever ever on
>> Under cloud and under star,
> Yet feet that wandering have gone
>> Turn at last to home afar.
> Eyes that fire and sword have seen
>> And horror in the halls of stone
> Look at last on meadows green
>> And trees and hills they long have known.

Gandalf looked at him. "My dear Bilbo!" he said. "Something is the matter with you! You are not the hobbit that you were."

And so they crossed the bridge and passed the mill by the river and came right back to Bilbo's own door.

"Bless me! What's going on?" he cried. There was a great commotion, and people of all sorts, respectable and unre-

spectable, were thick round the door, and many were going in
and out—not even wiping their feet on the mat, as Bilbo noticed with annoyance.

If he was surprised, they were more surprised still. He had
arrived back in the middle of an auction! There was a large
notice in black and red hung on the gate, stating that on June
the Twenty-second Messrs Grubb, Grubb, and Burrowes
would sell by auction the effects of the late Bilbo Baggins Es-
quire, of Bag-End, Underhill, Hobbiton. Sale to commence at
ten o'clock sharp. It was now nearly lunchtime, and most of
the things had already been sold, for various prices from next
to nothing to old songs (as is not unusual at auctions). Bilbo's
cousins the Sackville-Bagginses were, in fact, busy measuring his rooms to see if their own furniture would fit. In
short Bilbo was "Presumed Dead", and not everybody that
said so was sorry to find the presumption wrong.

The return of Mr Bilbo Baggins created quite a disturbance, both under the Hill and over the Hill, and across the
Water; it was a great deal more than a nine days' wonder. The
legal bother, indeed, lasted for years. It was quite a long time
before Mr Baggins was in fact admitted to be alive again. The
people who had got specially good bargains at the Sale took a
deal of convincing; and in the end to save time Bilbo had to
buy back quite a lot of his own furniture. Many of his silver
spoons mysteriously disappeared and were never accounted
for. Personally he suspected the Sackville-Bagginses. On
their side they never admitted that the returned Baggins was
genuine, and they were not on friendly terms with Bilbo ever
after. They really had wanted to live in his nice hobbit-hole so
very much.

Indeed Bilbo found he had lost more than spoons—he had
lost his reputation. It is true that for ever after he remained an

elf-friend, and had the honour of dwarves, wizards, and all
such folk as ever passed that way; but he was no longer quite
respectable. He was in fact held by all the hobbits of the
neighbourhood to be "queer"—except by his nephews and
nieces on the Took side, but even they were not encouraged in
their friendship by their elders.

I am sorry to say he did not mind. He was quite content;
and the sound of the kettle on his hearth was ever after more
musical than it had been even in the quiet days before the Un
expected Party. His sword he hung over the mantelpiece. His
coat of mail was arranged on a stand in the hall (until he lent
it to a Museum). His gold and silver was largely spent in pres
ents, both useful and extravagant—which to a certain exten
accounts for the affection of his nephews and nieces. His
magic ring he kept a great secret, for he chiefly used it when
unpleasant callers came.

He took to writing poetry and visiting the elves; and
though many shook their heads and touched their foreheads
and said "Poor old Baggins!" and though few believed any of
his tales, he remained very happy to the end of his days, and
those were extraordinarily long.

One autumn evening some years afterwards Bilbo was
sitting in his study writing his memoirs—he thought of call
ing them "There and Back Again, a Hobbit's Holiday"—
when there was a ring at the door. It was Gandalf and a dwarf;
and the dwarf was actually Balin.

"Come in! Come in!" said Bilbo, and soon they were settled
in chairs by the fire. If Balin noticed that Mr Baggins' waist
coat was more extensive (and had real gold buttons), Bilbo
also noticed that Balin's beard was several inches longer, and
his jewelled belt was of great magnificence.

They fell to talking of their times together, of course, and Bilbo asked how things were going in the lands of the Mountain. It seemed they were going very well. Bard had rebuilt the town in Dale and men had gathered to him from the Lake and from South and West, and all the valley had become tilled again and rich, and the desolation was now filled with birds and blossoms in spring and fruit and feasting in autumn. And Lake-town was refounded and was more prosperous than ever, and much wealth went up and down the Running River; and there was friendship in those parts between elves and dwarves and men.

The old Master had come to a bad end. Bard had given him much gold for the help of the Lake-people, but being of the kind that easily catches such disease he fell under the dragon-sickness, and took most of the gold and fled with it, and died of starvation in the Waste, deserted by his companions.

"The new Master is of wiser kind," said Balin, "and very popular, for, of course, he gets most of the credit for the present prosperity. They are making songs which say that in his day the rivers run with gold."

"Then the prophecies of the old songs have turned out to be true, after a fashion!" said Bilbo.

"Of course!" said Gandalf. "And why should not they prove true? Surely you don't disbelieve the prophecies, because you had a hand in bringing them about yourself? You don't really suppose, do you, that all your adventures and escapes were managed by mere luck, just for your sole benefit? You are a very fine person, Mr Baggins, and I am very fond of you; but you are only quite a little fellow in a wide world after all!"

"Thank goodness!" said Bilbo laughing, and handed him the tobacco-jar.

*If you are interested in Hobbits you will learn a lot mor about them in The Lord of the Rings:*

1. THE FELLOWSHIP OF THE RING
2. THE TWO TOWERS
3. THE RETURN OF THE KING

# Kafka: A Study

An educational edition of this book is available in the Student Guides to European Literature series, general editor Brian Masters.

*Other Titles in the Series*

*Molière*, by Brian Masters
*Sartre*, by Brian Masters
*Goethe*, by F. J. Lamport
*Rabelais*, by Brian Masters
*Corneille*, by J. H. Broome
*Böll*, by Enid Macpherson
*Saint-Exupéry*, by Brian Masters

# Kafka: A Study

*by*

ANTHONY THORLBY

*Professor of Comparative Literature*
*University of Sussex*

HEINEMANN
LONDON

Heinemann Educational Books Ltd

LONDON EDINBURGH MELBOURNE AUCKLAND TORONTO
HONG KONG SINGAPORE KUALA LUMPUR
IBADAN NAIROBI JOHANNESBURG
NEW DELHI

ISBN 0 435 38895 9

Published by
Heinemann Educational Books Ltd
48 Charles Street, London W1X 8AH
Printed in Great Britain by
Richard Clay (The Chaucer Press) Ltd
Bungay, Suffolk

# Contents

# Foreword

This book is intended to help students of literature in schools
and universities, as well as others who read Kafka for pleasure.
As so many people have come to know and be fascinated by
his work in English translation, all quotations in this book are
given in English, although page references have been given
to the German edition. For the most part the standard English
translations have been used, but in some cases a new translation of a phrase or word is offered. Kafka makes much play
with the multiple and metaphorical meanings of words, and
adequate equivalents cannot always be found in another
language. Some illustrations of this difficulty are given in the
chapters that follow, and the German original has been included in such cases.

Kafka is of special interest to any student of modern literature in no matter what language. This is because he was so
extraordinarily intelligent in his understanding of the generally
unspoken assumptions that underlie many tendencies and
techniques in modern writing – intelligent, that is, in self-understanding of his position as a writer.

A.K.T.
University of Sussex

# Acknowledgements

To acknowledge all that I have learnt from other scholars who have written about Kafka would be impossible. So much has been written about him that it is difficult even in the bibliography at the end to give anything like a fair selection of critical books; to have referred to other scholars' views in detail in the text would have taken up much space, which I have preferred to use for an analysis of Kafka's work that is, I hope, as original as can be expected at this already late stage in the debate. Sometimes my own view differs only slightly from that held by others; sometimes, however, it differs radically. I have indicated the main points of difference between my own and some earlier interpretations, though without attempting to refute the specific arguments of other scholars, many of which I have found valuable in arriving at my own conclusions.

I wish to thank S. Fischer Verlag and Schocken Books, New York, for permission to quote from the German edition of Kafka's work and to make translations from it, and Secker and Warburg for permission to quote from the English translations – and also to depart occasionally from these.

# Biographical Note

Franz Kafka was born on 3 July 1883, in Prague. He was the son of a successful, self-made merchant who had known hardship as a boy in the country. Both Kafka's father, Herrmann, and his mother Julie (*née* Löwy) were Jews; many of his family died as a result of Nazi persecution.

At university, Kafka studied literature briefly, then took up law in which he received his doctorate in 1906. He took a job with one insurance company, soon moved to another, the Arbeiter-Unfall-Versicherungs-Anstalt (Workers' Accident Insurance Company), with which he remained until he was pensioned off as a result of ill-health in 1922. His health was always weak, despite his persistent and even strenuous efforts to improve it; he visited several sanatoria, and died on 3 June 1924 in the Wienerwald Sanatorium in Vienna after suffering from tuberculosis first diagnosed seven years earlier.

Kafka passed almost all his life in Prague, making only short trips abroad and to the country, where he enjoyed particularly staying with his sister, Ottla, at Zürau. He several times made plans to marry, becoming officially engaged to Felice Bauer in 1914 and again in 1917; his last liaison was with Dora Dymant, with whom he lived for a while in Berlin in 1923, and who stayed with him till he died.

Only a small part of Kafka's writing was published during his lifetime, and he entrusted his unpublished works to Max Brod, his closest friend and a writer of some note, whom he asked to destroy them – although Max Brod had told him that he would not do so. Kafka remained relatively unknown until after the Second World War (for notorious reasons in the German-speaking world), but since then he has gained an international reputation as one of the greatest writers of the twentieth century.

# 1

## Life and Work

**Kafka's extraordinary achievement, and aims, as a writer**

Karl Kraus, who was Kafka's contemporary and also a citizen of the Austro-Hungarian Empire in its last decades, once wrote: 'The understanding of my work is made more difficult by a knowledge of my material.' The same is true of Franz Kafka. Editors, critics, and biographers have made available every scrap of information, every traceable manuscript, even remarks remembered by other people, that might throw light on Kafka's fiction. It cannot be said that all this material has helped very much – and yet it is in a certain sense indispensable. The sense in which it is helpful is largely a negative one: it makes clear the extent to which Kafka has made the autobiographical element in his work unrecognizable. But, of course, we need to know something about what he and his life were actually like in order to recognize how strangely both have become transformed in his writing.

Whether it is *permissible* that Kafka's life, and particularly his inner life, his fantasy world from which he drew his inspiration, should be pried into, is another question. Kafka asked his close friend, the novelist and critic Max Brod, to destroy his unpublished manuscripts. Max Brod did not comply, for reasons that he explained in a postscript to one of the novels of Kafka's that he published posthumously (*The Trial*). Had he complied, we should possess now only a handful of stories, and it is unlikely that Kafka would have achieved the kind of international fame that has been accorded to him since the Second World War. The letters Kafka wrote, especially those to the women who meant most to him, Felice Bauer and Milena Jesenská, might still have come to light. Some material and – what is incomparably more tragic – many persons related to Kafka's existence have perished without trace as a result of Nazi persecution of the Jews. It is in these exceptional circumstances, both intimately personal and globally political, that the question arises of what is the 'right' way to understand Kafka.

Suppression and oppression are part of the process that has made Kafka famous. His prose narratives contain to a unique degree symbolic statements of what civilized men have had to suffer in this century. These statements are not realistic descriptions of persecution in modern society. Kafka's fiction is not realistic in the normal sense of that word, and his own interest in politics and social conditions was, as regards his writing, very slight. The problem that has prompted so many critics to write more about Kafka than about any other writer since the war is this: how has it come about that an author so apparently indifferent to the world about him, so apparently turned in on himself, should have symbolized so profoundly events that occurred, and were increasingly to occur, outside his own experience and above all after his death? The English language even looks like accepting as an adjective, having a meaning familiar to a considerable number of people, the word 'Kafkaesque' (a distinction conferred for a while on the name of Shaw, and more lastingly on that of Dickens). The answer to the problem raised by Kafka's work has indeed a lot to do with what words mean, and particularly with the different kinds of meaning they can have – including, as we shall see, the dreadful possibility that they have no ultimately reliable meaning at all.

In saying this, we meet again the same kind of paradox that we mentioned at the start. In order to recognize an ultimate inadequacy in language, we must have something to compare it with. We need to be able to see that words seem to mean something at one level that at another level they do not. In real life we may often feel that words are inadequate; in some cases other forms of objective verification may be used to check their correctness. But if a writer wants to make clear in words the inadequacy of words, he faces a peculiarly difficult task. For he has both to evoke their meaning and to suppress it at the same time. This is one way of describing Kafka's literary technique. He presents a story, often no more than a simple incident or situation, which has an apparently realistic, surface meaning. As we look at it, however, we seem to see through it, as though it were also unreal, weird, nightmarish. We cannot then say for sure what other meaning we have glimpsed, and as a result *positive* interpretations of Kafka's symbolism have provoked wide disagreement amongst critics. Perhaps the only point of agreement is that Kafka's fiction cannot be taken at its face value and read like conventional novels about the real world. Realist writers generally want to make us believe in and understand the world as they describe it. Kafka wants to do this too, of course, since he too is a writer; but he also wants to do the opposite – to make us aware that the reality before us is incredible and incomprehensible.

Kafka knew well enough how paradoxical his aim and method as a writer were. He recalled and recorded in later years his ambitions as a young man:

> [I was sitting once] thinking over the things I wanted in life. What seemed most important and attractive was the wish to achieve a view of life (and – necessarily connected with this, of course – to be able to make other people believe in it by writing), in which life would still preserve its natural, solid course of ups and downs, but at the same time would be seen just as clearly to be a nothing, a dream, a weightless movement. A good wish perhaps, if I had desired it aright. Rather like wishing to hammer a table together with painstaking care and skill and at the same time to be doing nothing; and not in such a way that people could say: 'He doesn't take hammering seriously',

but so that they would say: 'When he hammers he really
means it but it is also nothing to him.' And the act of
hammering would thereby have become still more daring,
more determined, more real, and also perhaps more mad.
                    (*Beschreibung eines Kampfes*, pp. 293 f)

This passage illustrates the way Kafka's creative intelligence
works. He is, as the opening sentences make clear, talking
about the art of writing, which will make the real world both
real and unreal, a 'nothing' (*ein Nichts*). In order to grasp what
kind of activity his writing will be, he chooses a simile, likening
it to carpentry. Immediately a scene takes shape before his eyes,
with people speaking, commenting upon his 'work'. This projection outwards of a mental activity, that transforms it into an
apparently concrete job in real surroundings, makes his work
both more serious and more mad. In the next sentence Kafka
refers to himself no longer as 'I' but as 'he':

> But he could not wish any such thing, for his wish was no
> wish at all, it was merely a defence, a civilizing of nothing-
> ness (*Nichts*), a touch of lovely humour that he wanted to
> bestow on that nothingness, where he had only just begun
> to consciously take his first few steps, but which he already
> felt to be his element. (ibid., p. 294)

We see here Kafka's ability to turn his self-reflections into a
concrete symbol, indeed into a whole symbolic world where
things and people take on an objective reality – so that 'I' becomes 'he' – *and also* to stand back and observe the impossibility of the task. This constitutes the essence of Kafka's
genius. In the language of existentialism, with which Kafka is
sometimes associated, it constitutes an exercise in self-
alienation. The obscure depths of meaning that are suggested
by Kafka's symbolism are empty or negative depths; their
psychological secret is the discovery of nothingness. The 'view
of life' Kafka wished to achieve was and is a nihilistic viewpoint. His fiction will seem true to us in so far as we share it,
that is to say, in so far as we see the world from out of empty

space. Kafka's positive lesson is that he teaches us just where we may be standing and looking from, and what are the consequences of this nihilistic position. He wrote a number of aphorisms about the figure called 'he', in which he observes his position as observer. One of them is as follows:

> He has found the Archimedean point, but has used it against himself; evidently this is the condition that has enabled him to find it.
> (In *Hochzeitsvorbereitungen auf dem Lande*, p. 418)

## Kafka's cultural and social background

The two-sidedness of Kafka's talent, which has produced a truly profound ambiguity in his writing (apart from simple disagreement amongst his critics), can be related to his situation as a Jewish writer in Prague at the beginning of this century. This is not to suggest that Kafka's gift for bestowing more than just 'a touch of lively humour' on nothingness, his combination of subtle intelligence and deep moral, even religious feeling, is not unique and personal in degree. But in kind there is something typical about it. Kafka was born into a distinctive social and cultural milieu that provided him with remarkable spiritual resources.

It is important to recall, for instance, how greatly Jewish intellectual life had been retarded in Europe, partly as a result of social constraints imposed from without and amounting at times to violent persecution, and partly as a result of a deeply conservative vein within the Jewish religious tradition itself. Kafka was born at a time and place where the possibility, and therefore the problem, of assimilation into non-Jewish society was still recent and acute (severely restrictive laws were in force against the Jews in the Hapsburg Empire until 1848, as regards such matters as residence, employment, marriage, and above all, education). Kafka's father was a self-made man from the country, and one of the steps he took to gain success in Prague was to adopt German as his language and hence make it the language of his family. This further complicated the situation of his sensitive son, Franz, who grew up to find himself speaking the language of an influential, largely upper-class minority.

Kafka himself never suffered any persecution, but he was inwardly unsure about whether he 'belonged' in the society in which he lived. Even without the complications of his Czech and Jewish background, it is likely that Kafka would have experienced this doubt in some form, for it had been growing into a major obsession amongst writers for over a century, ever since the first romantic moan about the poet's solitude had sounded so effective. Kafka's situation as a German-speaking Jew in Prague gave him fresher and deeper access to this no longer new source of inspiration.

With Kafka it was not a case of feeling spiritually superior to an unfeeling, ugly, or materialistic world. He was not interested so much in the inadequacies of the society from which he felt alienated as in the complexities of his own state of mind. Far from producing books that imply the world is at fault for failing to satisfy human expectations (as rather too many simple-minded books of recent times have done), Kafka meditated critically upon these expectations themselves. In his fiction it is not clear who or what is at fault. Critics have brought social, religious, and psychological explanations in, to show what Kafka 'really' meant. But as we have said, he is not a realist writer; he himself was not looking for some external frame of reference to which to refer the question of what existence 'means', and it seems somewhat inappropriate for critics to try and provide him with one.

What did fascinate Kafka was the possibility of finding an internal way of grasping the meaning of meaning (which in his case meant the meaning of writing, the meaning of words). If he could do this, he would be free of all the uncertainties that surround any fixed frame of reference. And we should note that a longing for freedom is the other face of the condition of solitude in Kafka's fiction; it is likewise rooted in his experience of being a writer.

The difference made by his being a Jewish writer can again be described as a problem of assimilation. Let us take, by way of contrast to Kafka's preoccupation with the meaning of meaning, a common-sense realist view of the question. If meaning is not accepted as referring to a context of experience or rules outside itself, the question could be said to fall into an infinite recession. (Once this type of question is accepted as itself meaningful, you can go on to ask: 'What is the meaning of the meaning of meaning?' And so on.) What may be described as an 'assimilated' mind will then feel justified in putting a stop to this type of inquiry, which clearly leads nowhere.

Kafka, as we have seen, was under no illusion about the fact that his destination, his 'element', was nowhere, *das Nichts*. But this in no way weakened his determination to go on, just as K. goes on towards the unattainable castle, where there await him, even if he got there, unimaginable hierarchies of 'authority', an infinite recession of 'trials' from which he will never be set free. The fact that Kafka could not, as it were, leave well alone and simply live in the world without asking such impossible questions is due to his having the sensibility not only of a writer but of a Jewish writer. No writer of any intelligence can be fully assimilated to his earthly condition, the condition of having a mortal mind. A Jewish writer is likely to feel doubly unassimilated, because the roots of his mental life reach back into soil that is quite different from that on which the traditions of Western reason and common sense have been erected. It is religious soil, and three things must be said about it that are relevant to Kafka.

First, Judaism is an essentially different kind of religion from Christianity. This is not simply because of the explicitly new departure recorded in the Gospels (a matter that is not relevant here), but because of the long centuries of effort on the part of the Christian church to assimilate religious truth to the truths

B

of reason as these were inherited independently in the West from the Greco-Roman world. This process of assimilation reached its apogee in the late eighteenth and early nineteenth century, passing over into modes of thinking from which the religious element was fast disappearing, being replaced by increasingly materialist and scientific conceptions of man's destiny.

This point was reached, therefore, at about the same time as Jewish emancipation began so very belatedly to take place in Europe. One result of this was that a Jewish intellectual was potentially endowed with a remarkable spiritual constitution and opportunity: one part of his mind might still be close to an archaic, unassimilated religious tradition, while another part found the sophisticated intellectual equipment of modernity at his disposal. In Kafka's case, we find a familiar form of modern rationality expressing itself, challenging the world with a typical mixture of religious scepticism, moral idealism, and egotistical determination; but we also find a deeper resonance behind this plausible surface – the resonance of a religious seriousness that lacks any positively religious commitment. We may say that Kafka believes in nothing, but feels that the condition of believing in nothing is dreadful.

Here a second point needs to be made, concerning precisely this word 'dread'. The insight that reason may not be assimilable to existence has by no means been the exclusive prerogative of Jewish thinkers; it has been the starting point for that type of philosophizing known generally as existentialism, and was the starting point in particular for the Danish theological writer, Søren Kierkegaard. Now, Kafka read some of Kierkegaard's work, recognizing how deeply it touched his own condition, and responding most evidently to his forerunner's 'Concept of Dread'.

Dread or *Angst*, as it has come almost internationally to be called, is perhaps the only significant discovery of a new component of the psyche in modern times, something between an emotion and a thought, and yet not classifiable under the conventional categories of earlier psychology. It is the experience evoked in a man by the awareness of his selfhood and of the infinite discrepancy between what he knows and what he is. It is the experience that is symbolized and to some extent communicated by Kafka's writing. Kafka approached this abyss of uncertainty from a background unlike that of Kierkegaard, who was after all a Christian apologist. But their psychological discovery is similar in that it springs from a confrontation between a modern self-conscious intelligence and the *mysterium tremendens* of temporal existence.

The third aspect of Kafka's Jewishness that requires comment can only be sketched here in barest outline. It concerns the association of ordinary, everyday existence in time with a mystery of religious, or in some other way spiritually binding, importance. The tendency of Christian theology was for centuries, as we have said, to identify things divine with universal principles of morality and truth that stood above the realm of time and change. The Judaic religion has remained more firmly grounded in historical lore; and it resembles less an ideology, in the sense of premises and arguments to be understood, than a way of life, a ritual established on the authority of precedent and custom. This is not to deny that the Talmud offers commentary, interpretation, and analysis in plenty; but the subtlety of Rabbinical intelligence (and humour) has lain rather in adjusting thought to the decrees of the inscrutable.

Kafka was not well informed about his own religion, and his feelings towards it were ambivalent; at various stages in his life he became deeply impressed by some aspect of Judaism – by the Zionist movement, for instance, by Hassidic literature, and on one occasion by a troupe of Yiddish actors. But it is not here that we find the most telling marks of Kafka's racial religion upon his writing (however many putative similarities, borrowings, and influences critics knowledgeable in Jewish lore may detect in Kafka's work). We find them rather in the 'faith-value', to quote Kafka's own term, that he sensed in the simple act of living. It is characteristic of Kafka that we find this expression not in a personal profession of faith but in an aphoristic dialogue, which is an extremely detached literary form – and a favourite one for telling Jewish jokes:

> 'It cannot be said that we are lacking in faith. Even the simple fact of our life is of a faith-value that can never be exhausted.' 'You suggest there is some faith-value in this? One *cannot* not live, after all.' 'It is precisely in this "cannot, after all" that the mad strength of faith lies; it is in this negation that it takes on form.'
>
> (In *Hochzeitsvorbereitungen auf dem Lande*,
> Aphorism 109, p. 54)

One other example may be quoted, this time from a letter to Max Brod. It shows again the kind of spiritual fascination aroused in Kafka by the appearance of security, of confident belonging, that he saw *in other people*:

> When I opened my eyes after a short afternoon nap . . . I heard my mother speaking to someone from the balcony and asking them in a quite natural way: 'What are you doing?' A woman answered from the garden: 'I am having tea on the lawn.' And I was amazed at the assurance (*Festigkeit*) with which people are able to bear life.
>
> (*Briefe 1902–1924*, p. 29)

## Freudian Neurosis

Kafka's own life was outwardly ordinary and secure enough – compared, for instance, with the Bohemian existence of many European artists and writers – but he never felt inwardly at home in it. Yet he lived in his family's home for many years, worked full-time in an insurance office most of his life, and repeatedly made plans to get married and settle down. His attempts and failure to achieve this latter goal constituted the one, long, complex adventure of his inner world, where it was inextricably bound up with his inspiration as a writer.

As we might expect with Kafka, the connection is both very clear and profoundly obscure, resembling almost a form of self-torture he could not do without. It certainly resembles the psychological state that Kafka's great contemporary, Sigmund Freud (whose early work he knew about), was in these same years defining as neurotic. Kafka even reached, independently of Freud, the same conclusion that the origin of such neurosis lies in a son's relationship to his father. At the age of thirty-six Kafka wrote a 'letter' to his father – which he never delivered – that is a small masterpiece of psychoanalytic writing. If Freud's theory of analytical self-understanding is true, then Kafka's astonishing clearsightedness, in which there appears to be no trace of repression or fantasy, should signify that he was cured. Indeed, at one point in his 'letter to his father'* Kafka describes all his writing as a form of psychoanalytic cure: 'a long-drawn-out leave-taking from you', he says to his father: and again: 'My writing was all about you.' Whenever some stories of his had been published and he presented a copy to his father, not even his father's indifference could prevent Kafka from feeling – and as he subtly observes, perhaps helped him to feel – 'Now you are free.'

Did Kafka's writing, did the self-knowledge displayed not only in this letter to his father but in so many other letters and journal jottings, set him free? Kafka himself goes on: 'Of course, it was a delusion; I was not, or, to put it most optimistically, I was not *yet* free.' Of his writing, perhaps of this letter, perhaps of all his books, he remarks: 'How little all this amounted to!' The ambiguity about what 'this' refers to increases in the following sentence, where Kafka says that 'in my childhood it ruled my life as a premonition, later as a hope, and still later often as despair, dictating – it may be said, yet again in your shape – my few little decisions to me'. What is this 'it' which ruled Kafka's life 'in the shape of' his father?

* Also printed posthumously in the volume entitled *Hochzeitsvorbereitungen auf dem Lande und andere Prosa aus dem Nachlaß*.

Freud too resorted to the same word, the *id*, to describe the force that ultimately rules men's lives, expressing itself through various channels and 'shapes', some of them seeming – according largely to local customs – more healthy or normal than others. Can any man be entirely free of 'it', unless he dies? And the very desire to be free: is that perhaps merely another expression of 'it', only disguised in some peculiarly fatal and self-destructive form? Is the life instinct ultimately inseparable, perhaps even indistinguishable, from a death instinct?

These are all questions that cannot be answered within the frame of reference constructed by modern psychology. Kafka knew as well as any psychoanalyst to what remote depths, inaccessible to the light of consciousness, all the processes of the mind may be referred. And he knew more; he knew that no certain, scientific knowledge can ever unlock the labyrinthine secrets of the soul, the truly crucial secrets of 'conscience' in the sense not merely of man's capacity to feel guilt but of all his closely related capacities for self-awareness, for knowledge, for creative aspiration towards freedom and truth and beauty. The mind cannot unlock its own secrets, because the more highly rationalistic, conceptual, and verbally precise its questioning becomes, the more inappropriate it is to the 'thing' it is asking about. The modern manner of handling life intellectually – and Kafka had a pre-eminently modern intelligence – makes the thing impossible to grasp. The mysterious origins of the spirit recede into the impenetrable murk of something that looks absurd, obscene, and even evil. No wonder that Kafka should once have noted down despairingly: 'Never again any psychology!'

The hope of cure, of being set free, which sustains Kafka's writing, remains inseparable from his sense of enslavement, his manifest neurosis, which (in his own eyes at least) reached psychosomatic proportions. He repeatedly interpreted the tuberculosis that finally caused his death as a self-inflicted wound. Writing again to Max Brod about his desire for 'freedom, freedom above all else', he goes on in characteristically ambiguous terms: 'Admittedly the wound is still here, of which my sick lung is only the symbol.' Where is 'here'? In the desire for freedom? In the village where he happened then to be staying with his favourite sister, Ottla? Or simply in life itself, where the nameable diseases that kill us are only symbols of an inescapable, inscrutable decree that all men must die?

In Genesis a story is told of why men have to die: because Adam was beguiled through Eve into wanting knowledge of good and evil. Kafka often meditated upon this Biblical story, and upon other mythological stories that symbolize the human condition. For such stories do enable us to grasp life as a whole, and (if we believe in them) to have faith in life's ultimate meaningfulness – even though the myth may be an account of how we come to be deprived of that meaningful life which would be Paradise. Kafka's own writing has a similar mythological quality, in that his imagination conceives symbolic stories of man's deprived spiritual state. His myths symbolize the ills of modern selfconsciousness, the self-destructive urge to know oneself, assert one's innocence and rights, and through knowledge and determination to achieve freedom.

Kafka's myths differ from those of ancient tradition, however, as he well knew. For those of tradition (whether classical or Judaic) are based on a belief in the reality of the gods, that is to say, in the objective reality of spiritual forces external to men, of spiritual values embodied *in* the world. Kafka's modern, sceptical intelligence did not allow him to believe this. His myths, like his seemingly religious attitude towards his writing, point not outwards towards the world but inwards against himself.

## Kafka's 'philosophy'

Kafka's mythology, then, is based not on observation of the world but on observation of the self. His extraordinarily subtle insight into this process does not constitute a psychology, in the sense that it illumines worldly passions such as love, jealousy, greed and the like. Kafka's imagination reaches beyond all particular contents of the self to form mythological pictures of the total process of self-consciousness. And he encounters, as a result, the inevitable limit of all efforts at total understanding, where words pass over into symbols whose meaning cannot be related to anything beyond themselves.

His symbols resemble a second myth of the Fall, with the difference that they are not set in the context of a God-created paradise man has lost, but of a man-made hell he cannot escape from. Apart from the stories that symbolize this situation, Kafka's notebooks contain many aphoristic speculations, which formulate it abstractly; they provide a kind of inverted theology to explain the inverted myths of his fiction. He writes, for instance:

> The observer of the soul cannot penetrate into the soul, but there doubtless is a margin where he comes into contact with it. Recognition of this contact is the fact that even the soul does not know itself. Hence it must remain unknown. That would be sad only if there were anything apart from the soul, but there is nothing else.
>
> (In *Hochzeitsvorbereitungen*, p. 93)

Kafka often repeats the assertion, which on the face of it seems highly improbable, but which forms a major premise of his 'theology' and is essential to an understanding of his fiction, that 'there is nothing besides a spiritual world'. Whatever reaction this may provoke in readers brought up in a more realistic tradition, it must constantly be remembered that Kafka found his inspiration by immersing himself totally in his mental world and trying to describe his 'dream-like inner life'. The conflicts that produce such suffering and despair in his stories have not been conceived in the rationally objective manner of most conventional writing, i.e. as conflicts between real persons or (what conventionally has been supposed to be at the base of these) as a conflict between man's bodily and his spiritual nature. The division within Kafka's world is a division of the mind against itself.

The spiritual character of Kafka's world is seen again in the following notes, which pass with a sudden and, at first sight, mysterious jump to a moral speculation, where one might not have expected there to be any grounds for moral judgements of any kind:

> Three different things:
> Looking on oneself as something alien, forgetting the sight, remembering the gaze.
> Or only two different things, for the third includes the second.
> Evil is the starry sky of the Good.
> (In *Hochzeitsvorbereitungen*, p. 90)

The starry sky, traditional symbol of Heaven, has become for Kafka a symbol of the opposite, of evil. What does this inversion mean? First, let us remark that Kafka often says similar things about evil, even though his symbolism varies. For instance, the phrase quoted above to the effect that: 'There is nothing besides a spiritual world', continues as follows:

> What we call the world of the senses is the evil in the spiritual world, and what we call evil is only a necessity of a moment in our eternal evolution.
> (ibid., Aphorism 54, p. 44)

Or again:

> Evil is a radiation of the human consciousness in certain transitional positions. It is not actually the sensual world that is a mere appearance, what is so is the evil of it, which, admittedly, is what constitutes the sensual world in our eyes.　　(ibid., Aphorism 85, pp. 49 and 102)

Kafka's next aphorism then concludes:

> ... the whole visible world is perhaps nothing other than a motivation of man's wish to rest for a moment – an

attempt to falsify the fact of knowledge, to try to turn the knowledge into the goal.

(ibid., Aphorism 86, pp. 49 and 103)

Evil, then, is for Kafka attributable in some way to human consciousness; it is a kind of mistake or failure within the evolutionary process of the mind. It seems to come about from the mind's desire not to evolve further, 'to rest for a moment', and to accept as final, as real, its knowledge of the world.

Since Kafka's time, the spread of existentialist philosophies has made more familiar such assumptions as these: that the world has no fixed reality, that existence is something which is eternally being created within human consciousness, and that the only evil is to deny this creative role and try to 'rest' with the fixity of appearances. Kafka himself could have become familiar with such assumptions through his reading of Kierke-gaard, or through his knowledge of Nietzsche. The weakness of existentialist thinking, just as much in Kierkegaard as in Nietzsche, and apparent again in Heidegger and Sartre, lies in the difficulty of establishing any valid morality, i.e. one having regard to the good of other persons or any real results in the world. To the existentialist mind, *whatever* one does (or thinks) will, as soon as it is embarked on and starts to become real, also start to appear wrong – or 'evil', in Kafka's phrase.

The redeeming feature of Kafka's inverted theology as far as his writing is concerned is that he was obviously aware of the fatal paradox embedded in it. 'The state in which we are is sinful, irrespective of guilt,' he writes; and in the same vein: 'The fact that there is nothing but a spiritual world deprives us of hope and gives us certainty.' (Aphorisms 83 and 62) As we have suggested, Kafka's ability to pronounce upon the pre-dicament of the modern intelligence, and above all to symbolize this in stories that have religious profundity and the archaic surrealism of myth, may have been due to a still deeply Jewish feeling for the God-ordained character of life. Aphorism 83 begins by declaring: 'We are sinful not only because we have eaten of the Tree of Knowledge, but also because we have not yet eaten of the Tree of Life.'

Kafka's conception of the sanctity of life, in contrast to which he saw the starry heaven of self-observing thought as evil, is quite distinct from the *avant-garde* cults of sex, vitalism, and the like, which were fashionable in his day. His values in this respect sound quite piously conventional. He writes to his father:

> Marrying, founding a family, accepting all the children that come, supporting them in this insecure world and even guiding them a little as well, is, I am convinced the utmost a human being can succeed in doing at all.
>
> (ibid., p. 209)

But as he wrote to the sister of another girl – Julie Wohryzek – with whom he broke off his engagement; 'We were both perfectly clear that I regarded marriage and children as in a certain sense the highest thing to be striven for on earth, but that I was quite incapable of getting married.' Doubtless it was from this incapacity, this betrayal of the highest good on earth, that Kafka's sense of guilt largely sprang; but so also did his inspiration as a writer.


## Conclusion

In conclusion, then, we may sum up the paradoxical relationship of Kafka's work to his life as follows: his fiction is not 'about' his life in any conventional sense, and yet it *is* a symbolic expression of his life to an unusually intimate and intense degree. To pore over the letters Kafka wrote to Felice Bauer, with whom he twice became engaged but never married, can tell a reader of *The Trial* little of interest above the level of indiscreet gossip, and may actually mislead him. For the one important fact that detailed knowledge of Kafka's unhappy love life is liable to obscure is this: novels like *The Trial*, or stories like *The Judgement*, which have some psychological connection with Kafka's affairs with other people, are not recognizably about those affairs. More important still, they are not about human affairs *of that kind*. That is to say, they are not descriptions of the kind of events that we (or Kafka) could observe in the world, with merely some of the details changed or invented.

The course of events in Kafka's fiction (i.e. the plot), together with the way the personages react (i.e. their character), are frequently trivial or incomprehensible when judged by common-sense standards of realism. A critic who tries to work out the connection between, say, Frieda (in *The Castle*) and Milena Jesenská, or Klamm and Ernst Polak (Milena's husband), is going in the wrong direction and undoing Kafka's intellectual work.

Kafka's work aims at understanding its own inward character, not that of other people. And we must stress again that it is the inward character of his life as a writer that he strives to understand. Kafka is not *describing* even his own life in its outward aspect, as so many writers have done with more or less exaggeration during the last two hundred years. He made a new departure in the already well-established business of ego-gazing that is based on a quite radical realization: namely, that one cannot know oneself in the same way that one knows things and people outside oneself. Thus he writes:

> How pathetically scanty my self knowledge is compared with, say, my knowledge of my room . . . Why? There is no such thing as observation of the inner world, as there is of the outer world. At least descriptive psychology is probably, taken as a whole, a form of anthropomorphism, a nibbling* at our own limits. The inner world can only be experienced, not described.                (ibid., p. 72)

Similarly, it makes not much sense of *The Castle* to assume that it is a satire on bureaucracy based upon Kafka's experience as an employee of an insurance company. Not only do large

* The German text has 'ein Ausragen der Grenzen', but the incorrect English translation still conveys Kafka's meaning.

chunks of the text become irrelevant or boring on this assumption, but the attitudes and experiences of the hero seem in detail inexplicable and inappropriate. Of course, there is plenty of evidence to show that Kafka found his job ever more frustrating and irksome. 'My job is unbearable to me,' he wrote to Max Brod, 'because it contradicts my sole desire and my only vocation, which is literature. As I am nothing but literature, and neither can nor want to be anything else, my job can never have any hold over me, though it certainly can shatter me completely.' The whole point of *The Castle* is that K., the hero, wants to reach, enter, and master some organization that has an immense hold over him – and not simply a material hold such as jobs have over anyone who has to earn his living.

K. would seem both in *The Trial* and *The Castle* to be in a position merely to ignore the mysterious 'authorities' if he wanted to. Again, the point is that K. does not want to; the authorities fascinate him and he is drawn to them with his whole being. And as the letter to Max Brod says, his whole being is literature; it is literature that draws Kafka to itself, and to the impenetrably guilty and locked – the German word for 'castle' (*Schloß*) also means 'lock' – recesses of himself. Kafka's satire (if that is the right word for his style of writing) is directed against the impossibilities and immoralities not of any organization in society but of the sources of 'authority' in his, an author's, mind.

As we have seen, his intellectual assessment of what he wanted his writing to achieve was ambiguous: he wanted it to achieve everything and nothing – and he thought that the predicament of self-knowledge was typified by this problem. Kafka's moral assessment of the situation is even more vividly divided. We sometimes find him expressing the hope that his writing will be able to 'raise the world up into [a state of] purity, truth, and immutability'. More frequently we find descriptions of his enterprise that reveal both to what spiritual victory it aspired and to what dangers he was exposed:

One can disintegrate the world by means of very strong
light. For weak eyes the world becomes solid, for still
weaker eyes it seems to develop fists, for eyes weaker still
it becomes shamefaced and smashes anyone who dares to
gaze upon it.*                                    (ibid., p. 91)

At the other end of the scale, however, we find Kafka judging
writing in the harshest terms:

Writing is a sweet and marvellous reward – but for what?
Last night it came home to me with the clarity of an object
lesson for children, that it is the reward for serving the
devil. This descent to the dark powers, this setting free of
spirits that nature meant to be held in check, questionable
embracings and all the rest of it that is probably going on
deep down, which one doesn't know about any more if
one writes stories by the light of day. Perhaps there is
another way of writing, but the only one I know is this: at
night, when I cannot sleep for *Angst* – that is the only sort
of writing I know. And it seems to me quite clear why it is
devilish. It is the vanity and pleasure-seeking practice of
whirling around one's own person all the time, or around
someone else's – the movement then reduplicates itself,
producing a solar system of vanity –, and of enjoying
them. The thing an ordinary, simple man sometimes
wishes: 'I'd like to die and see how people are sorry that
I've gone,' is what a writer actually keeps doing; he dies
(or doesn't really live) and is perpetually sorry for himself.
                              (Letter to Max Brod, July 1922)

* The ambiguity in this aphorism lies in the suggestion that Kafka both
aspired to possess the very strong light and yet knew what it was like to
suffer (spiritually) from very weak eyes. The difficulty introduced into his
writing by his playing opposite roles simultaneously will be discussed
further in the next chapter.

# 2

# The Short Stories

Myths are essentially short. They can be elaborated, of course, and be told in a sophisticated style, and be added to and varied; but all these elaborations and embellishments do not add anything of *mythological* interest to the original, simple story.

The mythological character of Kafka's imagination shows in his gift for conceiving a situation, a scene, sometimes a single image, that is replete with significance. These Kafkaesque situations 'speak worlds', as it were, and nothing that is said afterwards alters the essential shape of any of these worlds, no matter how much detail is added. Indeed, the reader may as a result have the impression that he is getting nowhere as he presses on through the unfinished chapters of *The Castle*, and wonder whether Kafka ever could have written a conclusion that would have put the hero into any position that he was not already in at the start. Certainly a reader who expects, from his experience of more conventional novels or of the drama, that the plot and the characters should develop in some necessary way, is likely to be uneasy at the thought that there could ever be serious uncertainty about the order in which Kafka intended to place the chapters he completed for *The Trial*, or about whether he might have written one or two more.

All in all, we may not be surprised if the verdict of posterity is that Kafka is at his best as a short-story writer, however valuable the novels may have been in establishing his fame (it could be argued that their power also rests at bottom on the simple situation from which they spring). The simple situation that Kafka's imagination repeatedly tries to grasp as a whole is the point where two incompatible, incommensurable things meet and conflict. What the two things are can only be stated symbolically, not realistically. For a realistic view implies that we are able to look on at the conflicting parties from outside. If, however, the conflict that Kafka is trying to imagine is the total one of the mind's situation in the world, there is clearly no outside position, in any realistic sense, from which he can look on. In Kafka's fiction we can usually not be sure (i.e. in terms of a realistic interpretation) what his symbols 'mean', in the sense of 'refer to'. But we can always see quite clearly that there is tension and conflict. Even his notebook jottings have this clarity, right down to a short sentence, such as: 'A shout arises out of a river' or even the single compound word: 'Pigsticking'.

## Beschreibung eines Kampfes ('Description of a Fight', 1904/5)*

Since there is no space to discuss all of Kafka's stories in detail, and enough general remarks about his work have now been made, the best course will be to look at a few of the stories as closely as possible, beginning with the earliest, 'Description of a Fight'. This is already a characteristic piece of Kafkaesque writing, in that it exists in more than one version, consists of vivid scenes that are strung together in no necessary order, and is unfinished. The fight takes place between two characters who are referred to simply as 'I' and 'he', and who have, by conventional standards, few memorable characteristics. For all that, their struggle is real and intense, and it occurs in a frozen landscape that is partly a recognizable part of Prague – it must be the Laurenziberg, which was the scene of Kafka's youthful meditations on his life's ambition (recorded above, pp. 3–4) –

* The dates given in parentheses after each title indicate when the work was written.

and is partly a fantasy landscape that one or both of the characters enter at various stages in the story.

This mixture of realism and fantasy is not always successful here, but it is typical of Kafka's style, which at its best produces an indissoluble fusion of the two, so that the reader begins to accept nightmarish absurdities as matters of fact. Where the style is uneven, as it is in 'Description of a Fight' and continues to be still in a later book like *America* (1912), the characters and environment appear now in one light, now in another: at one moment there is normal conversation in a bar, at another weird, dreamlike behaviour in forests and deserted squares.

Both 'I' and 'he' represent aspects of Kafka himself, but again it is difficult to define them; the only thing that is clearly defined is the rift and tension between them, the fact that Kafka is divided against himself. 'He', for instance, is probably not the intellectually detached 'he' of the aphorisms, who had reached the Archimedean point. This 'he' is a man involved in a love affair which 'I' feels called upon to sort out. 'I', in fact, rides on the back of 'he', whom he brings at the end to stab himself – an uncanny anticipation of the idea of a self-inflicted wound which was to recur to Kafka's mind when tuberculosis 'released' him from his obligation to marry. 'I' would seem, therefore, to be playing the role here of Kafka's intellectual self.

'I's' relationship to the 'he' who lives in society and falls in love becomes particularly understandable in this light in the scene where 'he' goes through the outward motions of prayer rather too ostentatiously and is criticized for being bogus – or inauthentic, in the language of more recent existentialism – by the critical, uncommitted 'I'. 'He' answers that he has to pray in public like this, because he needs the gaze of other people in order to feel himself 'hammered together'. We have already quoted Kafka's use of this striking image in connection with his own writing, where the hammering was to be taken with complete seriousness and yet to mean nothing at all. It is likely that this crucial image of the section entitled 'Conversation

C

with the Praying Man', which Kafka published as a separate
story (in *Hyperion*, March–April 1909), was important to
Kafka less as a realistic psychological insight into the way any
man actually prays than as a symbol of the relationship between
reality and writing with which he personally was so deeply concerned.

If we look at the story, 'Conversation with a Praying Man',
on its own, however, we find that the definition of the roles
played by 'I' and 'he' is not entirely consistent with what has
been said above, and might even be said to be the other way
round. For instance, it is 'he' who tells the anecdote of the
woman calling out that she is having tea on the lawn (quoted
above, p. 10, from a letter of Kafka's to Max Brod); and it is
'he' who finds it extraordinary, and 'I' who protests that it is
not. 'I' plays the part rather of a rational psychoanalyst who
knows what the experiences of 'he' are like: they suggest 'he'
is in a state of existential 'nausea' – Kafka actually used words
similar to those employed by Kierkegaard to describe dread,
though he had not then read Kierkegaard, and similar to those
made famous since by Sartre – and 'I' is the one anxious that
'he' should conquer it.

The story concludes by 'he' making flattering remarks about
'I's' worldly appearance and suggesting that 'confessions become most clear when one recants them'. All this is very much
in contrast with the impressions of the world that 'he' has just
been recounting, which makes things and people seem so insubstantial that they could be swept away by the wind. Evidently by recounting them and forcing 'I' to accept his story,
'he' has recanted in some therapeutic way the sickness that
troubles his soul.

The German word for 'recant' (*widerrufen*) has faint philological undertones of repeating something over again, rather as
the English 're-cant' has. Kafka, as we shall see, makes much
use of the double meaning of words, which comes about as a
word passes to a higher, metaphorical level of significance. For

he knows that it is in this way that the structure of thought is built up, partly providing a greater spiritual mastery over the world, but partly also producing a sense of increasing separation from it, accompanied by feelings of insecurity as language fails to fasten on anything real. The conversation that Kafka here holds with himself through the two voices of 'I' and 'he' is typical of all his future work which explores precisely this ambiguity in the nature of language. His writing might be described as an effort to set himself free from the insecurities and inauthenticities induced by his being an author. It is a kind of re-cantation of literature itself, that is, of the impression that words grasp reality.

## Hochzeitsvorbereitungen auf dem Lande ('Wedding Preparations in the Country', 1907)

'Wedding Preparations in the Country' is another story that exists in two versions, neither of which is complete – evidence again of Kafka's greater interest in the statement of a situation than in the development of a story. The story, such as it is, concerns the visit of an office worker to his fiancée in the country, an engagement about which he feels reluctant and guilty, and a journey that plunges deeper and deeper into rainfall and nightfall. Kafka is experimenting here too with those stylistic effects that are already beginning to be distinctively 'Kafkaesque', and such things as the progress of the plot or realistic characterization are almost irrelevant to this undertaking.

The conversation might be about Kafka's own attitude towards the conventional story-interest of fiction when Raban, the central figure, says: 'When one is about to embark on some enterprise it is precisely the books whose contents have nothing at all in common with the enterprise that are the most useful. For the reader . . . will be stimulated by the book to all kinds of thought concerning his enterprise. Since the contents of the book are precisely something of entire indifference, the reader is not at all impeded in those thoughts and he passes through the midst of the book with them, as once the Jews passed through the Red Sea.' This is how the reader of Kafka will pass through his ever more inscrutable *œuvre* (inscrutable, that is, from a realistic point of view), being stimulated to all manner of thoughts about the enterprise of telling even the simplest story, of telling in words what any experience is actually like.

In this connection, Raban makes one still more illuminating observation, and one which throws further light on Kafka's interest in the interacting points of view of 'I' and 'he'.

> So long as you say 'one' instead of 'I', there's nothing to it and you can easily tell the story, but as soon as you admit to yourself that it is you yourself, you feel as though transfixed and are horrified.
>
> (*Hochzeitsvorbereitungen auf dem Lande*, p. 8)

The remark reaches at once to the heart of existentialist understanding of the world. It is like a hollow, frightening echo of Kierkegaard's more positive assertion that the individual is higher than the universal. Language, however, is by nature 'universal'; it reduces what are essentially distinct and different individual experiences to a standard set of shared words. Moreover, the standard set by language enables the individual to judge the value of things, and above all what he himself is, according to socially acceptable norms. He will understand his place in the world so long as he uses its language with confidence, believing that what is generally said about people is true also of his own experience. But he may develop the capacity and desire to dissociate himself from the common code; he may feel that he is acting a part when he performs society's routine. And once he can self-consciously act the role of living, able to see it and play it in his imagination, he is no longer really bound by its conventions, but can look at it all from the outside. He can see it all with a new vividness and judge it by no conventional standard at all.

This position of being an outsider has been much idealized by minor exponents of existentialism, who have tended to confuse a nihilistic source of judgement with a positive one. Kafka certainly does not idealize it, as must be clear from the extraordinary simile he uses to describe Raban's imaginative position when he feels that he need not really go to the country in person to get married but will simply send his body:

> Can't I do it the way I always used to as a child in matters that were dangerous? I don't even need to go to the country myself, it isn't necessary. I'll send my clothed body. If it staggers out of the door of my room, the staggering will not indicate fear, but its nothingness . . . For I myself am meanwhile lying in my bed, smoothly covered over with the yellow-brown blanket . . . As I lie in bed I assume the shape of a big beetle, a stag beetle or a cockchafer, I think. (ibid., pp. 11 f)

It is an image we shall meet again in one of the best-known stories that Kafka ever wrote, 'Metamorphosis', where its significance will become even clearer.

Here we may conclude by stressing the extraordinary sharpness of visual perception that Kafka associates with this strange state of hallucinatory detachment from his body, and from the body of everyone and everything about him. It is because he sees their nothingness that he sees them so clearly. But just as it was difficult to define consistently the roles played by 'I' and 'he', so it is difficult to decide whether it is the external world that should be evaluated as 'nothing', or Raban's inner world. Kafka's technique in this early fragment is simply to juxtapose, and alternate, totally impersonal passages of objective detail with passages of totally subjective reflection. There is a disturbing lack of relevance or connection between them, and it is probably to this indefinable area, this metaphysical gap in the phenomenon of existence, that the word 'nothingness' most appropriately applies. Kafka's skill as a writer lies in his ability to make us aware of the presence of this nothingness. Whether the things on one side of this gap should be considered more real than the human consciousness on the other side is a question that cannot be answered; and for this reason reality and nightmare are ready to become confused, indistinguishable, and ultimately identical in Kafka's later work.

## Das Urteil ('The Judgement', 1912)

Neither of the fragmentary pieces discussed above is a love story, but both of them begin from a love situation, which then stimulates thoughts going far beyond itself. When Kafka wrote them he had, though not innocent of any amorous encounters, not yet met Felice Bauer. Their apparently harmless meeting took place on 13 August 1912; but a few days later Kafka recorded the occasion in his diary, concluding his sharp, unflattering description of her appearance with the words: 'As I was sitting down I looked at her for the first time more carefully, and when I was seated I had already an unshakeable judgement' ['*hatte ich schon ein unerschütterliches Urteil*'].

How fateful that look was, and how ambiguous that clear judgement! Was it a judgement on her or on himself? Earlier in the diary entry he remarks against himself how alienated he felt 'from everything good in its entirety'; and the first masterpiece Kafka wrote, having the title 'The Judgement', deals with the fatal consequences – to himself – of a young man's announcement of his engagement in a letter. Two days before Kafka composed this story during a single night of unprecedented inspiration, he had written for the first time to Felice Bauer.

Of this composition, which was to remain Kafka's favourite, partly because of the compelling power with which it had come to him, Kafka nevertheless used the painful image that was to haunt him five years later as a symbolic way of expressing the connection between his writing, his engagement, and his (in his view) self-inflicted tuberculosis: 'Then the wound broke open for the first time in one long night.' That not only this story, but also probably 'Metamorphosis' and above all *The Trial* are intimately connected with Kafka's relationship to Felice Bauer there can be no doubt. Unfortunately, this biographical information does not make the story, perhaps the most mysterious that Kafka ever wrote, any easier to understand.

The transition in this story from a description of commonplace events (a young man writing about his engagement to a friend living abroad), to an equally matter-of-fact account of very uncommon events (the son's being condemned to death by his father and going out to execute the sentence), is perfectly treated; the texture of the narrative, which is both normal and terrible, is quite seamless. The doddery old father of the first half who rises up at the end to pronounce judgement with the authority and effectiveness of a God-figure still remains at the same time a grotesque old man. His actions and remarks make no more and no less sense at the end than they do at the beginning, but they gradually acquire the power of life and death.

Why does Georg's father have this power over him? About six months after writing the story, Kafka felt prompted to 'write down all the relationships which have become clear to me as far as I now remember them' – he was then engaged in reading the proofs – and this particular question of the father's authority he answered as follows:

> . . . only because he [Georg] has lost everything except his awareness of the father [*Blick auf den Vater*] does the judgement, which closes off his father from him completely, have so strong an effect on him.
>
> (*Tagebücher*, 11 February 1913)

The diary entry as a whole stresses the obvious fact about the narrative that at the beginning Georg believes that he has a bond with his father through the figure of his friend, whereas at the end the bond seems to exist only between father and friend to the exclusion of Georg. If we ask again why this should change the father's position of initial weakness into one of such formidable strength, we find that what has really changed is the plausibility and effectiveness of Georg's position; it is his authority, his 'version' of his marriage, his friendship, and his filial devotion, which has collapsed. The reality of existence rears up in the shape of his father, rending the fabric of Georg's carefully considered thoughts (the letter writing doubtless symbolizes his belief that he has made sense of his life in words), brushing aside his last few strands of spoken protest, and destroys him.

The truly Kafkaesque quality of this story, in which Kafka for the first time fused the elements of his inspiration – hitherto expressed in fragmentary form – into a perfect whole, is easier to identify than to explain. It lies in the fact that Georg cannot see how monstrous and absurd his father's 'judgement' is. Or rather, he *can* see this, tries to defend himself with some facetious observations, but nevertheless obeys the judgement as though it were – in the words of his own diary entry – 'unshakeable'. What has collapsed is Georg's bond with commonsense normality; he is drawn by some inexplicable compulsion, which is as unhesitating as love and as irresistible as the urge to create, towards what he partly knows to be monstrous and absurd.

Doubtless it was in some such way that Kafka, who definitely identified his own fate with that of Georg Bendemann, remained neurotically obsessed with his father, his writing, and his fiancée. This similarity with the circumstances of Kafka's life has led critics to interpret the story in biographical terms. There are, however, some particular difficulties of detail involved in doing this; but before we look at these, there is one more general comment that must be made. The most disquieting question presented by 'The Judgement' is this: on what grounds does any judgement about what is monstrous and what is normal ultimately rest?

In the first instance, a man's judgements rest on convention, and at a deeper level they rest on faith. At the beginning of the story Georg gives a conventional account of his life to a friend. At the end, his faith in having the friend – that is to say, convention – on his side is shaken. Then psychological insecurities about the nature of his feelings for his parents and his bride drive him to commit suicide, while still mentally in alert possession of his faculties. Such subconscious compulsion, which reason is powerless to resist, is exactly what psychoanalysis regards as neurotic. In this connection two observations of Freud's are pertinent: first, that the private codes of behaviour and fantasy in neurotic patients often resemble actual moral codes, religious beliefs, and works of art, but are caricatures of them. Second, that where an obsessional neurosis is shared by a whole community it need no longer be regarded as sick and may very well be accepted as a religion.

In giving this account of the story, we have already come close to saying what the various characters 'stand for'. We did not quite interpret the friend as 'standing for' convention, however, but interpreted rather the psychological importance to Georg of having a friend, and hence of supposing (mistakenly) that he has a friendly relationship with his father through his friend. The psychological relationships within the story are clearer, in fact, than the characters of the persons between whom they exist; indeed, it is uncertainty about the latter that make the former so compelling. Much of Kafka's effect derives from the impossibility of interpreting – in the sense of 'referring to an external convention of meaning' – the three main personages.

On the simplest level of biographical interpretation, for instance, Kafka's actual father generally welcomed, rather than resisted, Kafka's marriage plans; and he did not claim (as the father in the story does) that his son's friends were really his own – these Herrmann Kafka did dislike. The friend represented in the story, moreover, does not appear to be an intel-

lectual of any kind, as Kafka's few friends actually were; the
most that we can be sure of is that he is a not very successful
business man, destined to 'irrevocable bachelorhood', and that
he is somehow not respectable in the eyes of Georg's fianceé. If
the father is a good family man (and has really been a businessman like Kafka's own father, even though not a very efficient
one in the son's eyes – another biographical detail that does not
'fit'), then his preference *for* the friend over his own son appears
to conflict with the fiançe's prejudice *against* Georg's having
such disreputable friends. Of course, one may interpret one's
way around these difficulties by saying that what the father
really wanted was an unmarried son, and that Kafka's 'letter to
his father' shows how deeply the son felt his father had made
it impossible for him to marry. Before venturing onto this un-
certain psychological ground, however, one simpler point has
to be made.

In the story Georg appears to be a very efficient businessman,
and he finds no problem from his point of view about marrying,
whatever difficulties there may be in getting his friend, his
fiancée, and his father to accept his plans. It is therefore
puzzling to see how Kafka can be identified with this character.
The only solution is to regard all the characters – including the
fiancée, for Felice Bauer (Kafka's fiancée) can scarcely be
supposed to have disapproved of Max Brod (Kafka's friend)! –
as relationships within Kafka's mind, as projections of different
aspects of his own psyche, and not as real people at all, or even
as symbols standing for anything outside himself.

Looked at like this, we can say that a *part* of Kafka was
conscientious and competent at the office, and did, as we have
seen, earnestly plan to marry. But in another part of his mind
Kafka had, as it were, emigrated abroad and had only a remote
and unsuccessful relationship to business; this part he knew
was doomed to 'irrevocable bachelorhood', and to imaginative
exposure to all kinds of danger. The crucial relationship with
the father also becomes intelligible once we regard the old man

not as an independent character, but again as part, the pro-foundest part, of Kafka's psychological make-up.

A glance again at the 'letter to his father' will remind us how little it portrays of an objective person (though it pinpoints a few doubtless real characteristics) by comparison with the subtlety of its portrayal of inner tensions within Kafka, who pursues the ramifications of the relationship entirely within his own mind, writing an imaginary answer from his father, then answering that himself, and so on. Similarly, the father in 'The Judgement' does not symbolize at all realistically a businessman, or a family man, or any sort of bourgeois moral code or Jewish belief (which Kafka's actual father did perhaps represent for him). But this Kafkaesque father figure may symbolize Kafka's private *relationship* to some or all of these things: his relationship to the sources of his own life, to the inscrutable and frightening fact of being alive, which he – like the rest of us – tried to 'cover up' in conventional platitudes, pretending it was normal when deep down he knew it was monstrous and absurd.

The scene of 'covering up' is, as every critic has said, the crucial turning point in the story. It is described as being done with blankets because the German word for to 'cover up' (*zudecken*) readily – and perhaps basically – suggests the idea of a blanket (*Decke*); and as we have seen, it is by means of this kind of linguistic association and concretization that Kafka's creative mind works. But it is not a real man or literal father that is covered up in any actual bed; it is the 'bed' or source of Kafka's creativity which a part of himself tried to smother with conventionality, at this moment in his career when he had be-come established in his job and considered marrying. The part that was in danger of being smothered, the creative part, in other words, which Kafka knew to be deeply associated with *his* relationship to his father – although Herrmann Kafka, the man, was in reality hardly a very inspiring figure – then rose up and 'killed' Kafka. The 'wound', as he described the experience of writing this story, was mortal. He was now a true writer; and a writer, as Kafka wrote to Max Brod, 'dies (or doesn't really live) and is perpetually sorry for himself'.

## Die Verwandlung ('Metamorphosis', 1912)

'Metamorphosis' was written only a month or two after 'The Judgement', in the same period of intense inspiration that produced also substantial parts of a novel – later called *America* – to which Kafka gave at the time the significant title, 'The Man who Died Away' (*Der Verschollene* – another example of a word that has come to be used metaphorically in everyday speech, to mean 'missing' or 'forgotten', but which is in fact the past participle of the verb *verschallen*, to 'die away' of sound; sounds and silence, noises and listening, had all kinds of symbolic overtones for Kafka's imagination, as we shall see later). This story is again about a man who dies, 'or doesn't really live', and it is conceived in such a way as to extract the maximum of humour and pathos from this piteous fate. It indeed expresses the writer's desire to be 'sorry for himself', but certainly in no romantic or idealized way; the device of having the hero wake up to find himself transformed into a beetle renders the whole situation absurd.

Alas, all too many critics have treated 'Metamorphosis' with humourless solemnity, defending the beetle's point of view as though it provided a serious criticism of bourgeois society with its narrow-minded conventions and false values. The story seems to me to provide nothing of the kind. If it carries any criticism at all, then it is directed as much against the beetle as against anyone else. And to the extent to which Kafka identified himself with Gregor Samsa – he saw similarities between the hero's name here, as with Georg Bendemann's in 'A Judgement', and his own; and we have noted already that the early hero, Raban, also felt like a beetle, besides having a name that can be associated with Kafka's own (a 'raven' resembles a 'jackdaw', which is what *kavka* means in Czech) – the criticism is directed once more against himself. It is, however, less a moral criticism, let alone a social one, than a psychological critique, or analysis, of what writing does to the world and to the self. It 'transforms' both of them beyond recognition, as the title of this story (in German) already implies.

Laboriously to point out each of Kafka's humorous–pathetic effects would be to ruin them every one. Suffice it to say that they result from everybody's efforts, including the beetle's, to do something appropriate to the situation. Since there is no known cure for having turned into a beetle, nothing is appropriate and every response is absurd. This is not to say that every response is the same: the chief clerk's pompous speeches are clearly different from the mother's sentimental sighs and shrieks, the father's self-assertive hostility from the sister's selfless sympathy. But they are all engulfed in the same absurdity, and while this gives them a momentary 'depth', they quickly sink to the bottom where nothing matters any more.

It is remarkable how Kafka manages to sustain our interest for as long as he does, giving to the story an illusion of suspense and movement, as Gregor and his family show signs of coming to terms with what has happened, and even hope that something else will. The reader almost forgets what it is that has happened and that it is absurd to expect anything could be done about it to make it bearable. Is Gregor beginning to feel a little better as he learns to beetle about the walls and ceiling, does his sister care about him more or less, will the family survive . . . ? But what on earth are we talking about – the family has a beetle in the house instead of a son! There can only be one solution to this absurd problem and all the equally absurd personal re-actions and domestic crises to which it gives rise; and that is death.

Astonishingly, Kafka even contrives to give to this foregone conclusion a hint of further, even positive meaning. It is as though Gregor's final disillusion, suffering, and death had become a kind of self-sacrifice, almost an act of expiation, which has redeemed the whole family in some way. It is no more than a hint, and it too trembles on the brink of nonsense; for the way this family has been 'saved', if that is what the ending means, is by first turning one of its members into a beetle and afterwards getting rid of it.

But naturally we know better nowadays than to deal with a work of literature, and especially a modern work, in so simple-minded a spirit. We have learnt to recognize symbolism when we see it. And the symbolism of this story is plain: here is modern man in his alienated condition, treated as an insect by his fellows who think only of appearances, frustrated in his inner longings which he is unable to communicate, swept away good-humouredly but forcefully by the unsqueamish prole-tariat, and all the while an unacknowledged religious victim . . . or words to that effect.

Now, it is worth reminding ourselves that we do not have to accept the effect of words as true just because they have been used 'symbolically'. Symbolism has become for students of literature a magic concept to conjure with: find the symbolism in a poem or story, its 'deeper' meaning, and its value is estab-lished (and the value of literary criticism). But if literary criti-cism is not to degenerate into a lesson in sophistry, teaching in effect that anything can mean anything, we have to judge for ourselves not just whether there is symbolism in a work but whether we accept that symbolism as true, whether the symbol has been well chosen, i.e. on what grounds and for what pur-poses.

There is nothing particularly mysterious about the way Kafka achieves his effects in 'Metamorphosis': he simply con-tinues to describe Gregor's thoughts and feelings as though they were human, while everything connected with his bodily condition, such as his physical ability to see and speak is reduced to the level of an insect. The device could hardly be more artificial; it is certainly no less so than the allegorical make-believe and puppet shows of medieval literature. The difference in Kafka's case comes about from his having used a realistic style of presentation; but this should not deter us from asking what the purpose of his patently absurd invention is. Simply to jump to the conclusion that it shows symbolically how absurd conventional living is, would be to remain entirely uncritical in the face of a particular kind of literary effect.

What, then, is the literary effect produced by Kafka's grotesque invention? Strange to say, the predominant one is rather familiar, rather old-fashioned, and not at all symbolic: it is what in English we might call 'Dickensian' – and Kafka was much impressed by Dickens – and are inclined to regard as an amalgam of sentimentality, humour, and pathos. The swooning mother, the bemedalled father, the sweet-natured sister playing the violin: this is the stuff of which a certain kind of Victorian novel is made. Indeed, a large number of novelists throughout Europe in the nineteenth century were drawn towards the subject of poverty, lower-class family life, and the psychological problems of a social code based on money and respectability, even if they did not all go to the harrowing lengths of describing the womenfolk ruining their eyesight over badly paid sewing and lodgers lording it over a humiliated household, as Kafka does here.

Quite apart from these emotionally obvious themes, there is the detailed description of quite commonplace events that is common to all novels written in the style known loosely as 'realism' – as though opening a door or crossing a room or the words people actually use in daily speech or the clothes they actually wear were more 'real' than anything recorded by writers about life before. Kafka writes sentences crammed with observation and suspense to describe Gregor's efforts to open a door. It is a breathless, climactic passage: will he manage it? What will happen next? Now, if we ask why this scene is so gripping, we see at once that it is solely because 'he' is a beetle. And the pathos, humour, and sentiment of all the scenes mentioned above are due of course to the same cause. The symbolism of this story, that is to say, the literary device upon which it is based is undoubtedly important and illuminating. But what it illumines is not so much any real defectiveness in society as one source of realistic effectiveness in literature.

In reopening the question of what Kafka's symbolism means, we are in danger of starting too soon on a much larger problem of interpretation, before we have looked at enough examples of his writing. The larger issues will be left till the last chapter, therefore, and the immediate question of what 'beetledom' meant to Kafka pursued further here. The words Kafka uses to describe Gregor's state (*Ungeziefer, Insekt, Käfer*) doubtless had connotations and associations for him that are less evident in English: a dirty little monster, a creature divided into sections, a being imprisoned – the word *Käfig*, a cage, has alliterative similarity to *Käfer*, and it was through hints of other meanings hidden in words, which in this case again resembled his own name, that Kafka transformed the world.

He was also interested in the ambiguity of a closed-in state: did it imply a stronghold and security, or imprisonment and deprivation? A notebook entry reads simply: 'My prison cell: my fortress.' The postures in which Kafka later describes his 'hero' elaborate these associations. Gregor is now imprisoned in his room which gets into a more and more filthy state; he is divided in two, in that he has the mind of a man and the body of a beast. The most revealing features of Kafka's symbolism, which are at the same time entirely 'naturalistic', come from the beetle-man's ability to lie on the ceiling, a position where he feels 'more free', and from the concession he gains from his family after he has been *wounded* (an idea associated with writing for Kafka, as we have seen), to watch their everyday life through a chink in the slightly open door. Nothing could symbolize more exactly the position of the writer as an outsider looking on, a situation in which many of Kafka's contemporaries found themselves and also found their inspiration:

Proust and Mann (whose *Tonio Kröger* Kafka admired), Joyce, and Yeats, who also declared, 'I must lie down . . . in the foul rag-and-bone shop of the heart.' It is to the conditions under which 'he' has been 'allowed to find the Archimedean point' of effective literary portrayal that Kafka's beetle symbolism points above all.

Kafka forces us to ask a question that has only recently started to receive much critical attention: from what *point of view* does a novelist write, on what attitude to life is fiction based? The question is of acute importance because the amount of 'social' criticism contained in many realistic novels seems to be high, and has come to be accepted as useful for purposes of education and even of sociological research.

The implication of 'Metamorphosis', then, is that the novelist's viewpoint is unnatural and even disgusting. The one fatal thing to do (for someone in Gregor's 'position') is to let oneself be carried away by the deceptive lure of art, by its sweet suggestion of an emotionally and imaginatively more satisfying world: Gregor's death results from the scene where he leaves his prison in response to his sister's performance on the violin. He wants to bring her back to him, who truly appreciates her, to be with him in his foul beetle-room, to really live with her again. He forgets what he is – which is to say, he forgets what the condition of art is. The outrage he feels at the philistine human beings who are listening to her as well, but do not (he senses) appreciate her, together with his desire to save and possess the promise of beauty he hears in her music and remembers in his heart, are vitiated, of course, by his monstrous appearance as a beetle. If we interpret the symbolism of *this* situation, we see that Kafka is casting the gravest doubt upon the emotional responses of the artist, and upon his indignation at society. He is saying 'in effect' (that is, by showing from what point of view such literary effects are achieved) that the pathos and satire of the realistic novel are the products of a degraded and deluded vision – a beetle's vision.

D

Kafka reveals, by his grotesque reproduction of Dickensian effects, to what extent the sentiment they evoke differs both from that of moral satire and from that of tragedy. There is nothing besides sentiment in the protest of realistic fiction of this type: beneath the surface of humorous–pathetic satire there is a *totally* hopeless situation – beetledom. The effect of realism is to make us feel that something ought to be done to improve men's misfortunes in society – and so it should! – but Kafka betrays the literary secret of this way of writing. It makes something appear to be society's fault, and so capable of improvement, that is in fact past all remedy: beetledom. And here we have to ask whether we believe Kafka's symbol to be generally valid (and it is a matter of religious faith), for what it implies is that man is as hopelessly and inappropriately situated in the world as a beetle would be in a human family. And that the most he can hope to achieve is an impression of that family's being better off – redeemed – in some way when it has got rid of an unwanted spiritual perversion in its midst. We have to decide how trustworthy we find a beetle's point of view to be.

## In der Strafkolonie ('In the Penal Settlement', October 1914)

Kafka lived through the period of the First World War, which was to put an end to the Austro-Hungarian Empire and to make the social order of most European countries look like an *ancien régime* that could never return; but even in his diaries and letters he rarely mentions this cataclysm, the world's first experience of modern war, which was soon to alarm the imaginations and conscience of so many – although at one time Kafka considered volunteering for military service, from which he was officially excused on grounds of poor health.

'In the Penal Settlement' is a story, however, that might be interpreted as an exception to Kafka's customary reticence on the subject of the war and of the public world generally. It is certainly a story that concerns bloodshed and discipline, and the conflict between an old-fashioned military code and new attitudes of liberal humanitarianism. The fact that it is not about trench warfare, or indeed about warfare at all, need not discourage interpreters of a later generation, who have grown used to hearing war described in terms not of heroism and duty – the rhetoric still heard publicly in Kafka's day – but of a 'machine', a war-machine, which is the metaphor that forms the basis of this gruesome story. The metaphor is presented literally, of course, in the imaginative manner with which we should now be becoming familiar in Kafka. 'In the Penal Settlement' is about an actual machine, a horrible invention of Kafka's, that puts men to death in accordance with ancient law and custom.

The old law, for which we see a prisoner about to die, is very simple; it is based on obedience to the law which itself turns out to be supported by illegible or otherwise incomprehensible writings; for the prisoner is illiterate and the narrator, who is represented as a detached, scientific observer, can also make nothing of them. The officer who champions the old order claims that the machine is so designed that the condemned man will, as the machine slowly tortures him to death, 'get the point' of the law whose meaning or verdict has never been explained to him in words. This metaphor – though it happens not to be available in German (others are) – has, as it were, been taken literally in Kafka's story: the meaning of the deadly punishment is slowly cut deeper and deeper into the body of the victim by the sharp points of the machine.

The judgement to be thus physically 'borne in upon' the man on this occasion is: 'Honour thy superiors!' (*Ehre deinen Vorgesetzten!*) which carries in German perhaps a clearer suggestion that an old order of things, and not just a chain of command, has to be maintained. Now, as the story continues, we see how this order is already being undermined, cannot be maintained, and eventually goes to pieces. Again, these meta-

phors are illustrated literally: the machine has not been kept in
good working order, and eventually the mechanism goes wrong
and murders in a quite unforeseen fashion the officer who has
always believed in it. The reasons why the upkeep has been
neglected might very well be seen as an allusion to actual
political developments in Europe generally before 1914. In
Germany and Austria, for instance, the approval of the military
budget had for years been a major political issue; so had the
whole question of the role of parliament and the spread of
democratic ideas; and in England the cause of women's votes
was also involved. These are the factors also at work in the
'penal settlement' that have quite changed the way in which
ritual executions are carried out. There was a time when each
execution was a public occasion, almost a festival, watched and
applauded by women and children. Even the victims were
ecstatic in their agony, to judge anyway from the expression the
officer recalls seeing on their faces as they got the point of the
time-honoured code.

There are many such details having a possible relevance to
the 1914 war, which revealed its murderous character already
in its opening months (on the Marne, at Tannenberg, on the
Galician front). Even the grisly humour of the story, which
depends on the same kind of contrast exploited in 'Metamorphosis' between attitudes of sensible, human concern and
a basically inhuman situation, might be said to apply to the
way the army 'takes good care' of the very men it will sacrifice
as cannon fodder. But there are also, of course, several important features of the story that do not seem to have any connection with the war, or if they are meant to have one, represent
it falsely. For instance, the officer class in no sense sacrificed
itself *instead of* its men, even if it (in some cases) entered the
fray to prove the justice of its cause. Perhaps it was possible to
believe in 1914 that 'the war to end all wars' would release the
common people and put an end to the military caste; Kafka
had certainly read revolutionary writers like Bakunin, Herzen,

Kropotkin, and attended occasional meetings of the anti-
militarist 'Klub mladých' and the working-class 'Vilem
Körber'. But why is the Old Commandant, who actually invented the dreadful machine, buried in the local tea-house,
having been refused burial by the church? After all, military
men in the past were generally given splendid funerals by
church and state alike; why *this* suggestion of disgrace here? By
telling us that 'the priest wouldn't let him lie in the churchyard'
and showing us the grave in a tea-house 'that made . . . the
impression of a historic tradition of some kind', Kafka inevitably starts off in our minds thoughts of a quite different
interpretation. This interpretation is strengthened as soon as
we glance again at Kafka's biography.

July 1914 had been a fateful month in Kafka's life for quite
personal reasons. The shots fired in Sarajevo were unimportant
beside the sentence he felt had been passed on himself in the
Berlin hotel where, before witnesses, his engagement to Felice
Bauer was formally dissolved. Kafka likened the occasion to a
court of law (*ein Gericht*) at which he kept silent. This silence is
stressed as a feature of the story, where it distinguishes the last
moments of the machine as it goes wrong and murders the
officer: scarcely a very appropriate detail to characterize any
aspect of the First World War, but rather more relevant to
Kafka's experience of writing – at night, in solitude, and silent.
And the detail which makes least sense as regards the war and
the military, namely, that the officer subjects himself to punishment by the machine, makes most sense when interpreted in
autobiographical terms: this was exactly how Kafka described
his extraordinary viewpoint as a writer 'that he had turned it
against himself'.

The result of Kafka's turning of his intelligence on himself,
instead of upon life, was to put an end to the long-drawn-out
torture of a love story that was no longer capable of producing
the ecstatic sighs of tradition – another puzzling detail if the
story is supposed to be about war – and to abruptly kill the man

in charge. Who, then, is this man, and what is the machine he operates; and why does the machine go murderously wrong under the gaze of the rationally detached onlooker – and who anyway is he? A biographical interpretation leads naturally to the answer that all represent parts of Kafka's personality. The machine, in particular, looks very much like a pictorial representation of the self-torturing process of writing as Kafka experienced it. The part with the points is called by Kafka in German *der Zeichner*, and it writes the words of the 'judgement' into the flesh of the condemned man (*der Verurteilte*) – expressions which recall Kafka's conception of artistic activity. And not only Kafka's. His contemporary, James Joyce, with whom he has more similarities than has generally been recognized, describes in *Finnegan's Wake* how Shem the Penman writes world history as he cowers in his pitchblack house O'Shame, using his own skin as paper and his own bodily fluids as ink:

> . . . with this double dye, brought to blood heat, gallic acid on iron ore, through the bowels of his misery, flashly, faithly, nastily, appropriately . . . [this] first till last alshemist wrote over every square inch of the only foolscap available, his own body, till by its corrosive sublimation one continuous present tense integument slowly unfolded all . . . cycle-wheeling history (thereby, he said, reflecting from his own individual person life unlivable, transaccidented through the slow fires of consciousness into a dividual chaos, perilous, potent, common to allflesh, human only, mortal) . . .

Kafka likewise, beginning from his 'own individual person' and finding 'life unlivable', condemned to a slow death of shame for some unknown guilt, transformed this experience 'through the slow fires of consciousness' into a story that is not the 'dividual chaos' of Joyce's *œuvre* but is in some way related to a turning point in world history.

If we assume that 'In the Penal Settlement' is not so much *about* any single, identifiable reality, in the sense that realistic literature usually appears to be about some one thing, but is a symbolic 'world' in its own right, then it is possible to refer it *both* to Kafka's biography and to the First World War. The onlooker, whose visit to the settlement provokes the crisis of the story, has only one word to say: 'No.' He rejects the traditions on which the cruel machinery – of writing and of war – has been justified. When the disciple of these traditions turns the machine against himself, it not only kills him but 'no sign was visible of the promised redemption; what the others had found in the machine the officer had not found'. Some part of Kafka, then, did not believe either in war or in writing.

This part was what we have called Kafka's essentially modern, sceptical intelligence. And the strength of his negative belief, his 'no', his inverted theology (as we have called it) was such that it could establish a bond between private and public experience, between poetry and war: a negative bond. The cruelty of existence is, after all, merely intensified by war, not created by war. Men suffer in any event more or less; and all must die. The crucial question for a writer is not whether he has got his historical facts right, whether his realism is true; the reality of suffering and death is known to him through his imagination, and the question he must decide is what it means – i.e. his symbolism must be true. Literature has since the earliest times offered symbolic statements of life's cruelties, which in art appear irradiated by beauty, a convention that has been publicly accepted as meaning that human suffering is redeemed when the point of life's law is borne in on us in this way. But to the sceptical onlooker of 'In the Penal Settlement', whose gaze is fixed upon the sun, as though upon the bright light of a higher truth, all the beautiful writings of the past, like the skilled workmanship that went into designing the now dilapidated machine, have become unintelligible and unacceptable.

Finally, then, we can say who the Old Commandant 'is' and

why he is buried in the tea-house. He designed the machine, which is a perfect expression of the skills of the old order. He is the man who was once so idealized in European culture, the artist who beautified life's pain, and who (in this story) did so not only in exquisite – even if now incomprehensible – writings and designs, but executed them in life besides; or more accurately, executed other people by this means, thus persuading everyone to see that justice was done and life redeemed. He could symbolize, therefore, that ideal man of the Renaissance, skilled equally in art and in living, a 'complete' man like Leonardo da Vinci, or more recently, Goethe. It was a type, and an ideal, much discussed by Kafka's intellectual contemporaries, often in the terms made fashionable by Nietzsche who called this secular redeemer 'the superman'.

Such a type would necessarily be refused burial by the church, not only because he stands for this-worldly redemption, but because he had, as Nietzsche recognized in his feud with Wagner (whom he once thought possessed such superior greatness), great similarities with the actor. The church used to refuse burial to actors, because men who spent their life play-acting could not be trusted to have authentic souls. Their place of rest, in Kafka's imagination if not in any real instance, is appropriately enough a tea-house, a *café*, such as had been the non-home of all rootless intellectual life in Europe since the mid-nineteenth century. That is where the spiritual idealism of Europe's cultural tradition had been buried, driven out by more modern trends of a democratic, liberal kind – trends that Nietzsche despised with an aristocratic disdain typical of many writers of Kafka's generation, though probably not of Kafka himself.

Kafka sensed rather some danger that the old order might be revived. There is a vague sense of menace about the inscription on the Old Commandant's grave, set up by 'his adherents, who must now be nameless . . . There is a prophecy that after a certain number of years the Commandant will rise again and lead his adherents from this house to recover the settlement.' Let critics beware, who have been struck by phrases like 'rise again', 'redemption', and even mingling of 'blood and water' in this story, and not jump to the simple-minded conclusion that Kafka is prophesying the return of Christ. Doubtless the old order he has described was religious in origin, but he has discredited it thoroughly. The kind of reactionary revivals that were likely to issue from the intel-lectual atmosphere of the *Kaffeehäuser* of central Europe, let alone from the sleezy *Bierkeller* which this tea-house rather resembles, were not in the least Christian, though they certainly had a bogus religious–aesthetic appeal.

## Der Bau ('The Burrow', 1923/4)

'The Burrow' is one of the two last stories that Kafka wrote – the other, *Josefine, die Sängerin*, will be discussed in the last chapter – and its symbolism points unmistakably towards his own life and work, and (by comparison with 'In the Penal Settlement') to very little else besides. It is about an animal which works with its head and hands to construct a sub-terranean dwelling. This is what in English is naturally called a 'burrow', but the German word suggests a more concrete edifice. The ambiguity brought out by the difficulty in trans-lating the title is illuminating and helps to explain a puzzling passage at the core of the story.

For a burrow is essentially a hole made in solid ground; at the same time that it is a construction it consists of nothing at all. It is thus an altogether fitting final symbol for the kind of writing Kafka had striven to produce from the start: some-thing that would be of real importance to him and yet also nothing at all. Burrowing is a metaphor for thinking and writing, which creates an insubstantial inward realm, a spiritual labyrinth beneath and within the hard ground of existence. Here the self who is the narrator, has tried to make

48    KAFKA: A STUDY

himself secure, both from the predatory animals that live and hunt for food above ground, and also from a dread beast, an unknown enemy that likewise burrows from within, and one that the self knows in the end he cannot evade.

Kafka's narrator says of his burrow: 'I built it for myself and not for visitors,' a declaration that reminds us again of his desire to have the bulk of his writing destroyed, and makes us hesitant to pry into these transparent symbols. For what can the last enemy be in this story but the tuberculosis that had for so long been undermining Kafka's health and was by this date about to bring about his death? And what can the 'small fry' represent if not the minor ailments that also lurk within any body, but cause no concern because they do so little damage to the system. The pathos and interest of this story depend, as they do in 'Metamorphosis', on the hopelessness of trying to do anything about the basic situation. The burrower tries this device and that, pins his hopes on some truly impregnable work, experiments with leaving the burrow for ordinary life above ground, but is drawn back and left desperately regretting that he had not worked on a different plan from the beginning.

Kafka's metaphor enables him to describe the most subtle perceptions of existential psychology in the most lucid images. For instance, the burrower recalls 'happy periods in which I could almost assure myself that the enmity of the world towards one had ceased . . . or that the strength of my burrow had raised me above the destructive struggle of former times'. He finds, however, that it is impossible to rest upon 'the strength' of any spiritual achievement, although he admits that the desire to do so is 'a fancy [which] used to have such a hold over me that sometimes I have been seized by the childish wish never to return to the burrow again, but to settle down somewhere close to the entrance, to pass my life watching it, and gloat perpetually upon the reflection – and in that find my happiness – how steadfast a protection my burrow would be if I were inside it'. In other words, the mind longs to possess its own achievements, the self (of a writer at least, so Kafka explained in the letter to Max Brod already quoted above, p. 20) cherishes the childish fancy of wanting to get outside itself and enjoy itself from without.

Kafka is describing an impulse that Kierkegaard and Sartre have defined in much more elaborate language of despair and bad faith – terms that are necessarily negative because the self-conscious mind can only recognize its *inability* to achieve identity with spontaneous being. Kafka visualizes the same desperate situation in terms that have the positive vitality of a story, and thus do, in a sense, achieve a positive triumph over the very negativity of the spirit's position that they characterize.

The most remarkable instance of Kafka's imaginative transcendence of his own dilemma comes in the central passage where he gives an account of his plan for the castle keep (*Burgplatz\**). The name of this central stronghold of his burrow recalls his largest, but incomplete draft for a novel, *The Castle*, and Kafka makes us feel here what the writing of this novel meant to him and what he wanted to achieve with it:

> One of these favourite plans of mine was to isolate the Castle Keep from its surroundings, that is to say, to restrict the thickness of the walls to about my own height, and leave a free space, and not without reason, as the loveliest imaginable haunt. What a joy to be pressed against the rounded outer wall, to pull oneself up, let oneself slide down again, miss one's footing and find oneself on firm earth, and play all those games literally upon the Castle Keep and not inside it; to avoid the Castle Keep, to rest one's eyes from it whenever one wanted, to postpone the joy of seeing it until later and yet not have to do without it, but literally hold it safe between one's claws,

---

\* An English reader is likely to imagine a solid, heavily fortified tower when he reads of a 'Castle Keep'. The German word, however, suggests primarily an open space albeit within castle walls. (The 'castle' is, of course, a closed, 'locked' place, in either case, even though Kafka here uses the word *Burg* rather than *Schloß*.

a thing that is impossible if you have only an ordinary open entrance to it; but above all to be able to stand guard over it, and in that way to be so completely compensated for renouncing the actual sight of it that, if one had to choose between staying all one's life in the Castle Keep or in the free space outside it, one would choose the latter, content to wander up and down there all one's days and keep guard over the Castle Keep.

(In *Beschreibung eines Kampfes*, p. 202)

The description is, of course, very similar to the one quoted earlier describing the burrower's desire to possess his burrow from outside. The paradox of this desire is better brought out here for the simple reason that the plan to build this moat of freedom around the Castle Keep is more clearly an absurdity: it is a hole built around a hole, and at one point in the description Kafka plays nicely on the German word for 'foundation' and 'reason' (*Grund*) that would be good enough to support such an extraordinary project. Once we try to focus our imagination on the kind of wall that could separate one hole from another, so that he could 'play all those games literally on the Castle Keep and not inside it . . . [and] literally hold it safe between one's claws', we realize that Kafka is giving a precise symbol for the mysterious, insubstantial nature of language: resting on who knows what real foundation. Source of some mysterious source of comfort, creating the illusion that one can hold some essential meaning safe between one's claws, and inspiring in Kafka particularly the desire to play 'games' on the literal meanings of words within whose metaphorical realms we normally dwell on trust. Kafka was ready to leave what is for most of us the closed 'castle-square' of the mind, inside which language imprisons us, in the hope of embracing it in freedom and unassailable security from outside.

The more closely we look at this and other stories by Kafka the more we discover, of course, that he is for ever narrating, in a basically static, symbolic manner, the same situation. All his narratives are in a sense disguises and delays, a 'postponing of the joy of seeing and yet not having to do without'. And as he says, this is a 'thing that is impossible if you have only an ordinary open entrance', that is, if the reader is allowed to penetrate openly into the stronghold of Kafka's language. That is why we are told, in the opening sentences of the story, that: 'all that can be seen from the outside is a big hole; that, however, really leads nowhere; if you take a few steps you strike against natural firm rock'. This hole is the remains of an 'abortive building attempt' – an attempt on Kafka's part to write openly about himself, as he often appears to do; but as he shows, his writing is impenetrable in 'natural' or openly biographical terms.

At a considerable distance, yet still 'in the vicinity', there lies the real entrance, covered only by 'a movable layer of moss' where he is completely vulnerable. He is vulnerable because he wants to be able to 'leave at a moment's notice if necessary', i.e. because he cannot commit himself totally to his inner world, nor yet live a life above ground either. Kafka was not, in fact, an aesthete in the sense of a writer who believed he could bury himself totally in the ivory cave of his art. His strength, and superiority to many modernists, lie in his profound feeling for the reality of life against which the negative phenomenon of consciousness and all its works contrasted for him so strongly. Indeed, the vivid value of his writing, so full of dreadful tension despite being so apparently empty of real content, was inspired by Kafka's readiness to keep alive this sense of contrast, moving to and fro between the realms of art and life like the creature in 'The Burrow'. What he achieved was a uniquely heightened sense of awareness – an awareness not so much of anything concrete in the external world as of a very real state of danger in man's spiritual condition. 'Is not full awareness the true definition of a state of danger?'

# 3

# The Novels

That Kafka's genius may have been better suited to the short story form is an idea that we took up briefly at the beginning of the last chapter. We may add here that memorable parts of the novels could be considered as short stories in their own right, and several of them were actually published on their own (whereas the novels only appeared after Kafka's death and none of them is complete). Thus, the first chapter of *America* was published in three separate editions of Kurt Wolff's series *Der jüngste Tag* (1913, 1916, 1917/18) under the title *Der Heizer* (*The Stoker*). Admittedly, it is there called 'A Fragment', but in a letter to Wolff, Kafka suggested that this piece would make an ideal book if published together with – not the rest of the novel, as we might expect! – the stories, 'Metamorphosis' and 'The Judgement', for they 'belong together both inwardly and outwardly, there is an obvious and, even more, a hidden connection between them . . . The unity of these three stories together is just as important to me as the unity of any one of them.'

A similar situation exists with regard to that part of *The Trial* which Kurt Wolff published as an individual story in 1915 and again in 1917 under the title *Vor dem Gesetz* ('Before the Law'). And at least one part of *The Castle*, the main sections of Chapter XV, has all the makings of a Kafka story; the very fact that these sections have individual titles 'Amalia's Secret', 'Amalia's Punishment', and so on – could indicate perhaps that Kafka himself was thinking of possible publication separately from the novel. Nevertheless, it is on his incomplete novels that

Kafka's international reputation now rests, despite their unfinished state and the uncertainty about whether Kafka wanted them to be published at all, and we must now turn to *The Trial* and *The Castle* and consider to what extent they represent genuine extensions of Kafka's accomplishment. Lack of space forbids discussion of *America* (*Der Verschollene*); this is a pity in that it achieves some striking 'surrealistic' effects – German critics have likened them to those of the contemporary school of expressionist writing and even painting in Germany – but they are not typical of Kafka's future development and the novel is considerably inferior to the other two.

## Der Prozeß (The Trial, 1914)

Kafka's fame began to grow fast with the interest aroused above all by *The Trial* in France soon after the Second World War. It was discussed by writers of the stature of Sartre and Camus, dramatized for a successful stage production, and clearly spoke to the imagination of a considerable French public. The reason is obvious, of course: here was a story, by a Jewish author, of unjust, insane persecution, with a hero who resists the tyranny of arbitrary and inscrutable authorities, even though he cannot hope to break their total power of life and death. The relevance of this symbolism to recent history in Europe seemed so profound that it was hailed as prophetic, while the similarities between Kafka's manner of thinking and existentialist philosophy, which had likewise acquired a reputation for political commitment to the cause of freedom, also helped to establish him as a forerunner and an ally. Whatever the merits of French existentialism as a political philosophy (which have been cast in doubt by Sartre's later development), the political relevance of Kafka's novels, and particularly of *The Trial*, has gradually come to be seen as rather more questionable.

*The argument against treating* The Trial *as political satire*

The details of the novel do not, in fact, throw much light, not even satirical light, upon the way in which political and social persecution actually occurs. The most inappropriate feature of the story from a realistic point of view is the way the hero is left so largely free in public life, able outwardly at least to go about his ordinary business. When he is 'arrested' he is free to telephone a lawyer if he wishes, and later in the novel he discovers he can engage as many lawyers as he likes. He is even asked whether *he* has any objections to the proceedings against him being conducted on Sundays or during the night; and these all-powerful authorities that 'persecute' him inhabit old attic quarters to which they seem almost ashamed to summon their victim. These are *not* characteristics typical of any secret police yet known to the world; nor is it very common for any members of any persecuting organization to suffer corporal punishment when one of their victims complains about the way they have treated him.

The chapter entitled 'The Beater' (*Der Prügler*) is crucial in this context, because the justification given by the beater of his activities – 'I'm employed to beat people, so I beat them' – has been seized on again much more recently (for instance, at the time of the Eichmann trial) as epitomizing the inhumane mentality inculcated by a modern bureaucracy, where people do their jobs, no matter how cruel these may be, simply because they are employed to do so. The machine they serve relieves them of any personal sense of responsibility. Now, as a psychological insight into the way actual employees behave in the world, Kafka's remark is not particularly original; it does not differ greatly from Shakespeare's observation regarding the callousness of a gravedigger (in *Hamlet*), to the effect that: 'Custom hath made it in him a property of easiness.' What is original and disturbing in Kafka's beating scene are the weird circumstances in which it takes place – in the hero's own office, in an old store-room he had never been in, and apparently being repeated every time he opens the door – and the no less strange behaviour of the hero himself.

Although he makes some attempt to stop the beating from being carried out, he does so by resorting to private remonstration, even bribery, although he is in a public building where help could easily be found. But K. does not want help, he slams the door shut upon the disgraceful scene, because he evidently feels implicated himself in its disgrace. It is, in fact, K.'s disgrace, and he feels it to be his private responsibility in a way that makes it impossible for him to call for help from other people. There is, however, one thing he can ask the office clerks to do: 'Clear that lumber-room out, will you? We're being smothered in dirt!' K. obviously does not expect the clerks to find any actual people in this little room, let alone any beating going on. The place has another symbolic dimension for K., which it does not have for them; its symbolic suggestiveness causes this scene to occur in K.'s consciousness.

Let us accept, then, that *The Trial* cannot be read as even a symbolic account of totalitarian persecution, simply because the whole of the uncanny train of events narrated here are responded to by the hero in a manner that makes no political sense. Kafka creates the impression that K. is himself provoking and even controlling these events, from the fateful moment when he presses the bell in his bedroom at the beginning – police agents do not wait for a citizen to press the bell to call them in – until the moment near the end when he is told: 'The court receives you when *you* come and it dismisses you when *you* go.' (My italics.) It might be possible to persist with a political interpretation to the point where it is held that the victims of persecution themselves provoke their fate, but there is no historical evidence to support this view. (This argument sounds a little like the mad logic of tyrants who are ready to see everything a citizen freely does as suspicious and 'evidence' of a guilty state; it is an argument that cannot be used to interpret

E

Kafka's novels, however, since these are written from the standpoint of the victim, not of the persecutor.)

*The biographical background*

What other kind of interpretation can be offered of this novel, once its relevance in detail to the historical circumstances that brought it fame is ruled out? Who or what is it that has 'arrested' Joseph K., the doomed hero of our time? We have met this question before, in fact, in our discussion of Kafka's stories. Why does the doomed creature of *Der Bau* go back to his burrow? He says already well before the end, 'Someone whose invitation I shall not be able to withstand will, so to speak, summon me to him.' Why does Georg Bendemann in *Das Urteil* execute his father's mad sentence of death? The only explanation of his guilt that is given is that: 'You were really an innocent child, but still more really you were a devilish human being.' What is this more than real reality in which Kafka's heroes are 'sinful irrespective of guilt'?

It is tempting to return to the facts of Kafka's life for a fuller explanation of the mystery. This novel is all about a 'trial', albeit in a most unusual court of law; but the 'court of law' (*Gerichtshof*), as Kafka called it, was also most unusual when sentence was passed on him – as he felt – in the Berlin hotel, the Askanischer Hof, on the occasion of his breaking off his engagement to Felice Bauer. We know also that this novel was written in the months following that break and would appear, with its obsessive theme of some private guilt, to have been largely inspired by it. A modern critic, accustomed to the dependence of a work of art on the psychology of the artist rather than on the reality of the world, will inevitably start to notice such 'revealing' details as that the initials of Felice Bauer are the same as those of the girl who, at the start, means a lot to Joseph K. in his trial, Fräulein Bürstner; or that a minor but attractive part is played in the novel by a girl called Erna, which was the actual name of Felice's sister; and so on. Yet this kind of information does not help us very much, for the obvious reason already given, that Kafka has made such a strange use of whatever autobiographical material he may have incorporated in the novel, and it is precisely the significance of this strange use that we should be endeavouring to understand.

## Kafka's use of language

The problem the novel raises for us is indeed connected with the significance of names, persons, and even events in Kafka's life; but the problem is a linguistic, rather than a biographical or even psychological one. What do the words mean with which Kafka has represented what happened in his life, thereby distorting it so strangely? This is a problem of truly general, and essentially philosophical interest, for it makes us wonder at the process by which language makes experience comprehensible to ourselves and communicable to others. How well do the words we use actually 'fit' the reality of what happens in the world? This is a question to which we must have an answer – or else a sense of trust that conventional language does mean something – and yet we ultimately cannot answer it. Kafka is writing in this novel, and to some extent in all his work, about this problem: about what words 'really' mean, about their conventional meaning often smooth with well-worn metaphorical usage, and about the dark, inscrutable background that lies behind this reassuring facade.

When Joseph K. discovers the scene of a beating in the office store-room, he not only slams the door on it, he goes over to a window and gazes out. He has had a glimpse of some deeper reality and now he tries to penetrate its meaning – 'to pierce the darkness of the courtyard', or more explicitly in German: 'mit den Blicken in das Dunkel eines Hofwinkels einzudringen'. Let us not labour the symbolism of what 'court' (*Hof*) this now is, but simply ask what K. is trying to do in this moment of penetrating contemplation, when we might have expected some

more conventional action from him. He is making 'a vow not
to hush up the incident', a phrase that does not reveal to an
English reader what Kafka's commonplace German expression
plainly states: 'Er gelobte sich, die Sache noch zur Sprache zu
bringen' – to put the thing, or case, or cause, into words. It is a
matter of language.

Inasmuch as this is what the novel explores, namely, the linguistic, and not the legal or moral, essence of K's. case (*Sache*),
a great deal of its significance gets lost in translation. Even the
title of the book is misleading, for although the English 'trial'
has more than one meaning, the connotations of the word are
different from those of the German one. *Der Prozeß* is cognate,
of course, with the English 'process', and Kafka uses the term
interchangeably with *das Verfahren*, which means 'procedure',
but also has undertones of 'entanglement' and even 'muddle'.
Joseph K.'s trial is thus a verbal process, the process whereby
we try to investigate with language what the matter with our
lives is, getting hopelessly entangled 'in the process'.

It is, as James Joyce knew, quite simple to construct an
'action' out of plays on words, but it is probably impossible to
produce the same pattern of verbal 'cases' with English words
as with Kafka's original German one. For instance, it is just as
easy for an English as for a German reader to see that the
initials for Fräulein Bürstner are the same as Felice Bauer's,
but no amount of ingenuity can communicate the sexual echoes
of *bürsten*, a word that Kafka would surely have known as a
vulgar expression for intercourse. Similarly, the mysterious
'authorities' who try Joseph K. symbolize verbally the spiritual
predicament a man finds himself in as soon as he asks questions
about language. For the German *Behörde* has a philological
groundwork, a foundation in a more 'real' reality, which is of
the greatest interest. Cognate with it is the word for 'to belong'
(*gehören*), which in turn goes back to the basic word for 'to
hear' (*hören*), and to words describing ancient conditions of
servitude (*Hörer, Hörigkeit*); *gehörig*, on the other hand, is a

common modern word for 'appropriate' or 'relevant', with legal overtones of competence and admissibility.

The authorities before whom K. stands, therefore, are a symbol for some of the most fundamental questions raised by man's capacity to reflect about his position as a thinking, word-using animal in the world. To whom does he belong, who hears him, what words are appropriate to his situation, whom should he obey and who is competent to judge him? The consistent way in which Kafka's language creates an appearance of concrete action and character out of his basically spiritual, abstractly philosophical preoccupation with the 'world' of consciousness, becomes still more apparent when we look at other words closely connected with the above. K., for instance, is subjected to cross-examination, which in German is *Verhör*, with undertones of hearing incorrectly. Yet another train of words is based on the process of exploration downwards (*untersuchen*), as well as on concepts of what is right, embodied in persons K. only hears about but never meets (*Untersuchungsrichter*).

## Interpretation of the action and the characters

Once we assume that this is in part what *The Trial* is 'about', we can go on to interpret various aspects of the 'action' and of the 'characters' accordingly. For example, Joseph K. has to decide whether to get a lawyer to represent him, and then when he grows dissatisfied with this character's ability properly to represent his case, whether and how to get rid of him. Who is this character and why is he presented as a sickly, bedridden old man, who would be of no interest to K. at all if he did not have a sexy girl in his house to look after him? The answer is that he represents a character called in (ad-vocatus) to represent K.'s case; this he is too feeble to do, however, because K. is instinctively interested less in tiresome discussions of meaning than in its dependence on sex, which seems to have some intimate relationship with it. The lawyer thus 'represents' a character in a new sense: he represents Kafka's feeble reliance on characters (other than his hero's – and not even on his in any naturalistic sense) to further the 'action' of his unique kind of spiritual inquiry. Kafka uses the word *Vertreter* (representative) interchangeably with *Advokat* (lawyer), and we learn that there is a 'difference between a lawyer for ordinary legal rights and a lawyer for cases like these . . . The one lawyer leads his client by a fine thread until the verdict is reached, but the other lifts his client on his shoulders from the beginning and carries him bodily without once letting him down until the verdict is reached, and even beyond it.'

There are many clues in this chapter to show the reader that this passage, and the characters and situation described in it, represent different kinds of literary, rather than legal, practice. One of them lies in the word *Eingabe* (petition), which it is the representing lawyer's task to handle; a very similar German word from the same root means 'inspiration' (*Eingebung*). K.'s attitude towards his representative is unconventional, by comparison with that of an ordinary client like Kaufmann Block. The word *Kauf-mann* (business or tradesman) is given overtones of venality, because Block has apparently bought the services of many representatives; he is like a hack novelist, always looking for a new way to put his case. And the kinds of representative that he chooses are doubtless the ordinary ones referred to above, who lead him on through a rather tenuous tale. Kaufmann Block is simply a rather poor writer – his 'petitions (inspirations) turned out to be quite worthless' – who turned to matters like these only late in life, after his wife had died. He has no business to invoke the help of an *advocatus* like K.'s, who has specialized in the much more difficult kind of 'practice, in which after a certain moment nothing essentially new ever occurs'.

K.'s *Advokat*, however, is surely one of those lawyers who wants to 'lift his client on his shoulders and carry him bodily, without letting him down, until the verdict is reached and even beyond it' (. . . trägt ihn, ohne ihn abzusetzen, zum Urteil und noch darüber hinaus). This is a description of Kafka's 'practice', or at least of the one he has been looking for from the beginning, and it recalls details from the stories, from the early 'Description of a Fight' in which his first characters rode one upon the other's back, to the inescapable verdict of 'The Judgement', where there was no longer any possibility of being 'put down' again on to the ground of common-sense reality; a world in which metaphor, the process itself of language, becomes a nightmare-reality in its own right.

In ordinary literary terms the verdict to which a writer is exposed is merely the verdict of the public on his work. He does not 'do' anything criminal, but simply goes on with the process of writing, and this 'process' – as the priest explains to K. near the end – 'gradually passes over into a judgement' (geht allmählich ins Urteil über). In Kafka's case, we know that this verdict, which essentially he passed on himself, however he might represent it in writing (as being, for instance, the 'judgement' of his father), had the force of a 'life-sentence' – a play on words that is not possible in German but comes near to the spirit and goal of Kafka's work, just as it does to that of James Joyce whose *Finnegans Wake* is also a kind of never-ending 'life-sentence'.

It is significant that Joseph K., like his author, declares that he is not interested in knowing 'the meaning of the sign' that causes his public, at his first interrogation, to applaud or to hiss. He is aiming (like his author) at something more serious than ordinary literary success. He has a spiritual cause to champion: the cause, the case, of all individuals who have been 'arrested' like himself. For here everybody and 'everything belongs to the Court', even though most of the people he meets seem quite unconcerned at the fact, even unaware of it. (Kafka evidently thinks like Kierkegaard that all men are in despair and anguish at their human condition no matter whether or not they realize it.) But the fact that all men are subject to the process of living, which most of them do not think about enough to realize that it is (metaphorically) a nightmare, does not make the plight of the individual less grievous. The more desperately he pursues his case, the more inevitable the verdict becomes.

Thus, K. cannot make common cause with other men: 'combined action against the Court is impossible', which is to say that mankind cannot achieve through the solidarity of some public convention or belief any release from each man's private 'trial'. Nor can he dissociate himself from other men entirely. As with the animal in 'The Burrow', who can neither stay up above in the world or down below on his own, so Joseph K.'s case is inextricably bound up with his having a public existence which he keeps up right to the end: 'had he stood alone in the world, there would have been no case'. In other words, he realizes the nature of his own individuality through contact with other people. They have a part to play in the process through which the fateful verdict is reached. It is through this relationship to the others that the self realizes what it is.

It is not solely through a relationship to another person that we come to realize the unique character of the self as a state of consciousness; we may discover it more immediately through our relationship to our body. This is how Joseph K. first discovers it. For the figures who break in on him one morning, eat his breakfast and steal his clothes, are certainly not secret-policemen but rather representatives of his own body. They beg K. to stop protesting about his position and asking for their 'warrant' for being there. Why on earth, they exclaim, 'can't you accept your position and why are you so intent on pointlessly annoying us, who are probably closer to you than any of your fellow human beings!' The symbolism could scarcely be more obvious, and it is supported by many associated details, that call attention to the base, bodily character of these men, 'bodyguards' (*Leibwächter*) of the spirit, who later have to be ascetically punished and chastised for taking liberties to which they are not entitled. The liberty that K. desires is a pure, spiritual freedom, a total *Freisprechung* (absolution) through words. It was, of course, Kafka's own desire as a writer, an aspiration to emerge victorious over the monstrous 'process' (trial?) of being a thinking, speaking person in a world where language does not ever seem to 'apply'.

This novel is about the futility of man's 'applications' (*Bittschriften* – indeed, the novel is itself a *Bittschrift*), and about the very serious consequences to his body of repeatedly making them. We know how ruinous to Kafka's health writing was, and how he associated literature with illness; K.'s health similarly suffers as the 'process' continues – and in the last scene he is put to death 'like a dog'. These famous final words suggest that it is a bodily fate, which he cannot control, that at last overtakes him, even while his mind is battling to argue still and hope. The last thing he sees are his strange executioners observing the *Entscheidung*, an almost untranslatable word in this context, for it means the outcome of the story, but also suggests a decision or judgement of some kind, and has undertones of division and separation. The separation is between K.'s mind and body; the decision is his own; the outcome inevitable. The logic of this situation is 'unshakeable' (*unerschütterlich* – the word Kafka used to describe his sense of 'judgement' on looking again at Felice Bauer), but 'it cannot withstand a man who wants to go on living'. Alas, the novel has made it quite clear that K. did not simply want to go on living; he wanted to know. The outcome, decision, separation was for Kafka inevitably fatal.

The style of the final chapter – to the extent to which it is finished – is particularly grotesque. Two more men are sent to execute K., who are less realistic, more absurd characters than the warders who came to arrest him in chapter one. They look to K. like 'tenth-rate old actors', then again like tenors. Outside in the street they grapple hold of him in such a way that the three become a unity – 'a unity such as almost only lifeless matter can form' ('wie sie fast nur Lebloses bilden kann'). The trio move wherever K. wants to go; he catches sight of Fräulein

Bürstner, or a girl resembling her, and like a single man they follow her: 'that he might not forget the warning that she signified for him'. The lesson is plainly stated: 'he suddenly realized the futility of resistance. There would be nothing heroic in it were he to resist . . . to snatch the last appearance of life by struggling.' So K. does not resist, but co-operates, even getting himself and his executioners past a policeman who might have intervened. Only at the last he cannot seize the knife, 'as it was his duty to do . . . and plunge it into his own breast . . . He could not relieve the authorities of all the work, the responsibility for this final mistake lay with him who had denied him the last bit of strength necessary for the deed.'

While a biographical interpretation could explain this scene perhaps by reference to the grotesque 'performance' in the Berlin hotel, when Kafka's fateful separation from F.B. was conducted largely by others, the question still remains why Kafka has presented it like this at the end of *The Trial*. From a literary point of view, the scene is a travesty, a deliberately non-heroic ending. The executioners who are even more closely linked with K.'s person than the warders, symbolize his rapidly ailing state. When K. was first 'arrested' (*ver-haftet*), his spirit was brought to a halt in mid-career; both the German and the English word suggest this coming to a standstill and being held fast. Throughout Kafka's writing there is a constant play on images (often very common words) of movement and standstill; their conflict is as fundamental as that between freedom and imprisonment, or silence and noise. What is ambiguous is which is the better state. This last chapter describes a series of sporadic movements as K. half runs to meet his fate, half tries to stop it still. But since, after a year of futile 'trial', he no longer knows what he wants to stop it for (certainly not for F.B.), he can only acquiesce as his body performs the inevitable last act. In just this way Kafka was to describe his outbreak of tuberculosis three years later: as his lungs taking on the burden of suffering which his spirit could no longer bear.

*The material and the spiritual*

In making this kind of interpretation, we are beginning to distinguish between what 'is' (or stands for) body and what is spirit in Kafka, between reality and consciousness, in a way that his manner of writing renders finally impossible. Thus, the ubiquitous organization that has arrested K., with its endless hierarchies of officials, can be looked at symbolically as meaning either or both of two totally different things. One interpretation might see these authorities as symbolizing the infinite ramifications of consciousness, with airless corridors of thought, and impenetrable realms of speculative inquiry. Why else should people wear cushions on their heads, if not to symbolize the pressure upwards of the mind, always eager to break out of any constriction?

Many other details concerning the Courts suggest, however, that they are anything but a symbol of man's spiritual state. Their law-books are obscene, their practices corrupt, especially in their claims on women. The reactions of the women themselves, both in this novel and in *The Castle*, are equally ambiguous. They seem to have intimate connections with the courts, even belonging to them in some ill-defined sense; at the same time they fall in love with men who are accused and 'arrested', i.e. men who are in conflict with the Courts. Finally, the attitude towards women of the hero in each novel confirms this ambiguity. K. finds Fräulein Bürstner and Leni – later it will be Frieda and Pepi – attractive because he has been arrested and the women seem (at first) to offer something that he deeply needs. This something could be the solace and promise that have always been associated with love; but Kafka's love scenes give a more sordid impression of mindless sex.

Now, again, we have to be clear about what is original in Kafka's representation of ambiguity in the nature of love, and more broadly in the nature of reality. It is not the ambiguity itself, but Kafka's way of representing it, that disturbs us.

Indeed, by making it appear to be totally a problem of representation, he makes it appear quite hopeless, irrational, and fatal. That is to say: we do not need to look very far in literature to discover that love has another side that is hostile to the spirit – 'the expense of spirit in a waste of shame'. Nor (to be more precise) that a writer will be particularly sensitive to the question: 'What boots it with uncessant care / To tend the homely slighted Shepherd's trade, / And strictly meditate the thankless Muse? / Were it not better done as others use, / To sport with Amaryllis in the shade, / Or with the tangles of Naera's hair?' But the problem that confronts K. no longer appears in this light, and it is Kafka who has changed the lighting.

The biographical experience from which he started, of uncertainty and even incapacity concerning marriage, is not in itself so extraordinary – to the extent to which we can talk of an experience 'in itself' apart from a man's reaction to it – as Kafka well knew from reading of similar experiences in the lives of Grillparzer, Kierkegaard, and Flaubert. Kafka places this experience in a new and unrecognizable light, and in so doing puts it beyond man's moral control or even rational comprehension. All forms of moral or rational presentation assume that we can recognize what is right and wrong, better and worse, in the world; even if we make the wrong choice, we can know when we do. And this in turn assumes that the character and meaning of reality does not depend entirely on our interpretation of it; that the world is distinct from human consciousness, which can thus hope to penetrate and master its laws. Kafka's writing totally undermines these assumptions. We are no longer sure what is 'there' in reality, and what exists in K.'s mind. Does he confront a symbol of the natural world, physical existence in its sordid, obscene inscrutability? Or a symbol of his own consciousness, a projection outwards of his own muddled nature, which takes on a semblance of evil reality? Kafka's literary achievement consists in his having made it possible to distinguish between these two things. His symbolism is, as we have said, total, and leaves nothing outside itself to which it can confidently be referred, or on which a distinction between reality and consciousness can be based.

## The meaninglessness of meaning

The impenetrability of the world's law is summed up most brilliantly in this novel in the separate story already referred to: 'Before the Law', which is preached by a priest to K. as a parable. He has already been warned by the artist, Titorelli, that the court before which he is being 'tried' is 'completely impenetrable by argument' or more exactly: 'Impenetrable by arguments that one brings before the court . . . It is quite a different matter with one's efforts behind the public court, that is to say in the consulting rooms, in the corridors, or for instance in this very studio.' The word 'impenetrable' is in the German *unzugänglich*, which the first translator (Edwin Muir) rendered as 'impervious'. Whatever undertones an English reader may find in these words, it is important to notice how much more readily concrete the German *Zugang* is; it can mean an entrance or gateway, as well as 'access' in a more metaphorical sense. In Kafka's parable this situation is visualized concretely: a man waits before the entrance to the law all his life, and never gains admittance. The situation seems hopeless partly because the man insists on waiting for access. But when, after the parable has been told, K. himself tries to argue his way into the meaning of the story, he is unable to base any conclusive arguments on it, i.e. to reach any conclusion in either a negative or a positive sense.

K. cannot even prove, for instance, that the man who waits away his life has been deceived; that would at least establish a rational criterion of truth external to the story. However, at the same time that no truth can be established literally, so that in this representative symbol (if it is one) the mind's situation before the law of existence is hopeless, the story itself captures this very situation perfectly – and that, as the artist says, 'is quite a different matter'. This parable is preached to K. for a *good* reason: it is his story. Literally speaking, in terms of the novel as a whole, this parable does not do K. any good; it does not help him to evade his fate, does not procure for him the total 'acquittal' (*Freisprechung*) he seeks.

What, after all, would total release from the 'charge' of living mean? 'The documents relating to the case are said to be completely done away with, they vanish entirely from the proceedings, not only the charge, but the trial and even the acquittal itself is destroyed, everything is destroyed.' It sounds like Kafka's wish that his own manuscripts should be destroyed! But even while he knew that literally his writing could not save him, Kafka could imagine perfectly the hopelessness of desiring that it should. This parable represents a moment when the mind totally grasps its own situation, a moment of pure freedom such as the animal dreams of in 'The Burrow', an impossible and 'untenable' position like the Archimedean point only to be reached on condition that it is turned against its possessor. At this point in the book, the meaninglessness of the whole 'trial', the process not only of writing – as we have provisionally interpreted *der Prozeß* here – but of existing consciously at all, is concretely symbolized. The novel grasps itself in a symbol that passes beyond any interpretable meaning, for it symbolizes the impossibility of interpretation. 'The text is unalterable and the opinions [of critics] are often only an expression of despair at this fact.'

## Das Schloß (The Castle, 1922)

*The Castle* is Kafka's *magnum opus*; though it is flawed, unfinished, and perhaps unfinishable (whatever Kafka may have told Max Brod about his plans for a conclusion), it establishes its own imaginative world on a scale and with a unity of atmosphere that are unmatched by the earlier novels. Even *The*

*Trial* moves between two worlds still, one of them that of an ordinary office worker, the other a Kafkaesque realm of spiritual experiences that have become more real than everyday reality. When K. enters the frozen village of the Castle, he has left behind for ever the world of normality, though he can remember one and occasionally refers to it (did he have a wife, a job, a home there? Could he leave the Castle precincts again and emigrate to some normal country with a name?). The completeness with which Kafka's hero has severed his connections with the ordinary world is reflected in his loss of any name: the hero of *America* is called Karl Roßmann, the hero of *The Trial*, Joseph K., the hero of *The Castle*, simply K.

The action of the novel is likewise less attached to recognizable situations in 'life' – as the cathedral scene is in *The Trial*, for instance, where Joseph K. is sent by his real-life boss to accompany a visitor to the firm on a sightseeing tour of the town. The reality in which the Castle is located resembles far more that of the parable preached in the later course of the cathedral chapter. The whole of this novel is a projection of the concept of impenetrability (*Unzugänglichkeit*), of waiting 'before the Law'. And a large amount of the novel is taken up with interpretative discussion, similar to that which followed the narration of the parable in *The Trial*. The difference in *The Castle* is that the problem of interpretation is not discussed in a reality distinct from that of the stories K. hears, nor does such discussion take place in a reality distinct from the one in which K. works (as is the case with *The Trial*). There is only one reality in *The Castle*; the stories K. hears are about events that have actually taken place there, and his discussion of their meaning implicates him in their outcome.

### K.'s struggle for freedom

This is not to say that the kind of interpretation we have made of *The Trial* cannot be applied to *The Castle*. On the contrary, it must simply be taken further. *The Castle* is just as much

about the mind's efforts to grasp its own activity; and it is as
deeply embedded in the paradoxical limitations of language and
thought, which can 'know' that something lies beyond themselves but cannot reach it, and which cannot procure the
services of any other instruments – 'employees' or 'servants' are
Kafka's typically concrete symbols here – more dependable
than themselves, more 'in the know', in order to attain this end.
All that can be ascertained for sure is that in trying to attain it,
in trying to 'get above himself' spiritually, in order to pin down
the answer to his own existence, he fails, and achieves nothing
but humiliation, guilt, and finally – to judge from the way the
novel is going – a kind of defeat by self-attrition.

Kafka is less concerned in this novel with the guilt aspect of
this problem, although some critics have interpreted the book
realistically as showing K.'s treatment of Frieda to be morally
wrong (and even referred the story to the quite real relationship
of Kafka to Milena Jesenská, which may have inspired some
of it, though these facts bear little resemblance in detail to those
in *The Castle*). More important here than his desire to prove
his innocence is K.'s fight to get the upper hand and be free –
though, as we have already seen, the word used in *The Trial* for
'acquittal' (*Freisprechung*) suggests the idea of getting free from
entanglement in the muddled proceedings (*Verfahren*). Guilt is
incidental and hardly provides a plausible explanation of why
K. fails. His failure lies in the nature of the 'case', or in the
nature of 'the Castle' (*Schloß*), the locked, inaccessible place, to
use the metaphor on which this novel is based. All the hero can
accomplish is to clarify the fact that everything he knows about
the castle is confused, contradictory, and senseless. By putting
up a steady rational struggle against its confusions and contra-
dictions he does achieve a kind of freedom – but it is a negative
freedom, such as that described at the end of chapter eight:

> . . . as though he were now indeed (*freilich*) more free than
> ever, and at liberty to wait here as long as he desired, in

this place usually forbidden to him, and as though he had
won for himself this freedom such as hardly anyone else
had ever succeeded in doing . . .; but – this conviction
was at least as strong – as though at the same time there
was nothing more senseless, nothing more desperate, than
this freedom, this waiting, this inviolability.

(*Das Schloß*, p. 145)

*Kafka's use of language in* The Castle

Unlike many modern philosophers – Wittgenstein, it should be
remembered, was Kafka's near-contemporary in time and cultural milieu – Kafka knew that a mind that has disentangled
itself from the confusions of language, and detached itself from
the closed rules of mental 'structures' and language 'games', is
in a state not of positive freedom but of despair.

The use Kafka makes of the double meanings and deeper
associations of words has been more widely and clearly recognized with regard to *The Castle* than with regard to the rest of
his work. Apart from the title, and the suggestive name of
Frieda, whom K. woos as a 'Freier' (again implying one who
frees), K.'s questionable role as a Land Surveyor (*Landver-
messer*) has undertones of foolhardy boldness – 'getting above
himself'? – as well as of measuring inaccurately. *Klamm* is not
only an adjective meaning tight and hemmed in, but has
associations with the word for 'brackets' (*Klammer*), an important concept at the time in the phenomenological philosophy
of Husserl, who was similarly exploring the possibility of
'bracketing' reality, in the sense of grasping its meaning immediately, without reference to outside, metaphysical postu-
lates of understanding and evaluation.

A thought which particularly interested Kafka was the
mind's dependence upon the way in which it first receives, or
conceives, an idea; so much else seems to follow inescapably
from the context in which a word or image arouses our attention. Kafka expresses this thought concretely, of course, as an
actual situation of arrival in a place from which traditional

F

preoccupations of the world have (as Husserl might have said) been 'bracketed off'. Here Kafka's hero 'is received in a way that perhaps had determined the direction of everything that followed' ('daß der Empfang vielleicht allem Folgenden die Richtung gegeben hatte'; *Empfang*, it should be noted, is a word that associates the two ideas of reception and conception). Kafka says the same thing in the context of another story – 'A Country Doctor' (1916/17) – when he writes: 'Once answer a false ring at your night-bell and you can never repair the damage.' To some imponderable degree K.'s fate depends upon the fact that a character called Schwarzer 'happened to have' a girl-friend at the inn where the story of K.'s struggle with the Castle begins.

We should not, however, wax too ponderous over this problem, however much it may exercise K. himself along with the other accumulating details that he tries to make sense of. For we can see, as K. cannot, that we are reading a book in which the author is inventing these details. If we ask to what purpose he invents them, we can only answer: in order to symbolize the inscrutability of the mind's inventions. 'Inventions' are things which 'come in' from outside. Like K., they find themselves at the Bridge Inn, a place of transition, where a first thought begins to develop into something else. Like the *Bittschriften* in *The Trial* which represent what the novel also is, so this opening scene of *The Castle* represents symbolically the process of opening a novel – or of beginning on any train of thought. The hero can thus wonder whether he is playing the right role: should he perhaps have come as something other than a Land Surveyor – after all, it seems that no land surveyor is needed, there is no job for him to do – and is his engagement in this role, as he says, 'only a pretext, they were playing with me'?

## Similarity to earlier works

There are many features besides these in *The Castle* that recall Kafka's earlier work and reinforce the interpretation we are making here. K. stands alone, confronting a 'singular' reality, not a plural one, as he thinks at first. There is no difference between the world of the castle and the world of the village; everything belongs to the castle, as it did to the courts of *The Trial*. The apparently tri-partite division of the world, which Kafka first symbolized in 'The Judgement' and then analysed in his 'Letter' to his father, turns out to be a bi-partite one at best: for the other two parts beside himself are united against him, being in league despite all appearances to the contrary. They may quarrel, abuse, seduce one another, and generally present to K.'s mind a picture of universal injustice. But these others scarcely seem to mind. K. is amazed that a castle official like Erlanger summons people in the middle of the night, keeps them waiting on his whim, and that nobody objects, though their discontent is general. Of the whole relationship between castle and village he is told: 'In your opinion it's unjust and monstrous, but you're the only one in the village of that opinion.'

K. plays again the solitary role here that the narrating voice plays throughout so much of Kafka's work: that of the upright, rational, self-willed individual who demands his rights, and especially his freedom, in the face of an absurdly distorted and corrupt world, wherein he can find *no one like himself*: no one who can represent his case, no one – in the language of *The Castle* – who can act as a messenger, a contact, with the reality beyond his own mind. Kafka's ability to symbolize this state of mind, divided from the public world to the point of schizophrenia, refusing to compromise with anything that the world finds normal, protesting therefore about everything because the protesting gesture of refusal is the only one he knows, has made him the foremost myth-maker of the twentieth century. The myth does not describe very well the social facts of totalitarian persecution, as was at first supposed. But it does symbolize most profoundly the spirit of a hopelessly protesting generation, a generation of individualists without a public cause.

*The insoluble paradox*

So, we find here again that K. wants everything to be done on his initiative and on his own terms. 'I don't want any act of favour from the Castle,' he declares, 'but my rights.' The reader cannot help wondering, as with the man who passed a lifetime waiting 'before the Law', why K. does not simply go away. The question is even raised in the novel, and K.'s answer is (equally simply) that he has come in order to stay. There are characteristic shades of Jewish humour in a reply that says only that he would not have taken all this trouble to come, if he could be satisfied with merely going away again – shades that darken into profounder thoughts about what the difference is ultimately between a question and an answer: life *is* like that, and where should we go away to out of life?

K. is struggling for 'official' permission to stay – and there is much play with words like *hierzubleiben*, *standzuhalten*, *festzustehen*. But this is a permission that is not given to the kind of bold, inquiring, self-conscious mind that K. typifies; once a man no longer takes it for granted that he has a place 'here', he will never obtain any explanation of what his place is – except on his deathbed perhaps, when it will have to be recognized that he has in a sense possessed it all along. Why, then, the reader may wonder (as various critics have done) does not K. simply settle down in the village? Are there not hopeful signs that he is learning to do so towards the end, where he seems to acknowledge his mistake?

> I'm not sure if it's like this, and my guilt isn't clear to me either, but when I compare myself with you [Pepi] I do seem to get the idea that perhaps we've both been trying too hard, too noisily, too childishly, too ingenuously . . the way a child clutches a tablecloth but gets nothing besides knocking down the whole treat, which it has then made unobtainable for itself forever.
>
> (*Das Schloß*, p. 407)

Close reading further reveals that in the last chapter of *The*

*Trial* K. likewise recognizes how he has always wanted 'to reach out into the world with twenty hands' (mit zwanzig Händen in die Welt hineinfahren) and that 'this was wrong'. But close reading should also reveal that K. co-operates with his executioners in the end; that he sees the futility of resistance (*Widerstand*); and that he finally admits to them: 'I really didn't want to stop' (*stehenbleiben*). And plain common sense should tell us that a mind like K.'s cannot possibly 'settle down' in this crude and primitive village with its low-browed, sullen peasants, rank bathhouses, and orgiastic pubs. Even if, as seems most probable, the village is not meant to be believed in as any real place, but accepted rather as a symbol of Kafka's inner world – where icy conditions of intellect coexist with the physical crudities of bodily existence – it is still impossible for a Kafka-esque intelligence to find its earthly condition anything but utterly strange and unacceptable.

### The fantasy of fulfilment

The only times that K. ever feels himself at one with anything are when his conscious mind is lost. For instance, he enjoys in his first encounter with Frieda 'hours in which they breathed as one, hours in which their hearts beat as one'; but at the same time K. knows that he is 'losing himself or wandering into a strange country, farther than any man had been before'. He enters this strange country (*Fremde*) again much later in the novel when he falls asleep on Bürgel's bed. The scene has some similarity with the one in *The Trial* where K., at a moment of critical interest to himself, just when his uncle and his lawyer are discussing his case, goes off to 'sleep' with Leni. In the *Castle* scene, K. merely goes off to sleep (by himself) just as Bürgel is about to explain to K. how he might gain access to the castle. If this were a realistic novel, we should feel disappointed that the hero had missed this opportunity to gain his goal; we might even feel that some moral criticism was implied, and that we had been shown some tragic flaw in human nature. But since the novel is not of this conventional type, such criticism would make no sense. We have no confidence that anything really worth having could come from this, more than from any other, encounter with a character employed by the castle; Bürgel is as implausible, bedridden, and tedious as the rest. We can ultimately not even be sure whether K. has missed or got what he wants when he goes off to sleep. For his sleep 'was not a real sleep, he heard Bürgel's words better perhaps than before when he had been awake but dead tired, word for word beat upon his ear, but his burdensome consciousness had vanished, he felt himself free, it was not Bürgel who held him any longer, only he groped occasionally out for Bürgel, he was not yet in the depth of sleep, but he had gone beneath the surface'.

If K.'s experience here is to be related to anything in the real world, then it must surely be to Kafka's experience of writing late into the night, trying to gain access to the castle of his mind, encountering fictitious personages and situations that are in every sense mere diversions, and finally being no longer 'held' by one, so that his conscious attention wavers, sinks beneath the surface of consciousness, gropes for this murmuring figure once or twice more, then plunges into pure fantasy. K.'s fantasy is one of triumphant conquest, a struggle with some now archetypal artistic figure who cannot resist K.'s 'advances'. In this semi-conscious realm 'beneath the surface' the components of K.'s (or Kafka's) psychic world are laid bare as in a depth analysis. K. wins applause, a public toast in champagne – a banally obvious symbol of success. The figure whom he conquers 'looks very like a statue of a Greek god' – the classic model of accomplishment in Western art. At the same time this figure is a 'secretary', a castle employee, that is to say, Kafka's symbol for a servant of the literary imagination; the very word has philological undertones of secrecy – *secretarius*, a confidential official. And this secretary now vainly tries to cover his 'secret parts', giggling like a girl. Is *this* what K. wants, then? Is his desire a sexual one? Up to this point, K.'s dream might

have been invented by Freud, but here Kafka's intelligence
goes beyond that of his great contemporary. K.'s fantasy takes
him further: the girlish, secretarial god disappears, so too does
the applauding public, and K. discovers he is alone, eager to
pursue the struggle but unable to find his adversary. To find
him again, K. must wake up (woken by a pricking sensation –
he dreams it is a *broken* champagne glass: i.e. his subconscious
rouses him with a sense of failure). And once he is awake again,
trying to focus his conscious mind upon its impossible task –
impossible because the focus *is* so concentrated – K. 'understands completely' that there is nothing else he can do except
go completely to sleep: to sleep and not to dream, and thus 'go
away from everything' (*allem entgehen*).

K. is now 'dead to the world' ('abgeschlossen gegen alles, was
geschah'). Bürgel meanwhile goes on talking, and what he
describes is something very like K.'s own situation viewed from
the outside. K. is no longer the hero, but is in Bürgel's words
about to turn into the client who 'has never yet been seen, but
always expected, expected with true thirst, and always regarded
as unobtainable, which is only logical'. Bürgel has longed for
just such a client as this, whose 'silent presence is an invitation
to penetrate into his poor life, to transmute oneself into him as
though into a possession of one's own and to suffer with him in
this pretended guise'. If Bürgel could achieve this he would
have 'ceased to be an official employee' (*Amtsperson*), he would
be 'unable to refuse any petition' (*Bitte*), he would be 'in
despair, or looked at more accurately very happy'.

What is the meaning of this imagined situation, so strikingly
resembling K.'s own, which is preached over his uncompre-
hending head, like the sermon in *The Trial*? Why does Bürgel
say that here, 'in this very situation, the client in all his helpless-
ness . . . can master everything, and need do nothing to achieve
it except produce his petition', only to conclude, as K. wakes up
and hurries to another official who hammers on the wall, that:
'Thus the world corrects itself in its course and keeps its

balance ... There are opportunities indeed which are simply too great to be made use of, there are things that are destroyed by nothing but themselves'? As in the sermon story, the language has a prophetic or oracular ring, Greek this time rather than Hebraic, as though some ultimate mystery of human existence were being formulated, some ultimate limit of human endeavour, beyond which nothing mortal may go, however much imagination may desire it. And so it is. The limit here symbolized is that which prevents just this: prevents a man from becoming a creature of his own imagination, and wakefully in all conscience enjoying the fulfilment of his dreams. It is a state of despair and happiness to be able to imagine what it would be like to be another person, to find another character for oneself. Kafka here imagines the still more complicated possibility of what character he (as K.) might assume in another character's eyes. But however many reflections upon himself a man makes, he is not the same as any of these images. Fully to enter into the opportunities offered by any imagined reflection, the real man would have to be 'dead to the world'. A man cannot consciously possess himself, i.e. be identical with his longed-for fantasy-image of himself.

*Semantic ambiguities*

While Kafka's ability to symbolize this impossibility, this limit of consciousness, does not depend on any unique characteristics in the German language, he is very sensitive, of course, to those aspects of German that reflect his preoccupations. Thus, he remarks, for instance, on the fact that the word for 'his' in German is the same as the verb meaning 'to be' (*sein* \*). Kafka picks up this detail because it could be said to typify the kinds of ambiguity and confusion to which all language gives rise, inviting us to build structures of thought, and hence apparent

---

\* The point is very difficult to translate. Aphorism 46 reads: 'Das Wort "sein" bedeutet im Deutschen beides: Dasein und Ihmgehören.' (In *Hochzeitsvorbereitungen*, p. 44)

opportunities or possibilities of living, out of the reflected images of things. Everything in and about the castle is confusing and ambiguous in this way. Is it, in fact, a castle at all? It looks more like a rambling collection of low outhouses; its tower looks as though a madman had broken through the roof. What are we to 'make' of this? Everything we subsequently find out about its personnel and workings 'makes for' quite contradictory interpretations (as with the law-courts of *The Trial*). The castle officials are overworked night and day; yet Klamm himself sleeps most of the time. All the talk of tireless and efficient management is belied by the way documents are handled in the Village Superintendent's room or distributed amongst the officials at the inn. There is besides a grotesque lack of proportion between the size of this administrative apparatus and what is actually there to be administered. And there is a less comic, more disturbing lack of relationship between the supposedly superior intelligence of high-ranking officials and their coarse sexual demands, not to speak of the licence they permit in their underlings. Sex altogether 'means' something in the world of the castle of similar importance to its meaning in *The Trial*. But to be aware of its importance within this context does not make it any easier to say what its meaning is in words not taken from Kafka's actual text.

The problem of interpretation raised by *The Castle*, then, is ultimately insoluble because the thing itself has contradictory characteristics. Kafka's lucidity and genius lie in his allowing us to see that they are contradictory – which is to say, that the thing itself is self-contradictory. To say that the thing itself is 'life' or 'mind' will not do, because any such single interpretation implies that we have a larger frame of reference within which what is life and what is mind can be clearly located and related. Kafka has no such frame of reference. What he represents is the totally ambiguous character that existence takes on in these circumstances. My body alone, not to speak of the vaster physical universe beyond myself, is a tirelessly over-administered nervous organism – messages hurrying to and fro, cells endlessly having to be replaced, appetites sordidly to be satisfied . . . And yet the mind itself mostly sleeps, while the self can never be sure that it is wanted here. Do I possess my body, or my body me? Who or what is struggling with whom or what for recognition in this unidentifiable place? All that I can be sure of is the wanting and the struggle. Thus, it is not only impossible to interpret, say, the Assistants in this novel; it is not even necessary to interpret them in order to see what sort of role they play.

The role is very similar to that played by the warders, and later by the executioners, in *The Trial*. K. is told that they have been assigned to him, but he tries to disown them, complains about them, ill-treats them, gets a stick ready to beat them, and briefly drives them away – only to find that one of them has won Frieda's sympathy and perhaps usurped his place with her. It is tempting to interpret them here again as representing 'the body' (intended not so much to assist K., for the body generally seems to assist the rational self very little, but at least to cheer him up, and win a bit of feminine sympathy besides). But any close reading of Kafka's text will reveal that this kind of interpretation steps outside it, leaving behind quite inexplicable details – as, for instance, why the assistants should be perched on the bar *watching* K. who has been making love to Frieda. In the closed world of *The Castle* we cannot say what is bodily and what is spiritual, indeed nothing possesses one of these qualities to the exclusion of the other; everything rather is ambiguously compounded of both. But so, from Kafka's point of view, is life, and it is a confusion arising from the use of language (and of thought) to suppose that we can make such distinctions.

## Guilt and defiance

For Kafka, something worse than confusion and ambiguity resulted from the mind's perverse efforts to rise above its mortal condition. To question and resist the conventional 'processes' of existence, as K. does in *The Trial* and Amalia does in this novel, involves an apparently fatal guilt. K. is also guilty in *The Castle* because (to quote from the protocol drawn up by the Village Secretary): 'It was clear that the Land Surveyor did not love Frieda. . . . It was simply out of calculation of the vilest kind that K. made up to Frieda and stuck to her so long as he still had hope that his plans would succeed.' Here, in a few words, is the core of the plot, of which Amalia's story is a variant. What the two stories have in common, apart from a biographical foundation in Kafka's life (for his favourite sister, Ottla, had resisted the family convention as he had done), is that both K. and Amalia defy the castle, Amalia disinterestedly, K. in a more devious manner involving other people. The inclusion of Amalia's story, and its similarity to K.'s, suggests that the guilt involved is not of any conventional moral kind; the circumstances in which K. finds himself make it almost absurd to judge his behaviour by standards valid for any real social situation. K. is guilty not because of the way he actually treats Frieda – he is ready, after all, to marry her – but because he is interested in her for the wrong reason.

The protocol quoted above gives one description – which Kafka later deleted from the text – of K.'s 'wrong'. It does not appear to be a very accurate description, in fact, if we compare the word 'calculation' with what is described earlier as actually happening when K. and Frieda first meet. 'Calculation' describes better the protocol itself, and indeed all K.'s subsequent efforts to work out where he stands. It was this activity which Kafka considered wrong and impossible of success. It was to him a setting of himself over against life, opposite to it and therefore outside it. And what he meant by 'life' was primarily his own inward awareness of it, so that this opposition was a quite solitary struggle of himself with himself. 'O to be opposite myself alone,' he exclaims in his diary, and describes this wish as a desire 'for solitude beyond all consciousness of anything else' (*nach besinnungsloser Einsamkeit*). K. and Klamm

are ultimately the same 'person', therefore: the vain pursuit by
the self of itself as though it were something other, 'out there',
to be possessed. Women, not as persons, but as sexual experiences, seem to offer K. access to this 'unconscious' goal, and to
the extent to which Frieda or Pepi are realistic persons, he
doubtless treats them wrongly. But the wrong that K. incurs is
to be thought of not so much in moral terms as in metaphysical
ones.

The sense of guilt, the wrong, that inspires Kafka's fiction
derives not from any injustices he saw being perpetrated in
society – though these he saw too and held views about them
like many another socially responsible citizen – but from his
self-observation as a writer, a thinker, a user of words. The
wrong that he saw 'man' (if K.'s world is meant to represent a
generalization of Kafka's experiences) perpetrating in this
context was that man already *is* the thing that he tries to lay
hold of, conquer, and justify as *his* through knowledge. He runs
the risk, certainly, of destroying the thing he already has and is,
his life, in his vain intellectual efforts to penetrate its mystery.
But the damage he will do will be 'merely' psychological, as
Amalia's parallel story shows.

All the Barnabas family needs to do is to stop worrying; they
only cannot obtain pardon from the world because no offence
has been committed by Amalia's refusal of life's impersonal
demand for sexual perpetuation. They are guilty only of feeling
guilt. Amalia herself evidently feels none and is content to live
selflessly in the village. Above all she is capable of feeling no
doubt and no curiosity about her position. She talks with no
one about it, and no one talks to her. K. cannot be satisfied
with any such silent state of being. He is for ever interrogating
the world, and cannot settle quietly in the village, not only
because it is so 'low-browed' (a visual symbol of its mindless
state) but simply because: 'It would say nothing to me.' The
German phrase he uses is the idiom: *Es würde mir nicht
zusagen*, which in English has to be translated as: 'It would not

suit me.' But the English idiom, deriving from a quite different philological root meaning 'to follow', fails to remind us of the state of confrontation, opposition, and exclusion which for Kafka explained why the world can never 'suit' the thinking mind. Life 'speaks' to the writer largely because he opposes and will not quietly take his place in it.

# 4

# Conclusion:
# The Problem of Interpretation

It may seem perhaps superfluous to insist on a conclusion, dealing with the problem of interpreting Kafka, when this entire
study has from the beginning been concerned with just this
question. Kafka himself writes about nothing else; all his works
are essays in the problem of interpretation. As we have seen,
he presents his readers with a single, but usually also weird
situation, and then explores its significance, partly by actions
resembling (not very closely) what in more conventional
literature constitutes the story or plot, but mainly by speculative discussions of great length, subtlety, and lucidity – which
get absolutely nowhere. No advance in 'positive' understanding
is made, and the working out of the initial situation is on the
verge of appearing (and perhaps will appear to later generations
of readers) as exceedingly tiresome and negative. That is why a
case can be made for rating Kafka's short stories as superior
works of art, more likely to endure as masterpieces than the
novels that have recently enjoyed most fame. One suspects that
the fame of his longer fiction is partly due to its providing a
gymnasium for the favourite pastime of modern thinkers –
especially academic ones, and without the contemporary enthusiasm for literary criticism as a means of education, Kafka
would not have become as famous as he is – which is to exercise
the intellect with much personal earnestness and little public
relevance. This suspicion brings us back, however, to the more
fundamental question raised at the outset: how has it come

about that an author who was himself so apparently indifferent to the world about him should have produced stories that have enjoyed a serious claim to be considered as the most relevant myths of the modern age?

Several of Kafka's stories deal quite explicitly with the subject of the individual's relationship to the community, of private interpretations to public life, and it will be appropriate to look at them here. They are: *Beim Bau der chinesischen Mauer* (1917, 'The Chinese Wall'), *Forschungen eines Hundes* (1922, 'Investigations of a Dog'), and *Josefine, die Sängerin oder Das Volk der Mäuse* (1924, 'Josephine, the Singer, or The Mouse People'). 'The Investigations of a Dog' is particularly interesting in this connection, because it tells of a lifetime of solemn research 'into the simplest questions', and describes how the arduous process of research has not led to any scientific conclusion – the narrator is, he says, 'incapable of science' in the normal sense, and persists in the name of a higher 'ultimate science, prizing freedom above everything else' – but how it has led him to something quite different, namely, an ecstatic vision of a dog who sings. He never actually finds the answer to his question, 'what the canine race nourishes itself on', but he does experience music again, which was what made him ask his question in the first place. The visionary scene at the end harks back to a remembered occasion in childhood, when the narrator saw a troupe of performing dogs (just as Kafka had been impressed by the troupe of Yiddish actors) and was overwhelmed 'by their courage in facing so openly the music of their own making'. These dogs not only made music but stood upon their hind legs, 'as if nature were an error', and caused the narrator to feel that 'the world was standing on its head'. In other words, the mystery of what art is, and the overwhelming effect that beauty has on us, prompts other, 'simple' questions about the way we live, and what we are 'nourished' on.

Now, these basic questions, whose answer the community takes for granted, and which are bound up with the oldest moral codes and religious rituals of the race, are of a kind that scientific research cannot possibly answer. The greater part of this story is taken up with discussion of the problems involved in 'research'. The investigating dog, as a result of his persistent inquiries, has 'felt outlawed in my innermost heart and run my head against the traditional walls of my species like a savage'. He has 'asked no assistance from the dog community, and indeed rejected it in the most determined manner'. This does not mean, however, that he does not care about his fellow-creatures; on the contrary, 'all that I cared about was the race of dogs, that and nothing else. For what is there actually except our own species?' This question points to the moral – or something more fundamental even than morality – as well as to the quiet humour of this story. For the reader knows that there are men as well as dogs, and that all these solemn mysteries about where dogs' food comes from are merely a dog's way of describing the (to him) inexplicable dishing out of nourishment 'from above' by human beings.

As with all fables, however, this translation of the story to another level only confronts us again with the same problem in another form. What are human beings nourished on? By bread alone? And here again the fundamental assumption of the questioner is of crucial importance: 'What is there actually except our own species? To whom else can one appeal in the wide and empty world?' Kafka then describes the predicament of the modern mind as it tries to make sense of its condition without appeal to anyone else:

> All knowledge, the totality of all questions and answers, is contained in the dog. If one could but realize this knowledge, if one could but bring it into the light of day, if we dogs would but own that we know infinitely more than we admit to ourselves . . . But the one thing that you long to win above all, the admission of knowledge remains denied to you. To such prayers, whether silent or loud, the only answer you get, even after you have employed your

powers of seduction to the utmost, are vacant stares,
averted glances, troubled and veiled eyes.

(*Forschungen eines Hundes*, in *Beschreibung eines
Kampfes*, p. 255)

The narrator then goes on to ponder on the still greater
mystery that, after all, he himself is a dog, and the answer he
seeks as to the nature of dogdom is contained within himself.
This gives him a feeling of solidarity with his fellow-dogs: 'You
also have the dog knowledge; well, bring it out, not merely in
the form of a question, but as an answer. The great choir of
dogdom will join in as if it had been waiting for you. Then you
will have clarity, truth, avowal, as much as you desire. The roof
of this wretched life, of which you say so many hard things,
will burst open, and all of us shoulder to shoulder, will ascend
into the lofty realm of freedom.' Kafka perceives, however,
that this ideal of solidarity – which reflects his own renewed
interest in the last years of his life in Zionism and the Jewish
faith – is false. While he admits that the knowledge he desires,
'and the key to it as well', he cannot possess 'except in common
with all the others, I cannot grasp it without their help', he has
to admit also that: 'If I remain faithful to a metaphor, then the
goal of my aims, my questions, my enquiries, appears monstrous.' For the enthusiasm he feels for collective solidarity
amongst his people, which will make manifest the secret embodied in their bones, does not express any genuine readiness
to join them. What he would really do is to dismiss them
utterly, 'to the ordinary life they love', and to remain himself
quite alone, feeding on the marrow of his entire race.

The metaphor expresses vividly Kafka's guilty sense of being
a parasite as a writer, and he makes his judgement doubly clear
when he concludes: 'The marrow that I am discussing here is
no food; on the contrary, it is poison.' He cannot commune
with his neighbour, even though he knows that every dog must
in some degree 'have like me the impulse to question', indeed,
'it is the peculiarity of dogs to be always asking questions'. But

G

they ask them 'confusedly all together; it is as if in doing that they were trying to obliterate every trace of the genuine questions'. The genuine questions are asked by himself alone, and he pursues them with a passion akin to that of a 'scientist'. This does not mean that he thinks of his research as a material science * (for which he has an 'instinctive' incapacity); his inquiry has the spiritual seriousness of religious tradition, to which he also feels himself to be rather superior, for he looks down on his own generation of dogs as being in a state of spiritual decline. He looks back nostalgically to the earlier period of his race:

> Dogs had not yet become so doggish as today, the edifice was still loosely put together, the true Word could still have intervened, planning or replanning the structure, changing it at will, transforming it into its opposite; and the Word was there, was very near at least, on the tip of everybody's tongue, anyone might have hit upon it. And what has become of it today? Today one may pluck out one's very heart and not find it.          (ibid., p. 268)

It should now be becoming fairly clear what kind of 'research' the narrator is engaged in, and what kind of interpretation he is making of his canine culture in decline and of his own place in it. It is a kind of interpretation that lies between – and even pretends to combine – pure science and religious prophecy; it investigates simple but fundamental questions, drawing its primary evidence and inspiration from the experience of art. This manner of thinking about metaphysical and moral questions in social, historical, and cultural terms may be said to be typically German. It derives from the idealist metaphysics of Hegel, Schopenhauer, and Nietzsche; by Kafka's time it had permeated the minds of the most diverse thinkers, from Freud to Spengler. He himself might have picked it up from reading

---

* The German word *Wissenschaft* does not have the same connotations as the English word 'science', which refers almost exclusively to the natural or empirical sciences. *Wissenschaft* refers to learning in the humane, as well as in the pure, sciences.

Hegel's protesting disciple, Kierkegaard, or from contact with almost any of the cultural pessimists of his age, which is to say, almost any of his intelligent contemporaries. For it had taken hold of the spiritual life of Europe like a fever; indeed, the oppressive mood of cultural self-consciousness that it induced seemed particularly conducive to creative thought. While its home was Germany and central Europe, many French intellectuals were seduced by it (and since then still more have been); it spread as far as Spain in the writings of an Ortega y Gasset, and echoed in the Hegelian foundations of Marxism. Perhaps England and Italy have proved most resistant to it, but the academic world of America has fostered it in many later varieties. As a form of intellectual critique of life's meaning and civilization's value, it speaks with an authority that is devastatingly negative, for it is founded neither on faith nor on fact but on the unassailable ground of psychological analysis. Kafka's distinctive virtue as a writer in this tradition consists in his ability to render visible, in symbolic form, the way this type of thinking operates. He lays bare the state of mind, the motivation, and the attitudes on which its interpretation of the world is based. The symbolism Kafka uses to do this is graphic and lucid: the dog fasts, abstains totally from the food whose secret he is determined to have.

Kafka is more critical of the cultural critic's position than most writers have been. He keeps his feet on the ground as the 'hovering dogs', whom we may imagine to be his more highfalutin intellectual contemporaries, have not done. He has never actually seen them hover; he has seen dogs get two of their feet off the ground, but not all four. Such an existence would be entirely senseless in his view, but not for that reason not worth investigating. On the contrary, 'the most senseless seemed to me in this senseless world more probable than the sensible, and moreover particularly fertile for investigation'. The sentence sounds like a garbled pronouncement by Aristotle on art, and later the narrator tells us that 'someone now and then refers to art and artists' to explain these hovering creatures, who have 'no relation whatever to the life of the community'. That they are intellectuals of some sort seems clear enough from the fact that 'they are perpetually talking, partly of their philosophical reflections with which, seeing that they have completely renounced bodily exertion, they can continuously occupy themselves, partly of the observations they have made from their exalted stations'. This almost 'unendurable volubility' is to be explained, the narrator thinks, by their need to obtain pardon for their unjustifiable way of life; and here the criticism implicit in the gentle irony of the text would seem to extend to Kafka himself, who was always guiltily doubtful about the value of his activity as a writer. His research into this question has led him to the entirely negative conclusion that the only thing research can clarify is falsehood:

> The truth can never be discovered by such means – never can that stage be reached – but they [inquiries of this kind] throw light on some of the profounder ramifications of falsehood. For all the senseless phenomena of our existence, and the most senseless most of all, are susceptible of investigation. (ibid., p. 262)

This, too, might be a description of Kafka's own writings: an investigation of the senseless, a clarification of what is not the truth. As we shall see presently, the value of this strange exercise is to expose the way in which the interpretative intelligence works. This can only be grasped negatively, in isolation from the world.

'Investigations of a Dog' exposes, then, the psychology of the modern critical intelligence, driving itself to total abstinence from life, in both a physical and material sense, totally committed to an utterly wearisome task, 'but for that very reason resolved to pursue it indefatigably . . . so as to be left free to regain the ordinary, calm, happy life of everyday'. That the narrator will never regain it is obvious from the way the story is told as a parable about dogs. But the (human) reader is released by the symbolism from the dog's delusions, and thus indirectly raised up above the typical 'delusions' of the modern mind. One by one, the great themes of modern literature and thought are rehearsed. This dog has had some tremendous aesthetic experience when young which determined his fate, 'making me feel sorry for myself; it robbed me of my childhood . . . but perhaps I have the prospect of far more childish happiness, earned by a life of hard work, in my old age than any actual child'. Might we not think of Proust trying to recapture the lost paradise of his early years? Then we find Kafka's dog obsessed with the limits of language, the futility of expression, and the menacing challenge of silence. 'I only want to be stimulated by the silence which rises up around me as the ultimate answer . . . We survive all questions, even our own, bulwarks of silence that we are.' Might not Beckett have spoken thus? And when the strange hound appears at the end, 'not at all extraordinary' in himself, but transfigured in the delirious gaze of the narrator who is lying in the blood he has vomited, we think inevitably of Kafka himself, and of the piercing, monotonous, unendurable note of 'music' that the most ordinary existence, indeed the mere fact of existence, emitted 'solely for my sake' when he was, as the dog puts it here, 'quite beyond myself' (*außer mir*). But we might think equally of other modern, and especially German, writers who have attained this mystical awareness of reality as something unbearably terrible and beautiful – writers like Nietzsche and Rilke. And finally, there is the basic theme of the story, so fundamental to this and all Kafka's work that we might overlook it as a cliché of modern literature altogether: the solitary hero, set in opposition to all the world, who asks a question of metaphysical importance that his society cannot answer. But this story, like the other two we shall briefly look at here, puts this familiar modern motif in a new light.

The ironically metaphysical question about the provenance of dog's food that obsesses the narrator – a question which was originally inspired, as we saw, by an overwhelming artistic experience – not only sets him apart from the rest of his race, making him feel prematurely alone so that he loses his childhood; it also gives him a peculiar power of perception as regards his fellow-beings. He begins to see everything that they do as inadequate, and their very appearance as disgusting. Even though he knows that it is in their nature to ask questions, he finds their questions and their answers, which 'enable them to bear this life', to be inauthentic, evasions rather than confrontations. The narrator declares that the 'burden of my complaint, the kernel of it', is summed up in the doubt whether he has any 'real colleagues', or 'real *comrades*', as he sometimes puts it. What prevents him from believing 'that all dogs from the beginning of time have been my colleagues, all diligent in their own way, all unsuccessful in their own way, all silent or falsely garrulous in their own way, as hopeless research is apt to make one'? The only answer that follows is the reflection that his whole life of solitary investigation would in that case have been a waste of time: 'But in that case I need not have severed myself from my fellows at all, I could have remained quietly among the others, I had no need to fight my way out like a stubborn child through the closed ranks of the grown ups.' Kafka touches here on the critical problem of modern society, the crisis that has caused classes, races, groups, and generations to tear one another apart. And we touch here in Kafka's work the point of discovery that enabled him, despite all his preoccupation with seemingly private and psychological problems to create myths that embody so much of twentieth-century man's most disastrous experience. Kafka needed only to study his neighbour, like the dog in this story, needed only to reflect upon the relationship that existed between himself and his father, or between himself as a person in society and himself as a thinking, solitary mind, to perceive the motivations that would drive others to torture, deceive, and destroy themselves – and not just in imagination, but in reality.

The differences that separate the narrator from his fellows are all matters of convention. In his first encounter with the musical dogs as a child, it is he who is appalled, not they, by what they are doing, he who is amazed at their 'courage in facing so openly the music of their own making', and morally shaken that they should expose themselves in this un-doggy way. It is he who breaks out of the 'labyrinth of wooden bars' that should have kept him in his place (as conventions are meant to do), to confront these artists with protests about the enormity of their performance, about which they seem so unconcerned, being totally absorbed (as artists generally are) by the technical difficulties of their art. Later, when he considers discussing with his neighbour the questions that are obsessing him, he desists simply because he knows 'what course the conversation would take. He would . . . agree – agreement is the best weapon of defence – and the matter would be buried.' It is his neighbour's, his people's ability to bear without worrying these basic questions, to accept them as answers, as 'agreements', rather than as questions, that 'fills me with dejection and confuses me', so the narrator tells us. 'Their belief that it is simple prevents further enquiry.' And when finally the narrator, in his inability to accept that 'it' is simple, embarks upon his unheard-of course of inquiry by fasting, he breaks the unwritten law – and what else is convention? – of his race. The vision with which he is rewarded is quite literally a creation, a projection (in psychological terms) of his spiritual hunger. 'In the midst of pain I felt a longing to go on fasting, and I followed it as greedily as if it were a strange dog.' This is then exactly what appears to him in his fainting state: a strange dog. No analysis could be more exact of the way in which Kafka's creative imagination responded to the world. It happens also to be a prophetic description of the spiritual hunger and hallucinations of the modern age.

The almost automatic assumption of Europe's intelligentsia for the last century or more has been that the conventional

values or 'agreements' of society are false. This habit of mind
has grown amongst aspirant intellectuals at an ever-younger
age and on an ever-increasing scale. Kafka was by no means
the first writer to anticipate and express it; but he remains
remarkable for his ability to rise above and reflect upon this
mental attitude, not taking its criticisms of the world literally,
that is, as if it showed what was really 'wrong' in some still conventional sense, but showing instead how questionable this way
of thinking in itself is. The criticism of the world inspired by
such metaphysical uncertainty cannot be proved on purely
objective grounds; what is seen in the world is a reflection of
the viewer's state of mind. The collapse of convention, that
cliché of contemporary thought, is a psychological collapse,
rather than something that has happened 'out there' in society.
Or rather, Kafka teaches us to see that the ultimate terror
brought about by such a collapse is that we feel trapped inside
a deluded consciousness of the world, regarding *all* conventional representations of existence as false, but for that very
reason unable to extricate ourselves from them. Kafka's
mythology makes us aware of the impossibility of distinguish-
ing between what happens 'out there' and our consciousness of
it. This is like living in a nightmare, knowing it to be a nightmare, but being unable to wake up. Kafka's myths illustrate
the psychological pattern of the urges that move men in this
spiritual situation: the revolutionary urge to break the illusions
of convention, contempt for the scruffy, conformist neighbour,
who accepts the dream as true, and desire for a nobler solidarity
of the race and a higher type of individual. The fantasies of the
dog in this story, who dreams of ascending shoulder to shoulder
into freedom and who hears in his sick despair a sublime
transcendent voice, are the product of the same imagination
that is disgusted by his bourgeois neighbour and outraged by
the moral inadequacies of his society.

A similar psychological pattern underlies the story 'The
Great Wall of China'. The narrator is again a scholarly in-

vestigator set apart from his people, who for him are guilty of 'a certain feebleness of faith and imaginative power'. In the end he desists from further research because 'to set about establishing a fundamental defect here would mean undermining not only our consciences, but, what is worse, our feet'. In studying the great wall that everyone believes to protect the empire, he alone has sought for 'an explanation of the system of piecemeal construction that goes farther than the one that contented people then'. In the early days, people had not meditated on the mystery of the wall's construction, which is so obviously inexpedient since it consists of as many gaps as ramparts, because they were content with a maxim that assumed human thought must correspond to nature, the order of meaning to the order of the world, and science to the law of God. The narrator stands above all earlier beliefs about the wall, especially those of a religious character; for him 'no lightning flashes any longer from the long-since vanished thunder clouds'. But he comes to a kind of religious conclusion nevertheless, though it is founded on different grounds now. He believes there must always have been a 'high command'; the conventions of the world cannot be regarded as merely secular, sociological arrangements. That the wall – of human achievement, perhaps in a metaphorical sense, of knowledge – is so full of holes is to be explained by the psychological wisdom of the 'high command':

> Human nature, essentially changeable, unstable as the dust, can endure no restraint; if it binds itself it soon begins to tear madly at its bonds, until it rends everything asunder, the wall, the bonds and its very self.
>
> (*Beim Bau der chinesischen Mauer*,
> in *Beschreibungen eines Kampfes*, p. 72)

The result of this subjectively wise, even if objectively crazy, method of construction is to prevent any such outbreak of destructive despair and to preserve feelings of the greatest solidarity amongst the people. They labour on, confident that 'every fellow country-man was a brother for whom one was building a wall of protection . . . Unity! Unity! Shoulder to shoulder, a ring of brothers, a current of blood no longer confined within the narrow circulation of one body, but sweetly rolling and yet ever returning throughout the endless leagues of China.'

As we recognize the same pattern of events and responses in 'The Great Wall of China' that we have seen in so many of Kafka's stories and novels, we can begin to sum up the problem of interpretation that they present. Kafka *might* be writing here of a political 'high command', which understands the psychological needs of its citizens so well that it can produce a state of popular national brotherhood by cunningly manipulating the economy while leaving the people in ignorance. (Later in the story the extent of this ignorance is made quite plain.) Or Kafka *might* even here be thought of – as he has been thought of in connection with his major works – as writing about God, the structure of Creation, and the part played in it by human beings. As he describes the problem posed by the vastness and uniqueness of this edifice, and of 'the many legends to which the building of the wall gave rise, which cannot be verified, at least by any man with his own eyes and judgement, on account of the extent of the structure', Kafka *might* be taking up in his own picturesque language a problem that has exercised philosophers and theologians: namely, by what standards can human beings judge metaphysical questions concerning the whole universe, of which they are a mere subordinate part and outside which they have nothing to judge it by. On the other hand, Kafka *might* well be writing metaphorically about something rather different, as we have already hinted. The story could be about the piecemeal character of human learning, which is to say, of thinking and writing. Words themselves, which can be built into coherent stretches of 'wall', or sentences, leave huge holes and gaps between one and the next, and cannot ever protect us fully against the menace of reality. Sometimes, of course, in the enthusiasm of building some small piece of wall, a few impressive sentences, a poem perhaps, or a story, a writer may produce in all his being, and in his hearers too, a sense of 'Unity! Unity!' A surge of meaningful feelings unites the words in the sentence – or equally we might say, unites the readers of the poem; we are, after all, taking Kafka's story in a metaphorical sense, way beyond its literal meaning, and who shall say what is the 'right' meaning of a word? Language itself gives rise to legends 'which cannot be verified, on account of the extent of the structure'. Kafka *might* simply be telling a literal story about the Great Wall of China, and who shall say that this is not interesting enough as it stands? Why do we have to interpret it? Why don't we just read it?

Exactly the same question can be asked, of course, about life itself. Why don't we just live it? The answer is that it seems to be saying something to us. The situation is summed up for us in the parable told in the second half of 'The Great Wall of China'. The Emperor has sent a message to you, the humble subject, from the centre of the world; but the messenger cannot get through, the clutter and refuse and sheer 'overpopulation' of existence prevent him from reaching you. So 'you sit at your window when evening falls and dream it to yourself'. In the passages before and after this beautiful parable, Kafka plays with the idea that the Emperor is really dead, but that this makes no difference to what the people dream; the Empire itself goes on, indeed, it is 'immortal'. To the detached observer there is no rational connection, no true correspondence, between what the people believe and what the case is. But it makes no difference, life goes on, indeed 'it' is immortal. Only one thing might seriously threaten it, 'undermine our consciences and what is worse our feet' (that is, our real ability to 'stand' it at all), and that would be to discover the truth, or rather the total absence of it, the lack of any possibility of it, in all human endeavour. And so the inquirer, the author, desists from further inquiry. Did Kafka, then, desist, and should we likewise not persist? The paradox of this intellectual situation is that he and we could only do this by either not beginning at all, or destroying everything at the end, or – if a third alternative is permissible – by writing in such a way that what is written both means something and means nothing at one and the same time. And this, as we remarked at the outset, was Kafka's extraordinary intellectual project. When he was in a mood to believe that in much of his writing he had not succeeded, he fell back in despair on the second alternative, and asked that it should be destroyed.

Kafka's strangely symbolic fiction, which presents so obvious a challenge to interpretation, resembles real life to the extent to which living too is felt to present a similar challenge. What Kafka is 'imitating', in the same way that all artists may be said to be making a likeness or copy of something real, is the experience of this challenge. He is not representing the world according to the rules of some convention that purports to tell us what it means; he is representing the process of describing the world when no convention is available to tell us what it means, not even a convention that will enable us to distinguish what is there from what we think is there. In such a situation of profound spiritual doubt, Kafka certainly does not provide *an* interpretation of the world, and criticism cannot consequently provide *an* interpretation of Kafka's work. What he provides is an image of how experience looks when all interpretations are called in doubt. He does not write simple-minded existentialist literature of the kind that supposedly exposes the artificiality of human values, psychic structures, language games, and the like; Kafka is too desperately – and humorously – aware of the absurdity in the claims of any mind that judges everything to be absurd. What standard is it judging by? Where does it stand? Kafka's writing is directed against the absurdity not of the world, but of writing. It reflects its own activity, its own reality – and utter artificiality. The fact that the resulting symbolism bears some resemblance to events in the outside world tells us less about those events than about the way we are in the habit (perhaps) of thinking about them. If we have no social or political conventions we really believe in, if we have no faith in any value more positive than to gaze without bias or commitment upon the truth, then the truth will become a nightmare.

Many writers, and amongst them some of the greatest, like Dante, and Shakespeare, and Goethe, have recognized the limits of what writing may achieve in the face of life's mystery – and death's. But none has described these limits more modestly or wittily than Kafka in 'Josephine, the Singer'. The story forms a contrast and companion piece to 'The Burrow', and in it Kafka reveals the secret of his art's success, instead of its hopeless failure. But his ironical aesthetic theory makes success and failure ultimately indistinguishable. For the singer, he says, cannot actually sing any better than other people; if anything, Josephine sings rather worse. The only difference made by art is that it is a self-conscious and deliberate imitation of what everyone else does spontaneously.

> To crack a nut is certainly not an art, therefore no one would dare to bring an audience together and crack nuts before them in order to entertain them. But if someone should do this nevertheless, and if he successfully accomplishes his 'art', then the thing does cease to be a mere nutcracking. Or rather, it continues to be still a matter of cracking nuts, but it becomes apparent that we have normally overlooked what an art this was, because we could do it so easily, and that this new nutcracker was the first person to show us what the real nature of the business was; and it might then even be more effective if he was a little less good at cracking nuts than the majority of us.
>
> (In *Erzählungen*, pp. 270 f)

# Bibliography

GERMAN EDITIONS

*Gesammelte Werke*, ed. M. Brod, 2nd edn, New York/Frankfurt am Main: *Der Prozeß*, 1950; *Das Schloß*, 1951; *Tagebücher 1910–1923*, 1951; *Briefe an Milena*, ed. W. Haas, 1952; *Erzählungen*, 1952; *Amerika*, 1953; *Hochzeitsvorbereitungen auf dem Lande und andere Prosa aus dem Nachlaß*, 1953; *Beschreibung eines Kampfes. Novellen, Skizzen, Aphorismen aus dem Nachlaß*, 1954; *Briefe 1902–1924*, 1958.

*Sämtliche Erzählungen*, ed. P. Raabe, Frankfurt am Main, 1970.

*Briefe an Felice und andere Korrespondenz*, ed. and introd. E. Heller, Frankfurt am Main, 1967.

ENGLISH EDITIONS

*The Castle*, tr. W. and E. Muir, 1930; rev. edn, 1953.

*The Great Wall of China and Other Pieces*, tr. E. and W. Muir, 1933.

*The Trial*, tr. W. and E. Muir, 1937; rev. edn, 1955.

*The Metamorphosis*, tr. A. L. Lloyd, 1937.

*America*, tr. W. and E. Muir, 1938.

*The Penal Colony: Stories and short pieces*, tr. W. and E. Muir, 1948.

*The Diaries of Franz Kafka*, tr. J. Kresh, 2 vols, 1948–9.

*Letters to Milena*, tr. J. and T. Stern, 1953.

*Wedding Preparations in the Country, and other posthumous prose writings*, tr. E. Kaiser and E. Wilkins, 1954.

*Metamorphosis and other stories*, tr. E. and W. Muir, 1961 (Penguin).

WRITINGS ON KAFKA

(*In German*)

H. Järv, *Die Kafka Literatur*, Malmö–Lund, 1961.

M. Brod, *Über Franz Kafka*, Frankfurt am Main, 1966.

W. Emrich, *Franz Kafka*, Bonn, 1958.

W. H. Sokel, *Franz Kafka. Tragik und Ironie*, Munich, 1964.

K. Wagenbach, *Franz Kafka. Eine Biographie seiner Jugend*, Bern, 1958.

(*In English*)

G. Anders, *Franz Kafka*, London, 1960.

A. Flores and H. Swander, eds., *Franz Kafka Today*, Madison, 1958.

R. D. Gray, *Kafka's Castle*, Cambridge, 1956.

R. D. Gray, ed., *Kafka: A Collection of Critical Essays*, Englewood Cliffs, 1962.

H. Politzer, *Franz Kafka. Parable and Paradox*, New York, rev. edn, 1966.